SHAMELESS ABANDON

"You are my woman, don't you know?" Shane whispered against her lips. "Now that I have met you, you have become my life. Only you."

A sweet current of warmth swept through Melanie. Unable to resist, she twined her arms around his neck. "Shane, oh, Shane," she whispered, then emitted a soft moan of passion against his lips as his mouth closed hard upon hers. A need familiar to her only since she had met Shane was rising up inside her, spreading and swelling. She clung to him as he lowered her to the ground. The spongy green moss beneath her cushioned her back. Shane's hands, busy disrobing her, were setting fires along her flesh as it became exposed to the afternoon sunlight that was drifting like spiraling, golden ribbons through the trees overhead.

Cassie Edwards
WHEN PASSION CALLS

With appreciation and admiration I dedicate *When Passion Calls* to Leisure's publisher, Jerry Brisman, a man who kindly gave me that most-needed helping hand at the beginning of my career. Having returned to write for Leisure I have come full circle in my career. I am enjoying working with Mr. Brisman again and look forward to being a part of Leisure's bright future.

—Cassie Edwards

I will not let thee go.
The stars that crowd the summer skies
Have watched us so below
With all their million eyes,
I dare not let thee go.

I will not let thee go.
Have we not chid the changeful moon,
Now rising late, and now
Because she set too soon,
And shall I let thee go?

I will not let thee go.
Have not the young flowers been content,
Plucked ere their buds could blow,
To seal our sacrament?
I cannot let thee go.

I will not let thee go.
I hold thee by too many bands:
Thou sayest farewell, and lo!
I have thee by the hands,
And will not let thee go.

—ROBERT BRIDGES

· PROLOGUE ·

Spring—1827

The sun was low in the sky, casting orange reflections upon two fifty-foot keelboats making their way up the Mississippi River. They were filled with settlers bound for the untamed territory of Minnesota. The two-week journey from Saint Louis had been tedious and uncomfortable for the men, women, and children on board, yet it now looked as though the journey were nearing an end. The Land of Many Lakes had finally been reached.

Four-year-old Shane Brennan sat on his mother's lap in the second boat, straining his neck to see the lead boat as it disappeared round a sharp bend in the river. He wanted to get another glimpse of his father, Jared, and his twin brother, Josh, before the boat was lost from his sight. It had

1

been his father's decision to separate the family into two different boats, hoping that in the event of an Indian attack, at least some of the family would complete the journey safely.

No longer able to see the boat, Shane looked up at his mother, Amy, who was cloaked in a dark, hooded cape. "Are all Indians bad, Mama?" he asked. "If they come, will they take our hair?"

"Hush, Shane," Amy scolded. "You've heard too many of the bigger boys telling tall tales. They only tell you such things to frighten you."

"Then if I see an Indian, I don't have to be afraid?" Shane asked, his blue eyes wide.

"I believe there is some good in everyone," Amy said. "Even Indians."

Shane fell silent, satisfied with his mother's answer. He snuggled more comfortably against her, but was thrown from her lap when the boat jolted suddenly. As his mother lifted him back up, he looked over the side of the boat and saw that the craft had run aground on a sand bar.

Amid shouts and confusion, the men began helping everyone from the boat onto the sand. The weight of the vessel had to be lessened so that it could be freed from the sandbar.

Shane looked over his shoulder at his mother as a man carried him from the boat. Amy followed. When Shane was set down on the sand, his mother took his hand and moved with the others to more solid ground.

"Will we see Indians, Mama?" Shane asked, looking trustingly up at his mother. "Will we?"

"Oh, Shane," Amy said, sighing heavily. "Why

are you so full of questions today? I'm so weary of traveling. So weary!"

Shane hung his head, sad, then raised his eyes and began to look around while the men struggled to free the boat. The air was fresh and cool, smelling of the Norway pines that lined the sandy shore of the river. Chipmunks scolded and bluejays squawked from somewhere close by.

Shane's attention was drawn to a covey of partridges that were just within the darker shadows of the forest. They were feeding on the bright red clusters of pigeon berries that were thrusting through the carpet of brown pine needles beneath the trees. Shane slipped his hand free of his mother's and moved slowly toward the birds.

There was a great whirring of wings as the partridges took off, fast and low, disappearing into the lengthening shadows of the tall pines. Then everything around Shane became strangely quiet. The chipmunks were silent. The bluejays no longer squawked.

Suddenly, terrifying screams and shouts of pain filled the silence. Instinctively, Shane crouched down in the thick underbrush. Terror gripping him, he watched men, women and children dropping to the ground as arrows hissed through the air, piercing the bodies of those who were still alive.

Then it was all over. Frozen to the spot with fear, Shane looked at the carnage. His pulse racing, he saw his mother among the dead. He wanted to run to her, but instinct told him to stay hidden. As far as he could tell, he was the only survivor.

Trembling, sobbing quietly, Shane watched as several white men dressed in fringed buckskin emerged from the forest carrying bows and arrows. He bit his lower lip in frustration as he watched some of them begin to steal from the dead while others carried their victims' belongings from the boat.

Shane covered his mouth to stifle a gasp of despair. A large, burly man was bending over his mother. He was removing her wedding band and slipping it into his pocket.

When the man straightened to his full height and looked suddenly in Shane's direction, the boy thought discovery was certain. The man stared for a moment, yet did not seem to see Shane. Frozen with fear, Shane felt a tremor go through him as he looked into the man's gaze. Why, the man had one blue and one brown eye! Never had Shane seen anything like that.

And he would never forget. All of his life he would remember those eyes—the eyes of the man who had killed his mother, the eyes of the man who stole her wedding band!

Shane huddled low behind the bush until the men left. When he felt it was safe enough, he went to his mother and looked solemnly down at her. The evening air was becoming damp and cold. It seemed to be grasping at Shane with icy, groping fingers. Kneeling down beside his mother, he touched her face, then her hand. Some warmth remained. He snuggled down on the ground beside her and began to cry.

4

"Papa, Papa," he sobbed. "Where are you, Papa?"

A shadow fell over Shane. He looked slowly up into the dark, fathomless eyes of an Indian. But Shane was not afraid. Only a short while ago, his mother had taught him not to be afraid of Indians.

· CHAPTER ONE ·

The Territory of Minnesota—1852

Melanie Stanton stood beside her horse, a white-faced bay gelding with white hind legs, smoothing on her butter-soft leather gloves one finger at a time. With defiance, she looked from her brother, Terrance, to Terrance's best friend, Josh Brennan, as they mounted their horses.

"Terrance, no matter how much you fuss at me, I am accompanying you into St. Paul," she said firmly. The soft morning breeze blew down the front of her white cotton blouse, billowing it away from her breasts. "I want to learn the cattle business. I want to have a say in our choice of cattle. Why shouldn't I? It's my right. The farm is partly mine."

Terrance's spine stiffened as he glowered at Melanie. He circled his reins so tightly around his

6

fingers that the leather cut painfully into his flesh. He could not help but resent his sister. She was eighteen, still a mere girl. He was twenty-five. Yet she had been given an equal share in the inheritance when their father died. Terrance had felt his manhood stripped away at the reading of the will. It was a man's place to run things; a man ought to have full control of his destiny.

"Melanie, must you remind me of your rights again?" Terrance asked, sliding his wide-brimmed hat back from his brow, revealing dark, wiry hair. He toyed nervously with his narrow mustache. "Pop's been dead a year and since then you've been nothing but a nuisance."

His gaze raked over her. She was slim and exquisite, with soft, perfect features. Her face was framed by lustrous, auburn hair that fell in drifts to her waist. Her neck was like a swan's, long and graceful; her eyes were brown, wide and innocent. His eyes fell to her high, well-rounded breasts. There was no denying that she had developed into a woman.

But although she was beautiful and feminine in appearance, Melanie was still a high-spirited tomboy who enjoyed taking dares. She liked to show her strength and agility. For as long as Terrance could remember, he had been in constant competition with her. The fact that she now equalled him in wealth and possessions galled him unbearably. Lately, it had driven him to drink and gamble more than ever. And even before his father's death he had gained the reputation of being a hell-raiser.

"Just look at you," Terrance scolded. "Where

did you pick up that godawful outfit? A fringed buckskin skirt? Moccasins that reach up to your knees? You look like a savage."

Hurt by her brother's reaction to her new riding outfit, which she had chosen for comfort rather than appearance, Melanie ran a gloved hand down the front of her skirt. "Maybe I would look better in skin-hugging breeches and chaps like you and Josh are wearing," she said, defying her brother with another stubborn stare.

Then she looked over at Josh and offered him her most winning smile.

"Josh, you think I'm dressed appropriately enough for riding horseback, don't you?" she asked, then wished she hadn't included him in the debate after all.

Of late, Josh Brennan had become a thorn in her side. Though they had been neighbors for years, she had never cared much for him. As far back as she could remember he had been spoiled and arrogant. Though Terrance scoffed at Josh, saying that he was ignorant when it came to negotiating business deals, Melanie thought Josh was skilled enough at getting what he wanted.

Though his blond hair and blue eyes were attractive, Josh was almost intolerable to be around. He was a gambler and a womanizer. And now he had the nerve to say that he had never gotten married because he had been waiting for Melanie to grow up so he could marry her!

Josh circled a hand around the pommel of his saddle and leaned down closer to Melanie's face.

"Hon, as far as I'm concerned you can wear any damn thing you want," he said in a lazy, teasing fashion. "Or better yet, you don't have to wear anything at all."

Melanie's face grew hot. She set her jaw firmly and glared from Josh to Terrance, annoyed at her brother for allowing Josh to make such personal remarks to her. But she knew her brother would not correct anything Josh Brennan said or did. Terrance had his heart set on her marrying Josh, so that he could gain a hold on the Brennans' riches.

She wondered if her brother had always been so scheming, so power-hungry. If he could, he would hand her over to Josh Brennan this very moment! Josh's father was on his deathbed. Josh would soon own all of his father's land. All of his father's cattle. His father's entire empire!

Stubbornly, Melanie placed her foot in the stirrup and swung herself up into the saddle. She took up her reins and straightened her back as she looked pensively at Terrance. Though he was just as greedy and calculating as his friend, Josh, she could not help but love him. She had no choice but to keep an eye on him and the farm. She had to make sure that at least her portion of the inheritance was protected. If Terrance got unlucky at the poker table, he might be forced to gamble his portion of the farm away.

Yes, she had to learn all of the details of how to run a cattle farm and make sure that Terrance never got hold of her portion. Their father had worked himself into the grave to make this farm what it was today. She could let nothing take away his dream, for his dream was now hers!

"Well? What are we waiting for?" she said impatiently, her eyes dancing. "Let's go to St. Paul. The riverboat should be arriving soon with that new shipment of Texas longhorns. Those that have endured the trail drive from Texas to New Orleans and the boat ride to Saint Louis will be the sort we can be proud to own. They will be the strongest of the lot. But they've already been picked over at New Orleans and St. Louis. We don't want to have the last of the pick here in St. Paul."

Terrance sighed heavily and shook his head in exasperation. "Melanie, ever since Pop died you've been behaving more like a man than a woman. Now get down off that horse and go back inside the house. Mary Ellen is making bread today. Watch her and learn how it's done. If I have to force you at gunpoint, you're going to be someone's wife one of these days. You can't spend the rest of your life outdoors playing around with the cattle. It's a man's job, damn it. It's my job. Allow me to do it?"

Again Melanie's eyes sought Josh for support. "Josh, can you see why Terrance is so mad at me?" she asked, her lower lip curved into a pout. "Wouldn't you think he'd be happy that he has someone besides mere cowhands to help him with the farm? Don't you sometimes wish that you had a brother or sis—?"

Melanie's words trailed off when she saw a

guarded look enter Josh's eyes. She had forgotten again! It had been twenty-five years since Josh had seen Shane, his twin brother, but it still seemed to unnerve Josh when Shane's name was brought into the conversation. Though Josh's father, Jared, enjoyed talking of the son who had disappeared so many years ago, Josh never wanted to discuss him.

Was it because the loss was still so painful? Or was it because his father had never let one day pass without talking about Shane as though he were there, alive? Had Josh been driven to drink and gambling because of his resentment of Shane?

"I'm sorry," Melanie blurted out. "I always forget. I know that you don't like to think of your brother . . . and . . . and the massacre."

Josh shifted his weight in his saddle. "The past is best left alone," he said. "Today and tomorrow is all I'm concerned about."

He turned aside so that Melanie could not read the truth in his eyes. For many years now he had known that Shane was alive and well. It always made him uneasy, even a bit guilty, when he was forced to think of Shane, for Josh had not shared the discovery with anyone. Not even his father.

When he discovered that Shane had been rescued by a band of Chippewa Indians, he had realized how difficult life would be for him if Shane returned home.

Josh already felt as though he were an outsider in his own home. He hated living in competition with the ghost of a brother who most thought was dead. In Josh's father's eyes, Shane was perfect. If Josh's father knew that Shane was alive, Shane would end up with everything! Josh would lose his control over the Brennan riches.

"Yes, I know how precious each day is to you while your father is still alive," Melanie said softly. "How is your father, Josh? Is he better this morning?"

"I don't see how Father can last much longer," Josh said, repositioning his hat so that the brim shadowed his cool blue eyes. "He wastes away a little more each day. I sometimes think I shouldn't leave the house. I'd hate to be gone when . . . when he needed me."

He looked over his shoulder, across the stretch of land that separated the Brennan farm from the Stantons'. A two-storied mansion loomed up, a pillared facade with a wide porch and mansard roof, white and stark. It was a large, empty home. His father had chosen not to remarry, but had instead mourned for the wife he had loved so intensely.

Josh hungered to fill the house with many laughing children. His and Melanie's.

"At least he's not alone today," he said thickly. "Mike Green, his attorney, is there. He should be there a good portion of the day. They have much to discuss." He frowned darkly, knowing that a will was being drawn up. His father had mentioned including Shane in the will. The thought of his father actually doing that grated at his nerves.

How could his father be so foolish as to include a dead man in his will?

Again Josh would be in competition with the

ghost of his brother. As far as Josh was concerned, his brother would remain a ghost. Forever!

"Enough talk about illnesses and dead brothers," Terrance said, visibly shuddering. "It's too pretty a day to be so morbid." He shook his head as he looked at Melanie. "I guess there's no talking you out of coming with us, is there?"

"Not on your life," Melanie said, stubbornly lifting her chin.

"Then let's be on our way," Terrance said, sinking the heels of his boots into the flanks of his black stallion. "Just don't stray from us, Melanie. I'd hate like hell to have to go and rescue you from a renegade Injun."

Ill and wasting away with tuberculosis, Jared Brennan trembled beneath his blankets with each painful breath. Mike Green, his attorney, sat at Jared's bedside, taking down everything that Jared instructed.

Then Mike paused and looked questioningly at Jared. "Jared, don't you think it's a bit foolish to include Shane in your will?" he asked in a low voice. "Surely you have accepted Shane's death by now. After you discovered the massacre that day, and Shane's disappearance, you searched everywhere for him. There's never been any indication that he's still alive." He cleared his throat nervously. "Be sensible, Jared. You have only one surviving son. Josh should be the only one mentioned in this will."

Jared glared at Mike. "I pay you well," he said,

13

stopping to inhale a shaky breath. "You write what I tell you."

"But Jared, this time you must listen to reason," Mike argued.

Jared lifted a bony hand from beneath the warmth of the blanket and pointed a trembling finger at Mike. "Either you do it my way or not at all," he said, his face flushed with anger. "There are more attorneys in St. Paul now than you can shake a stick at. I'll just have Josh find me someone who doesn't ask questions, who does as he is told and earns his pay because of it."

Mike sighed deeply. He nodded. "Whatever you say, I'll do," he said. "No need to get yourself all worked up. I just wanted to help."

"I don't need that kind of help," Jared sputtered as a sudden seizure of coughing overwhelmed him. He coughed until his face turned blue, then stopped, exhausted. He closed his eyes and panted for breath.

Mike laid his note pad aside and wrung a washcloth out in a basin of water, then sponged Jared's sweaty brow with it. "I'll write up the will just as you've instructed," he said in a soothing tone of voice. "It will state that half of all you possess goes to Shane if he ever shows up to claim it."

"Yes, that's what I want," Jared said hoarsely. "Until my son's body is brought before me, I will consider Shane to be alive. And if he is, he deserves everything that I've set aside for him. It's the least I can do after letting him down the day of the massacre. Damn. If only I could have gotten back to him that day. If only the rapids in that damn river hadn't complicated everything. Perhaps no one would have died. His mother would still be alive. Shane would be here as healthy and happy as Josh. It's all my fault, Mike. All my fault."

Mike continued bathing Jared's brow, acting now as a friend, not a lawyer. "Jared, there wasn't anything you could do about those rapids," he said, having heard the tale repeated over and over again. "You did what you had to do. You had to take your boat from the river and carry it past the worst of the rapids. You know how long that took. There was no way of knowing the other boat was in trouble."

"But it shouldn't have taken me or anyone else so long to realize that something was amiss when we stopped and began waiting for them. I recall being so tired," Jared said with a sob. "I was enjoying that time of rest before we ventured onward in the water again. I was selfish, Mike. Selfish! While I was resting, my wife was being slain. My son was being abducted. I can hardly bear to think of it now."

"Yes, I know," Mike said, dropping the cloth in the water and taking Jared's hand to comfort him. "The way you found your wife must haunt you something terrible. But you must stop blaming yourself. You've lived a lifetime of regret. Try to spend your remaining days in peace. Please, Jared. You deserve so much more than you have allowed yourself. You cannot turn time back now, no more than you could stop those rapids that interfered with your life that day. Let it go, Jared. Let it go."

Jared looked wild-eyed up at Mike. He clasped his friend's hand hard. "Just make sure that Shane gets his fair share," he said, tears spilling from his eyes. "Do that for me, will you, Mike?"

Mike nodded. "You know that I will," he said. He watched Jared's washed-out blue eyes close as he fell into a restless sleep. He eased his hands from Jared's and went to gaze out the bedroom window. He looked toward the neighboring farm and watched three horsemen riding down the dusty lane. He leaned closer to the window, correcting his thoughts. The riders weren't all men. One was a lady, more than likely Melanie Stanton.

But one of the two men was Josh. God. How was Josh going to take the wording of this will? It would be humiliating, but no more humiliating than having to live under the shadow of a long-lost brother all these years.

Though Mike did not care much for Josh, he could not help but pity him.

· CHAPTER TWO ·

The sun was barely over the treetops, pulsing and glowing. In the shadows of early dawn stood a tall, lean man with broad shoulders, his sun-bronzed face revealing strong lines and a kind of savage eagerness. His eyes were crisply blue, his shoulder-length hair was the golden color of summer wheat. Though he was dressed in fringed buckskins and beaded moccasins, and stood among the Chippewa Indians as though one of them, he was white.

All around Shane Brennan men and women labored hard cutting birch trees and erecting wigwams. The Chippewa had traveled for two sleeps but now had arrived at the location of the village they had left behind many moons ago.

Across the land, bare bent birch poles reached up from the ground like skeletal fingers. At one time in the past many wigwams had housed families of Chippewa here. When the decision was made for the village to move north, the poles had been stripped of their buckskin coverings and left behind, a graveyard of memories.

Resting the handle of his axe on his shoulder, Shane stared into space. He had his own memories to contend with. They had only recently been brought to the surface in his mind. He and the Chippewa with whom he had been living these past twenty-five years had stopped to rest and parley with other bands of Chippewa on their way back from Canada, sharing stories over a campfire long into the night. When Shane was asked how he had come to be with the Chippewa instead of his true white family, he had explained about the massacre and the man who was partly to blame—the man with the peculiar eyes, one brown and one blue.

It had come as a shock to Shane when some of those who had listened intently to his tale of a dying mother and her stolen wedding band said they had heard rumors of such a man. He had been seen trapping in the area. They even supplied Shane with the man's name.

"Trapper Dan!" Shane whispered in a hiss. "He calls himself Trapper Dan!"

Shane lifted his axe and began chopping a birch tree with angry swings, pretending the tree was the evil, murdering trapper. As soon as he had erected his wigwam, he was going to go and search for him. Finally, Shane's mother's death would be avenged!

18

He lifted the axe for another blow to the tree, but stopped when a shadow fell in his path. Not offering a smile, he turned and faced Chief Gray Falcon. Ever since Gray Falcon's father had died, Shane had felt his coldness toward him deepen into something more intense. Though they had been childhood friends, things had begun to change as they grew older. Gray Falcon had become jealous of Shane because Shane had become so close to his father, Chief Standing Tall.

Did Shane have to expect this jealousy to intensify even after the old chief's death? He hoped not, yet it was in Gray Falcon's dark eyes even now, the smoldering fire of his hatred of someone he had decided not to accept as one of his people.

"Stop!" Gray Falcon ordered flatly. "You have no need to build an *ayn-dah-yin.*"

Shane's blue eyes widened with surprise. The muscles of his tanned, bare shoulders tensed. "I don't understand you," he said in Chippewa, although he still spoke in English quite well. He had kept the ability by sharing much time with trappers and traders while living in Canada. He had even learned the French language from those who had taken the time to teach him. He was proud to be fluent in three different languages.

Shane looked around him. Many wigwams were nearing completion. He looked back into Gray Falcon's cold, fathomless eyes. "What have you not said that you are feeling in your heart?" he asked. "Tell me why I have no need for a wigwam."

Gray Falcon folded his arms across his bare

copper chest. He lifted his chin smugly. "You have no need, because you will no longer be a part of my people," he said sternly. "It is time for you to return to your people. Leave me in peace with mine!"

"What did you say?" Shane gasped. "You are ordering me to leave? You do not see that I am happy with the Chippewa? I have no family but Chippewa!"

Shane gestured with a hand toward himself. "Do I not wear my hair unbraided to prove my mourning for your father? Do I not wear narrow strips of braided buckskin around my neck and waist during this period of mourning?" he said, his voice drawn and disbelieving of what was being forced upon him.

He doubled a fist to his bare chest, resting it over his heart. His gaze lowered and he looked at himself and how he was clothed in fringed buckskin leggings and moccasins. "Have I not always dressed and acted as though a true Chippewa?" he asked, looking slowly up at Gray Falcon. "As children, we rode side by side in the hunt, Gray Falcon. Did you resent me even then? Did you?"

"It is because of you that my people were moved north from the peaceful land of many lakes," Gray Falcon said sharply. "It is because of you my father chose to move his people north. He grew tired of hiding you when white people came asking for you. He knew that it was best to take you north because he knew the white people would not venture that far from their own land. He did this to his own people to protect your identity from yours!"

"That is not the only reason your father moved north," Shane said. He had been told later in life about Chief Standing Tall having always hidden him when he was a child from anyone who came searching for him. At that time Shane had been too small to understand why he was whisked away at the sound of approaching horses. When he was older, he was already in Canada, and hiding was no longer necessary. "Your father was not content with the land and the game that was offered him in the south. He was in search of a better way of life. Never would a chief as strong-minded as your father let a mere boy stand in the way of what was best for his people!"

"I am more astute than you. I saw a father whose heart drifted from strong love for a son to care more deeply for one who was not a blood relation. Though you did not live in the same dwelling as my family, my father became your father," Chief Gray Falcon said. "He enjoyed your company more than mine, his true son. Did he not even play the white man game of cards that you call poker with you? Sons and fathers should share—not sons and strangers!"

"I have not been a stranger since the day your father rescued me from the forest," Shane said, setting his jaw firmly. "I became one of your people that day. I grew to love all of your people. When your father gave me to Little Dove to raise as her own, and when I was even blessed with a

21

sister many moons later, my past life was forgotten. I did not mean to cause resentments. I am sorry for that, Gray Falcon, but now let us forget the past and live as a family. This is what your father would want."

Gray Falcon firmed his jaw. "No," he argued. "It is time for you to seek your true destiny. You were not born with the blood of the Chippewa running through your veins. You are white. You have a family who are white. *Mah-szhon*—go to them now."

Anger rose within Shane and he felt as though he were being banished from the tribe because of having been deceitful. He met Gray Falcon's steady stare with his own. "I go," he said. "But not to a white family, for I have none. They were lost to me many years ago. To them I am dead. To me they are dead!"

"You have a brother and father who are alive," Gray Falcon said, his eyes unblinking. "For many moons my father has known of your true father and where he resides. Before Father died, he confided this truth to me. I was not to tell you unless you had reason to know. My father showed two of his braves where your family resides and instructed them to keep the secret until the time came for you to know. One of the old braves is still alive. He will guide you to your true family. There you will live. Not here with the Chippewa."

Shane's head was spinning with all that he was discovering—not only that Grey Falcon, who had

22

once been as close to him as a brother, resented him so deeply, but that Chief Standing Tall had known all along where Shane's true family was! When Shane was first told about being hidden from his family when they had come searching for him all those years ago, it had been hard to accept. But he had grown to understand that Chief Standing Tall had acted this way because he had grown to love him. No true father could have ever loved as strongly or devotedly!

Yet, for Chief Standing Tall to have known through all the years where Shane's true family resided, surely grieving for him, made his heart begin a slow ache. In a sense, Chief Standing Tall had deceived him. Though done in love, it was still no less than deceit!

Han-tay-wee, Cedar Maid, the daughter of Little Dove who had been raised as Shane's sister, came to stand beside him. She took his hand and gazed up into his eyes the color of the sky, then looked slowly at Gray Falcon. She grew cold inside when she saw Gray Falcon's stiff reserve as he glared at Shane. Since Chief Standing Tall's death, she had feared what might transpire between the new young chief and Shane. She knew the depth of Gray Falcon's resentment.

"Gray Falcon, what is wrong with you?" she asked softly, yet fearing to hear the answer. "Why are you *nish-ska-diz-ee?* You should be happy, not angry, that we have arrived to our land that you were eager to return to. Our people are preparing their wigwams with much love and pride in their hearts. Now that you are chief, you have guided your people here, to the place of your boyhood dreams. Why are you not happy, Gray Falcon?"

"You read my mood wrong, Cedar Maid," Gray Falcon said, frowning down at her. "It is not an unhappy face you see. It is the face of a chief who is giving an order that must be carried out."

"What order?" Cedar Maid asked, glancing at Shane, then back at Gray Falcon. "You tell Shane something? What is it? I know him well. I read his mood right and I see that he is not happy!"

"While our people build themselves new wigwams, Shane is to move onward," Gray Falcon said, stubbornly lifting his chin.

Cedar Maid gasped. She turned quickly to Shane. "Where will you go?" she asked, her dark eyes pleading. "Shane, tell me that what Gray Falcon says is false. You cannot leave. Cedar Maid will go with you if you do!"

Suddenly realizing what banishment meant—leaving the way of life that he had grown to love, and leaving Cedar Maid behind also—Shane felt as though his heart was being pierced by many arrows. Already he missed his sister. Their mother had gone to the hereafter many moons ago, and Cedar Maid had depended on Shane for protection.

Now who would she have? He could not take her with him. She would not be happy away from her people. Would she be treated fairly by Gray Falcon when left alone without Shane's protection? Or would Gray Falcon's resentment not be cast aside when Shane was gone? Would he not also hold the same resentment against Cedar Maid because she was Shane's sister?

Shane placed his fingers gently to Cedar Maid's shoulders. He swallowed hard, her gentle loveliness today almost stealing his breath away. Her white, fine buckskin dress clung to her wondrous curves; her hair was loose and worn very long down her back. Many said that, at the age of fifteen winters, she was the most beautiful maiden among all the Chippewa villages in both Canada and the Land of Many Lakes. Her beauty made her even more vulnerable, for she would be sought out soon by many willing to pay a high bride price for her. Shane wanted to be there to decide if the brave who paid for her was good enough for her!

But that was not meant to be. Because of Gray Falcon's jealousies, Shane would have to say farewell to Cedar Maid, and when he did, he would not look back. He would never return to this village and beg for permission to see Cedar Maid! If he was forced to leave the Indian life behind, he would also leave everything about this way of life behind. He would no longer speak in Chippewa. He would never wear his hair in braids again.

He was glad that he had retained his rightful name. If he had been forced to take an Indian name—ah, how hard it would be to leave it behind!

"Shane, tell me you are not going," Cedar Maid said, breaking into soft sobs. "Tell me it is not so!"

"I've got to go now," Shane said thickly. "I

25

should have not stayed so long with your people. It is time for me to break my ties now and return to my own people. Please try to understand."

Cedar Maid broke away from his grasp and flung herself into his arms, hugging him tightly. "My people, the Chippewa, are your people!" she cried. "Do not abandon us just because you hunger for the white man's way of life. Oh, Shane, please take me with you if you must go!"

Feeling torn apart inside, Shane held her close, then eased her away from him. He firmed his jaw and looked down at her. "Deep inside my heart the Chippewa will always be my people," he said, fighting back a sob that would make him look less than a man. "But my true people live not even a sleep away, and I must go and make acquaintance with them again. It has been twenty-five long winters since I last saw them. It is time to make all wrongs right."

He looked over Cedar Maid's shoulder at Gray Falcon. "Though you do this thing because of ill feelings between us, I will pretend that you do it because you think it is best for me," he said. "I will go. I will entrust Cedar Maid in your care. Do not let harm come to her. She deserves a good life. She is nothing but sweetness."

Cedar Maid grabbed his hands. "Let me go with you," she cried. "My brother, my heart will break with missing you!"

Again Shane drew her within his arms. "Cedar Maid, I have no idea how the white man's world is going to treat me, and I am white," he said softly, weaving his fingers through her long, drifting hair.

"But I suspect how you, an Indian, would be treated. It is not best for you to leave your people. Stay. A husband will come soon and pay a great bride price for you. Be content in being a wife."

Cedar Maid jerked free from his grip and turned and defied Chief Gray Falcon with fire in her eyes. "It is all your fault!" she stormed. "You know that your father looks down from the hereafter disapproving of this that you do. You must change your mind. Do not force Shane to go!"

"Stop arguing!" Gray Falcon hissed. He drew an imaginary line in mid-air that signified that was the way it had to be and he would not listen to any further argument about it.

Cedar Maid spun around on a heel and looked pleadingly up at Shane again.

"I will come to see you some time," Shane said, lying. Even if it meant abandoning Cedar Maid, he would not look back. He would never try to combine two such different lives. If he were going to be forced to live in the white man's world, it would be as a white man!

Cedar Maid lunged into his arms again. "Oh, do come often," she sobbed. "My heart will be so lonely with missing you!"

Two braves on horseback approached, leading Shane's white stallion, already saddled behind them. Shane looked up into the eyes of his best friend, Red Raven, then at the old brave, Flying Wing. It was apparently Flying Wing who carried the secret of where Shane's true family lived. He looked at Red Raven. It was in his eyes that he knew what was occurring—and that he would soon lose his best friend to the white man's world. He had even painted black marks of mourning across his cheeks and brow.

"You have come to accompany me to my new world?" Shane asked, making the brother sign by touching two fingers to his lips and swinging his hand straight out from his mouth.

"*Ay-uh,*" Red Raven said, his eyes wavering. "Now our plans to search for Trapper Dan together cannot be. You will be gone, my friend."

Shane tensed, having for the moment forgotten the plans of friends. They had spoken often on the journey from Canada about how they would join forces and find the evil trapper. Now even that was being denied Shane because of Gray Falcon's command. Shane and Red Raven were being forced apart, their camaraderie a thing of the past.

From the moment he said farewell to his best friend, Shane would be forced to eat, sleep, and hunt alone. Though he would be shown where his true family resided, that did not mean that he would want to share the intimacies of his life with them as he had with Red Raven. The ultimate that could be shared between friends would be an enemy found and dealt with properly, and now this would never be.

Shane would have to search for Trapper Dan alone. But first he could not help but be curious about his true family and where they resided. He would accompany Red Raven and Flying Wing there, but he would choose for himself just when he would go and meet his brother and father face-to-face. Knowing that Trapper Dan was somewhere near lay too heavily on his heart to make plans to establish a whole new life for himself at this moment. His mother's death must be avenged, and soon!

"Yes, all of our plans must be forgotten," Shane finally said, resting a hand heavily on his friend's shoulder.

"Let us make the miles stretch out before us slowly, my friend," Red Raven said solemnly. "While we can, we shall cling to this world that we have shared for many moons."

"Yes, we shall travel slowly," Shane said, nodding. He lowered his hand from Red Raven's shoulder and looked down at Cedar Maid. Seeing her remorseful tears, he drew her into his arms and gave her a soft kiss on the brow, then turned away from her. He gathered together his buckskin bags which held his belongings. Reaching inside one of them, he made sure that the old chief's deck of cards was still there. How many times had they sat before a fire in the chief's great lodge, playing poker, smoking pipes, and drinking whiskey? The old chief had liked nothing better than his smoke, cards, and whiskey after having been introduced to them by a trapper who had come and spent many sleeps with them in the village. Shane had learned to enjoy these pastimes too and had accepted the old chief's cards as a remembrance as he had lain on his death bed.

Shane would guard the cards with his life. They were all that remained of the chief's devotion and friendship.

He slipped a fringed buckskin shirt over his

head and eyed the carved bow that he was so proud of having made himself. He set his jaw firmly, choosing not to take his bow, reminding himself of his vow to make a clean break with the Indians now that he was being banished from the tribe.

With an angry determination, he slipped his long Kentucky rifle into a leather gun boot at the side of his horse and sheathed a knife at his waist. He secured his bundles of belongings on his horse, then mounted.

Shane gave Cedar Maid a lingering stare. "Cedar Maid, I have to go now," he said thickly, vowing to himself that those were the last Chippewa words that he would ever speak. "Be happy."

He could not stand the despair in Cedar Maid's eyes any longer. He wheeled his horse around and rode away, feeling the same emptiness that he had felt the day his mother died. He already missed Cedar Maid almost as unbearably and he had not been gone from her for more than two heartbeats!

As Shane rode between the old brave and his best friend, he forced his thoughts from Cedar Maid. He was going to be starting a new life again. The first time he had been forced into such a change, he had wondered if he could learn to adjust to life among the Indians. Now, ironically, he was wondering if he could adjust to the white man's way of life. Could they adjust to him? He knew that prejudices existed and that if anyone realized that he had been raised among Indians, he might be looked down upon, as still a part of them.

He feared many a battle ahead, but surely most would be within his heart and mind!

His horse was a large, clean-limbed, very swift white stallion. He rode at a trot, occasionally broken by a short lope. Less than one sleep away, if he wished, he could be talking with his true father again. And what of his brother?

He frowned as he tried to recall his brother's name.

Josh?

Was it Josh?

Did his brother remember him? Or had he given up long ago on ever seeing Shane again?

Shane could not help but wonder how his brother would react when he discovered that his twin was still alive. Would he be pleased?

Or would he resent a brother who was in a true sense no brother at all?

Too many years divided them.

Perhaps it was best not to return at all!

Downcast, torn with indecision over what he should do, Shane rode onward.

· CHAPTER THREE ·

Shane dismounted in a grove of cottonwoods and willows and led the white stallion to the Rum River, which crept narrowly through the pine forest. Cascading water gurgled in little rills and spills through natural rock gates where minnows flashed in the red glow of the setting sun.

While his horse drank greedily, Shane sank to one knee, cupped his hands together, and lowered them into the river. He lifted his hands to his mouth and drank the water in slow gulps, feeling rather than seeing Red Raven come to stand beside him.

The time of parting was near. The farewell would be hard. At the age of eight winters, Red Raven and Shane had opened wounds on their arms with sharp knives to mingle their blood. In every sense of the word they were brothers; the bond between them was stronger than Shane's with his real brother, whose name he had almost forgotten during the years of separation.

So many of his memories had been robbed by the passing of time. Only four years old at the time of his rescue, he had even forgotten his own last name! If he had known the name, he would have gone searching for his true family long ago.

As it was, he had learned to live with one name, with one family of Chippewa. He had never guessed that his life would ever be any different. He had thought to die and be buried in the Chippewa tradition.

Shane doubted if he could ever feel the same about anyone as he did about Red Raven. They had shared their first hunt, the first vision, and how it felt to be with a woman for that first time.

Because of Gray Falcon, Shane and Red Raven would never share anything again.

Shane would never again have good feelings about Gray Falcon, but he would not hate him. Gray Falcon was the son of Chief Standing Tall and the old chief would not want hate between two men who should love one another as brothers.

But Shane would always resent Gray Falcon for separating him from his Chippewa family.

His thirst quenched, Shane rose to his feet. Wanting to delay the parting, he stepped past Red Raven and went to the edge of the butte. The river hurried down the gentle slope of the butte and cut across a wide, fertile pasture alongside a split rail fence that marched across the land as far as his eye could see.

Shane looked down upon the green river valley that stretched out below him. A feeling of pride swept through him. His father had achieved great things. Everywhere he looked cattle grazed on the soft green grass. He knew of the longhorns that had been introduced to the Land of Many Lakes by boats, which had carried them from a place called Texas.

He had seen longhorns before, but never in this quantity. They made a striking sight. Most were coal-black and clean-limbed, their white horns glistening as if polished. Some had bodies so long their backs swayed; their dewlaps swung in rhythm with their steps. They were mightily antlered and wild-eyed.

Shane looked beyond the cattle. His shoulder muscles tensed when he saw two massive houses in the distance. Flying Wing had pointed out his father's house, and it was as nothing Shane had ever seen before. It was a house built by a man of many riches. Was Shane ready to become a part of such a life?

"My friend, it is time for Red Raven to leave," the young brave said, interrupting Shane's troubled thoughts.

Shane turned slowly to his friend. He willed away the tears that would show signs of weakness in his character. "Yes, it is time to go separate ways," he said, placing his hands on his friend's shoulders. "Though we say farewell you will live within my heart forever. Be happy, Red Raven.

Find a woman and let her fill your dwelling with sunshine. Soon Cedar Maid will be needing a man to warm her bed. Go to her. She will make a good wife."

"*Ay-uh*. Red Raven has been watching Cedar Maid with interest," Red Raven said, smiling at the thought of her loveliness. "Already I have decided on the bride price I will pay."

Shane's eyes brightened. He dropped his hands to his sides. "You plan to offer a bride price soon?" he asked, his voice displaying much gladness. "You never told me. It is not like you to keep secrets from your blood brother."

Red Raven looked away from Shane, lowering his eyes to the ground. "It was in my plan to tell you soon," he said thickly. "Never did I expect you would be gone when the time came to share this special secret."

Shane doubled a fist at his side. "Nor did I expect to be gone," he growled. "Chief Gray Falcon is the most skilled of all at keeping secrets. He must have known for many moons that he was going to banish me from the village of Chippewa."

"And what of Trapper Dan?" Red Raven asked. "You will still search for him?"

Shane's eyes narrowed in hate. "You ask a question you already have an answer to," he said flatly. He looked determinedly at Red Raven. "Soon I shall travel through these forests until I find the man with the peculiar eyes. I have only temporarily been sidetracked from this quest."

"Your search will be a lonely one without Red Raven riding at your side," Red Raven said, then suddenly lunged into Shane's arms, hugging him. "Everyone will miss you, Shane. You will come often to see your people, the Chippewa?"

Shane patted Red Raven on the back, then stepped away. "No," he said firmly, again surveying the land of his true father. "It is over. Never will I return. I have been banished. I shall stay away. It is time to begin a new life—a life that was stolen from me when I had seen but four winters."

"You do not mean it!" Red Raven gasped. "You will not return to the Chippewa? Ever? What of your feelings for Cedar Maid? You will miss her. She will miss you!"

"I have spoken," Shane said firmly. "It is up to you to make Cedar Maid forget me. Make her happy, Red Raven. I cannot depend on Gray Falcon to see to her welfare. I believe he sees me every time he looks at her. I cannot trust him where she is concerned."

"I will make things right with her," Red Raven said, nodding.

Shane placed a hand on Red Raven's shoulder. "That is good," he said softly. "That is good."

Shane turned away from Red Raven and once again looked down at the shadowy valley.

"You are eager to see your true father?" Red Raven asked as his eyes followed Shane's steady stare. "You are eager to own the land? The animals?"

"No, I am not eager for anything at this moment," Shane said, his voice quiet. "I am filled with sadness."

Flying Wing, the old brave who had accompanied Shane from the village, rode up to Shane and Red Raven. He frowned down at Red Raven. "It is time to go," he said. "We have many miles to ride through the darkness. Let us begin now."

Shane and Red Raven turned and faced each other, then Shane tore the braided buckskin strips from his neck and waist and tossed them to the ground. "My mourning is over, as is my old life," he said. He pointed toward Red Raven's horse. "Go. Do not look back. Go now."

Red Raven swallowed hard, then spun around and hurried to his horse. Looking straight ahead, he urged his horse away in a strong gallop.

Shane placed a hand on his heart and doubled it into a tight fist. He looked up at Flying Wing, for a moment gazing at the old chief sitting on his saddle of blankets. "Farewell, old friend," he said, then turned his back as Flying Wing rode away from him.

To busy himself, Shane began gathering firewood. This was as close as he would get to his father's house tonight. He was not quite ready to test his father's or brother's feelings. Surely they thought he was dead. Would it not be the same as seeing a ghost when they first caught sight of him?

Perhaps it would be best if he did not even go to them.

He would take the full night to ponder his best course. Nothing was ever gained by making hasty decisions.

In a matter of minutes Shane had a fire burning. He looked at the river. He was hungry. He would spear a fish with his knife and fill his stomach, hoping that would help fill the emptiness that he felt inside him.

Once a fish was caught, Shane knelt down beside the fire. But something kept him from cooking the fish. The strange bellowing and moaning of the longhorns drew him back to his feet and to the very edge of the butte, silhouetting him against the blazing sunset.

He looked down at the restless animals. They seemed to be an extension of his own restlessness. At this moment he was straddling two worlds, torn between two life paths.

Melanie brushed her horse eagerly. The day spent in St. Paul had been inspiring. She had showed both Josh and Terrance that she knew how to transact business as skillfully as any man. They hadn't known that she had studied the ledgers beforehand, familiarizing herself with the cost of cattle.

"Their eyes almost popped out of their heads when I quoted the cost of shipping the longhorns," she whispered. "They could hardly believe it when I told them that it costs about a dollar a head to ship an average herd from New Orleans to Minnesota."

The bellowing of the cattle drew Melanie's attention from her bay gelding. Placing the brush on a shelf, she left the barn and went to stand at the fence, viewing the animals. Some cows were chewing their cuds; others were licking their calves.

She could almost smell the cattle's strong, good,

and wholesome breath. She could hear the placid moos with which each calf was greeted as it came through the gate from the calf pen to suck from the cows.

Then Melanie looked out at the big pasture. Restless longhorns were tossing their heads high in the air, bellowing and nervously swishing their tails back and forth. It was as though they smelled something in the air that was not familiar to them.

But what?

Melanie inhaled deeply, tensing when she smelled a slight trace of smoke, the kind that came from an outdoor fire. Shielding her eyes with her hands to keep the rays of the bright sunset from blinding her, she looked up at the butte in the distance. She gasped and took a shaky step backward when she saw the silhouette of a lone man atop the butte, smoke spiraling up from a campfire behind him.

"Who could that be?" she whispered harshly. "Why is he alone and staring down at the farms?"

She glanced over her shoulder at her home. Terrance had left only a short while ago to spend the evening drinking and gambling in town. He had left before supper. Except for the cowhands, who were occupied with their evening chores, and the household servants, Melanie was alone.

She looked past her farm, at Josh and Jared's house. Josh had accompanied Terrance into town, and she would not trouble Jared with the news that a stranger was closely observing their adjoining lands.

"That leaves only me," she said, turning her

eyes back to the butte. "I'll go and investigate myself. With my rifle I should be safe enough."

She frowned when she discovered that the man was no longer in view. But the smoke spiraling upward from the fire was proof enough that he was still there.

"I will go," Melanie said, hurriedly bridling and saddling her horse. She slipped her rifle into the leather gun boot at the horse's side, then swung herself up into the saddle.

The wind was becoming cool as the sun dipped low behind the distant hills. Hiking her fringed skirt above her knees, Melanie urged her horse into a gallop. Her hair whipped across her shoulders, then around her face. Her white cotton blouse was not heavy enough to ward off the chill that engulfed her as she reached the dampness of the forest and began climbing the gentle incline that led to the butte. The scent of the fire grew stronger, intermingled with the fragrance of cooking fish.

"He's sure making himself at home on property that does not belong to him," Melanie muttered to herself. "Who does he think he is? Anyone who knows anything about cattle would know that it makes folks nervous to have a stranger so close. What if he plans to steal a few in the night? Whose would he choose? Ours or the Brennans'?"

Not wanting to be noticed, Melanie drew her horse to a halt and secured the reins to a tree. Taking her rifle from the gun boot, she made her way stealthily through the forest. Up just ahead, a small campfire cast flickering shadows against the dark trees.

Her heart pounding, Melanie stopped to take a deep, quivering breath. Then she moved onward. She was now close enough to see the man sitting by the fire, eating. But his back was to her. All that she could see was long golden hair, his fringed buckskin outfit, and moccasins. If not for his golden hair, she would think that he was Indian because of the way he was dressed.

She had to see more. She had to see his face!

Just as Melanie started to move behind some flowering bushes to get a look at the stranger's face, he sprang to his feet, as lithe as a panther. His knife was drawn and poised in the air.

Melanie's breath was stolen away by his quickness and by the threat of his knife. Yet she calmed herself, knowing that she had the true advantage. She was pointing a loaded rifle directly at his chest!

Then she had another shock. The light of the fire flickered on the man's face, revealing all of his features to Melanie. He looked so much like Josh Brennan he could have been his double! He had the same sky-blue eyes, the same golden hair the color of summer wheat, the sculped jawline and lips.

The only differences were in the length of the hair and the man's build. The stranger was a tall, lean man like Josh, but his shoulders were much broader and his muscles rippled beneath his skintight buckskin clothes.

Melanie was so taken aback by the resemblance, that she was at a loss for words. She stared openly at Shane, and he at her. Neither lowered their weapons.

"Who are you?" Shane finally asked, his eyes flashing dangerously. Yet though this woman was a threat to him, he could not help but admire her bravery. And her ravishing loveliness. Her hair was the color of the sunset; her eyes were dark brown, wide, and daring. She was slim and exquisite and had perfect, soft features. In many ways she reminded him of Cedar Maid, except that this woman's skin was white.

"It is I who should be doing the asking," Melanie said, finally overcoming her astonishment at his resemblance to Josh. She looked down at his knife, then back up into his eyes. "You are trespassing. I'm sure you know the dangers. I could shoot you right here on the spot and be within my rights."

"Why don't you?" Shane dared. "I am an easy target."

His gaze raked over her again. He was puzzled by her attire. She wore a fringed buckskin skirt and knee-high moccasins. Why did she prefer Indian clothes over those of the white people? Was there some wildness flowing through her veins? Did she prefer the outdoors to the white woman's fancy house? Did that not give him even more reason to admire her? Was she from the house that adjoined his father's? Or was she from his father's house, perhaps married to Shane's brother?

"I won't have to shoot you because you are

going to agree to move on, away from my land," Melanie said, swallowing hard when she realized that he was studying her far too closely. It unnerved her.

"Your land?" Shane said, slowly lowering his knife to his side. "And how is that you lay claim to land that once belonged to only the Indian and wild animals?"

Melanie shuffled her feet nervously. This man was not only dressed like a savage, he thought like one! Who was he? Where had he come from? What did he want?

"Are you saying that I have no right to claim this land that my father paid for and nurtured as though it were a child until he died?" Melanie asked, her voice tense. She slowly lowered the rifle to her side.

Shane's eyes wavered. He still didn't know which house she lived in. What if Shane's father had remarried and a daughter had been born to him? What if this woman was the daughter? What if she was Shane's sister? She had just said that her father was dead. Could that mean that his father was dead?

The thought caused him a deep inner turmoil, bringing the realization that he did want a chance to see his true father again. The pain he felt now was the pain of loss. He had felt the same long ago when he had lost his mother, and again recently when the old chief died. He knew the feeling well.

In his mind's eye he could see his father again as he had looked to an adoring little boy—big, strong, his eyes filled with love for his son. If his father was dead he would never know that love again.

Even if he were alive, Shane might not find love in his father's eyes.

Shane was no longer an innocent boy of four. He was a man—a man who had been raised by the Chippewa. His feelings about life were Chippewa. Could a father with white skin and the ideals of a white man ever accept the fact that his son thought differently, behaved differently?

"Your father is dead?" Shane asked finally.

Melanie saw sudden alarm in the depths of his magnetic blue eyes and wondered at it. Why would this stranger care about her father? Had he known her father? If so, when? "My father died a short while ago," she murmured. "Why do you ask?"

"His name," Shane asked, gazing raptly down at her. "What was your father's name?" He could not remember his own last name no matter how hard he tried. But he recalled his father's first name. He had heard his mother address him as Jared too many times ever to forget it!

Melanie was shaken by the stranger's resemblance to Josh now that a similar cold determination had entered his eyes. How could it be? Melanie had met all of Josh's close relatives and none had resembled him, and none had been this man, for she would never have forgotten him!

This man. Why, he looked enough like Josh to be . . . his brother!

Melanie's hands went to her throat and she grew pale. Sudden remembrances of Jared Brennan talking about a son who had been abducted by Indians twenty-five years ago came to her mind. He had been four. Today he would be twenty-nine. This man who was awaiting her reply could be that age.

Could it possibly be . . . ?

But why was he so adamant about wanting to know her father's name?

"My father's name was Duane," Melanie said softly, watching him carefully for his reaction. "Duane Stanton."

She saw the muscles of his face contort strangely, then go slack, and his chest heave with a deep sigh, relief evident. Knowing her father's name had meant something.

But what?

"Your name?" she blurted. "What is your name?"

A warning shot through Shane. He was not sure if he was ready to disclose his true identity to anyone just yet. Though he now understood just how eager he was to see his father again after all these years of having been denied him, he did not want to rush right into it. He had to ready himself. He had only found out today where his father and brother resided. Only today had he found out that he had another life still awaiting him.

"My name is not important," Shane said, squatting down on his haunches before the fire. He picked up his baked fish and bit into it.

Unable to banish the thought of Jared's long-lost son from her mind, Melanie dared to bend down beside the stranger. She had heard Shane's name spoken so often by Jared Brennan, it was as though she had known him all of her life. If she spoke the name out loud to this man, would it—could it—mean something to him?

"Shane?" she said suddenly, her insides tremoring with anticipation as she watched him for his reaction. When his head jerked around and their eyes met and held, he did not have to answer her, for she knew that it was he.

· CHAPTER FOUR ·

Shane rose slowly to his feet; Melanie followed his lead. Her eyes were still fixed on his; her mind was aswirl with questions but she dared not ask any of them, for even though she was certain this man was Shane Brennan, he had not yet openly admitted it to her.

Oh, why didn't he say something? His silence was unnerving! She did not know what to do now, or say. He had to say something about her having called him Shane. What could she expect? What if he denied it? What then?

Full of wonder of this woman who seemed to look right into his heart and discover answers that he had not wanted to share with anyone just yet, Shane looked for only a moment longer at her, then spun around and walked toward his horse.

47

He had to get away, to think! He had to put a distance between himself and this woman who not only knew who he was but also had a way of disturbing him as no other woman had before her. Never had he met any woman who was such a combination of beauty, knowledge, and courage! It would be too easy to love such a woman.

Shane realized that there were dangers in his feelings, for even though he now knew that this woman was not his sister, she could be married to his brother. And though he need only ask her a few simple questions to get the answers he wanted, he was too torn by other things that moved him to go and commune with the Great Spirit, to ask for strength.

Stopping suddenly, Shane realized where his thoughts had taken him. He was ready to pray to the Great Spirit—but that could not be! He had been banished from the Chippewa tribe and from their lives; he had vowed to place all Indian thoughts and habits behind him. That meant even the Great Spirit!

Melanie had almost run after Shane when he had turned away from her, yet something held her back. She had seen how Shane looked—as though he was being torn by feelings. Since he had come this close to returning to his family, she could not let her interference change his mind. Surely he wanted to go to them in his own time, in his own way. Her questions about where he had been and with whom could wait.

But ask them she would! Something told her

that he needed a friend and she would be there for him when he realized it, too.

Melanie's heart skipped a beat when Shane suddenly stopped and made no more effort to leave. Her pulse raced when she saw him double his hands into tight fists at his sides. He was battling so much within him—she could tell! She could not just stand by and ignore it. He needed someone.

Walking slowly toward him, Melanie's knees were weak with anticipation. "Shane, please don't leave," she murmured. "Tell me all about everything. Where have you been? How have you lived these past twenty-five years?"

When she reached his side, she moved her hand slowly toward his. When she touched his bronzed skin it was as though a current of warmth moved between them. She had expected him to jump with a start at her touch, but instead he loosened his fist and let her twine her fingers through his. When he turned and looked down at her and their wondering eyes met, she felt her heart melting into his.

"Come and sit beside the fire," Melanie softly urged, almost hypnotized by his soft stare. "Let's talk. If you want, I will promise not to tell anyone. You will go to your father and disclose to him that you are alive whenever you feel the time is right."

Saying this, giving him this option, made a sort of desperation rise inside Melanie, for she knew that his father could be taking his last breath of life at any moment. Shane shouldn't wait too long.

Yet she did not feel free to tell him anything so

upsetting. He was obviously already emotionally overwhelmed by everything that had brought him here now.

But why *was* he here now? Why hadn't he returned sooner to see his family? Had he only just discovered where they lived?

Shane still did not speak, but only looked down at her with his magnetic eyes that disturbed her in unfamiliar ways. Again she thought of Josh and how strange it was that Shane could look so much like Josh, the man she despised, yet could affect her so sensually. Was it because there was a challenge in knowing, perhaps in even eventually loving this man who had a wild, savage side to him?

She had never known such a man before.

Or was it because she felt so deeply for him, knowing that these past twenty-five years had surely been anything but easy? It was apparent by his attire and behavior that he had lived in the wilderness.

"How do you know my name?" Shane suddenly blurted. "Why do you care about me now when earlier you were ready to shoot me?"

A great relief flooded Melanie, almost making her dizzy with happiness, for Shane had finally confessed to being Shane!

Could it truly be?

Shane. Shane Brennan! The little boy of four who had disappeared those twenty-five years ago now was face to face with her!

How wonderful the news would be for Jared Brennan. He was going to have his last wish in life—of seeing his son whom everyone else had sworn was dead.

"How do I know you?" Melanie said, looking adoringly up at him. "Oh, Shane, your father has kept you alive within not only his heart, but mine also. He has talked so much about you, I feel as though I have known you all my life. Somehow he knew that you would return to him." She grabbed his other hand and squeezed it affectionately. "And you have! He will be so happy, Shane. So happy!"

"My father," Shane said, absorbing the softness of Melanie's hands within the coarseness of his own, feeling the bond between himself and Melanie strengthening. It surely was destiny that they should meet this way. He could see so much in her eyes. He could hear so much in her voice. "My father is still alive?"

Melanie's smile faded.

Should she tell him?

No!

She thought it best not to disclose such a sad truth to Shane at the very moment he was finally opening up to her.

She forced another smile. "Yes, your father is alive," she said, nodding. "Also your brother, Josh."

Her gaze swept over him, then looked into his eyes again. "You look so much like your twin brother," she marveled. "There are some differences. But not so much in appearances. The difference I see is in your hearts."

Shane's gaze raked over her, familiarizing himself with her loveliness. Then his eyes locked with hers again, afraid of his feelings. "And what is my brother to you?" he asked, his voice drawn.

Melanie blinked her eyes nervously, not wanting to disclose to Shane just how much she despised his brother. "Josh and your father are my neighbors," she said quickly. "Our lands adjoin. Do you remember, when you looked down from this butte, all the cattle you saw? Half belong to my family and half belong to yours. The fence you saw divides the two pastures."

Shane's eyes wavered. When she referred to his father's land as also his, it was not a reality he could yet face. Was it real? Would his family truly want to share with him? Could he be a part of the family again? Did he even want to be?

Yes, he wanted to see his father and embrace him as sons embrace fathers, but to be a part of a life that he had never known was a disturbing idea to him. For many years he had known only one way of life.

Melanie saw Shane's uneasiness and hesitation. Afraid that she was not handling this delicate affair right, she turned and looked over her shoulder at the campfire, then back up at Shane. "Let's go and sit by the fire," she said, easing her hands from his. She hugged herself, the damp evening breeze penetrating her thin blouse, chilling her. "We can talk a while and then I must leave. If my brother returns from town and finds me gone he will become alarmed."

"You live with your brother?" Shane asked,

already relieved to have heard her refer to his family, especially his brother, as neighbors, nothing more.

Melanie's eyes lowered, her father's death not that long ago that mentioning it did not always cause her pain. "Yes, I live with my brother," she murmured. "Ever since my father's death it has been only my brother and myself."

Shane recognized the pain that speaking of her loss caused her. He could sympathize with that. He was still feeling the pain so recently caused by the old chief's parting. Something urged him to give her a soft comforting. He clasped his fingers gently to her shoulders.

"Death is but a change for the better. It is time borrowed until loved ones meet again," he said. "Do not be sad. You will be with your father again. And what of your mother?"

His hands and voice, his nearness, flooded Melanie with a strange sort of sweetness. She slowly lifted her eyes to him, then melted inside when she saw how warmly he was looking down at her.

"Your mother?" Shane repeated. "You have not spoken of your mother." He moved a hand to her cheek and stroked it with his thumb. "You have not even told me your name."

Unable to shake this rapture that was spinning around inside her, suddenly afraid of it, Melanie stepped back away from Shane. She flinched when she saw that her action caused a sudden hurt to trouble his handsome face.

"My mother has been dead ever since my birth," she said, her voice quavering. "My name? It's Melanie. Please call me Melanie."

"Melanie?" Shane said, as though testing its meaning on his lips as he spoke. He smiled down at Melanie and shook his head in approval. "Yes. I like that. Like you, it is a gentle name."

Shane saw Melanie visibly shiver. He looked at the fire, then back at her. Taking her by the elbow he walked her toward the fire. "It is sad that you, too, have lost a mother," he said gently.

Renewed pain entered his expression as he recalled that fateful day. Though so many of his childhood memories had been lost to him by the passing of time, the moment of his mother's death and the strange color of the eyes on the man who was responsible for her death, were etched onto Shane's brain like the fossil a leaf onto stone.

But Shane felt compelled to learn more of Melanie first, and of his true brother and father who were now only heartbeats away! What could it hurt to delay the search for Trapper Dan a few hours? It had already been twenty-five years!

Melanie glanced at Shane as he urged her down to the ground beside the fire, then sat down beside her. "I know of your mother," she said, almost afraid to let him know that she was aware of that most intimate detail of his life. "It had to be unbearable, Shane. I am sorry for you for having to experience it."

"The day she died my life was changed," Shane said, picking up a stick and idly stirring it around in the ashes that had fallen away from the fire.

"My family as I had always known it was lost to me. Another family took me in, and that is all I have since known. Until today, I had no knowledge of where my true family resided. Until today, I was content to live without them. But now? Suddenly everything has changed in my life again and I am confused."

"Shane, I want to help—if you will let me," Melanie said, placing a hand on his arm. "Do you want to tell me where you have been? And with whom?"

Shane looked down at her hand resting on his arm, then up into her eyes. She was not only courageous and beautiful, she was compassionate. He looked into the fire and began talking in a monotone, seeing his life being relived in his mind's eye as he spoke.

"The day my mother was murdered by white men dressed as Indians, I watched for my father to return and rescue me, but he never came," Shane said thickly. "I recall very little about my early life, but I do remember lying down beside my mother for warmth that day after she was slain. I fell asleep crying and was awakened when strong arms lifted me up from the ground. It was not my father. It was a Chippewa Indian. I was taken to his village and there I became as a part of his people. Until today, I was happy to be a part of them. But the old chief who rescued me that day died not long ago and his son did not want me to be a part of the village any longer. I was sent away."

Melanie was stunned by his story. Yet she now

understood so much about him—why he had a sort of savage eagerness about him. He had lived with Indians all these years. She was surprised that he could still speak the English language.

There was so much that she would have liked to know, but she did not want to pry him too deeply for answers. She wanted him to trust her—not become angry or suspicious of her.

"Shane, I know why your father didn't arrive in time to rescue you after the massacre," she said, recalling Jared's torment when he had relayed the story to her more than once. "Shane, your father's boat had gone ahead of the one you traveled and was almost overturned in severe rapids," she began, telling him the whole ordeal of his father that day.

Shane's heart pounded. It was good to finally know that his father had tried to rescue him that day, that when people came searching for him as a child, his father may have been among them.

"For many years your father searched for you," Melanie said, as though she had read Shane's troubled thoughts. "After a while he quit searching, but within his heart he never gave up hope that he would see you again one day." She moved to her knees and faced him. "Shane, he will be so happy. When will you go and see him? When?"

Doubt of himself and his acceptance assailed Shane. He brushed past Melanie and rose to his feet. He went to the edge of the butte and looked down at the darkened land below him; in the moonlight he could still see the dark forms of the longhorns grazing lazily.

Melanie went to Shane. She followed his gaze, and when she looked at the lamplight flooding from the windows of her house, she grew anxious. If Terrance had arrived home and discovered her gone he would become alarmed and would come looking for her. It was best that Terrance didn't see Shane until Shane had made his appearance at the Brennan farm.

Turning to Shane, Melanie again placed a gentle hand on his arm. Though she felt the urgency to leave, she still wanted to know just a little bit more about him and if he wanted her to go to his father and tell him that he was near.

"Shane, you said earlier that you only found out today where your father resided," she said softly. "Why didn't you know earlier? Why didn't you come looking for him?"

Shane swallowed hard. He turned and faced Melanie and placed his fingers gently to her shoulders. "So much of my memory as a child of four was scarred by sadness and death," he said. "I forgot my last name, even my brother's first name. All I could recall was my father's name because I had heard my mother address him as Jared so often. I could not recall where my father was traveling. It could have been to Canada as far as I knew. A child of four is only aware of what makes him comfortable from day to day. Hardly anything more. So through the years I was only called Shane because that was the only name I knew to tell the Indians to call me."

"You speak kindly of the Chippewa," Melanie

said, again looking at his fringed buckskin outfit. "They were good to you?"

"They took me in and raised me as one of their own," Shane said, nodding. "I would still be there today had the old chief's son not resented me through the years because his father treated me like a son. Jealousy led him to make the decision to send me away. He was told by his father shortly before his death exactly where my true family resided. So now I am here."

"But the old chief's son did you a favor," Melanie said. "By sending you away, you have found your true family. Doesn't that make you happy, Shane? You can live a normal life now."

She stood on tiptoe to come closer to his face, and smiled. "Shane, your father is very wealthy. You can share in the wealth," she said softly. "You will never want for another thing. You can have all the comforts that you have been denied through the years."

Shane did not like her referring to the Indian way of life as not normal, but he understood her feelings. They were as most white people's feelings toward the Indian. This could be the hardest part of living in the white man's world again. Resentments and prejudices.

But now he knew that he could stand up against any ridicule—because he wanted to be near Melanie. Though they had only just met, he knew that she was going to be his woman!

With her lips so close and her eyes smiling so warmly into his, Shane could not help himself. His steel arms enfolded her, drawing her into his arms.

"Melanie," he whispered. "Sweet Melanie. I am grateful for what Gray Falcon has done, for if he had not done it, I would never have found you." He locked her against his body and kissed her with a fierce, possessive heat.

Melanie was too weak with desire to protest. She twined her arms about Shane's neck and clung to his rock hardness, giving herself up to the rapture. It was as though she had known him forever. The kiss, the embrace, the wondrous feelings were so right! How his kiss inflamed her heart!

• CHAPTER FIVE •

The sound of an approaching horse drew Melanie and Shane quickly apart. Torn with feelings, Melanie's heart was thundering wildly. She was stunned by Shane's kiss and her reaction to it. But she did not have much time to wonder about it, for suddenly her brother was there on horseback, staring in dismay down at her, and then at Shane.

Melanie paled and blinked nervously up at Terrance. Caught in the aftermath of passion, she wondered how she could possibly explain Shane's presence there. She should have just left long ago. There would have been nothing at all to explain.

But if she had left, she would have been denied the rapture of Shane's kiss. Anything was worth that marvelous moment of bliss—except seeing

Shane put in the position that he was now in—caught offguard by Melanie's brother.

Fire was in Shane's eyes, and his jaw was set. She tensed when he glanced down at his knife, perhaps feeling naked without it in a time of threat.

"What the hell's going on here?" Terrance asked, leaning his full weight on the pommel of his saddle. "I saw the campfire from the stable. I had to check it out. God, Melanie, why are you here?" He smoothed his hat back from his brow and eyed Shane even more closely. "Who is he? What are you doing with him?"

Feeling the need to protect Shane from Terrance's questioning stare, Melanie stepped in front of him. She held her chin stubbornly high, yet did not know what to say. Would Shane want Terrance to know who he was? Or did he prefer his father to be the first to know that he had returned? It was apparent that Shane had wanted more time before approaching his family, for he had chosen to spend the night before a campfire instead of in his father's house.

"I also saw the campfire," Melanie said, trying to force her voice to remain smooth and even. "Since you were gone, I saw no choice but to see who had built it. I have found that this man is no threat to us. He means us no harm. He just needed to rest the night before going on his way. We can go back home now, Terrance."

Her brother dismounted and went to Melanie and lifted her bodily from in front of Shane. He then took a closer look at Shane, the glow of the campfire golden on his face. "If I hadn't left Josh just moments ago, I'd swear you were him," he said, kneading his chin contemplatingly. "Who are you?" His gaze raked over Shane, then again looked him square in the eye. "Who in the hell are you?"

Melanie stood by, helpless. She placed her hands to her throat, wondering just how long Shane would let Terrance question him in such a way. She could see anger flaring in his eyes.

"You say I resemble Josh?" Shane said suddenly, his voice void of feeling. "That is because we are brothers."

Terrance gasped. He looked to Melanie, then back to Shane. "You're Josh's brother?" he said, his voice drawn. "That's impossible. Everyone knows he's dead. It's been too long, too many years. You can't be Shane." He toyed nervously with his thin mustache and let his gaze take in every feature of Shane's face, unable to deny how much he resembled Josh. "Yet—God, you are Josh's double! There's no denying that."

Melanie moved to her brother's side and touched his arm gently. "No, he's not Josh's double," she murmured. "He's Josh's brother. His twin. This is Shane. Shane Brennan."

Dumbfounded by the discovery, Terrance was at a loss for words. It was as though Shane had returned from the dead.

"Well?" Melanie said, taking a step closer to her brother. "Don't you have anything to say? Don't you think it's wonderful that Shane is all right? Everyone gave up on his being alive long ago."

Terrance smiled an awkward, lopsided smile. "Yes, so they had." He looked past Melanie, at Shane. "I guess a welcome is in order," he said, forcing himself to offer a handshake. "I'm glad you're safe, Shane. Welcome back."

Shane hesitated, recognizing when a man spoke with a forked tongue. This man, Melanie's brother, was anything but happy that he was alive. Shane could understand why he would disrupt his own family's lives. But how could he matter to Terrance's?

Shane glanced at Melanie. Yes, it was because of her. Did not all brothers love and protect their sisters? Had he not always protected Cedar Maid?

Lifting a hand and solidly clasping his fingers around Terrance's proffered hand, Shane returned the handshake of friendship. "It is good of you to welcome me back," he said, smiling stiffly.

Terrance felt the solid steel grip of Shane's hand, painful in its intensity. He looked into his eyes, seeing a distant coldness. Both caused a strange sort of fear to ripple through him. He wanted to ask Shane so many questions, but something held him back. He felt suddenly uncomfortable beneath Shane's steady stare. It was as though he were able to look clear through him, reading his every thought.

What sort of man had Shane become? Where had he been all these years? Why had he returned now? Had he heard that his father was dying? Had he returned just for his piece of the pie?

Relieved when Shane released his hand, Terrance slipped an arm around Melanie's waist.

"It's time to go home," he said, giving Shane a guarded look over her shoulder. "Damn it, Melanie, you shouldn't be here in the first place. Don't you know the dangers of leaving the farm unescorted this time of night? You could've been raped and murdered!"

Melanie stepped away from him and went to Shane. "My brother is right, you know," she murmured. "I did take risks coming here. But, oh, Shane, I'm so glad that I did." She ignored her brother's gaping stare and took Shane's hands, holding them tenderly.

It was hard for her to understand her sudden attraction to this man and his sensual effect on her. But she could not deny it. Even now she wanted to ease into his arms and hug him. Her lips burned for his kiss.

"You will return tomorrow?" Shane asked, his insides melting as she looked up at him with such adoring, trusting eyes.

"Will you still be here?" Melanie asked, her eyes questioning. "You don't plan to go to your father tonight?"

Again she wondered if she should tell Shane about his father's weakened condition. She knew that Shane needed more time to sort things out inside his head. She did not need to complicate things any more than they already were by telling him that his father was dying.

If only Jared would last another night! He must! He had clung to life this long with hope in his heart that he might see his long-lost son—surely he would not give up just as the son had come within a heartbeat of him!

Shane looked at Terrance, then at Melanie. "This land belongs to you and your brother," he said hoarsely. "It is all right that I stay a full night? I do not wish just yet to go to my father and brother. I would like another night to acquaint myself with all that has happened today." He leaned closer to her, his breath hot on her face. "And also tonight."

A weakness claimed Melanie's knees as their breaths mingled. Then Terrance was suddenly there, jerking her away from Shane.

"Good Lord, Melanie, what on earth are you thinking?" Terrance roared, gripping her painfully by the shoulders. "Even though you know who this man is, it isn't right for you to behave so—so brazenly with him. He's a stranger, Melanie. A stranger! What's got into you? I've never seen you behave so loosely before."

Terrance's fingers dug even more painfully into Melanie's shoulders. She tried to get free, but couldn't. "Terrance, you're hurting me," she cried. "Unhand me this minute. Do you hear?"

She gasped and stumbled free of her brother when Shane moved swiftly and jerked Terrance away from her. She watched in dismay as her brother cowered from Shane's threatening fist.

"You do not treat your sister with the respect that she is due," Shane growled. "Never lay a hand on her again. If you do, you will pay, for I shall be near to protect her from such abuse!"

The color had drained from Terrance's face. His heart felt a strange sort of iciness encircle it, as though he had been threatened by a savage, not a white man. He began inching his way backward, fumbling in the air behind him as he blindly searched for his horse's reins. "Melanie, I'm not going to tell you again," he dared to say. "Get your horse and come home with me. Now!"

Melanie looked from Terrance to Shane, afraid of these dangerous feelings that flowed between them. Yet Terrance did not have the backbone to fight back. She knew him well enough to know that once he rode away from Shane and his threats, he would not return. He was not the sort who would choose a fight—not even when he had been humiliated.

"I truly must go, Shane," she said, touching his cheek gently. She so wanted to kiss him goodbye, but that would be stretching her brother's contempt too far. "I'll be back tomorrow. Perhaps then you will let me accompany you to see your father and brother."

"Perhaps," Shane said, devouring her with his eyes, wanting her so badly it caused a cutting ache in his gut. He reached a hand to her hair and twined his fingers through it. Not fearing her cowardly brother, Shane drew her lips to his mouth and gave her a fleeting kiss.

Shaken, Melanie slipped free and ran past Terrance to her horse, unaware of the murderous glares being exchanged between her brother and the man that she knew she was destined to love.

* * *

Restless, too much on his mind to be able to go to sleep, Shane looked down from the butte at his father's house outlined in the distant darkness. It would be hard to wait the long night without at least a glance of the man he had worshipped as a child. He could go and take a brief glance through a window. Perhaps he would even see Josh, the man who was said to look so much like himself.

But he did not yet want to meet either his father or brother face to face. He would be committing himself to a new life by letting them know that he was alive. Though he never stepped back from a challenge, this time it was different. Many other hearts than his own were involved.

His eyes moved slowly to the other massive house in the valley below him. Melanie's home. He looked from window to window, seeing them golden with lamplight. She should be home by now. In which room would she be? Was she, like himself, entranced over the discovery that they shared so many feelings? Would she be as restless as he was tonight? Would it be because of him?

Shaking thoughts of Melanie from his mind, troubled enough by having been so affected by a woman for the first time in his life, Shane began running in an easy bounding gait through the forest, then down the steep embankment.

Not wanting to stampede the cattle, he moved in a wide circle around them, his eyes on his father's house that was growing closer in the distance. His heart thudded wildly at the thought of looking upon his father's gentle face again. It was hard to believe that any of this was happening.

It had been so long, so very long. . . .

Melanie watched Terrance pacing back and forth in the parlor, a half-emptied bottle of whiskey clutched in his left hand. Her insides tightened when he tipped the bottle to his lips again and took several long gulps, then stared angrily at her as he slammed the bottle onto a table.

"I hardly know you anymore," Terrance said in a drunken drawl. "Ever since Pop—"

"Yes, say it again," Melanie said, sighing resolutely. "Ever since Pop died, I've been nothing but a thorn in your side."

Her brown eyes flashed stormily as she glared up at him. "Terrance, maybe that's because you never saw me as a threat before Papa died," she said. "Now you watch every move I make as though you're afraid I'm going to cheat you or something. Why, Terrance? Why is there no trust between us anymore?"

Terrance threw his head back in a laugh, then met her steady, angry stare with his own. "You speak of trust when you've just come from the arms of a stranger?" he shouted. "You flaunted your independence in my face when you let him kiss you in front of me. Where is your self-respect, Melanie? Who knows where that man has been all these years? Why, he could be a thieving outlaw. He dresses no better. How could you have let him touch you? Or do you let all strangers paw you and I just never caught one doing it before?"

Melanie had taken all the insults that she could stand. She raised a hand and slapped her brother hard across the face. "How dare you!" she cried. "You've become even more insulting since Papa's death. Terrance, you have changed for the worse —not I!"

Terrance's eyes widened in disbelief as he rubbed his burning cheek. "Melanie, no matter what you say, I'm not going to let you get involved with Shane Brennan," he told her.

Terrance had been doing some serious thinking since they left Shane behind in the forest. It had suddenly dawned on him that Shane had appeared out of nowhere just in time to complicate everyone's lives. Josh needed to be warned! Josh would surely throw a fit when he discovered that he was now more than likely going to have to split his inheritance down the middle with a brother he had been parted from since the age of four!

And Shane was going to wreck not only Josh's plans—but Terrance's too!

He grabbed his hat. "I'm going to go warn Josh about the brother he thought was dead," he blurted out. "He deserves to be warned before Shane comes to his front door. Fair is fair."

Panic rose inside Melanie. This was not the best way to handle this as far as Shane was concerned, and since nobody had looked after his interests these past twenty-five years, she would just appoint herself! No matter how much her brother tried to insult Shane in front of her, to turn her against him, she had seen the good in Shane and would not let anything go awry for him. He was too close to discovering his family again. She would not let her brother spoil the reunion.

And she also had to think of Jared. A shock could kill him. Terrance would not even think about that. He would more than likely storm into Jared's house with the news and cause utter confusion.

Melanie rushed to Terrance and took his hat from him as he staggered toward the door. "You're in no shape to go anywhere," she said, guiding him back into the parlor. She helped him down onto the sofa before the fireplace. "If you insist that Josh be told tonight, I can do the telling."

"Like hell . . ." Terrance growled. He tried to get up but fell back down as his wobbly legs gave way beneath him.

"If you even try to ride a horse in that condition, you'll kill yourself, Terrance," Melanie said, reaching for a blanket. She urged Terrance to stretch out on the sofa, then pulled the covering over him, up to his chin. He was so drunk she could expect him to sleep not only the night away, but most of the next day.

Melanie stepped back from the sofa and shook her head in disgust as Terrance hiccoughed crudely and then closed his eyes, snoring almost as quickly as his eyelashes locked together.

"Terrance," Melanie whispered. "What's happening between us? I love you so much. Can't you see that?"

She turned and tiptoed from the room and closed the door. She gave strict instructions to the servants that he was not to be disturbed. She ordered another servant to ready her horse and buggy. She would make a call on Josh and Jared Brennan.

But she would not tell them anything about Shane. She was mainly going to see how Jared was. If he seemed worse, she just might have to go and get Shane tonight and take him to his father after all. As Terrance had said, fair was fair.

In her mind, it was time for someone to be fair to Shane!

Shane moved stealthily through the night, avoiding any open spaces so that he would not be seen. He was now close enough to his father's house to see shadows moving around inside. His pulse raced. Was he truly going to see his father in only a matter of moments? Had he changed much through the years? Had the years been good to him?

The sound of an approaching horse and buggy startled Shane into jumping behind a tree. His heart pounding, he watched as the buggy drew closer on the gravel road only a few feet away from him. In the moonlight, he could make out the driver. His eyes widened. It was Melanie! She was going to his father's house. Why? Was she going to tell everyone about him? Surely not. He had thought that she understood that he was not ready, that he wanted to wait until tomorrow.

But if she were not coming to his father's house for that reason, why was she?

He watched as Melanie stopped the buggy in front of the massive house and hurried up the front steps. Breathless, he watched her knock on the door. His heart fluttered nervously as the door opened widely, and the man who greeted Melanie drew her briskly into his arms and hugged her.

Jealously inflamed Shane's insides when the man swung away from Melanie and the bright lamplight flooding from the opened door settled on his face. It was unnerving for Shane to see a man who resembled himself so much that it was like seeing his own face reflected in a pool. It had to be Josh! The man who had greeted Melanie so ambitiously was his brother Josh! Did she care for him in ways that she had shown she cared for Shane?

Were they lovers . . . ?

A gnawing ache swept through Shane at the thought that Melanie could be so deceitful. Yet, he knew her not at all! How could he expect so much of a woman he had only just met?

Disillusioned, Shane spun around and began running back in the direction of his campsite. He did not care to see any more shows of affection between his brother and the woman of his desire! Perhaps he should even leave the area tonight and not look back. Was he not foolish to have thought any good could come from having found his true family? From a woman who stole his heart away at first glance? Was it meant for him to be denied these special feelings, forever?

He broke into a mad run, blinded with anguish.

Melanie brushed Josh away and frowned up at him. "Good heavens," she scolded. "Josh, what do you think you're doing, grabbing me like that? Surely you know that I've come to see your father, not you."

Josh stepped aside and let her storm on into the hall, then closed the door behind her. He took her shawl and handed it to a servant. Walking around her, studying her in the bright lamplight, he smiled smugly at her.

"What has happened to put the glow on your face if not my fond embrace?" he asked teasingly. "My dear, I've never seen you look so radiant. If I am the cause because I greeted you in such a fashion, I shall remember to do that every time you come for a visit."

Melanie felt a hot blush rise to her cheeks, knowing exactly what had caused her to look different. Shane! Only Shane!

Trying to throw Josh off the track, she took a step closer to him and sniffed. "Yes, just as I guessed," she said, looking up at him as smugly as he was looking at her. "Just like my brother, you've had a mite too much to drink tonight. It's causing you to imagine things."

She walked on past him, the softness of her moccasins making scarcely a sound on the hardwood floor. "I've come to see your father," she said, already headed for the sick room. "How is he?"

"The same," Josh said, catching up with her. He opened the door for her. "He seems to stay the same these days. Just hanging on."

Melanie entered a room that was dimly lighted by low-burning kerosene lamps. The aroma was strong with medicine. The sound was that of a man fighting for every breath.

Melanie went to Jared's bedside and looked down at him. As always, her heart went out to the man who had dwindled away to mere flesh stretched tautly across bone. When his eyes opened and he saw her there, he reached a bony hand to her and managed a smile.

"Melanie, it's so good to see you," Jared said, wheezing between words. His blue eyes were faded with time and illness. "Sit down and visit a spell. Did you do anything exciting today? Josh tells me you rode into town with him and Terrance." He laughed a throaty, scratchy laugh. "I knew ever since you were a mere sprite of a girl that you'd have spunk. You're going to give a husband fits one of these days, aren't you?"

Melanie's eyes wavered. She was immediately reminded of Shane and how she had been catapulted into feelings for him so quickly. Could anything ever truly come of it? Was Jared, without even knowing it, speaking of his own son when he made reference to a husband?

She so badly wanted to spill out the truth to this trusting, ailing man! It would be so easy to tell him that his son had returned and that he was a caring, gentle man. In only the short time Melanie had become acquainted with Shane, she knew that. She knew that she was in love with him!

If she could just share that secret with Jared, as through the years she had shared so many things with him. He had been like a second father to her.

But for now, she had to just be there for him, be

someone he could take comfort in. Tomorrow, he would have his son. Tomorrow!

Melanie eased down onto a chair beside Jared's bed. She clung to his hand and smiled at him. "Today was special in many ways," she murmured. "But it's only girl stuff, Jared. You wouldn't be interested. Tell me—how are you feeling?"

Jared glanced up at Josh, then at Melanie. He wanted to confide in her about the will, about Shane's portion of the inheritance. But he couldn't. Josh was already aware of the stipulation and was upset over it. No sense in causing the hurt to deepen by talking about it openly to Melanie in front of him.

Tomorrow. He would tell her tomorrow. Besides Jared's lawyer, someone else had to be aware of how strongly he felt about Shane, should Shane ever come home. He could trust Melanie to see that Shane was treated fairly.

"I'm faring well enough," Jared said. "But I'm not sure how much longer I can hang on. This old ticker of mine gets weaker every day."

"You're going to live forever," Melanie said, pretending to scoff at his resignation to dying. "Just think of all the tomorrows and the surprises that each tomorrow may have in store for you. You're going to be here to enjoy them all."

Melanie and Jared exchanged warm smiles. It took a lot of willpower not to tell him the wonderful news. But she had to reserve tomorrow for Shane and Jared. It would be one of those days of special surprises that she had just promised Jared.

Josh stiffened behind them, then swung around and left the room. He went to the parlor and poured himself a shot of whiskey and swallowed it in one fast gulp. He could not get the will off his mind. Damn his father. Josh had lived in Shane's shadow forever and would still feel it on him after their father was dead!

That will would haunt him forever.

· CHAPTER SIX ·

Gilding the edges of clouds, the sun lazily stretched its early morning rays over fertile fields. After a restless night, Melanie was awake and eager to go to Shane. She must, before Terrance had a chance to tell Josh everything!

Stepping lightly down the stairs, she held a lacy shawl around her shoulders and peered intensely at the parlor door. It was still closed. She had gone and checked on Terrance when she first awoke, to make sure that he was still there after passing out in his drunken stupor the previous night. She had found him snoring and still sleeping. Sleeping this soundly, he would surely not awaken for several more hours.

Time. Melanie needed all the time she could get to go to Shane and get him to his father's house.

Any more interference from Terrance could easily send Shane away, perhaps never to be heard from again. Melanie could not help worrying that even Shane's one confrontation with Terrance the night before might have been enough to send him running. . . .

She had given orders to a stable hand last night to have her horse saddled and ready for travel at sunup this morning, and she had chosen a dress that would stand up under the roughness of traveling on horseback.

She had not wanted to wear the buckskin skirt and moccasins today. To look more ladylike for Shane, she had chosen a yellow cotton dress with white roses embroidered on the skirt. White, delicate lace edged the cuffs of the long sleeves and the scooped bodice. For warding off the chill of the early morning she had drawn a lace shawl around her shoulders. If not for the racket it would make, possibly awakening Terrance, she would have prefered going to Shane in her buggy.

Melanie hurried from the house and found her horse secured to a hitching rail close to the porch. After tying the end of her shawl into a neat, small bow so that it would not slip from her shoulders, she placed a foot in the stirrup and pulled herself into the saddle. Then she wheeled her horse around and rode away into the shiny mist of morning.

Shivers ran up and down Melanie's spine as the damp, cool air stung her cheeks and seeped through her light clothing. Her hair whipped around her face, then tumbled back down and swirled around her shoulders. As she rode more quickly across the straight stretch of green land, she fought the skirt of her dress that kept fluttering up above her knees, revealing a lacy petticoat.

Then the meadow was left behind. Melanie's body strained against the slope of land as she began the steady climb upward. She held more tightly to the reins and hugged the horse's body with her legs. Her heart began to pound, knowing that in only a matter of moments she would be seeing Shane again.

Oh, Lord, why did Shane disturb her so much in ways that Josh, his twin, never had, or could? Why had she allowed it? Why couldn't she at this very moment decide not to get caught up in further feelings for Shane, somehow knowing that she would be better off for it?

"I know why I can't," she whispered, a rush of pleasure soaring through her at the thought of Shane's wild, passionate kisses. "He makes me feel more like a woman than any other man has been able to. He's awakened me to feelings that I never knew existed—feelings that I thought people never truly experienced, but only read about in books. I never want to lose these feelings. Never!"

In truth, she never wanted to lose Shane. She had to make sure that she didn't!

At the top of the hill, Melanie sank her heels into the horse's flanks and rode onward through the forest, peering ahead for any sign of Shane or his campfire. An uneasiness began to creep over her, for not only did she not see any campfire, she didn't smell any smoke.

Had he left? Had she been wrong to think he had felt something special for her—and proved it by the way he kissed her? Or had she been nothing but a passing fancy for him? Was he more like Josh than she had guessed?

Now upon the campsite, Melanie eased out of her saddle, numb. A keen disappointment assailing her, she looked down at the campfire that had sunk into a pile of damp coals. And though a blanket and Shane's fringed buckskin shirt still lay beside the firepit, he wasn't there.

Then Melanie's eyes were drawn to something that seemed peculiar in this setting. She tied her horse's reins to a tree, then went and knelt down on the blanket and picked up a deck of cards. She turned it over and over in her hands, studying it. They were the kind of playing cards most generally used for playing poker. She ought to know. Both Josh and Terrance were gamblers.

These cards had to be Shane's.

But he did not seem the sort to indulge in . . . .

A crushing of leaves behind Melanie made her drop the cards and rise quickly to her feet. Turning, her breath was stolen away when she saw Shane walking toward her. She was engulfed with a shameless passion when she gaped openly at him. He was shirtless. His long, golden hair was dripping wet over his shoulders, and his muscled chest was sleek with water. Surely no man could be as handsome, as seductive as Shane was at this moment.

"Shane!" Melanie said, her shameful thoughts causing color to rush to her cheeks. "For a moment I thought you had left. You have no fire—"

He interrupted her. "I allowed the fire to burn itself out last night because I feared that someone else would see it," he said stiffly. "It had already attracted too much attention."

Melanie was stung by his coldness and stiff reserve. It was not the way she had expected to be greeted by him. She wanted to ask why, yet was afraid to hear the answer. He had surely spent the long night thinking through his decision of what he should do in the light of everything he now knew about his family, and had decided it was best to move on. That meant he would place her from his mind and life as well!

A chill ran through Melanie as the damp breeze penetrated her thin cotton dress. She looked at Shane and the wetness of his hair and body, drawing her shawl more comfortably around her shoulders. "Shane, you're wet," she murmured. "Aren't you cold?"

"During my teachings as a child with the Chippewa, I was taught to practice endurance," he said, still standing stiffly, looking at Melanie with something close to contempt. "More than once my adviser put dry sunflower seeds on my wrists. These were lit at the top and I had to let them burn clear down to my skin. They hurt and made sores but if I had knocked them off or cried, I would have been called a woman."

He held his shoulders proudly squared. "In comparison, the cold air and water are no more than the sting of a tiny fly on my skin."

Melanie winced at the thought of what he must have had to endure in his lifetime. He even acted as though she were now something else he had to endure.

But why?

Last night he had behaved so differently toward her. What had caused him to change?

She couldn't stand not knowing any longer. She went to Shane and placed a gentle hand on his arm and looked up at him with pleading eyes. "What's wrong, Shane?" she blurted. "Why are you acting so distant, so cold, toward me? If I have done something wrong, I need to know."

Shane looked down at Melanie, trying to stifle the yearnings for her that were gnawing away at his heart. He had tasted her lips. He had smelled her sweetness. Even now, she smelled like roses that grew wild in the forest.

His gaze raked over her. Unlike yesterday, she wore feminine clothing, and her shawl did not cover her entirely. He could see her ripe, curving breasts where her dress dipped low in front, causing a slow burning ache in his loins.

His gaze moved slowly upward. The early morning light bathed her face in a soft reflective glow, limning her throat and slender neck. Her long and lustrous auburn hair was fluttering gently in the breeze; her lips were slightly parted as their eyes locked and momentarily held.

He wanted to draw her into his arms and kiss her, and tell her how he felt about her. He had waited a lifetime for a woman to speak to his heart in the way that she did.

But now?

He had to refuse himself this woman who had left his arms only to go to his brother's. What had she told his brother about Shane? That she had made a fool of him? Had they laughed about it together? Was he something to laugh at, since he had not had a white man's education or upbringing?

Shane placed his fingers to Melanie's shoulders and pushed her aside, then went and pulled his shirt over his head. Bending to one knee, he picked up his deck of cards and blanket and began moving away from Melanie. He had carefully hidden his white stallion within a thick stand of trees. He could not get to it quickly enough, for another moment with her and he would have not been able to resist her.

It was best that he leave. He now knew that he should have gone sooner. Seeing Melanie again was pure torture.

But he could not shake the memory of her in Josh's arms. If she loved Josh, why had she kissed Shane so intimately? Why?

Melanie was numb as she watched Shane walk away. She had seen too much in his eyes not to know that he had special feelings for her. When he was gazing raptly down at her, it was as though they were melting together, two people becoming one in both heart and soul.

But then he had turned away from her.

She had to know the reason he was compelled to turn his back on her and what they had found together!

"Shane!" Melanie cried, breaking into a run toward him. "You can't leave like this. You've got to tell me what's wrong." A loud, torturous sob tore from the depths of her being. "Shane, I couldn't bear it if you left. I don't know how it could happen so quickly, but I know that I love you! Do you hear me? I love you! Please don't leave me!"

Her words of love hit Shane with the impact of a fall off a horse at full gallop. His heart thundering wildly, he stopped and turned to Melanie just as she caught up with him. Bewildered, he looked down at her as she lunged into his arms and clung to him, her tears wetting his buckskin shirt.

"Shane, oh, Shane," Melanie sobbed. "Don't you see? It's as though we have known each other forever. Don't you feel it? It's such a wonderful, warm feeling that comes over me when I am near you. Tell me that you feel the same. Tell me you aren't going to turn your back on what we have found together."

Shane recalled how Melanie had embraced Josh. It had not been with the same enthusiasm as she was now holding onto him. If he recalled correctly, she had not even instigated the embrace and had stayed within Josh's arms for only a brief moment. With Shane it was different. She embraced him with the fierceness of someone in love! She did not love Josh. She loved Shane!

Shane dropped his blanket and cards. Twining his fingers through Melanie's hair he held her face back from his chest and gazed in rapture down at her.

Melanie blinked back her tears and returned his gaze openly, fearlessly, lovingly.

Slowly, Shane drew her lips to his mouth, then kissed her with fire.

Melanie was catapulted into a world of spinning sensations that flooded her whole body. She was not even aware of being lowered to the ground; that Shane was still kissing her and holding her was all that mattered. Nothing could be sweeter or more beautiful. He was the world . . . the universe. . . . He was her every breath!

Shane held Melanie up with one arm while smoothing his blanket along the ground beneath her with his free hand. Then he lay her on the blanket and rose above her, his lips now sending feathery kisses along her face and then the hollow of her throat.

Watching Shane, loving him so deeply, Melanie caught her breath when he leaned partially away from her and untied her shawl and laid it aside, then reached behind her and began unsnapping her dress. Her pulse raced, realizing his intent. His burning need was in his eyes. His desire matched her own.

But hers was a desire never tested before. He was the first for her. Yet she knew that he had surely had many women. Would her inexperience disappoint him? Should she stop what she had begun here?

But she could not stop wanting him to make love to her anymore than she could exist without breathing. She wanted him. With all of her heart she wanted him, and not later.

Now.

Everything within her cried out to experience the ultimate feelings with him now.

Though her breasts were bare, Melanie was no longer aware of the damp chill of the morning air. A surge of tingling heat flowed through her breast as Shane's mouth found her nipple and drew it taut between his sucking lips. Melanie closed her eyes and heard someone making a whimpering sound, then realized that it was herself. Desire raged and washed over her as one of Shane's hands kneaded her breast while the other managed to get her dress and petticoat away from her.

Then Shane was suddenly everywhere at once. His lips and hands were caressing all of her secret places. She was becoming delirious with sensations, her entire body heating up, all of her senses yearning for the promise he was offering her.

Hardly able to stand much more, finding herself ready to reach a peak that was unfamiliar to her, frightening her, Melanie gently touched Shane's smooth cheek. "Shane, my love," she whispered. "What are you doing to me? Oh, what are you doing to me?"

Shane framed her face between his hands and drew her lips to his mouth. He brushed her lips with soft kisses while he spoke softly and reassuringly to her.

"What am I doing?" he whispered huskily. "You told me that you loved me. I am showing you that I love you. I will ask for nothing myself this time, my love. Let me just give you pleasure. I shall wait. I was taught early in life the art of restraint."

"This is all so new to me," Melanie said, emitting a sigh when he placed a hand at the juncture of her thighs and began softly caressing her again. "Please don't think that I have done this before with other men. I am not a whore, Shane. I have only done this with you because it is you. Please believe me, Shane."

Shane slipped a finger up inside her tight sheath and felt her womanhood still intact. He smiled and eased his finger back from inside her and began caressing her again. She spoke the truth. No man had entered her. No man but he ever would!

Shane continued to move his fingers along her swollen mound, feeling it becoming tighter beneath his touch. He looked up at her. He could tell by the haze in her eyes that she was nearing that point of no return. He was glad to be the first to introduce her into the pleasures of a woman. He remembered the time he had been shown what it felt like to be a man. It had been with an older woman. She had known just the right moves to make with a boy of thirteen winters. When his insides had exploded with the first wondrous feelings of a young man, it had been as if every star had fallen from the heavens!

He wanted it to be the same for Melanie.

"Think of nothing but how you are feeling at this moment," Shane said, making his way down her body with his lips. "Enjoy this first time, Melanie. Remember that it is only the beginning. From now on I will be there for you to show you every way to make love. But for now, there is only one way."

Melanie's ragged breathing became slower as she felt Shane's lips and tongue travel lower than her belly. She gasped in shocked pleasure as he found her throbbing center and paid homage to it. She closed her eyes again and held her head back, going over the edge into ecstasy as a strange spinning sensation rose up and flooded her whole body. . . .

· CHAPTER SEVEN ·

When Shane leaned over Melanie and drew her up into his arms and held her close, she clung desperately to the magic of the moment, not wanting to let shame spoil what she had just discovered with the man she could not help but adore.

When Shane wove his fingers through her hair and drew it back from her brow, gently kissing her, she twined her arms around his neck and returned the kiss with a fierce passion. Then a sensual shiver raced up and down her spine as his hands moved downward and he again began smoothing his fingers across her flesh, stopping to softly knead her breasts.

The bellowing of cattle in the distance made Melanie's eyes fly open and her heart skip a beat.

For a while she had let herself forget everything but Shane and the ecstasy of being with him.

But the cattle were a crude reminder of the real world and the chore that lay ahead of her—that of introducing a long-lost son to a dying father.

And how could she have forgotten Terrance? If he got to Josh first, it would not only be awkward for Shane, but perhaps deadly for Jared! If the telling weren't handled right, he could die from the shock.

Easing from Shane's arms, Melanie blushed as she realized her nudity for the first time since Shane had sent her mind out of the real world, into another realm. She reached for her dress and petticoat and held them against her body.

"What I have done is shameful," she said in a rush of words. "What must you think of me?"

"I think that you have proven to me that you are a woman," he said, picking up his blanket. He folded it and placed it and his deck of cards in one of his buckskin bags on his horse.

He went to Melanie and took her clothes from her arms. His gaze went slowly over her, setting his insides on fire with need, yet he looked away from her and slipped her petticoat over her head, and then her dress. "I wandered from my campsite last night," he said, turning her around so that her back was to him.

"I had the strong desire to get at least a glimpse of my father," he said, fastening her dress. "As I was on my way to his house, I saw you arrive there. I witnessed an embrace shared by you and my brother."

Melanie gasped and spun around to face him. "You were there?" she said, searching his face with her eyes. "You saw Josh embrace me?"

"Yes," he said thickly. "This I witnessed. Nothing else. I left. At that time I did not understand the embrace. But now I do."

Melanie combed her fingers through her hair, straightening it around her shoulders. "What do you mean?" she asked. "You understand now, but you didn't then?"

"I was so hurt and angry over seeing you in my brother's arms that I did not stop to look for the meaning behind the embrace," Shane said, smiling down at her. He ran the palm of his hand along the slender column of her neck. "Today, when you embraced me, I knew the difference. You embrace me with enthusiasm. You embraced my brother with no feelings. I was wrong to become disillusioned so quickly with you. I am sorry, Melanie. I almost left because of this."

He placed his hands to her waist and drew her against him, his eyes filled with warmth as he gazed down at her. "You are my woman," he said huskily. "You have proven that to me today. Nothing will cause me to leave you. Ever. We have much to share. Forever."

Melanie's insides were aglow with ecstasy. His words were so sweet, they caused tears to flood her eyes. But this was not the time for tears. She knew that too much time had been wasted. A man lay dying. Each heartbeat now brought him closer to death. Melanie felt selfish for having taken up even these last wonderful moments with Shane when they should have belonged to his father.

"Shane, we do have forever," she murmured, placing a hand to his cheek. "But your father doesn't. Shane, how can I tell you?"

"Tell me what?" Shane asked, his eyes wavering.

"Before you go and see your father today, you must be told his condition," Melanie said, clearing her throat nervously. "Shane, I didn't tell you sooner because you weren't ready to see your father yet. But now that you are, you must know that he is a dying man. He doesn't have much longer."

She felt Shane tense within her arms. She hugged him tightly. "Shane, oh, Shane," she murmured. "He is not at all the man you remember. He has wasted away almost to nothing. He has consumption, Shane, a terrible disease of the lungs."

While clinging to Shane, her cheek pressed against his chest, Melanie could hear the rapid beat of his heart. "I'm sorry, Shane," she said softly. "But I had to tell you. If you had gone into your father's bedroom and had seen him without first being warned, it would not have been good for him. Your reaction could have killed him."

"It is hard for me to recall much of my childhood," Shane said. "But I do remember my father well. He was my idol. He was a strapping sort of man. He towered over me as tall as a tree. I enjoyed walking around and chasing his shadow. When I caught up with it, I would pretend it was me, a grown man already."

He eased away from Melanie. Downcast, he went to his horse and took the reins, stepped a foot into the stirrup, and swung himself into his saddle. He looked down at Melanie. "Now I am that grown man," he said dryly. "With a grown man's duty to perform." He gestured toward her horse with a hand. "Come along. We shall go and see my father together."

Almost choked with emotion, Melanie looked up at Shane for a moment longer. It was quite obvious that he was hurting inside, yet on the outside he was a picture of courage. He had twenty-five years to catch up with, and he now knew that there was little time allowed for it.

So much in life wasn't fair!

Picking up her shawl, Melanie placed it around her shoulders and tied the ends together to secure it. Feeling anything but ladylike and unable to keep her dress from hiking up above her knees as she placed her foot into the stirrup, she hurried into the saddle.

Draping the reins around her hands, she sent her horse into a soft lope and followed Shane down the gentle slope, then across the pasture. They were leaving the palisades of pine trees behind them. Clouds of split-tail swallows were flying all around above them.

Melanie was hardly able to keep her eyes dry as she looked at Shane when her horse caught up with his beautiful white stallion. "You are going to make your father's last days so filled with happiness," she reassured him. "Shane, since I met your father he has talked of nothing but you and your mother. That you are alive is a miracle, Shane. It's as though your father willed it, and that alone has made it so."

"You will be at my side when I see my father?" Shane asked, glancing over at Melanie.

His heart warmed within his chest. The sun that was now brightening the land with its radiance was full on Melanie's face, making her flesh take on the look of rich, warm satin. Her auburn hair was even more red in the sunlight and bounced lustrously on her shoulders as she rode alongside him. Her brown eyes were luminous. Her parted lips were vivacious. She was nothing less than beautiful. But not only was she beautiful, she was a woman filled with compassion.

"If that's what you want," Melanie said, looking away quickly when the Brennan mansion came into view at the end of the lane. "I want to do whatever I can to make it easy not only for you, but also for your father. He's a wonderful man, Shane." She glanced at him. "Your brother will be shocked. Let me warn you that he will not be all that happy to see you. You see, he's . . . he's . . ."

She turned her eyes away. How could she tell Shane that his brother was a most unpleasant, greedy man? How could she tell Shane that Josh would not want to accept his brother's return because it would mean losing half his inheritance? Just as Terrance had been forced to accept sharing equally with his sister, Melanie, so would Josh be forced to share with a brother.

But Melanie knew the difference. Josh was going to be sharing with a man he had thought was dead.

"What were you going to say?" Shane asked, forking an eyebrow. "Josh is what?"

"Well, I guess you could say that he is not a very pleasant man," Melanie blurted, giving Shane a quick glance. "Shane, you and Josh may resemble one another in appearances, but that is as far as it goes. He's selfish and thinks of only one person—Josh Brennan. Don't be surprised by his attitude when he sees you. Just remember your father. He is all that matters."

Shane's eyes wavered as he stared at the house that stood directly ahead, and he cast thoughts of a jealous brother aside. He was used to jealousies and the harm they brought to one's soul. Instead, he was in awe again of the house in which his father made residence. Could it be true? Had Shane been born into a family of such wealth? Had he truly been denied all of this because of the man whose peculiar eyes would forever haunt him?

He could not help but wonder how different his childhood might have been had he not witnessed a massacre at age four.

Would he have had an education?

Would he have been rich in his own right by now?

Guilt splashed through him when he suddenly thought of Chief Standing Tall, who had guided him since boyhood, and how kind he had been to Shane all through the years. Shane could not make less of this relationship in his mind than it was. If not for Chief Standing Tall, he would probably be dead.

Melanie saw that Shane was filled with reservations about the coming moments that would change his life forever. Shane was kind, gentle, and compassionate. Being all of these things, would he be able to stand up to his conniving brother, to accept the share of the Brennan inheritance that would be rightfully his?

Or would he be afraid to stand up for himself in a world of white men, a world that might condemn him as an Indian because he was raised by them?

Sighing heavily, taking a deep, shaky breath, Melanie saw much responsibility in introducing Shane into the world of the white man. Without her, he would be alone. She had to see that he would have his rightful share in life. He had suffered a lifetime already of injustice because of the senseless massacre by men who had given no value to life, only to that which could be carried away from their victims to sell for profit. It was time for all of this to be made up to Shane. She would see that it was!

They rode on toward the house. Everything was quiet. Melanie eased from her saddle to the ground. Shane seemed unsure of himself as he gazed up at the house, looking from window to window.

Then the front door swung open suddenly, revealing Josh. Melanie watched Josh step shakily out onto the porch, growing pale as he stared unblinkingly down at Shane. Except for the cut of his hair and their different attire, surely Josh felt as though he was looking into a mirror.

Shane met Josh's steady stare with stiff reserve as he slipped out of his saddle. Melanie hurried to

Shane's side and took his hand and began urging him up the steps to the porch. When they came face to face with Josh, Melanie swallowed hard, then urged Shane even closer.

"Shane, this is your brother, Josh," she said, her voice lilting. "Josh, this is your brother, Shane. As you can see, Josh, you've been wrong to think that Shane was no longer alive. He's very much alive and has come to see you and your father."

Josh was stunned speechless. Suddenly, he turned his back to Shane and Melanie, feeling as though he might retch at the shock. All these years that he had suppressed feelings for his twin brother, even knowing that he was alive, were now behind him. This was the present, and damn it all to hell, Shane had somehow found out where his true family lived.

And wasn't it all so well planned? The long-lost son arriving just in time to get a piece of the pie when his father died?

It was almost more than Josh could bear.

"Josh!" Melanie gasped, her cheeks flaming with embarrassment for Shane. "This is your brother. Can't you be glad that he's alive? God, Josh, he's not only your brother, he's your twin!"

Shane took Melanie's hand and drew her around to face him. "Melanie, it is not important," he said softly. "Did you not say that my father is all that matters? Take me to him. I am ready to see him now."

Angry with Josh, Melanie blinked back tears of rage. She looked up into Shane's blue eyes, marveling over how the hurt that his brother had inflicted on him did not show. He was a strong, controlled man, who surely could win against all odds. He had proven that he could overcome this first obstacle in his new life.

"Come with me," Melanie said, giving Josh an angry glance over her shoulder as she led Shane around him and into the house.

Shane's footsteps faltered as he stepped into the fancy foyer. Sunshine was pouring into the windows of the parlor at his right side, crowning all of the plush furnishings with its golden light. Shane took it all in, the gilt-framed pictures that graced the walls, the velveteen-upholstered furniture and expensive oak tables that were positioned around the room.

He then became aware of a strong medicinal smell emanating from a room to his left. Melanie went to the door and opened it, then turned to Shane and nodded. "In here," she whispered. "Your father preferred to have his bed in his library, rather than upstairs away from the activity of the house."

Shane moved to Melanie's side and looked into a room dim with shadows; the draperies had not yet been opened for the day. A candle was flickering beside a bed that had rows and rows of books behind it in built-in bookshelves that lined the wall.

"I shall go in ahead of you," Melanie whispered, touching Shane gently on the cheek. "I shall try to prepare your father before he sees you. No matter how we handle it, though, it's going to be a shock."

Shane nodded, his heart thundering wildly inside him. He watched Melanie enter the room, then he looked at the bed. He could not make out the figure of a man. All that he saw was a layer of blankets stretched out over something that was not all that large. It surely wasn't his father. His father had been gigantic! He would have filled out the bed and more! But he was recalling Melanie's warnings. His father was now only the ghost of the man that Shane remembered.

His pulse racing, he watched Melanie lean over the bed. He could hardly make out what she was saying. It was the tone of her voice that made his love for her grow stronger. She was gentle. She was sweet.

Melanie leaned down over Jared. She placed a hand to his brow and smoothed a gray lock of hair back in place. "Jared?" she whispered, seeing how soundly he was sleeping. Though his breathing was shallow, wheezing sounds surfacing from deeply within his lungs, he seemed no weaker than the last time she had seen him. That was good. Perhaps he could withstand the shock that was only moments away.

Jared opened his eyes slowly, then smiled up at Melanie. "Well, hello there," he said, coughing slightly. "It's been some time since I've awakened in the morning to smiling, seductive eyes. What brings you here so early in the morning, Melanie? Don't tell me it's me you're interested in, not my son, Josh." He laughed throatily as Melanie slipped her hand into his.

"I believe you'll be much happier for the true reason I'm here," Melanie said, giggling. "Jared, do you recall talking about surprises only last night?"

"Yes, seems that I do," Jared said, squinting his eyes up at her. "Now, Melanie, just what sort of surprise have you brought me this morning?"

Melanie swallowed back a lump that was fast growing in her throat. She glanced over her shoulder at Shane, who stood too much in the shadows for Jared to see.

Then she looked back down at Jared. "Jared, I've brought you the best of all surprises," she said, her voice breaking. "Oh, Jared, I've . . . I've brought you Shane."

Jared jerked his hand away. His eyes were wild as he looked past Melanie just as Shane stepped into full view. His head began to spin and his eyes became blinded with tears as he leaned shakily up on one elbow. "Shane?" he said in a low gasp. "Is . . . it . . . really you?"

Shane's knees grew weak as the candle cast its glow onto his Father's thin, drawn face. He had to stifle a wail, the sort that Indians cried when discovering something too hard to bear. This man who had spoken his name—this man who was looking at Shane with sunken eyes on a face with skin drawn tautly over bone—bore no resemblance whatsoever to the man Shane remembered.

Though Melanie had tried to warn Shane, the shock was no less. This man, his father, had suffered a lifetime, it seemed. It showed in the haunted depths of his eyes, in the haunted features of his face. Had all this suffering been the result of that one tragic day so long ago? Had he relived it over and over again in his mind's eye, as Shane had? Could they bear to live it over again with one another now?

Melanie went to Shane and locked an arm through his. She walked with him to Jared's bed. Tears streamed from her eyes as Jared stared openly up at Shane, his whole body trembling from the shock.

"Father, it is I," Shane finally said. He eased away from Melanie and leaned down over his father, enfolding him in a gentle hug. "Father," he cried, his voice quaking. "It is I, Shane. I have come home."

Jared flung his arms around Shane. Tears flooded from his eyes as he wept, clinging to Shane with all his might. "Shane," he cried. "I knew you were alive. Oh, Lord, I knew you were alive!"

Melanie turned her back to the emotional scene. She hung her head and wept into her hands, then lifted her eyes slowly when she felt another presence in the room. She looked across the room and saw Josh standing there, gaping openly at the reunion of father and son.

She could not help but see the hate in his eyes. She pitied him for it.

· CHAPTER EIGHT ·

Josh came on into the room and inched up next to Melanie. "Let's talk," he whispered. "Go with me to the parlor. We've got to talk this thing over about Shane."

Not liking his implication, as though Shane were something to be bartered over, Melanie glared at Josh. "There's nothing to talk over," she whispered harshly. "Shane has come home. He's going to stay." She shook her head. "Josh, he's your brother. Your twin. Can't you show some compassion for him?"

"It's true that Shane is my brother," Josh whispered, staring at Shane and then at his father. They were talking as though they had never been apart. "But only by blood. Nothing more. Shane's been gone too long for me to have any other sorts of feelings about him."

Melanie looked at Shane and his father, seeing how happy they were to be with each other again. It touched her deeply, this warmth flooding from father to son. She glared at Josh again. "The years of separation haven't lessened the love your father has for Shane, or the love Shane feels for your father," she said, her voice breaking. "Nor should it affect the way you feel about your brother. Josh, how can you be so cold? So heartless?"

A warning grabbed Josh at his gut as he realized just how he looked in Melanie's eyes. It could cause her to despise him more than she already did. The chances of ever marrying her were getting dimmer by the minute. "I don't mean to sound crass," he said, nervously raking his fingers through his golden hair. "It's just that—that this is all so sudden."

He started to reach for Melanie's hand, to try to smooth the waters between them, but a familiar voice surfacing from the foyer made him turn with a start. Terrance had arrived, and by the sound of his voice he was disturbed by something. Melanie heard it, too.

"I don't need this," she said, sighing heavily. She looked up at Josh, anger flaring in her eyes. "First you, and now my brother? This should be a happy day for everyone. Shane has come home. Shane isn't dead! What is wrong with everyone?"

She brushed past Josh and hurried to the corridor. She stopped and placed her hands on her hips and looked arrows up at her brother as he returned just as angry a stare.

"Terrance, what are you doing here?" she asked, trying not to cause any more disturbance than her brother already had. Her gaze swept over his unshaven face, then stopped at his eyes. They were bloodshot and swollen from his frenzied drinking of the night before. "Or need I ask? You're angry because I managed to get Shane here to see his father before you had a chance to intervene, aren't you?"

Terrance clasped his fingers to her shoulders. "I'm angry because you don't listen to a damn thing I say anymore," he growled. "Melanie, when Pop died, it became my duty to look after you. Damn it, you're making that impossible. Do you know that when I woke up and found you gone this morning it scared the hell outta me? You're taking chances riding off without someone escorting you, even if it was to go to Shane Brennan."

"I don't need a bodyguard," Melanie said, jerking free from his grip. "And you know that you aren't as mad at me for having gone to Shane again as you are for my having brought him here to see his father." She looked at Josh, then back at Terrance. "You and Josh should have been born brothers instead of Josh and Shane. You both have identical hearts of stone."

"Melanie, now that's a terrible thing to say," Josh said, intervening. "I explained how all of this has caught me offguard. I just need time to get used to the idea of having a brother again. That's all."

"That shouldn't be so hard to do," Melanie said, turning to look toward the bedroom. "It's nothing less than a miracle that Shane is here. I'm so happy for your father and Shane, Josh. So happy."

Terrance turned cold inside, hearing how fondly Melanie talked of Shane, and recalling how Shane had kissed her, and how she had allowed it. If he didn't know better, he would think that Melanie was in love with Shane, and he with her. Terrance saw Shane as perhaps more of a threat to his security and his future than Melanie having received half the family inheritance.

Damn, if she married Shane, that Indian-lover would eventually manage to get everything! It wasn't the same as with Josh. If Melanie married Josh, Terrance knew Josh's weaknesses and how to prey on them.

He knew nothing about Shane except that he had been raised by Indians, and Indians were known for their cunning, shrewd ways.

Melanie turned to Josh and placed a hand on his arm. "Josh, please and try to be as happy as your father is over Shane's return," she pleaded softly. "It would mean so much to your father. And it would help Shane adjust to his new way of life. You do realize how hard all of this must be for him. He has never known anything but living in the wilderness. Now he will have everything, but I'm not so sure he can handle it. Will you help?"

Feeling trapped, not wanting to do anything to further stir Melanie's contempt, Josh nodded. "I'll try my damndest," he promised.

Melanie eased into his arms and hugged him. "That would make me so very happy, Josh," she murmured. "So very happy."

Josh viewed Terrance over Melanie's shoulder. Terrance was looking at him with fire in his eyes and it was not hard to understand why. Shane had interfered in his life, too; he was a brother whose sister was captivated by a man who was hardly more than a savage. Josh's insides rippled strangely when he realized that he had just found himself an ally in his plans to get rid of Shane. Terrance. Perhaps he was the solution.

Josh shrugged at Terrance and smiled awkwardly, then stepped away from Melanie as she eased from his arms.

"Come on, Josh," Melanie said, taking his hand, tugging on it. "It's time you joined your brother and father." She smiled warmly up at him. "Just imagine, Josh, a family is reunited after all those years. Isn't it just too wonderful?"

"Yes, wonderful," Josh said in a low rumble. He cast Terrance a glance over his shoulder as he walked alongside Melanie into the bedroom. His insides knotted as she led him to Shane's side and he looked down at his father, whose face was pink with color, whose eyes were bright with happiness. No one but Shane had been able to do this.

Jealousy raged through Josh, yet he had to pretend differently—for Melanie. At least for the moment, he had to behave as though he were happy to see his brother again.

Jared looked up at Josh and lifted a trembling

hand toward him. "Son, what do you think?" he said, wheezing. "Your brother is home." He looked from Shane to Josh and smiled. "By God, it's just like it was the day you were born. Hardly a thing about you is different. When you look at one another it's surely like lookin' into a mirror."

Shane turned slowly and faced Josh. He was quite aware of how his brother felt about his return and he understood. Shane was a sudden unwelcome intruder in his brother's life, just as Shane had been an intruder in Gray Falcon's life.

Was it never going to be different for him? Was he destined to always be the one that was not wanted? Would he have been better off that day if he had just been murdered alongside his beloved mother?

Melanie slipped a hand into Shane's and squeezed it affectionately. He looked down at her, moved by her gesture of sweetness, reminding him of what they had shared together. How could he ever again think that he was not wanted? It was in Melanie's eyes just how deeply she felt about him. It had been their destiny to meet. He had surely been directed back to his father to say a final goodbye and to meet the woman of his midnight dreams.

"Shane, tell Josh where you've been these past years," Jared said, his eyes growing haunted at the thought of Shane living with Indians. "Tell Josh about the chief who always knew where we lived but chose not to tell you."

Shane looked at Josh. He knew his brother did

not care, but to please his father, he began the tale all over again, while Melanie looked up at him, devotion in her eyes.

A strange, sudden weakness, more overpowering than before, overcame Jared. He closed his eyes and gasped for breath, then coughed.

Panic rising inside Shane, he stopped talking and kneeled down on a knee beside his father's bed. "Father, what is it?" he asked, his voice trembling. He took his father's hand and held it, feeling the utter coldness of his skin. "Have I overtired you? Has this been too taxing for you?"

Jared forced his eyes open, yet found it hard to focus. He blinked his eyes nervously, then was able to make out Shane's face again. He smiled wanly. "I guess I am a mite tired," he said weakly. "Perhaps it would be best if you let me rest a spell. Come back and talk some more later. I love you, Shane. God, it's so good to have you home with me. Please don't ever leave again. Stay. Stay."

Shane slipped his father's hand beneath the warmth of the covers. "I love you, father," he said, finding the words strange as they breathed across his lips. He had never thought that he would have the opportunity to see his father again, much less to tell him that he loved him.

But in a sense, it was not his father he was telling this to. His father had wasted away, and was almost a total stranger to him. The feelings of love flowing from him were the same, though. Shane recalled quite vividly the love he had shared with his father all those years ago. That sort of love could never die.

"Shane isn't going anywhere," Melanie said, looking adoringly down at Shane. "Jared, you go on to sleep. Shane will be here when you wake up."

"Shane," Jared said, reaching his hand from beneath the blankets again. He touched Shane's cheek softly. "You're staying on, not only for now, but for always. You're entitled to. What is mine and Josh's, is also yours."

Jared looked past Shane, up at Josh. "Josh, you show Shane to a room," he said, wheezing. "You show him the ropes of running a cattle farm. Son, he's going to take my place at your side. Together, you're going to keep this farm going. Do you hear?"

Josh stiffened, yet forced a smile. "Yes, sir," he murmured. "Whatever you say, sir."

Jared patted Shane on the shoulder, looking at his buckskin attire. "And, Josh, take your brother into St. Paul and get him fitted with new clothes," he said flatly. "Get him the finest duds St. Paul has to offer. We're goin' to make a new man outta him, from his head to his toe."

Nodding toward a drawer in a table beside his bed, Jared looked up at Shane. "In that drawer, in my wallet, you'll find enough money to buy you several fancy outfits," he said, his voice growing weaker. He looked up at Josh. "Son, take Shane today. It's time for him to look like a Brennan again."

Melanie saw the look of utter contempt in Josh's eyes, knowing that he dreaded the chore of taking Shane into town to have him fitted with clothes.

He dreaded the chore of teaching Shane the cattle business. Well, she would show him! She would take over all of these chores and do them herself. Nothing would please her more than to be able to be with Shane while he learned to live his new life. She would make sure that all barriers were torn down for him.

"Jared, I need some things of my own in town," she said suddenly. "Shane could go with me. There's no need to trouble Josh. He's got things to do. All of the cattle that were purchased yesterday have to be branded. I know how Josh likes to oversee the branding, so that it is done properly." She turned to Shane. "Would that be all right? Would you mind going with me instead of Josh?"

Shane smiled at Melanie, his eyes gleaming. He understood her motive. She wanted to rescue him from having to be under Josh's thumb at such a vulnerable time. She had to know that he had never worn anything but buckskins and would know nothing about choosing white man's attire. She knew that Josh could use that opportunity to humiliate him.

"That would be just fine," Shane said gratefully.

"Then we shall go this afternoon," Melanie said, squaring her shoulders proudly. "Right after lunch." She leaned down and gave Jared a soft kiss on the cheek, then rushed across the room. "We can go in my buggy, Shane. Be ready right after lunch."

Shane nodded and watched her until she left the room, then looked down at his father, who was panting for breath. He slipped his father's hand

110

beneath the blankets and drew the blankets up to his chin. "Father, should I leave today, to go into town with Melanie?" he asked. His eyes troubled, he peered down at his father's face. In the last few moments Jared had grown ashen in color. "Will you be all right?"

"I sleep most afternoons away," Jared said weakly. "Just be here tonight. I'd like to go asleep knowing that you are here at my bedside."

"I will be here,' Shane said, his eyes misting with tears.

Jared nodded toward the table again. "In my wallet," he said hoarsely. "Get the money. Go and have a hell of a time in St. Paul." He closed his eyes wearily. "It's sweet of Melanie to take the time with you. She's a saint. A saint."

Shane watched his father fall into a deep, quick sleep. He watched his shallow breathing for a while, then rose to his full height. He eyed the drawer, then Josh.

"Take the money," Josh said dryly. "If you don't, father will have a conniption when he wakes up. When he sees you again, you'd best have on new clothes. I think he'd like to see you that way, instead of in buckskin."

Taking a wide step, Shane stepped up to the table. He slowly opened the drawer and lifted his father's wallet into his hands. When he opened the wallet, his eyes widened and his pulse raced. He was looking down at many bills that showed hundreds on them. His father was a rich man and he was not ashamed to show it.

"Take several," Josh said, going to Shane's side.

"It takes a lot of money to dress the part of a rich man." He cleared his throat nervously. "But, Shane, don't get any ideas that everything is going to be this easy for you. Take my word for it, things aren't going to be."

Suddenly, Josh leaned closer to Shane and whispered harshly, "Damn it, Shane, I'm not going to allow it! You just can't waltz in here after all these years as though you belong and take charge. I won't allow it!"

Shane turned and gave Josh a cold, icy stare. Josh's insides turned inside out when he saw the utter contempt in his brother's eyes. He felt as though his brother were nothing but savage at that moment. Was it safe to live under the same roof as Shane? Had he killed many men? Had he taken any scalps? Would it be easy to kill a brother who had shown nothing but contempt for him?

Josh feared that a sleepless night lay ahead of him.

· CHAPTER NINE ·

The sun stood high overhead as the morning evaporated. The streets of St. Paul were deep gulleys of dried dirt, heavily traveled by horse and buggy and men on horseback. False-fronted buildings of planked lumber lined the streets, saloons and bawdy houses the most prominent. There had been a rumor that the railroad would come through, but the main mode of travel was still the steamboat. Sixty-two steamboats could make more than a thousand landings in a year's time, bringing new settlers, mail, and supplies on the Mississippi River.

In her pale green, tailored walking suit that was smartly cut, accentuating the soft curves of her breasts and the narrowness of her waist, and with her straw bonnet and its matching green velveteen bow tied beneath her delicate chin, Melanie walked alongside Shane on the wood-planked sidewalk in St. Paul, proud of his transformation. He had been fitted for several fashionable suits. Many would take several days to be ready for him, but they had managed to find a few that were ready to wear, and the one he wore now fit him to perfection.

Out of the corner of her eye, Melanie looked at Shane admiringly. His black cutaway coat emphasized the broadness of his shoulders. His shirt was dazzling white against his tanned face, an abundance of ruffles spilling over his embroidered waistcoat. His fawn-colored trousers fit him like a glove and were worn down on his boots, even touching the sidewalk in the back, with a strap under the foot.

But one thing was amiss. He had refused to buy a hat or have his hair cut. His golden hair was drawn back from his brow and hung long, just past his shoulders.

"Shane, you look quite handsome," Melanie said, shifting her velveteen purse from one hand to the other. "I hope you feel comfortable in your new clothes. Do you?"

Running a finger around the collar of his shirt, stretching it away from his neck, Shane gave Melanie an awkward smile. "I know I have much to get used to now that I no longer live with the Indians," he said, his voice drawn. "Wearing these damnable tight clothes may be the worst of the lot,

Melanie. Nothing feels better than buckskin against the flesh. Nothing."

Melanie elbowed her way through a crowd of men standing in front of a saloon, relieved when Shane slipped an arm around her waist and helped her along, away from their leering, drunken stares. "Thank you," she murmured. "I have found that shopping in St. Paul can sometimes be quite challenging. If a riverboat has just arrived with an onslaught of new settlers to the community, one never knows what to expect of the men who seek out the saloons even before a decent meal. My father never allowed me to come to town alone. But since his death, I do pretty much as I please."

"Perhaps that isn't wise," Shane said. "You can't trust everyone the way you did me, Melanie. When your brother warned you against being reckless, perhaps you should have listened."

He looked over his shoulder at the saloon they had just passed. He had heard the clink of coins and the shuffling of cards. It was arousing a hunger in him that had begun the day he had learned the game of poker from a trapper. Though he had never played poker anywhere but in the Indian village, he could not help but wonder how far his skills would take him in a white man's establishment. He would give it a try the first chance he got.

Melanie looked up at Shane, aghast. "How can you defend anything Terrance says or does?" she gasped. "Shane, he has been anything but polite to you."

"I'm not defending him," Shane said, his eyes

locking with hers. "It's you I'm concerned over. Though I admire your adventurous nature, I would hate to see you let it get out of hand. Melanie, this world we live in isn't all that safe or nice."

Melanie sighed. Her shoulders drooped as she looked away from Shane. "Yes, I know," she murmured. "But it is a world I have learned to live in and have done quite well for myself, thank you."

Shane's attention was drawn to a huge, impressive house across the street, on the corner of Minnesota and Bench streets, where the American flag fluttered on a pole in front.

Melanie sensed his silence and followed his gaze. "That's St. Paul's Central House," she said. "That's where the Minnesota territorial legislature meets to discuss the tax laws, the territory's school system, and the plans for a capitol building that should be completed in a couple of years."

"Capitol building?" Shane said, forking an eyebrow.

"St. Paul is the capital of the Minnesota Territory," Melanie said. "One day soon, Minnesota will become a state. I am so glad to be a part of this thriving community. When I was small, before there was ever a trace of a city here, I had doubted there ever would be. Everything seemed so untamable."

She looked up at Shane and said softly, "Your future was changed because of everything being so wild. But I doubt if there are any men left in the territory who would do anything as horrible as those white men did who massacred the ship's passengers that day."

"Twenty-five years have passed, but I cannot believe the man with the peculiar eyes has given up his evil ways," Shane said. "I have dreamed of the day that I will avenge my mother's death and I plan to look into those strange-colored eyes again soon. It has been said by many Chippewa that he has been seen. I will search for him soon. He is the same as dead."

A shudder coursed through Melanie. She stopped and grabbed Shane's hands, stopping him. "Shane, I understand how you feel," she said. "But I'm sorry I brought up the past today. I've had such fun shopping with you. Let's not spoil it by talking about that terrible man." She looked down at a cigar that was barely visible in his waistcoat pocket. Her eyes twinkled. "Let's talk about that cigar you bought when I wasn't looking. My word, Shane, don't tell me you're going to smoke that thing."

A slow smile lifted Shane's lips. He glanced down at the cigar, then at Melanie. "I smoke a fine cigar every chance I get," he said, chuckling. "I've managed to get cigars on occasion when trappers or traders came to the village." His eyes took on a haunted look as he again glanced at the cigar. "The old chief even learned to like cigars. If he wasn't smoking his pipe, he was smoking a cigar. That old man liked nothing better than his smoke, cards and whiskey."

Melanie's eyes widened. "What?" she said incredulously. "An Indian chief who liked not only cigars and whiskey, but also cards? What sort?" In her mind's eye she was recalling the deck of cards that she had found close to Shane's belongings that morning when she had returned for him. In the moments of passion that followed she had forgotten to ask him about them.

"Poker," Shane said, shrugging casually. "What other sort of cards are there?"

Melanie was at a loss of words for a moment, then she laughed. "My Lord," she said, swinging back around to Shane's side, to walk alongside him again. "I guess I have much to learn about your friends, the Indians, don't I?"

"If you want to learn, I will be more than pleased to teach you," Shane said, his chin held proudly high. "Just as I accept your teachings about things that I have not had a chance to learn through my years of living away from the white man."

Melanie spied a millinery shop just ahead. Her one weakness was hats. She could hardly ever pass a window display of hats without going inside the shop to buy one. She looked anxiously up at Shane, then back at the shop. "Shane, I know how eager you must be to get back to your father," she said. "But I would like to make one last stop before returning home." She pleaded up at him with her seductive brown eyes. "Would you mind?"

"Father says he sleeps the afternoon away," Shane said, smiling down at her. "He doesn't expect me at his bedside until later this evening.

You take all the time you need. Where do you want to go?"

Melanie looked sheepishly at him. "Shane," she murmured. "It's a place that usually makes a man quite uncomfortable. It's a place where women go to choose a new hat. Do you think you would mind waiting outside for me while I go inside and choose one for myself? It wouldn't take long."

"Take your time," Shane said, stepping back from the crowd. He stood in the shadows of a saloon, and the sound of shuffling cards causing his heart to race. "I'll wait here for you." He cleared his throat nervously as he took a look over his shoulder at the men coming and going from the saloon. Then he smiled down at her. "You go and pick out a pretty hat. I'll be just fine."

Melanie looked from side to side, at the crowded walkway and street, knowing this would be the first time Shane would be alone in this environment. She blinked her eyes nervously as she looked up at him. "Are you sure?" she asked, placing her hand on his arm. "Really? Are you sure?"

Shane smiled reassuringly down at her. "Melanie, you forget that I'm a grown man," he chuckled. "I don't think someone is going to come along and abduct me, now do you?"

Melanie laughed awkwardly. She leaned up and kissed him quickly on the cheek. "I won't be long," she said. "The shop is just a few doors down."

His heart hammering against his chest, Shane

watched Melanie walk briskly away, then reached his hand inside his pocket to jingle the coins that he had left after his buying spree. Taking three wide steps, he went inside the saloon. He stood just inside the swinging doors, looking the place over slowly and calculatingly. It was smoke-filled. A bar, with many men standing against it, reached along one whole side wall; a picture of a sprawling naked lady hung above shelves lined with an assortment of alcoholic beverages. There were several tables in the room, around which more men sat, drinking and playing poker.

Shane ambled farther into the room and found a vacant chair at one of the tables. Without waiting to be invited, he sat down. Taking several coins from his pocket he placed them on the table before him. The man dealing the cards gave Shane a sidewise glance.

"You want to be a part of this game?" the man asked. A cigar hung limply from the corner of his mouth.

Shane felt all eyes turn his way. He tensed up, wondering if they realized that he was fresh out of the wilderness, more Indian at heart than white. But nobody seemed the wiser. With his new attire, he was even dressed better than most of the men at the table, who wore mainly faded shirts and coarse denim breeches. Some needed shaves. Most reeked of alcohol.

"Deal me in," Shane said, nodding. He slipped his cigar from his pocket and bit off the tip and spat it over his shoulder.

Placing the cigar between his teeth he leaned

into a match that was offered by the man who sat next to him. "Thanks," he said. He took several long drags until smoke spiraled from the end of the cigar.

"Whiskey?" the man on the other side of Shane asked, scooting a glass and whiskey bottle in front of him.

"Don't mind if I do," Shane said, pouring himself a glass. In his heart he was remembering with fondness those many times of sharing a smoke, whiskey and cards with the old chief. In his heart, the old chief was there, looking over his shoulder, sharing his enjoyment.

Tipping the glass to his lips and taking a quick drink of the whiskey, Shane looked across the table at the man who was shuffling the cards. He was not as friendly as the others at the table. He was puffing on a cigar and his dark eyes were squinted beneath the brim of a sweat-stained hat. His face was stubbly with whiskers—except for a scar that slashed through the whiskers on his left cheek. Even from this distance Shane could smell the man. He probably hadn't had a bath in weeks.

"This time it'll be five card stud," the man said in a slow drawl, still staring at Shane. "Jacks or better to open. Place your coins on the table. An ante of one dollar."

Shane scooted his coins out in the middle of the table along with the rest. He began picking his cards up slowly as they were dealt to him until he was holding five in his hand. He studied the cards. He hadn't drawn openers.

"Check," he said, placing his cards on the table, face down.

"Check," the man next to him said, slapping his cards on the table also.

No one had drawn openers. They threw their cards in a pile in the middle of the table. The man with the scar shuffled the cards again while everyone placed more coins on the pile. Again the cards were dealt. Shane took his up from the table, one at a time. When all of his cards were in his hands, his pulse began to race. He was drawing into a straight flush! If he could only be dealt an eight of clubs!

"What's your bet?" the dealer asked, glaring at Shane after the bet had gone around the table to him.

"I'll call you," Shane said, smiling smugly at the dealer.

"How many cards?" the dealer asked, chewing on his cigar.

Shane placed his cards face down in front of him on the table after throwing in his one discard. "One card," he said, taking his cigar from his mouth and flicking ashes on the floor beside him.

The dealer slid the one card over to Shane. Shane tried to act nonchalant when he picked the card up and saw that it was just as good as the eight of clubs he had been hoping for. He had been dealt a three of clubs. He was still holding a straight flush.

"I'll raise you two dollars," Shane said, scooting more money out into the center of the table with the rest.

"Okay, I'll call you," the dealer said, everyone else having already dropped out. The focus was on Shane and the man with the scar.

Shane placed the cards down on the table face up. He heard the man with the scar groan, then smack down his cards angrily.

"Deal 'em," the man with the scar said, shoving the cards to the man sitting next to him. "I'll show this stranger with the fancy duds and long hair that he's going to be lucky only once today."

Shane's eyes gleamed as he dragged in his winnings. "We'll just see about that," he drawled confidently.

· CHAPTER TEN ·

Proud of her purchase, the hat box in which it lay swinging at her side, Melanie strutted from the millinery shop. Eager to show Shane her new hat, she pushed her way along the crowded sidewalk— then panic rose inside her when she didn't see Shane standing where she had left him, where he had promised to stay.

Afraid for Shane, Melanie began to push and shove desperately at the people crowding around her. Her eyes were moving wildly from place to place and store to store, for any signs of Shane.

What was she to do? He wasn't used to the city, nor to the brusqueness of some of its people. Where could he have gone? Why had he?

Recalling his love of cigars and his mention of pipes, Melanie rushed into a shop that specialized in tobacco products. Her heart faltered in its beat when she didn't find him there.

She rushed back outside, looking wildly up and down the street. She began walking toward the spot where she had last seen him. "Where could you be, Shane?" she whispered, her heart thumping.

Her words faded from her lips as she looked up at the sign hanging over the door of the saloon. She recalled how he had talked of enjoying poker. "Lord, he wouldn't . . ." she whispered, paling. "He'll be eaten alive by the sorts of men that frequent those places!"

She had never been in a saloon before. Her knees weak, Melanie pushed the swinging door open and peered inside. Smoke was as thick as a low hanging fog, impeding her complete view of who was inside. But she did not need to see. Shane's voice was loud and clear from somewhere close by, followed by the most definite sound of the shuffling of cards.

"Oh, no," Melanie said, groaning.

Inching her way inside and ignoring the appraising looks of the men at the bar and at the tables she was passing, Melanie kept her eye out for Shane. When she saw him, she stopped cold in her tracks, for it was obvious that the man sitting opposite Shane was angry at him for some reason. She inhaled a shaky breath when, just then, all hell seemed to break loose. She stood her ground, afraid to speak or even move.

"You sonofabitch!" the man with the scar said, leaning over the table as he threw his cards down and slipped a hand beneath the table. "You're nothin' but a goddamn cheater. Fancy man, I ain't liked your looks since you sat down here. Somethin' ain't right about you. You dress fancy but I'd say you're part Injun. I've been around enough to know how they hold theirselves. Now I ain't ever liked Injuns or even white men who smell like 'em. Real easy like, hand over all the money you've won from me, or I'll shoot your balls off. My pistol is aimed directly at 'em."

"Scarface, I've been insulted before and I'm used to it, but I don't think I can tolerate any insults from the likes of you," Shane said, his voice harsh. Quick as a panther, he raised a foot and kicked the man's gun away, then with deliberation and accuracy gave the man a swift kick by planting the heel of his boot into his groin.

The man scooted his chair back, yelping with pain, then grabbed his pistol and limped from the saloon.

Melanie watched all of this with dismay, then smiled awkwardly at Shane as he rose from his chair, turned, and saw her standing there. He grabbed his winnings from the table and walked confidently to her.

"I hope I didn't delay you any," he said, stuffing money in his pockets and puffing on his cigar.

Melanie scampered alongside him as they left the saloon. "Shane, you could have been killed," she fussed. "I've never seen anyone as angry as that man." She looked incredulously up at him. "Shane, he had a gun on you. If you hadn't been fast enough, I know he would have shot you."

"But I was, and he didn't," Shane said, slipping an arm around Melanie's trim waist. His eyes were twinkling. "Damn, Melanie, did you see my winnings? It's more than I ever thought possible. Always before, when I won, it was usually only against one trapper or trader, or the old chief. I've never played with a large group of men before."

An icy coldness suddenly gripped Melanie's insides. She didn't like Shane's reaction to his victory at the poker table today. Was he going to be more like his brother after all? Would Shane grow to love to gamble as much as Josh? She could smell whiskey on his breath! Would he grow to love to drink as much as his brother? Would becoming a part of the white man's world change him that much?

They reached the horse and buggy. Silent, Melanie nodded a thank-you to Shane as he helped her onto the seat, then climbed aboard himself. Disillusioned about this man she had sworn to protect and guide, she snapped the reins and rode from the city. She could feel his eyes on her, studying her. She knew why. Since they had met, she had never been this quiet. He had to wonder why.

Yet he did not ask.

Shane saw a troubled expression on her face and in her eyes. Did it stem from his having not stayed where she could find him after she left her millinery shop? Or did it stem from his having played poker in the saloon?

He could not take this silent treatment much longer. When the city was far behind them and they were traveling down an isolated road shaded on both sides by stately elms, he grabbed the reins from Melanie's hands and stopped the horses.

Melanie looked at him, stunned. "Why did you do that?" she asked, her voice shallow.

"I will drive the rest of the way," Shane said. "Move over."

Seeing that he meant business, Melanie said nothing. Her eyes wavered when Shane snapped the reins and left the road, moving instead through the forest. Melanie clung to the seat as the buggy weaved around trees, beneath low-hanging branches, and finally came to a halt beside the Rum River, not all that far from the Brennan and Stanton farms.

Her eyes wide, Melanie watched Shane jump from the buggy and come around to her side. Her breath was stolen away when he grabbed her by the waist and lifted her from the buggy and half dragged her to the riverbank. Turning her to face him, he glowered down at her.

"Now do you want to tell me why you're giving me the cold shoulder?" he demanded. "Why have you been so quiet since we left town? What did I do that did not please you, Melanie?"

Melanie blinked nervously up at him. "I'm sorry, Shane," she murmured. "It's just that— that—"

"It's just what?" he stormed. "I thought you understood me—what I was about. Was I wrong?"

"How could I know that much about you?" Melanie said. "Shane, we truly don't know one another at all. Today proved that I don't know you."

"Why today?" he said, searching her eyes for answers.

Melanie lowered her eyes. "Oh, Shane, it was the way you enjoyed your winnings so much after that card game," she blurted out. "Your brother Josh is a gambler." She looked quickly up at him. "He gambles and drinks so much of your father's money away! Even my brother Terrance is guilty of the same. Shane, I would hate to think that your life could be guided by such weaknesses! I love you so much, I couldn't bear to lose you to cards and whiskey. I have seen how it destroys a man's morals—his strengths. Please, please understand!"

Shane was taken aback by the violence of her feelings about cards and whiskey. He had never seen them as a problem, for he and the old chief had always indulged in both in moderation. He had been taught the art of restraint, of willpower. He would never let cards or drinking rule him. He understood the dangers.

Touched by Melanie's concern for him, understanding now why she had been distant with him, Shane drew her to him and cradled her in his arms. He untied her bonnet and lifted it from her head, then tossed it to the ground. He wove his fingers through her auburn hair, then lowered his mouth to her lips.

"Never worry about anything taking your place in my life," he whispered against her lips. "You are my woman, don't you know? Now that I have met you, you have become my life. Only you."

A sweet current of warmth swept through Melanie. Unable to resist, she twined her arms around his neck. "Shane, oh, Shane," she whispered, then emitted a soft moan of passion against his lips as his mouth closed hard upon hers. A need familiar to her only since she had met Shane was rising up inside her, spreading and swelling. She clung to him as he lowered her to the ground. The spongy green moss beneath her cushioned her back. Shane's hands, busy disrobing her, were setting fires along her flesh as it became exposed to the afternoon sunlight that was drifting like spiraling, golden ribbons through the trees overhead.

When Shane leaned away from Melanie as he withdrew her last garment, leaving her shamelessly nude beneath his passion-filled eyes, she could not help being alarmed by her willingness to let Shane remove her clothes. Even more than that— to share another intimate encounter with him. Only he could blot out all reason! Only he!

"Shane, we mustn't," she said, grasping at sanity for a fleeting moment. She reached for her dress and held it against her body. "Your father . . ."

"Today is ours," Shane said, easing the dress from her hands. "Tonight is my father's."

Melanie's eyes widened as he laid her dress aside and began undressing himself. Very soon, he had removed his clothes and was bending over her, reaching a hand to sweep her against him. Melanie was breathless. She was frightened. She had never seen a man undressed before and even now she could feel the hardened full length of his manhood pressing against her thigh.

"This moment is ours," he said, brushing his lips against the nipple of her breast, causing it to stiffen and throb with pleasure. "Close your eyes, Melanie. Let yourself enjoy the feelings that are blossoming within you. Let me take you to paradise and back."

She wanted to cry out and tell him that this was wrong, that this was shameful! But she could not find the words. She was being consumed with a hot, pulsing desire. She recalled how he had given her such pleasure before. Her body cried out for the same rapture. She wanted to give him the same, in return.

"My love," she murmured, arching her body as Shane caressed her skin lightly with his fingertips while his lips and tongue skillfully teased her taut breasts.

And then he was suddenly sculpting himself against her body, his hardness gently probing between her thighs. Melanie's heartbeat was so wild it felt as though she might be swallowed whole by it as she waited for that moment of his entrance inside her. She bit her lower lip to keep from crying out with pleasure as Shane began caressing her tight core of womanhood while he pressed himself farther and farther within her. A sudden burst of pain made her eyes fly wildly open, but in only an instant the pain was smoothed away into something wonderful as he began moving rhythmically within her.

"Relax," Shane whispered, his breath hot on her cheek. "Enjoy."

As Shane continued tantalizing her with his hands and mouth, Melanie moaned softly. Lifting her legs and locking them together at her ankles about his waist, she began to move against him, moving her hips to meet his eager thrusts.

His mouth seared into hers with intensity, causing delicious shivers of desire to race up and down her spine. Her body was turning to liquid, melting into his. . . .

Shane was molded perfectly to the curved hollow of Melanie's hips. As she responded to his touch, thrusting her hips toward him, he pressed deeper within her. Gathering her buttocks within his hands, he relished the softness of her skin against his flesh. The air heavy with the promise of what was to come, he was hardly able to hold back any longer that which he had desired from the moment he had seen Melanie. The need was ravaging him, heart, body and soul. White heat was traveling through him, vibrating in his bloodstream.

Taking a moment to get his breath before the final plunge into rapture, Shane drew his mouth from Melanie's lips and leaned back to look down at her. As his hands smoothed damp, perspiration-laced tendrils of her hair back from her face, their eyes met and locked in an unspoken understanding, a promise of ecstasy.

A surge of pleasure welled within Melanie as Shane gathered her fully against him again and began more heated strokes within her. She clung to him, pressing her lips to his sinewy shoulders. She closed her eyes, her breathing becoming rapid as she felt the wonders of rapture spilling over inside her, drenching her with warmth. She clung to Shane, only half aware of making whimpering sounds, as his body shuddered maddeningly into hers, then lay quietly against her.

Overwhelmed by the ecstasy, tears splashed from Melanie's eyes. She slowly opened them when she felt Shane kissing the tears away, then seared her lips with a kiss of fire. She clung to him, radiantly happy.

The aroma of medicine was almost overpowering as Shane sat at his father's bedside. A lone candle flickered on the nightstand beside the bed, casting dancing shadows on Jared's ashen face. Shane sank a washcloth into a basin of water, lifted it and wrung it out, then gently applied the dampened cloth to his father's brow.

"That feels good, son," Jared said, wheezing. "First I'm hot, then cold. If I didn't know better, I'd say my old ticker was about to give out on me. Every breath I take is such . . . such an effort."

"Father, you're going to last forever," Shane said, yet doubting his words. His father had worsened since he saw him last. He had not only slept the afternoon away, but most of the evening, as well. It seemed to be not only an effort for him to breathe, but to stay awake. "You'll see. You're much stronger than you give yourself credit for."

Jared reached a trembling hand from beneath his layer of blankets and patted Shane on the knee, appraising him as he looked him up and down. "Melanie has good taste in clothes," he said, chuckling. He winked slowly. "And men, also. Shane, don't let her slip from between your fingers. She'll make you a fine wife. It's as though she's been waiting for you to come back. She hasn't given any other man the time of the day." He chuckled beneath his breath. "Not even your brother Josh. Seems there's a lot of friction between them two. Ever since they've known each other they've argued about this or that."

He coughed, almost turning blue from the effort, then again patted Shane's knee. "But I saw how she looked at you, son. She adores you. Take advantage of it. Marry her. She's right for you." He closed his eyes as his words faded away. "Yep, she's right for you."

"Father?" Shane said, alarmed at how quickly his father seemed to drift back into sleep. He dropped the washcloth into the basin and took his father's hand and held onto it tightly. "Father, are you all right?"

Jared laughed a strangled sort of laugh and opened his eyes slowly. "Don't fret none," he said, nodding. "I'm not going to leave you just yet. We've much more to talk over, you and I."

Shane inhaled a shaky breath, relieved that his father had not slipped into a sound sleep again after all. He smiled down at his father, wanting so badly to share his moments with Melanie with him, knowing that he would be happy.

But it did not seem the proper thing to do—to tell a father about having made love only a few hours ago with the woman of his father's choice. These sorts of things were talked about between close, best friends, but not between fathers and sons.

"What do you want to talk about?" Shane asked, moving his chair closer.

"Tell me again about your life as an Indian," Jared said, his eyes wavering. "Tell me about those sonofabitch white men pretending to be Indians who killed everyone, about the Indian chief who took you away from the scene of the massacre. Did you ever call him father, Shane? Did he become a substitute father for you?"

Shane firmed his jaw as his eyes clouded with memories. It had not been that long since he had said his last goodbyes to the old chief, a father to him for so many years. And now he was so close to saying another goodbye, this time to his true father.

It tore at his heart, this torture of having to say so many goodbyes so often!

"Chief Standing Tall did not take me to raise me as his son," Shane explained. "I was raised with another family. The old chief and I became close, but never did I call him father."

"Tell me about this old chief and what he taught you," Jared said, gasping for breath as a sharp pain shot through his lungs, then his heart. He tried to stay calm, not wanting to alert Shane that the pain was so severe.

These last few moments were too precious.

Shane began his story again, repeating everything that he had told his father earlier. He ignored Josh as he came into the room and sat down at the bed opposite him, watching him with intent interest as he related the story of his Indian life.

Melanie paced back and forth in the parlor, the fire on the hearth warm at her side. She flipped her hair back from her shoulders as she looked up at the ceiling, sighing heavily. Something told her that she should be with Shane, that he needed her. Was it his father? Was he worse? Or was she concerned over leaving Shane alone with Josh and his humiliations and insinuations?

"Melanie, you're going to wear a hole in the carpet if you don't stop that damned pacing," Terrance said, pouring himself another glass of whiskey. He slouched down on the sofa, already glassy-eyed and lightheaded from too much to drink. "Sit down, damn it. You're driving me crazy."

Melanie stopped in mid-step and turned to look down at Terrance. She shook her head, disgusted at the sight of him. "Must you drink so much?" she said, glaring at him. "How can you even be aware of what I am doing? You're almost drunk again, Terrance. Don't you have any pride? Don't you see what you're doing to yourself?"

Terrance returned her glare with one of his own as he tipped the glass to his lips again and guzzled down the last of the whiskey. He looked Melanie up and down, seeing her as too ravishingly lovely in her fully-gathered pale green silk dress with its low-cut bodice. Shane had also seen how lovely she was and had taken advantage of it. Had he come back not only to claim his portion of the Brennan riches, but to get his hands on Melanie, as well, to gain control of her portion of the Stanton riches?

Melanie and Shane had surely shared in more than purchasing a new wardrobe for him this afternoon, for she had come home with stars in her eyes! Even now her cheeks were pink and her eyes were glowing. Had things gone farther than kisses between them? Would Shane dare . . . ?

Yes, he thought angrily. Shane more than likely had coerced her into intimacy! He had been raised in the wilderness, hadn't he? He had no more morals than a damn savage!

"You condemn me for drinking while you gallivant around town with a man who was raised by Indians, surely even thinks like one?" Terrance said, angrily tossing the glass against the brick fireplace, shattering it. He rose to his feet and grabbed Melanie by the shoulders. "Melanie, where's *your* pride? Where?"

Beneath her brother's accusing eyes, Melanie felt a hot blush rush to her cheeks. She was recalling her afternoon with Shane, and where it had taken them—to paradise, just as Shane had promised! And she would not let her brother make it ugly! She loved Shane. He loved her. In time, they would shout to the world of this love!

"Shane Brennan is more man than you can ever be. Ever!" Melanie said, jerking away from Terrance.

She went into the foyer and grabbed a shawl.

"And as for how much time I spend with Shane, and where," she stormed. "That's none of your concern."

Stumbling, Terrance went after Melanie just as she stepped outside onto the porch. He leaned heavily against the doorframe. "Damn it, Melanie," he shouted. "Where are you going?"

"To Shane," she said, squaring her shoulders proudly. "Where else?"

Terrance groaned. He doubled a hand into a tight fist and slammed it into the wall beside him.

"And that is how I came to find out about you, and where you resided," Shane said, completing his story. "Father, I—"

Shane's words came to an abrupt halt when he heard his father gasp for breath. He felt the tightening of his father's grip. He saw his father's locked eyes staring toward the ceiling. He saw no pulsebeat at his throat.

"No!" Shane cried, staring wild-eyed down at his father. "You can't be dead. You can't!"

Josh's insides became queasy. He looked away and swallowed hard to choke back the bitter bile that was rising into his throat. He had known for a long time that his father was going to die. But now that he had, it did not seem real. For so long, it had been only the two of them.

Until Shane came back.

Turning slowly around, Josh glared at Shane. Their father had nothing on his mind at the end except Shane! Only Shane! Hate swelled within

Josh for a brother who had robbed him of his father, even at the last.

Trembling, tears burning the corners of his eyes, Shane eased his fingers from his father's strong death grip and placed it beneath the blankets. "Farewell, *Gee-bah-bah*," he whispered, hanging his head sadly. "Farewell, father."

A rustling of feet and a chair falling over backward, crashing against the wooden floor, made Shane jump with alarm to his feet. He looked across the bed at Josh, whose face was red with anger.

"This isn't the place to be speaking that hocus-pocus Indian language," Josh growled between gritted teeth. "Shane, this isn't the place for you. Now that you've said your goodbyes to father, you can go on your way. He was the one who wanted you here. Not me. In my eyes, you are not my brother. You are—someone I don't even know."

"How can you say that, Josh?" Melanie said suddenly from behind them. "How can you look your brother in the eye and say that? Lord, Josh, it's the same as looking at yourself. Would you deny your own self the rights that you would deny Shane? Would you?"

Shane turned quickly as Melanie moved to his side and slipped an affectionate arm around his waist. She looked adoringly up at him, then down at Jared. "At last he's in peace," she murmured, her voice breaking as tears rolled down her cheeks. "Shane, he's no longer in pain and he was able to die knowing you are alive and well." She smoothed a tear away from her cheek as she looked closer at Jared. "Can you see? He died with a contented smile on his face."

Shane turned back around and looked down at his father. He had been too distraught to notice before, but, yes, his father had died with a smile on his lips. He had died happy!

"Josh, would you have denied your father that smile?" Melanie asked, looking accusingly at him. "Would you?"

Josh swallowed hard as he bowed his head, ashamed.

· CHAPTER ELEVEN ·

A lone grave beneath a towering elm tree not far from the Brennan mansion lay piled high with flowers. The soft summer breeze whispered gently through the leaves of the tree, and a mockingbird warbled on a low-hanging limb.

Melanie, dressed all in black, stood at the parlor window of Shane's house, staring out at the grave, remembering all too clearly another funeral not long ago. Her father's. She missed him today more than ever. With Terrance behaving so erratically, drunk one minute, sober the next, she felt as though the weight of the world was on her shoulders.

She turned slowly and looked across the room at Shane, who was sitting before the fire, staring into it. Her heart went out to him and she realized that she bore not only her own sorrow today, but his also. And didn't she also have his welfare to look after, as well as her own? Was she capable of seeing all this through? When her father was alive, she had been carefree. Now she had nothing but cares.

Except for Shane. Though he was a man of twenty-nine, she a mere girl of eighteen, her strongest instinct was to protect him. And she would.

Her gaze shifted and settled on Jared's attorney, Mike Green. He was on the sofa removing a legal document from a brown leather satchel. The will. Melanie had made it a point to stay after the funeral to see that Shane's interests were protected. If Josh had his way, Shane would have none of the inheritance.

Her gaze shifted to Josh, who was downing another glass of whiskey as he leaned an arm against the fireplace mantel, staring blankly down into the fire. Melanie sighed heavily. Immediately after the funeral, Terrance had left for town. It did not take much thought to guess where he was going. He would gamble and drink another day away while he left his responsibilities to the hired cowhands and his sister! And he wondered why Melanie was so determined to learn all of the particulars about running the cattle farm? Indeed!

"Shall we proceed?" Mike Green said, breaking the silence with his slight voice. He looked nervously at Shane, then at Josh. It was beyond his comprehension how Jared had been so sure that Shane would return—by God, though, he had been right. There he sat, all six feet of him, an exact replica of Josh.

Josh was drowning his problems in alcohol, as usual. Well, he would damn well need it when he heard the final changes in the will. Only yesterday Mike had returned and listened to Jared give the command to make the needed changes. Once Josh heard, all hell could break loose.

"Yes, let's get this over with," Josh said, glaring at Mike.

"Perhaps you can set your drink aside for a few moments, Josh," Mike said, running a finger nervously around his tight, ruffled collar. "This will needs some strong listening."

"I can listen just as well with a glass in my hand as without," Josh growled. He went across the room to the liquor cabinet and poured more whiskey into the glass. "What I do need is to make sure there's enough whiskey in it."

"As you wish," Mike said, his eyes wavering.

Melanie stood beside Shane's chair and placed a gentle hand on his shoulder. When he looked up at her and smiled, everything within her turned to mush. "It will be over soon," she whispered. "It won't take long for Mike to read the will." She glanced at Josh, who had slouched down into a chair opposite Shane. "But it may take a lifetime for Josh to accept what's in it."

Shane turned his eyes to Josh and felt a sadness sweep through him. His own brother. His own brother cared nothing for him. It was hard enough to accept Gray Falcon's rejection and he was of no blood kin. But to have a true brother, a twin, reject him?

It was as if his brother had taken a knife and stabbed him. Perhaps in time Shane could change Josh's attitude. But he had decided that he would not be run off. He was home. He was going to stay. His father had waited for him to come home before he drifted away to join his ancestors in the hereafter—waited to tell him how much he was loved and wanted.

His father wanted him here—and he would stay!

Mike stood up, with his back to the fireplace. He stretched the legal document out before him and began to read.

"This is my last will and testament," he began, continuing until he came to the part that he knew would shock Josh and surprise Shane. He paused, frowning, and glanced at Josh, who was refilling his glass again with whiskey, then focused his full attention on Jared's will.

"My son Shane has just returned home, alive and well, and to him I bequeath three-fourths of my land and cattle. It is only right that I do so, since Shane has suffered a lifetime of injustices since the day he watched his mother die. To Josh, my other son, I bequeath the remainder of my possessions except for my house, which is to be shared equally with Shane as long as Shane desires to live there. To Josh I must say that I do not do this to hurt him, but to make him a better man for it. Through my years of having Josh solely to myself, I have tended to spoil him by giving him everything a son might desire. He took it all willingly and grew careless with it by gambling and drinking too much of our riches away. With Shane holding the largest sum of the inheritance in his hand, Josh will have to learn to toe the line or lose everything in the end. To both my sons, it is only my intention to do what is best for you. You have a long life ahead of you. Make the best of it."

The room was deafeningly quiet as Mike re-folded the will. Melanie looked at Josh. She had never seen anyone as stunned. It was in the way he held his glass only halfway to his mouth, as though frozen there, and in the way his eyes were fixed on the will, glassy with shock. She knew that Josh had expected to have to share with Shane, but now he knew he would have less than an equal share.

Melanie stepped around in front of Shane and looked down at him. The show of tears in his eyes revealed that he was realizing just how much he had missed by not being with his true father all these years that had been stolen from him—and just how much his father had loved him.

Shane looked slowly up at Melanie. Tears streamed from her eyes as she bent to her knees before him and buried her head against his chest, hugging him. "Shane, oh, Shane," she murmured, warming all over inside when he twined his fingers through her hair and held her even closer to him.

Mike held the will out before him, motioning from Shane to Josh, offering it to them. "This copy of the will is for your files," he said, looking from Shane to Josh. "I have my own."

Josh turned his eyes away from Mike, holding

onto his glass so strongly it threatened to break. "You know what you can do with that goddamned piece of paper," he said between clenched teeth. He slammed the glass down on a table and stormed from the room. When he was outside the house, he inhaled several deep breaths, trying to stop the nervous beating of his heart. He raked his fingers through his golden hair and stared at the fresh grave beneath the elm tree.

"Father, why?" he said, a sob escaping from between his lips. "Was I that big a disappointment to you? Or did you feel you had to make it up to Shane for never having found him the day of the massacre? Which is it, Father? Which is it?"

Not wanting to think any more about it, feeling as though the world were tumbling down around him, Josh began running. When he reached the stable, he saddled his horse and mounted it shakily. He had already been condemned because of his drinking and gambling, so to hell with it. That's what he needed now to make him forget the follies of a dead father!

His hair flying in the wind, Josh rode away, hell bent for leather . . .

Melanie stood at the window, watching Josh. Mike went to her side and saw him ride away.

"He'll soon come to his senses and see that his father had only his best interest in mind," Mike said. "But at this moment, he probably hates Shane so much he could kill him. I'd keep my eye on him tonight. He's already reeking of whiskey.

When he returns from town, he'll be drunk as hell."

Mike turned and placed a hand on Shane's shoulder, looking up at him from his less than imposing height. "Son, I don't know how it happened that you came home when you did," he said, not wanting to accuse Shane of anything, certainly not of having heard that his father was dying and knowing that an inheritance could make him rich. "But it made Jared's last moments on this earth happy. That's all that mattered." He nodded down at the will. "What's written in that will is fair and square, but it's going to take Josh some time to accept it. Just go about your business. He'll have to come round, in time."

Melanie went to Shane and linked her arm through his. She looked Mike square in the face. "Do you truly feel that Shane could be in danger staying here tonight?" she asked softly. "I've known Josh almost all my life, but I've never seen him as upset as he is now. Would you advise Shane to stay somewhere else tonight? Until Josh has a chance to cool off and accept what has happened?"

"I would highly advise this young man to sleep elsewhere tonight," Mike said, picking up his satchel. "I've never seen a violent side to Josh, yet under these circumstances, who can tell?"

Melanie firmed her jaw and looked up at Shane. "That settles it," she said. "You're going to stay at my place tonight."

Shane shook his head, his jaw set just as tightly.

"My father has given me part ownership of this house," he said flatly. "I will not be a coward and leave. My brother and I share the same blood in our veins. He will not harm me. You will see."

Melanie wanted to blurt out that she would stay with him to make sure, yet she could not take away his pride by showing her lack of faith in his ability to keep himself safe. He had lived under questionable conditions these past twenty-five years and he had survived. She could not believe that Josh could be more of a threat than those other dangers Shane had been forced to face and endure!

"I must take my leave," Mike said, picking up his wide-brimmed felt hat from a chair and hiding his bald head beneath it. "If ever you have need of legal assistance, Shane—or Melanie—I shall always be there to serve."

Melanie broke away from Shane and escorted Mike to the door. "Thank you for everything," she murmured. "Have a safe journey back to St. Paul."

"Thank God it's not all that far," Mike said, glancing over at Shane. "You never know when a stranger is going to pop up out of nowhere."

Melanie blanched, then closed the door after him and went to Shane. She slipped into his arms and hugged him.

Many others would question the true reason for Shane's suddenly showing up at the time of his father's death. But she knew that he did not have a devious bone in his body. In time, everybody who concerned themselves about his sudden appearance would know the truth.

In time. . . .

The saloon was dim with smoke. The tinkling of a piano and loud, boisterous laughter filled the room. Terrance sat beside Josh at the bar, his arm slung around Josh's shoulder.

"Seems we both got rotten bargains," Terrance said in a drunken drawl. "First my sister havin' to share everything with me on the farm like she's a man, and now you havin' to take less than your brother. There ought to be a law against it, Josh."

His eyes blurred, Josh attempted to pour himself another drink, but spilled half of the whiskey on the counter. "Damn it," he growled, shoving the bottle away from him. "I still can't believe what my father did to me. It's damn humiliating, Terrance."

Terrance patted Josh's shoulder. "It's damn unfair, Josh," he said, burping loudly. "What'd we do wrong to be treated so unjustly?"

"Just exist, I guess," Josh grumbled, tipping the glass to his lips and taking a quick gulp.

"I love Melanie so much my gut aches, but there isn't much I can do about her having an equal share of everything," Terrance said, slipping his arm away from Josh. He poured himself another drink. "But we can do something about your brother."

Terrance could tell that Josh was seeing his hopes fading. More important to Terrance, if Shane stayed on at the Brennan farm, Melanie would more than likely end up marrying him, and Shane would get his hands on Melanie's share of the Stanton riches too.

Terrance had been thinking of how he could prevent that, to show up this man who had been raised by Indians. He had to find a way to make Melanie see how worthless he was!

"No matter what anyone says, Shane shouldn't be allowed to take charge at your farm," Terrance continued. "Perhaps there's something we can do about it. Are you game?"

"Do?" Josh said, looking quizzically over at Terrance. "Like what? What are you talking about?"

Terrance shook his head and sighed. He was right to see Josh as a bungler and expect that he would botch everything up. If he were smarter, he would narrow in on Shane and make friends instead of enemies, because Shane was now in possession of so much that he would like to own.

But Terrance didn't expect anyone could ever get anything out of Shane Brennan. He was a survivor. Hadn't he lived those many years with Indians and lived to tell about it?

Terrance moved his stool closer to Josh and placed an arm around his shoulder. "Josh, I've got a plan that could ruin everything for Shane, especially his relationship with Melanie," he said, chuckling. "I can't bear to think of her marrying up with that Indian-lover. But to guarantee that my plan will work, I need your help."

"What do you plan to do?" Josh asked, looking guardedly over at Terrance.

"I can't say unless you agree to help me," Terrance said, toying with his thin, black mustache.

"I don't know," Josh said, frowning. "I'm damn mad at Shane, but I don't want to do anything that might get me locked behind bars."

"You'd never get caught," Terrance said, smiling smugly. "Will you agree to help me?"

Josh stared down into his glass, then over at Terrance. "Naw, I don't think so," he said, shaking his head. "Let's just let things happen on their own. Shane knows nothing about farming. And Melanie will soon see the sort of man that he is. He'll leave again. It'll all be mine again. You'll see."

"God, Josh, you're even dumber than I thought," Terrance said. Disgusted, he got off his stool and lumbered from the saloon. Josh gaped openly after him, then ordered another bottle of whiskey and went to join a poker game.

· CHAPTER TWELVE ·

Someone cursing outside her bedroom door drew Melanie awake. She yawned sleepily, then winced when she heard the shattering of glass on the hardwood floor in the hallway, followed by more cursing. Her eyes rolled upward.

"Terrance," she groaned, knowing she would find a mess outside her door before the servants awakened. Her brother had returned home after his drunken bout in St. Paul and had more than likely brought another bottle of whiskey with him. In his whiskey-induced stupor he had dropped the bottle and broken it.

It would not be the first time, nor would it be the last.

Disgusted with her brother and now fully awake, Melanie rubbed sleep from her eyes and got out of the bed. Slipping a robe around her shoulders, she went to the window and pulled aside the heavy, white satin drapery. She moaned. Her brother had spent the whole night tom-catting around. The rising sun was barely tipping the trees with its lustrous orange light. Occasional strips of black still colored the sky that was softening to a pale blue.

Leaning closer to the window, Melanie peered through the hazy morning light toward Shane's house in the distance. A tingling heat rose from her toes at the thought of him. She wondered if he had slept safely. Josh had probably been no threat after all. He had more than likely been with Terrance the full night. They were known to frequent the same saloons, the same brothels.

"They are both no good," Melanie whispered, flinching when she heard the loud bang of Terrance's door as he finally reached his room. "I've grown used to it. Will Shane be able to? Josh can be intolerable at times, especially after he's had a few too many drinks."

Now that she was awake and eager to start the day, Melanie threw her robe aside. Today she planned to spend most of her time with Shane. He needed to know so much! Not only how to read and write, but everything about cattle farming. She wanted to be there for him, to teach him everything. Hadn't he taught her some valuable lessons in the short time she had known him? He had taught her the true meaning of compassion. He had led her down the path of true romance.

Going to her armoire, Melanie ran her hands

through her clothes. She stopped at the fringed buckskin skirt. It was the most comfortable. She would wear it. She planned to spend some time on her horse today, and the buckskin skirt would give her more freedom of movement.

With no further thought of Terrance, Melanie hurried into her skirt and white, long-sleeved blouse, then yanked on her knee-high leather boots. After taking several quick strokes with a brush through her hair, she tied it back from her face with a yellow ribbon. Ready to challenge this new day, she left the room.

But when she stepped out into the hallway and saw the broken bottle and the whiskey spread across the golden grains of the wood floor, her anger at her brother returned. Tapping the toe of her boot on the floor, she looked toward Terrance's room. He could not get away with this careless behavior forever! Something had to be done to make him aware of just how disgusting he had become!

"I guess that little chore is mine," she whispered, stomping determinedly to Terrance's room.

Angrily, she jerked the door open, then shuddered with distaste when she saw her brother sprawled across the bed, still fully clothed. His snores reverberated around the room. The stench of alcohol was so strong, it made Melanie's stomach feel as though it were being turned inside out.

Terrance was sleeping on his stomach, his face turned toward her. A growth of whiskers was dark on his chin, but not dark enough to hide the lipstick that was smeared across his mouth and cheek. His shirt was half unbuttoned and only partially tucked into the waistband of his breeches. His dark, tangled hair was sprayed across the bedspread.

"You had yourself quite a night, didn't you, big brother?" Melanie said beneath her breath. "You plan to sleep a good portion of the day away, don't you?" She looked toward the pitcher of water that sat beside the basin on his nightstand. "Well, we'll just see about that."

Melanie circled her fingers around the handle of the pitcher and lifted it from the table. Positioning it over her brother's head, she emptied the water from it onto his face.

Awakened with a start, Terrance yowled and bolted from the bed. His eyes were wild as he rubbed the water from his face. "Goddamn it all to hell, Melanie!" he screeched, looking at her through his fuzzy, drunken vision. "What'd you do that for?"

Melanie put the empty pitcher on the table and brushed past Terrance as she walked toward the door. "Seems I came in here for a drink and when I began pouring the water from the pitcher I just somehow failed to have a glass there to catch it," she said, smiling over her shoulder at him. "My, oh my, Terrance—seems I've awakened you. I couldn't be sorrier. Why, look at you. You look like something the dogs dragged in."

Laughing, she left the room. She rushed down the stairs and into the kitchen. Grabbing a carrot for her horse and an apple for herself, she stepped out into the brisk morning air. Inhaling deeply, she looked across the wide pasture at Shane's house. Was he awake also? Was he eager to see her? How soon would he come?

Going to the stable, she went to her horse's stall. "Good morning, Sugar," she said, offering her bay gelding the carrot. "And it will be a good morning. I'll be with Shane again!"

She led her horse from the stable and began brushing its mane, taking occasional glances at the road that led from Shane's house, to hers.

Sparrows were awakening and making a racket in the trees just outside Shane's bedroom window. This, and having to sleep another night on a mattress instead of on a soft pile of bear furs on the floor of his wigwam at the Chippewa village, made him awaken with a groan.

When he heard the creaking of floorboards out in the corridor, his spine stiffened and he slowly reached for his knife that he had slept with under his blankets. Slipping his fingers around the handle of his knife, he began easing his weapon along the side of his body.

Breathing shallowly, he watched the door open slowly. His eyes narrowed when the shape of a man filled out the spaces in the doorway, a man whose outline was defined by the soft lamplight emanating from behind him in the hall. It was Shane's brother, Josh. He had surely just arrived back home after being gone all night, gambling and drinking. Even with the full length of the room separating them, Shane could smell the powerful stench of alcohol wafting across the room from his brother.

Waiting to see what Josh was going to do, Shane did not move a hair, and the room was still too dark for his eyes to meet and challenge his brother's.

But the feelings were strong without words even being spoken. Shane could hear his brother's heavy breathing. He could feel the hate radiating from Josh and wondered why it had to be that way. Shane had no feelings one way or the other for his brother, for the years had stolen away from him his memories of a brother's love, but he saw no reason why this love could not be rekindled now.

But jealousy was at the root of many a falling-out, even between brothers. Recalling the lawyer's warning that Josh might try to harm him, Shane kept his fingers circled around the handle of his knife. But then his brother turned and stumbled away in a drunken stupor.

Shane perked up his ears and listened for Josh's door to open and close. When it did, he lay his knife aside and rose slowly from the bed. For a moment he hung his face in his hands, recalling the sadness of the previous day. He had lost a father he had just become acquainted with again. What in life was fair? What?

Stepping to the window and drawing aside the heavy drapery, Shane peered across the wide pasture at Melanie's house. At this early hour of morning, she was probably still asleep. Before going to meet her, he had time to ride into the forest for a time of meditation, to reflect on where he was in life. Although he had Melanie's devoted love and his dying father's assurance that his future was secure, Shane felt anything but comfortable with his new life. His thoughts strayed too often to the life he knew before. Only a few days separated him from what had been. His heart cried out to see Cedar Maid and to ride alongside his faithful companion, Red Raven. How could Gray Falcon have denied him so much? How?

And there was the constant nagging itch to leave everything behind to go and search for Trapper Dan. "Let him have a few more days to feel smug about life," he whispered, his eyes filled with fire. "That will give me more time to anticipate victory over him. Waiting always enhances the pleasure!"

Dropping the drapery back in place, Shane turned to look at the fancy clothes hung across the back of a plush, upholstered chair. They were stiff and cold compared to his buckskins. His buckskins were warm, like a second flesh. He saw no reason not to wear them, at least this one more morning until the other, more casual clothes were ready for him at the shop in St. Paul.

Shane dressed quickly in his buckskin attire, even his soft, comfortable moccasins. Fitting his sheathed knife at his waist, he left the room and moved stealthily along the narrow hallway. He looked toward his brother's closed door, hearing the rumbling of drunken snores. This brother of his had been a disappointment to his father and Shane now understood all too well why! Josh did not know how to do anything in moderation, especially drinking. When he gambled, did he also do that blindly, carelessly?

Perhaps one day Shane would get the opportunity to teach Josh the art of restraint. He would show him that a man played poker much more skillfully when he was sober!

Smiling, he rushed down the stairs and outside. Going to the stable, he took his stallion from its stall and patting the horse fondly he saddled it, led it outside, mounted it, and rode away.

The bellowing of cattle drew Shane's eyes admiringly to their long horns glistening in the early morning light. Then his gaze was averted. His heart skipped a beat when he saw someone approaching quickly on a horse, riding up the long lane that led to the house.

"Red Raven?" Shane said, his blood turning cold in his veins when he saw that his friend wore no smile of greeting on his face. He was somber, and streaks of black had been painted on his brow and across his high cheekbones.

Had someone died?

A feeling of foreboding washed over Shane. Red Raven would not have Gray Falcon's permission to come to Shane with any news of their people, for Shane was the same as dead to the new chief now that he had been banished from the tribe. Red Raven had come on his own.

To defy the new chief, the news that he carried to Shane could not be good.

Sinking his heels into the flanks of his horse, Shane sent his stallion galloping hard until he reached Red Raven. Drawing his reins tautly, he stopped alongside his friend, eying him warily. "My friend, why have you come?" he asked, his voice drawn. "I see much in your eyes that is not good. What news have you brought to me?"

Red Raven, attired in only a brief loincloth and moccasins, a beaded headband holding his coal black hair back from his face, reached a hand to Shane's shoulder. "Shane, *nee-mah-tah-bin*, it is good to see you," he said. "But I have not come for a friendly visit. You have guessed right. There is much that troubles me."

Shane shifted uneasily in his saddle. "Tell me, Red Raven, what is in your heart?"

"The news is about Cedar Maid," Red Raven said, lowering his hand from Shane's shoulder. He cast his eyes downward. "My bride price was not large enough. She has become another man's woman. She is no longer in our village. She was forced to leave with the man who paid many horses and pelts for her."

Shane flinched as though shot. With trembling fingers, he reached a hand to Red Raven's shoulder and pressed his fingers firmly into his bare copper flesh. "Gray Falcon did this?" he growled. "He traded her off as though she were no more than a—a dog?"

"That is so," Red Raven said, nodding. "She is gone."

"Cedar Maid is gone?" Shane said, easing his hand back to his reins, clutching them so hard that the leather bit into his flesh. He squared his shoulders. "Who was this man who came into the Chippewa village and paid for my sister?"

Red Raven rose his eyes slowly upward. They wavered when he found Shane looking at him so intensely. "Shane, it is not an easy thing to tell you," he said, swallowing hard. "How do I?"

"What do you mean?" Shane asked. "Why are you finding it so hard to tell me who paid the price for Cedar Maid? Is it someone I know and do not care for?"

"It is someone you have never met," Red Raven said. He rested a hand on the pommel of his saddle. "But you know of him. He is a man of your past and of your worst nightmares."

A shudder coursed through Shane. There was only one man of his past who had troubled his dreams! "You are speaking of Trapper Dan?" he said, almost choking on the words. He was dying a slow death inside at the thought of sweet and gentle Cedar Maid forced to be attentive to such a vile man!

"It was he," Red Raven said, nodding. "I was there. I looked into his eyes. They turned me cold inside, Shane, for I knew, at that moment, exactly who he was!"

"Did you tell Gray Falcon?"

"Yes, I told him."

"And he still accepted the bride price for Cedar Maid?"

"*Ay-uh*, that is so."

Shane looked quickly away from Red Raven, so distraught he could hardly hold himself at bay. He wanted to shout! He wanted to wail to the tree-tops!

But he would not. He had placed all of his Indian ways behind him.

However, he would use the skills the Chippewa had taught him to track down the trapper and kill him. He would take Cedar Maid away from him and bring her to his home. She would live in peace with him.

Red Raven sidled his horse closer to Shane's. "What do we do about Trapper Dan and what he has done?" he asked, his voice solemn.

Shane turned his eyes back to Red Raven. They were clouded with emotion. "Do you even have to ask?" he said flatly. "Do you travel with me? Or do I travel alone?"

"Need *you* ask?" Red Raven said, setting his jaw firmly.

"Then what are we waiting for?" Shane said, flicking his reins and sinking his heels into his horse's flanks. He rode away, Red Raven alongside him. All thoughts of Melanie—all thoughts of anyone or anything else—were banished from his mind. Only Cedar Maid and her welfare mattered now. If anything happened to her, it would be his fault, for he had placed everything else before finding the evil trapper who had been close to the village on the very day that Shane had been ordered to leave!

In truth, it would be Gray Falcon's fault if anything happened to Cedar Maid, for if Shane had been allowed to stay with the Chippewa, he would have been there when Trapper Dan had arrived. Trapper Dan would have never left the village alive. As it was, Gray Falcon had succeeded in total revenge against Shane by selling Cedar Maid to the man responsible for Shane's mother's death!

His eager stallion pounded the earth as they rode away from the farm.

Melanie looked toward Shane's house again, then dropped her brush with alarm when she saw him riding away alongside an Indian! Was he leaving? Was he returning to the Indians? Did Josh do something to him in the night to make him want to leave?

Fearing all of these things, Melanie's fingers trembled as she slipped the stirrup on her horse. She didn't take time for a saddle. She had to catch up with Shane. She had to know the reason he was riding away as though in desperation! She had to stop him. Somehow, she had to dissuade him from leaving!

Gripping her knees against the horse, Melanie snapped the reins and began riding in a strong gallop away from her farm. The brisk wind tore the ribbon from her hair. The early morning air seeped through her blouse, chilling her clean through. But her eyes never left Shane as he thundered away in his buckskin attire toward the incline that would take him upward, into the depths of the forest.

Afraid that she would lose sight of him once he blended into the forest, Melanie snapped her reins harder against her horse. She leaned low over her mount's flying mane. She was gaining ground! She was going to catch up with him.

"Shane!" she screamed, squaring her shoulders as she straightening her back. "Shane! Stop! Oh, please stop!"

Terrance had heard Melanie riding away on her horse. He stumbled from his bed and drew the drapery aside and peered through the window. He kneaded his chin as he looked at Melanie riding toward Shane, and frowned. Where was Shane going in such a hurry? Why was Melanie following him?

Then he focused his attention on the Indian riding alongside Shane. He smiled crookedly. "Well, I'll be damned," he drawled. "Shane's friend has come and got him. He's going back to the Indians!"

Dizziness claimed him. He reeled, catching himself as he grabbed the back of a chair. A sick feeling swept through him and he understood why. He had been ill many times before after a full night of drinking, gambling and womanizing. Today was no different. He needed sleep. That would make it all pass.

Forgetting Melanie in his need of rest, Terrance stumbled back to the bed and plopped face down across it.

Sleep quickly claimed him again.

Shane's spine stiffened when he heard Melanie's voice from somewhere behind him. He drew the reins tautly and wheeled his horse around. Breathing shallowly, he watched her riding hard toward him. He took her reins as she stopped alongside him, her hair tangled, her eyes wild.

"Shane, where are you going?" Melanie asked, breathless. She looked at Red Raven. Attired in only a brief loincloth and with black paint streaked across his face, he looked no less than threatening.

"Why are you leaving with him?" She implored Shane with tear-filled eyes. "Shane, please don't leave. You can't! Things will get better between you and your brother. Please give it a chance!"

"What I am doing has nothing to do with Josh," Shane said, his blue eyes filled with emotion. "Nothing at all."

"Then what?" Melanie persisted, reaching to touch his hand. "Why are you leaving so hastily? Where are you going?"

"My friend, Red Raven, has brought me troubling news," Shane explained quietly, casting Red Raven a glance as his friend edged his horse close to Shane's.

"What sort of news?" Melanie asked, looking guardedly at Red Raven.

"It is about Cedar Maid," Shane said.

Melanie was aware of the sudden pain in Shane's eyes at the mention of Cedar Maid. She could tell that the news about her could not be good. She was almost afraid to ask further about her, yet she had to know. Anything that had to do with Shane now, had to do with her!

"Shane, what about Cedar Maid?" she asked weakly. "What has happened?"

"She is no longer with the Chippewa," Shane said, anger suddenly flaring in his eyes. "A great bride price was paid for her. She now travels with a white man. This white man is the same man who stole from my mother's dead body! It is the man with the peculiar eyes! He has returned to steal from me again!"

Melanie grew cold inside at Shane's vehemence. "I'm sorry," she murmured. "That's terrible."

"He will not have Cedar Maid for long," Shane said, narrowing his eyes. "By nightfall she will be mine. She will make residence in my house. She will be safe with me, forever."

Jealousy stung Melanie's insides. Could Shane's strong feelings for Cedar Maid be more than that for a sister? She swallowed back a lump that was invading her throat. "Then you intend to go and take her from this man?" she asked, her voice drawn.

Shane nodded. "He cannot be allowed to molest someone as sweet and innocent as Cedar Maid," he said. He gave Red Raven a troubled glance, then peered intensely at Melanie. "Too much time is being wasted in talk," he said, reaching to touch her cheek gently. "I must go. Already Trapper Dan has the advantage. He has surely gone many miles since he took Cedar Maid away!"

"I want to go with you," Melanie said, grabbing his hand and holding on to it for dear life. She had the feeling that she was going to lose him and she had only had him for a short while. She could not bear the loss.

"It is not wise," Shane said, shaking his head. "Return home where you will be safe. I only wish to have one woman at a time to worry about."

Melanie flinched at those words, suspecting more meaning in them than he had intended. "I will not slow you down" she argued. "I ride a horse as skillfully as any man. And I can take care of myself! I will go with you, Shane. You can't expect me to return home as though nothing has happened."

She blinked back a tear. "Shane, I'm afraid for you," she said. "This man you are going after has proven to be nothing less than a fiend! He will not let you take Cedar Maid without a fight."

"It is my fight," Shane said flatly. "I will fight and I will win." He pointed toward the farm in the distance. "Go home, Melanie. I have no more time for arguing."

Stung by his actually giving her a command, Melanie gave him a hurt stare, then wheeled her horse around and rode hard away from him. Tears splashed from her eyes, fearing for more than just his safety. She feared that his past would always be there to interfere with his new life.

Hearing the thundering of hooves behind her, Melanie drew her reins taut and eased her horse around so that she could take a final look at Shane. Wiping tears from her cheeks, she watched him disappear into the forest.

"I can't let him go this easily!" she cried to herself. "I must follow. I must! He just won't know that I am there!"

Waiting just a moment longer, Melanie nudged her horse with her knees and urged it into a soft trot, keeping just far enough back from Shane so that she would not be noticed by him or his friend. When she reached the forest, she found cover behind the trees. She rode steadily, never letting Shane out of her sight.

· CHAPTER THIRTEEN ·

Unaware of Melanie following them, Shane and Red Raven rode endlessly onward. The shadows of the forest loomed around them, yet the air was warm as the sun rose higher in the sky.

"Are you positive this is the way Trapper Dan traveled with Cedar Maid?" Shane shouted, casting a troubled glance at Red Raven.

"The tracks of the trapper's horses led in this direction earlier," Red Raven shouted back. "But I lost them at the river! We can only hope now that we are still following them."

"I cannot believe that the same man can take two of the women I love away from me!" Shane said, his eyes haunted. "Why did he choose Cedar Maid for a bride? Why?"

"As the story was repeated to me by one of my

cousins, who sat around the fire with Gray Falcon while the bride price was being paid, the trapper said that he had heard about how beautiful this woman was who had just moved to the land of many lakes from Canada," Red Raven said. "He came. He paid well. Not only did you lose Cedar Maid, Shane, but I also. She was to be my bride!"

"Gray Falcon will pay for this," Shane grumbled, doubling a fist at his side. "It is only in spite that he sent Cedar Maid away. He wanted nothing in his village to remind him of me! Because of his jealousy and spite, Cedar Maid must now suffer!"

"Shane, Gray Falcon has won in the battle of the heart," Red Raven said. "Not only Cedar Maid is suffering, but also you and I!"

Hate welled inside Shane for Gray Falcon. He nodded. "Yes, that is so, Red Raven," he mumbled. "That is so." He thrust his heels into the flanks of his horse and urged it into a harder gallop.

Tired and hungry, her body feeling as though it were glued to the horse's back, Melanie continued her journey with watchful eyes. She sighed heavily, her hair lifting wildly from her shoulders as the wind whipped it about. "When will they ever stop?" she whispered, her lips parched with her need of water. "Do they have any idea at all where they are going, or is it all a guessing game? If they do catch up with the trapper, what then? Will I witness a side of Shane that I do not even want to know exists? Will he viciously kill the man?" She swallowed hard. "Lord, will he even scalp him?"

Weary, and too full of questions that she feared the answers to, Melanie chose to drop back away from the two determined riders and return to her farm. This was not a mission that she should be a part of, after all. She could not bear to think that Shane could have a savage side. It would tear at her heart to see him be anything but gentle and compassionate.

"I don't know what I was thinking by following him," Melanie said, drawing her reins tautly and stopping her horse. "It was foolish!"

Needing a moment to rest before traveling back, Melanie dismounted. Watching Shane ride farther and farther away from her, she felt empty and frightened. Perhaps this would be the last time she would ever see him.

Turning her eyes away and stifling a sob in the depths of her throat, Melanie took her horse's reins and led her steed to a great nestling of oak trees. After securing the reins on a tree limb, she stretched her tired and aching bones.

Just as she started to sit down on the ground for a much needed rest, however, she stopped short and took an unsteady step backward. Just ahead was something that did not look right. It was a pile of leaves that looked as though it had been put there purposely. And the form it took was that of a human body!

Paling, Melanie stared at the mound of leaves for a moment longer, then, scarcely breathing, she knelt to the ground and began brushing leaves aside.

When suddenly a face showed up at her through

the opening, Melanie jolted with fright back to her feet. And as she looked down at the lifeless dark eyes staring blankly up at her, she began to scream.

Over and over again she screamed.

The screams reached through the forest. When Shane heard them, chills raced up and down his spine. He stared at Red Raven for a moment, then both wheeled their horses around and began riding back in the direction from which they had just come. Everything was silent now, even the warbling of the birds in the trees.

After a moment of quick travel, Shane blinked his eyes, hardly believing what he was seeing. It was Melanie. But what was she doing there?

His jaw firmed angrily as he realized that she must have been following him. But what had happened to cause her so much distress? Where was her horse? Had it thrown her?

Puzzled, he watched Melanie running through the forest in his direction. Her eyes were wild. Tears streaked down her face.

"Shane!" Melanie cried, waving her hands desperately. "I'm so glad you heard my screams. Oh, Shane, it's so horrible! Someone—someone is dead back there. Someone has been buried beneath a layer of leaves. Oh, Shane, I saw the person's face! It was . . . a woman!"

Shane drew his stallion to a shuddering halt beside Melanie. He was filled with many questions —why she was there, why she had followed him!

Yet, nothing but what she had said was important. Who was buried beneath the leaves? A woman?

No! It could not be! Not Cedar Maid!

The trapper had paid well for her. Why would he take her as a bride, then kill her?

Reaching down, Shane swept Melanie up on his horse with him. Securing her on his lap and locking an arm around her waist, he rode onward. "How much farther?" he asked. He was so filled with fear of what he was soon going to find, his voice sounded strangled.

"I couldn't have run far," Melanie said, sobbing. The beautiful face of the woman, an Indian maiden, haunted her now, and probably would for the rest of her life.

Her heart faltered as she looked quickly up at Shane. She had failed to tell him that the woman was an Indian. He was looking for an Indian woman.

Oh, no, it couldn't be! It just couldn't be!

"I see your horse," Shane said, snapping the reins to urge his mount to go faster. "Did you find the body close by where your horse is reined?"

"Yes," Melanie said, turning cold inside at the thought of seeing the woman again. "Only a few footsteps away."

Shane drew rein beside Melanie's bay gelding. He helped her to the ground, then swung himself out of his saddle and followed her. When she pointed to the mound of leaves he hesitated, then went on to it. A dizziness swept through him when he found the beautiful doe eyes of Cedar Maid looking up at him, yet not seeing him. In those death-locked eyes he could see pain. He could see despair.

Crazed, Shane fell to his knees and began scraping the rest of the leaves away. Soon Cedar Maid's body was fully uncovered. Melanie saw the bloody wrists and turned her eyes away, bitter bile rising into her throat. She choked back the urge to retch as she hung her head in her hands.

Red Raven moved to Shane's side. He knelt down to one knee beside him and gazed down at Cedar Maid, unable to hold back remorseful tears. Shane picked Cedar Maid up and moved her from the grave of leaves and took her to a more pleasant spot close beside a flowering lilac bush.

Melanie regained her composure. She went to Shane and knelt down beside him. "This is Cedar Maid?" she asked, her voice breaking.

"Yes," Shane said, his voice filled with venom. "This is Cedar Maid." He lifted one of Cedar Maid's limp hands, studying her wrist. He could tell that the wounds on both of her wrists were self-inflicted. To keep from having to submit to the evil trapper, surely even before he had dishonored her, she had taken her own life!

"It is because of me that she is dead," Shane said, easing Cedar Maid's hand back to the ground. He reached trembling fingers to her eyes and gently closed her eyelids, then cradled her head against his chest. "I should have been there to protect her." He began to wail and chant, looking to the heavens.

Shaken, Melanie rose to her feet and stared

down at Shane, then at Red Raven. She felt out of place, as though an intruder, witnessing their terrible grief.

She looked at Shane again. His reaction to Cedar Maid's death was so intense. His reaction was that of a man in love.

Had he desired Cedar Maid but been denied the chance to marry her because he had been banished from the Chippewa village?

Had Melanie just been someone to comfort him in his loss, a handy substitute for the woman he could not have?

Turning her eyes away, Melanie cried softly—not only for herself, but also for Shane, and for the tragedy that had befallen this innocent woman.

So often she was discovering that not only was life hard, but so very, very cruel!

Red Raven dried his tears and placed a hand on Shane's shoulder. "It is best that we return Cedar Maid to my village," he said. "Then we must go and find the trapper. We must kill him, Shane."

Shane shook his head as he looked up at Red Raven. "The search for Trapper Dan will be futile," he said. "He knows the wrath of the Chippewa. He will not chance being caught after Cedar Maid is found dead. Did you not see the haste in which he left her? He did not even take the time to bury her except beneath a covering of leaves! He knew that quick escape was vital, or else he would have taken the time to bury her in the ground, to guarantee that no one would ever find her."

175

He looked down at Cedar Maid's lovely, quiet face. He rocked her within his arms. "And, no, she will not be taken back to Gray Falcon's village," he said softly. "She was sent away from the village against her wishes. She was disgraced in the eyes of all of her people by having to leave with the vile trapper. She would not want to be disgraced again by being returned to be stared upon with her death mask. No. She will be buried here. Where it is peaceful. Where she chose to die."

"*Ay-uh,* that is probably best," Red Raven said, nodding. "It is peaceful here and the fragrance from the flowers is sweet. Cedar Maid will enjoy it in death, as she would have in life."

"I always swore never to hate Gray Falcon because the old chief would not have approved of such ugly emotion," Shane said coldly. "But I was wrong. I do hate him. And I will avenge Cedar Maid's death!"

"Together we will avenge her death," Red Raven said, his eyes filled with sudden fire. "Whatever you say, I will do alongside you!"

"How many horses did Trapper Dan pay as bride price for Cedar Maid?" Shane asked, gazing down at her as she lay so limply in his arms. "Just how many pelts passed from Trapper Dan's hands into Gray Falcon's?"

"Five horses and at least ten very fine bear pelts," Red Raven said, moving to balance himself on his haunches beside Shane.

"Then tonight we shall go and steal this exact number of horses and pelts from Gray Falcon," Shane said. "He will lose everything that he found worthy of such a heartless trade. Tonight, Red Raven, if we ride hard, we can be there. As the moon rises high in the sky, it will cast our shadows along the ground as we take what should not be Gray Falcon's!"

Melanie had stood by, listening. Fear grabbed her at the pit of her stomach. If Shane did not return with her now to his new life, perhaps he would never return again!

"Shane," she said, kneeling down beside him. "Please don't do this. Let it be. If not, perhaps it won't only be Cedar Maid who dies needlessly. You could die, also."

She so badly wanted to replace Cedar Maid in his arms. She wanted to cling to him, whisper in his ear what they had found together!

Had it all been false? Would he ever turn to her again with tender, loving arms? Had his feelings for her all been pretense?

If so, she would never trust a man again. She would not even want to. He was her life.

Only he!

Shane rose to his feet, carrying Cedar Maid. "Melanie, you must return home," he said flatly, his voice cold and unfeeling as he gazed down at her. "I shall follow later."

"But how can I be sure?" she said, her voice drawn. "Shane, listen to me! You could die while trying to make things right for a woman who is already dead! I am alive, Shane. Alive! Please go home with me."

"You know that I can't," Shane said, his eyes holding hers. "Cedar Maid's death must be

177

avenged. Now that is all that I will say to you about it. Go home!"

"No," Melanie said, lifting her chin stubbornly. "I will go with you. I can help you steal the horses. I am skilled with horses. You know that I am!"

"I cannot allow it, Melanie," Shane said, impatience thick in his words. "You were told not to follow earlier and you chose to disobey me. But now it is different. You are right. What I have chosen to do has a measure of danger in it. If I cannot achieve this revenge, I would not want to think it is because you got in the way. Do you understand now why you must do as you are told?"

Melanie stared up at him unblinkingly, knowing that this time she had no choice but to do as he said. It was true that more than likely she would get in the way. And what of Terrance? Once he discovered her gone for much longer than usual, he would come looking for her. He might even bring the whole city of St. Paul to look for her!

There were more dangers here than she even wanted to think about.

"I'll do as you ask," she said, trembling. "But I shall not rest until I see you've returned home safely, Shane. Please make it soon."

"One sunset will pass and then I will return," Shane said, sighing heavily.

"I only hope that you are sincere," Melanie said, then rushed to her horse and jerked her reins from the tree limb. She pulled herself up onto the horse and wheeled it around. For a moment, she gazed down at the lifeless form in Shane's arm, feeling a deep remorse for the innocent woman who had been wronged.

She then looked up and let her eyes lock with Shane's. A cold rush of fear soared through her, for she was not seeing anything akin to what she usually saw in Shane's eyes when he looked at her.

Had Cedar Maid's death changed everything, forever?

Melanie turned her eyes away, swallowing back the urge to cry. She squared her shoulders and thrust her knees hard into her horse's side. "Sugar, take me home," she whispered.

She looked to the heavens and said a soft prayer for Shane.

· CHAPTER FOURTEEN ·

Moonlight spiraled through the dining room window, silvering the floor at Melanie's feet. Seated at a long dining table, a chandelier with melting, tapered candles above it, Melanie only picked at her food. She stared down at her plate filled with tempting morsels, but too many doubts and fears were getting in the way of a healthy appetite.

She couldn't get Shane off her mind, nor the Indian maiden he had held in his arms as he mourned over her! When she recalled Shane's wails, like those of an Indian in torment, she couldn't stop the jealousy that stung her heart.

Had he lived with the Indians too long? Was there truly a chance that he could change? If he did return to his farm, could he ever forget his past and live for the present? For the future? Was Melanie truly going to be a part of that future?

And, oh, Lord, where was he at this moment? Was he safe? Or had he been caught stealing from the Chippewa chief?

"Sis, you've barely touched your food," Terrance said, startling Melanie's eyes upward. He ran a finger around the tightness of his ruffle-splashed collar, his gold brocade waistcoat picking up the glow of the candles. He poured more wine into his long-stemmed glass. "I know what you're thinking about and it's a waste of time."

Terrance smiled smugly at her as he lifted his glass in a mock salute. "It's plain and simple, Melanie. Shane is gone," he said, his slow smile tugging at his narrow black mustache. "In time you'll see that you're better off without him. He could never become one of us. He was a part of the wilderness for too long."

A slow burn was beginning deeply within Melanie. She placed her fork on her plate. Grabbing her linen napkin from her lap, she slammed it on the table, then shoved her chair back and rose angrily from it. "Terrance, Shane will return and he will fit in to his new life," she said, her eyes flashing angrily. "You may as well get used to the idea of his being around, brother dear, because I plan to be his wife!"

Afraid that she had just confessed to something that would never be, Melanie swung away from the table and left the dining room in a rush. Her low-bodiced green satin dress rustled voluptuously against her lacy petticoats as she hurried to the parlor, away from Terrance's searching eyes. She went to a window and stared through the darkness at the forest. She had to believe in Shane and in his declaration of love for her. She had to believe that he would come out of this adventure tonight unharmed. He would return home! He must!

A strong hand on her wrist made Melanie's heart skip a beat. She winced as she was forced around to face Terrance. "What are you doing?" she asked, looking up at him. "Let me go, Terrance."

"Not until you are made to listen to reason," Terrance growled. "Melanie, you've been nothing but bullheaded since Pop's death and it's time for that to stop. I am your older brother. Pop depended on me to see to your welfare." He leaned closer to her face, the stench of alcohol heavy on his breath. "You know that Pop and Jared Brennan planned for you to marry Josh. Damn it, Melanie, that's exactly who you are going to marry. Do you understand?"

Melanie squared her shoulders angrily. She jerked her wrist away from Terrance. "You may be my older brother and Pop may have asked you to look after me, but, Terrance, Pop wasn't aware of just how much you drink," she hissed. "When he was alive you did a damn good job hiding this from him. You never let him hear you come in at all hours of the night, drunk. Somehow you managed to be there for him, to look after the farm like a devoted son. But since his death you've let yourself go to hell, Terrance! How on earth can you expect me to listen to anything you say?"

Placing her hands on her hips, Melanie looked up at Terrance defiantly. "And do you truly think I want to marry someone just like you? It's enough, Terrance, that I have to put up with *your* nonsense," she stormed. "I will not marry Josh, no matter what either of you says, or does!"

Terrance doubled his fists at his sides. His face was red with rage. "Well, my dear sister, you sure as hell aren't going to marry that Indian-lover," he shouted, turning and stamping away from her.

Melanie flinched as the front door slammed. She turned and watched through the window as Terrance went to his horse reined at the hitching rail and swung himself into his saddle. Scarcely breathing, she watched him ride away, his dark hair flying in the wind.

Wasn't it enough, Melanie thought, that she had Shane to worry about? Why did Terrance have to choose this moment to cause more problems?

Melanie lowered the wick in the kerosene lamps around the room, then left the parlor and wearily climbed the stairs. She hadn't been able to eat. She most surely would not be able to get one wink of sleep!

Until Shane returned home and convinced her that he truly loved her, a part of her was dead inside.

The moon sheened everything in silver as Shane moved stealthily among the fenced-in horses close to the Chippewa village. Red Raven quietly pointed out the ones that had been traded to Gray

Falcon while Shane slipped a rope over each of their heads.

Running alongside each other, Shane and Red Raven led the horses away from the village, then stopped and caught their breaths after tying the horses together and securing them to a post that Shane had pounded into the ground earlier.

"I will return with you to your farm with the horses and then I will have to say a final goodbye, my friend," Red Raven said, clasping his hands onto Shane's shoulders. "I can no longer find it in my heart to stay among my people. It would be hard to look at Gray Falcon's face every day and not see Cedar Maid's eyes locked in death, knowing that he is responsible."

"What will you do?" Shane asked, sadness engulfing him over these continued losses in his life. "Where will you go?"

"My horse will carry me far away," Red Raven said, swallowing hard. "Perhaps back to Canada."

"You don't have to go, you know," Shane said, glancing over his shoulder as the roped horses began to whinny. "You can go with me. You can learn with me the art of raising the cattle with the long, white horns. We could hunt together again. Perhaps one day we will hear word of Trapper Dan trapping in the forest again. Our hunt would be for him. We could live as brothers on land that is now mine."

"Land that is also your brother's," Red Raven growled. "Land that was once the Indian's! Land that is now fenced in!"

"Yes," Shane said, nodding. "It is all of those

things. It is the way of the white man." His eyes wavered. "I am a white man, Red Raven. My parents were white. And since I am not allowed to live with the Chippewa, I will now live like the white man!"

Red Raven dropped his hands to his side and stepped away from Shane. "That is why I cannot come to live with you," he said. "I am Indian."

"I understand," Shane said softly. He turned and looked at the stolen horses. Hidden in the shadows of a butte, they were grazing on knee-high grass. "You do not have to travel with me to my farm. It is I who chose to steal the horses. It is I who will take the responsibility for them."

"It is I who shared in the revenge," Red Raven said flatly. "I wish to see that you get the horses to your farm without any confrontation with Gray Falcon's braves."

"That is generous of you," Shane said, staring through the darkness at the outdoor fires in the Indian village in the distance.

"And now we will go and steal the pelts from Gray Falcon's wigwam?" Red Raven asked, following Shane's intent stare.

"It must be done to complete this act of vengeance," Shane said.

"We could be caught and slain," Red Raven warned him, drawing his knife from its buckskin sheath at his waist.

Shane slipped his own knife from its sheath. "It is the hour of night when everyone is asleep," he said. "Even Gray Falcon. We will come and go and no one will be the wiser."

"*"Ay-uh,"* Red Raven said. "But if Gray Falcon does awaken, it is I who will plunge the knife into his heart."

Shane heard the venom in Red Raven's voice, and knew he would kill Gray Falcon with pleasure. He hoped it would not come to that. Shane hated Gray Falcon with all of his being, but he did not want to be forced to participate in an act that would make Chief Standing Tall cry out from the hereafter. No. With luck, the remaining chore of the revenge would be silent and swift!

"Let us go," Shane said, grasping hard onto his knife. "Tomorrow Gray Falcon will realize that he slept too soundly tonight!"

Grim-faced, Shane ran alongside Red Raven through the night. On the outskirts of the village, he stopped and looked guardedly around him. Then he focused his full attention on the largest wigwam of all.

"I see no one," Red Raven said, leaning closer to Shane. "It is safe. Let us do it now."

Shane nodded and ran around behind the wigwams that were in his path. His eyes glittering with hate, he moved with the steps of a panther to the back of Gray Falcon's wigwam. Stopping to get his breath, he listened for any movements within. There were none. He smiled at Red Raven and nodded.

"Remember, take only the pelts that were given Gray Falcon in trade," Shane whispered. "He must understand why they are gone!"

"Ay-uh," Red Raven whispered back.

Together, they circled around to the front of the

wigwam. Shane held his breath as he lifted the buckskin entrance flap and peered inside. His heart lurched when he discovered that Gray Falcon was not alone. Sleeping on his pallet of furs alongside him was Blue Blossom, a dear friend of Cedar Maid's. The chief had chosen her to be his woman! Surely she did not lie with him from her own choosing. She must have hate in her heart for what he had forced upon Cedar Maid! If Blue Blossom knew that Cedar Maid was dead, she would not hesitate to take revenge.

Shane and Red Raven exchanged quick glances, then Shane stepped inside and moved stealthily around the two sleeping forms. From the glow of the orange, sunken coals in the fire space Shane could see well enough around the inside of the wigwam. He smiled at Red Raven when they both spied the pile of bear pelts at the same time.

Together they went and gathered the pelts in their arms and turned to leave but both stopped, alarmed, when they discovered two dark eyes watching them. Blue Blossom had awakened and was leaning up on an elbow, looking from Shane to Red Raven, then back to Shane again.

Shane moved slowly toward her, his heart pounding against his ribs as her eyes followed him. When he reached her, he knelt down onto a knee and leaned down into her face. "This I do for Cedar Maid," he whispered.

A gleam appeared in Blue Blossom's eyes as she smiled up at Shane. She reached a gentle hand to his cheek. *"Wee-weeb*—hurry and be safe," she whispered.

Shane took her hand and kissed its palm, his eyes wavering, for he did not have the courage to tell her about Cedar Maid's fate. It was enough that he and Red Raven were having to carry such a sad burden around inside their hearts.

"Mee-gway-chee-wahn-dum," he whispered in Chippewa even though he had sworn not to use their language again. But Blue Blossom spoke nothing but Chippewa. He had no choice but to converse with her in her own language. "Thank you."

Red Raven moved past Shane. Shane followed closely behind him. They broke into a run and then spilled the pelts from their arms and fell to the ground panting beside the stolen horses.

"It is done!" Shane said, his voice filled with a fierce exultation. "How easy it was! My blood is on fire with victory!"

Red Raven picked up one of the bear pelts and stroked its silken fur. "Do you realize, Shane, that Gray Falcon saw more worth in these pelts than he did in Cedar Maid?" he said, his voice drawn. "Perhaps our revenge tonight is not enough!"

Shane's eyes were hard. "For tonight it is enough," he said, moving back to his feet. "I made a promise to my woman and I must be sure and keep it. I feel that she already doubts me too much."

Red Raven rose to his feet. "Your love for her is strong?" he asked, placing an arm around Shane's shoulder.

"Yes, my love for her is as strong as the marriage

188

of the stars to the heavens," Shane said, looking to the sky. "And our love will be as everlasting."

The aroma of bacon and eggs wafted across the table to Melanie, yet all that she could eat was a piece of buttered toast. She watched Terrance shovel the food into his mouth, glad that he had not had a drink for a full day and night now. He had been spending most of his time with the cowhands, branding the new shipment of longhorns.

Or had he stayed around the farm just to keep an eye on her? To see if Shane did return? She knew he would never stop gloating if Shane was gone for good.

Terrance looked across the table at Melanie. "So? What do you have planned for today?" he asked, sopping up the last of the milk gravy from his plate with a biscuit. His eyes lowered, seeing her smart, fitted travel suit. "You're dressed for shopping in St. Paul. Am I right? What are you going to do? Buy yourself a whole new wardrobe to get your mind off Shane's deserting you?"

Melanie's eyes filled with sudden fire. "I'll have you know I am not going into town for myself," she said.

"Then pray tell, who are you going for?" Terrance said, poking the remainder of his gravied biscuit in his mouth. He smiled as he chewed. "Are you going to buy something for your dear brother? Do you think my wardrobe needs to be updated, too?"

Melanie pushed her chair back and rose to her feet. She leaned down, placing the palms of her hands on the table, and talked into Terrance's face. "No, it's not your wardrobe or mine that I'm going to update," she said in a silken purr. "It's Shane's. I'm going to go and pick up the clothes that he was fitted for the other day. They were supposed to be ready today."

Terrance's face flushed with a sudden anger. He slammed his fork down on his plate and glared up at Melanie. "You just won't give up on him, will you?" he snarled. "He's been gone a full day and night now. Do you honestly think he's going to come sniffing at your doorstep again? No. I think not."

Melanie straightened her back and went and looked out the window, toward the butte, where she had first seen Shane. "Yes, he's been gone a full day and night," she murmured. "And if his calculations were right, he'll be gone another full day. I expect him to arrive sometime tonight, probably at dusk."

Terrance rushed from his chair and gestured wildly with his hand. "You think you've got it all figured out, don't you?" he raved, not stopping to hear her answer.

Melanie continued to look at the butte in the distance. "I certainly hope so," she whispered. "Oh, God, I hope so."

· CHAPTER FIFTEEN ·

Her arms laden with packages, Melanie struggled through the throng of people rushing along the busy wood-planked walks. She had completed her business in St. Paul and was anxious to return home. The afternoon sun was lowering in the sky, casting the long shadows of the buildings along the rutted dirt streets. She wanted to be sure and be home when Shane arrived, for deep within her heart she had to believe that he would come home again.

She had to wonder if his mission had been successful. Would he be bringing home his spoils of war? If so, what would Josh's reaction be to the stolen horses?

So caught up in her thoughts was she that Melanie became careless and did not watch where she was stepping. Suddenly she collided with someone, the impact knocking her packages from her arms, and her from her feet.

Tumbling to the sidewalk, she cried out with pain as her wrist twisted beneath her. Sitting clumsily on the sidewalk with passersby stopping to stare down at her, Melanie eased her hand from beneath her and tested her wrist to see if it was broken.

When she found that it was all right, she became aware of a hand being offered her.

She looked slowly up at the massive hulk of a man whom she had collided with. Now she understood why the impact had been so deadly! The man was huge. A scruffy beard covered his face and sweat-stained buckskins his fatty flesh. He looked like a wild mountain man.

A sense of loathing coursed through Melanie as she became aware of the foul stench emanating from him. He was not the sort a woman would want to come in close contact with either by day or night! All she wanted was to retrieve her packages and be on her way!

"Ma'am?" the man said in a thick, gravelly voice. "Let me help you up. It's my fault you're lyin' there in the first place 'cept seems you just came out of nowheres."

Melanie ignored his hand. "I'll be just fine, thank you," she said, easing back to her feet.

As she smoothed out the wrinkles in her skirt, she looked shyly around her at the people continuing to gawk at her and the man.

Then suddenly she felt packages being thrust

into her arms. Lips parted, she watched the man picking up the packages and giving them to her until there were no more left on the sidewalk.

"There, that ought to do it," the man said, stepping closer to Melanie and smiling broadly down at her.

Mclanie smiled awkwardly up at him, first noting his jagged yellow teeth.

Then something grabbed her at the pit of her stomach as she looked into his eyes. She blanched, feeling a strange dizziness overcoming her when she discovered that one of his eyes was blue—and one was brown! This had to be the evil trapper that had caused Shane so much sorrow! It just wasn't that common for a man to have such peculiar eyes. And didn't he seem the sort that would have such little regard for human life? He had little enough for his own, it seemed, for no man had ever looked so unkempt or smelled so ungodly!

"Thank you," Melanie said weakly, backing away from him. "I appreciate . . . your kindness." She found those words hard to speak, for at this moment she was recalling Cedar Maid's dark eyes looking up at her from her grave of leaves.

But to protect herself from this man who might be offended by any show of repulsiveness toward him, Melanie had to put on a show of courtesy, then excuse herself and go on her way. She wanted desperately to go to the authorities and give them information about this man, but there was no proof. She would be wasting her time. And when she saw Shane could she—should she—even tell him? If he returned from his mission to the Indian village, wouldn't it be best to let all of this rest, so that he could get on with the rest of his life instead of living in the past? If he knew that the trapper was anywhere near his farm, he would go and find him. He would kill him. Then it would be Shane hunted down by the authorities!

No. The main thing for her to do was to get away from this man and forget that she had seen him!

Scarcely breathing, her heart thundering within her chest, Melanie gave Trapper Dan another fleeting glance, then brushed on past him and hurried toward her waiting horse and buggy. She could feel his eyes following her. Oh, Lord, what if he came after her? What if he followed her? He and Shane might come face to face!

Her pulse racing, Melanie dropped her packages in the back of her buggy. Without looking at the man who still stood watching her, she climbed onto the perch and lifted the reins with her shaky hand. Flicking the rein, she guided her horse out into the traffic, cursing the crowded street. It was impeding her quick escape from the watchful eye of the trapper.

Then her attention was drawn elsewhere. Elbowing his way through the crowded sidewalk was Terrance! He was dressed in his finest frock coat. A diamond stickpin glittered in the folds of his cravat. A cigar hung loosely from the corner of his mouth.

Melanie watched Terrance disappear into a saloon, then her insides tightened when the trapper sauntered into the same barroom. She dreaded the thought of Terrance and the trapper sitting at the same table, gambling, drinking, and sharing small talk. Terrance would have no idea the sort of man he was becoming friendly with.

Shaking her head, Melanie slapped her reins against her horse again and rode up one street and down the other, glad when the outskirts of the city were finally reached and she could send her horse along at a much brisker pace. She was anxious to get away from the city. Her only regret was that Terrance was still there. He never listened to anything anyone said anymore—especially his sister! Yet his sister lived in fear that one day something horrible would happen to him. Nothing good could come of the path Terrance had chosen to take in his life. Nothing!

Attired in a brief loincloth, his copper skin gleaming in the fading sunlight, Chief Gray Falcon strode square-shouldered toward his wigwam. Blue Blossom followed behind him, her eyes cast downward. She felt deceitful for having told Gray Falcon that it was Shane and Red Raven who had stolen from him.

But she had no choice! Gray Falcon had threatened to banish her from the tribe, to wander alone through the wilderness if she did not tell everything that she had seen the previous night. The fact that she had not awakened him and told him then had angered him terribly! She did not know what to expect now. She only knew that she must obey or she would end up like Cedar Maid—gone and forgotten!

Shy and petite, Blue Blossom trailed Gray Falcon inside his wigwam. She stood quietly by as he pulled his magnificent pelts from the back of the wigwam and began counting them.

"They took many!" he shouted, gazing at Blue Blossom with fire in his eyes.

"I have counted them, Gray Falcon," Blue Blossom murmured. "In pelts and horses, they took exactly the amount that Trapper Dan paid bride price for Cedar Maid. That is all, Gray Falcon. Please do not be so angry. I beg of you not to be angry with me!"

Gray Falcon tossed the pelts aside and went to Blue Blossom. "It is your innocent loveliness that saves you this time," he growled, drawing her against his hard body. "But do not make the same mistake a second time. I will throw you to the wolves."

Blue Blossom trembled with fear. She sobbed as Gray Falcon crushed his mouth to her lips and eased her down onto his pallet of furs. Gently, his hands disrobed her.

"Love me, Blue Blossom," he whispered, removing his loincloth. "Be my woman. I want a woman of courage. You proved that you are such a woman last night! You defied me, your chief!"

Blue Blossom could not deny how his body and hands always affected her. Warming all over inside, she reached for his hardness probing at the juncture of her thighs and led him inside her. She offered herself to him willingly, and hated herself for such a weakness!

She so badly wanted to ask Gray Falcon what he

was going to do about his stolen property, but she was too afraid to ask.

Would the revenge never stop?

Melanie stopped her horse and buggy in front of Shane's front porch. She peered toward the pasture, then the stable, seeing no signs of Shane's return. She glanced up at the sky. The sun was gone and the moon slowly slipping up into the sky to take its place.

Yet there was still no sign of Shane!

"Melanie?"

Josh's voice drew Melanie around. She looked up just as he took the last step to the ground, walking toward her.

"Hello, Josh," Melanie said, stepping down from the buggy. She went to the back and began taking packages from it. "I went into town, to the tailor's. I got Shane's clothes."

"Now aren't you the helpful one?" Josh said sarcastically. He smiled smugly as she brushed past him, ignoring his sarcasm.

"The fancy clothes won't be needed, you know," he said, following her up the steps. "He's gone, Melanie. He couldn't stay away from his Indian friends."

"We'll see, Josh," Melanie said icily. She gave him a frown over her shoulder. "I would appreciate it if you would help me with the door. Or would you rather I didn't take Shane's clothes to his room?"

Josh shrugged and opened the door for her. "It's

a waste of time," he said. "But go on, anyhow. Perhaps I can find something among them that suits my taste." He winked down at her. "Especially since you had a hand in choosing them."

"Josh, before you wore what I helped choose for Shane, I would burn them first," Melanie said, her voice drawn. She stepped inside and went up the stairs to Shane's room. She placed the packages on the bed, then spun around when Josh approached her suddenly from behind.

When Josh locked an arm about Melanie's waist and drew her around to face him, his blue eyes filled with lust, she froze inside. "Unhand me this minute, Josh Brennan," she hissed. "You know better than to expect me to appreciate being manhandled by you. I'd die first."

"Damn it, Melanie," Josh said throatily. "What do you see in Shane that you don't see in me? God, woman, he's nothing more than a savage, raised by savages. You've known me all your life, Melanie. Doesn't that amount to something?"

"I think that's the problem," Melanie said. "I have known you too long and too well. I know all of your faults, Josh, and there are plenty!"

"I could give you a loving no other man would know how to give!" Josh pleaded, leaning his face closer to hers. "Let me have a chance, Melanie. Good Lord, I've waited a lifetime for you. Don't tell me I'm going to lose not only my father to my brother, but also you!"

Melanie pushed at his chest with the palms of her hands. She smiled slowly up at him. "Why, Josh, I do believe you suspect Shane is going to come back home after all," she tormented him. "If not, you wouldn't be pleading your case so hard for me this evening. You would have plenty of time to plan a new strategy on how you could court and win me! But you feel pressured, don't you?"

Josh turned abruptly away from her, then rushed to the window when he heard the approach of many horses below, coming up the long lane that led to the house. He grew cold inside and his face paled. "Goddamn it all to hell," he gasped. "Shane. It's Shane."

Melanie felt a rush of relief flow through her. She went to the window and crowded in beside Josh. With pride and an immense flooding of happiness, she watched Shane as he dismounted out by the stable, while his friend, Red Raven, stayed on his horse. Her gaze went to the five handsome horses that were now being guided into the pasture and let loose.

"He did it," she whispered, placing a hand to her throat. She looked at the pelts thrown across the back of Shane's horse. "Not only did he succeed at getting the horses from Chief Gray Falcon, but the pelts too!"

"What on earth are you talking about?" Josh asked, squinting through the falling dusk.

Melanie did not take the time to respond. She was too eager to go and embrace Shane—to welcome him back home. His return had proved so much to her!

Breaking into a run, she left the bedroom. She did not even feel the steps beneath her feet as she rushed down the staircase. Breathless, she hurried from the house, down the front steps. Lifting her skirt up into her arms, she ran toward Shane.

When he saw her approaching, he met her halfway and drew her into his embrace, hugging her fiercely.

"As promised, I have returned," he said in a whisper into her ear. "It is good to feel you in my arms, Melanie. So good."

"What's this all about?"

Melanie and Shane drew apart quickly when Josh spoke up behind them. Shane took a step toward his brother and glowered at him.

"I said what's this all about?" Josh stormed, gesturing toward the horses that Shane had added to the others. "Where did you get those horses? Why did you bring them here? Damn it, Shane, where the hell have you been?"

"I owe you no answers about anything," Shane said. He walked past Josh and lifted a hand to Red Raven. They intertwined their fingers. "My friend, we will meet again. But until we do, ride with care."

Red Raven gave Shane a steady gaze, gripped his hand harder, then drew it away. He wheeled his horse around and rode off in a gallop.

Josh went to the fence and peered at the horses more closely. "These horses are stolen, aren't they?" he asked, giving Shane a glance over his shoulder. "Melanie said something about Chief Gray Falcon. Shane, did you steal these horses from him?"

Shane tightened his jaw. He turned away from Josh and began lifting his pelts off his horse. He stiffened when Josh came to him and grabbed him by an arm.

"Shane, are these horses stolen?" Josh shouted. He stared down at the pelts. "Are those stolen pelts? Are you trying to draw us into a war with the Indians? I should have expected something like this!"

Melanie yanked his hand from Shane's arm. "Josh, stop that!" she shouted. "You don't understand. You don't know!"

Josh stepped away from Melanie. He raked his fingers nervously through his hair, staring from Melanie to Shane. "I've had enough," he said, his voice drawn. "I've got to get away. I can't be a part of horse stealing. I won't be here when the Indians arrive to retaliate!"

He waved a hand wildly in the air. "For now, it's all yours," he said, his voice breaking. "I see now that there's no other way—no other way to prove that it's wrong for you to be here except to let you take charge. It won't take long for you and everyone else to see just how wrong it is. I'll be back and take over after you leave. That is, if the damn Indians don't burn down my house and steal all of my cattle first!"

Melanie's mouth dropped open. She stared disbelievingly at Josh as he broke into a run toward the stable and soon rode away on his horse.

Shane seemed not at all disturbed by Josh's abrupt decision to leave. He walked toward the house with the pelts.

Melanie watched, feeling suddenly helpless. Without Josh, everything—all responsibility for

Shane's welfare—had fallen into her hands. It would be up to her to teach Shane everything, or he would lose the farm! She knew that Josh would not stay away forever. He cared too much about his position in life to turn his back on it. Melanie had only till Josh's return to teach Shane everything that was required to run a cattle farm!

She looked up at the butte, where the land reached into the forest. Fear suddenly claimed her heart. Josh had been right to worry about a reprisal by Chief Gray Falcon.

But just what sort could be expected?

Melanie broke into a run after Shane. She had much to say to him. She had much to find out. There was the question about Cedar Maid. In what way had he loved her? And how deeply?

· CHAPTER SIXTEEN ·

Melanie followed Shane through the house and into his bedroom. Wide-eyed, she watched him lay his pelts aside, then remove the packages from his bed and place them on the floor. Without hesitation, he lifted the mattress from his bed and carried it past Melanie, out into the hall, then returned and dismantled the bed and, piece by piece, removed it from the room also.

Puzzled by his actions, Melanie watched Shane as he placed the many pelts on the floor where his bed had stood, spreading them out in a comfortable pile.

Shane stood up and studied his pallet of furs, nodding his approval, then went to Melanie and took her hand and led her to them. Snuggling her close in his arms, he eased her down onto the furs.

"I am being forced to conform to many things now that I live away from the Chippewa," he said, brushing his mouth lightly against her lips. "But if I am ever to have a full night of sleep again, I had to do away with that damn bed."

Now understanding, Melanie laughed softly. She twined her fingers through his blond hair, curving her body into his as he lay beside her. She looked up at his sun-bronzed, finely chiseled face as he gazed down at her. "Darling, however you choose to sleep is fine with me," she whispered. "I don't need a bed. All I need is you."

Shane turned to lie on his back and lifted her atop him. His loins grew hot as he felt the weight of her breasts pressing against his chest. "Melanie, how can I tell you how much it means to me to have you?" he asked, searching her face with his eyes, seeing her flawless features, how delicately sweet and sculpted her lips were. Her eyes, brown and soft, looked adoringly down at him, firing his desire.

"That you have returned assures me that I can believe what you say," Melanie murmured, gently placing a hand to his cheek, ignoring the two-day growth of blond stubble. "Yet, there are questions, Shane. I know that I should not ask them, but I must."

Shane brushed a kiss across her lips, then rolled her back down beside him. He leaned on an elbow and faced her, his eyes haunted with remembrance. "You need not ask," he said gently. "Let me tell you, for you see, I know your thoughts without your speaking them aloud to me."

Melanie's eyes clouded with tears. She waited anxiously for his explanation, yet as the moments passed, nothing but that he was there with her seemed all that important to her anymore. He could have been slain on his expedition to the Indian village to steal the horses and pelts!

But he hadn't been.

He could have decided not to return to his farm, knowing the obstacles that stood in his way.

But he had!

Not only had he returned, but he was now with her, proving to her that he was devoted to her— that he truly loved her. If he had loved Cedar Maid in that way, he would have never left her! He would have taken her with him when he was forced to leave the village. He would have made Cedar Maid his wife!

But he hadn't.

"You want to know about Cedar Maid, fearing that she was more to me than I have professed," Shane said. "Cedar Maid and I shared many secrets. Many times we bathed together in the river. We strolled through the forest, hand in hand. I knew everything about her. She, everything about me. But never did we touch in any way but as brother and sister."

"You loved her so very much," Melanie said, hearing the melancholy in his voice.

"Melanie, she was a sister to me," Shane said, smoothing a fallen lock of her hair back from her eyes. "We were raised in the same wigwam. Did I love her? No true sister could have been any dearer to me. But the love in her life belonged to

205

Red Raven. He was going to ask her to marry him. Soon. But the trapper offered the bride price before Red Raven had the chance. The trapper had more to offer, so if Red Raven had even asked Cedar Maid to marry him, she would have been denied him."

He moved over Melanie, resting on his knees above her. "So you see?" he said softly. "She occupied a large portion of my heart for many years, but never in the way that you do, now. You have given me a different sort of love—the sort a man would die for!"

He wrapped her within his arms and drew her against him as he stretched out atop her. His mouth came to her in a heated kiss. Melanie answered his kiss with abandon, a curling of heat tightening within her. She moaned against his lips as he kneaded her breasts through her dress, making her need for him grow with fevered intensity.

"Please let me undress you," she whispered, drawing her lips away.

Her hands went to his fringed buckskin shirt and slid it slowly up his broad, tanned chest and over his head. With a boldness she had never known in herself before, Melanie untied the leather laces of his fringed breeches and pushed this garment down, revealing his risen manhood to her, and she knew that his desire for her was great. With exquisite tenderness, she encircled his hardness with her hand and moved her fingers on him, watching his eyes become filled with a hazy, unleashed passion.

Her gaze swept over him, seeing his long, lithe body, slim-hipped and well-muscled.

And he was so very, very aroused!

Hardly able to stand the way she was maddeningly arousing him, Shane moved her hand away. He placed a hand to Melanie's waist and lifted her to her feet as he moved to his.

Slowly, meditatingly, Shane began undressing her. Once she was silkenly nude, he lowered his mouth to a breast and flicked his tongue over the nipple, causing it to harden into a tight, dark peak.

With slow deliberation, Shane's hands traveled over Melanie's slim, sinuous body. Her long, drifting hair cascaded across her shoulders as she held her head back, sighing langorously, when his lips replaced his hands, moving hotly down her body, drugging her.

"I must have you," Shane whispered, engulfing her within his arms, easing her back down onto the pallet of furs. "Now."

"Yes, my love," Melanie whispered, smoothing his hair back from his face as he rose above her. She drifted toward him, arching her hips to meet him. She placed her cheek on his chest. "You smell of spring rain." She licked his neck, then around his hardened nipples. "So sweet. Oh, Shane, you are so wonderfully sweet."

Shane's jaw tightened with pleasure. "It is good that I thought to bathe today in the river while the horses were watering," he whispered. "I shall remember to do that more often if it arouses you in this way." He gritted his teeth as her tongue swept into his ear, then again down, around a tightened nipple.

"My darling, don't you know that it is not because of your bath?" Melanie giggled, looking adoringly up at him. "It is you, Shane. Just being with you causes me to behave so wantonly!"

"Wanton?" he said huskily, his eyes lit with points of fire as he gazed down at her. "Never wanton. Just your sweet self learning more and more how to please your man."

Their bodies strained together as he entered her in one bold thrust. Shane's mouth came to hers with an explosive kiss, as his movements within her became more demanding. She responded in kind, her hips moving in unison with his thrusts. Their bodies jolted and quivered. Their mouths opened and their tongues met and danced.

The pleasure mounted within Melanie. It filled her with a crazy sort of spinning sensation that suddenly spilled over, filling her with ecstasy.

Shane moved his mouth from her lips. He burrowed his nose into the depths of her hair and emitted a loud groan of pleasure as his body tightened and stiffened, and then plunged further within her, releasing his love seed within her womb.

Their bodies pearled and sleek with sweat, Melanie and Shane drew apart. They each stretched out on their backs, their eyes closed. Then Melanie's heart soared with pleasure when Shane gently cupped the throbbing mound at the juncture of her thighs, slowly thrusting a finger in and out of her, arousing her anew.

Their eyes met, locking, promising ecstasy. "What are you doing?" she murmured, smiling drunkenly. Her pulse began to race as the same, dizzying pleasure began to spread through her that only Shane had the ability to arouse. She closed her eyes, trembling, and shook her head back and forth.

"Oh, Shane, Shane," she whispered, breathing raggedly. "What you do to me! Oh, what you do to me!"

In a matter of moments that same wondrous release soared through her, blissful in its sweetness. She cried out, then was glad when Shane was suddenly there, holding her and rocking her in his muscled arms.

She clung to him, a gentle peace engulfing her.

Starved after their time of intense lovemaking, Shane and Melanie sat before a roaring fire in his parlor, feeding each other fruit and cheese. "If only everything in life could be just as it is at this moment," Melanie said, her face flushed with happiness. She fed Shane a piece of apple, then accepted a grape as he slipped it between her lips.

"Life could never be like a fantasy," Shane said, his eyes wavering. "There is too much ugliness to contend with. Always."

Melanie moved closer to Shane. "Shane, please tell me how things went at the Indian village," she said, her smile fading. "Were you in danger? Did anyone see you steal the horses and pelts? Shane, how did you do it without getting shot?"

"Everyone was asleep except for Blue Blossom," Shane said, picking at the cheese and placing small bites in his mouth. "She watched as the pelts were stolen from Gray Falcon's dwelling. Upon arising the next morning, she would also know that Red Raven and I were also responsible for stealing the horses."

Melanie's heart skipped a beat. "Shane, if she knows, she will surely tell Gray Falcon! Aren't you afraid of what he might do in return?"

"Yes, Blue Blossom will tell," Shane said, frowning. "She will have no choice. She is Gray Falcon's woman. But it was enough that she did not awaken him the moment she saw us in the dwelling. For Cedar Maid's sake, she let us leave without awakening Gray Falcon, and warning him of our presence."

"But, Shane, what can you expect him to do?" Melanie persisted, clutching his hands.

"In time, he will arrive to make wrongs right for himself," Shane said, slipping his hands free. He moved to his feet and leaned an arm on the fireplace mantel, staring down into the fire. "Until then, I will not worry myself over it. There is already too much burdening my mind and heart."

Hearing the sadness in Shane's voice, Melanie pushed herself up from the floor. She crept an arm around his waist and cuddled close to him. "Are you thinking about Josh and how he behaves toward you?" she asked, gazing raptly up at him.

"That and so much more," Shane said, nodding.

"I am appalled by Josh's attitude," Melanie

said, anger flaring in her eyes. "But now he's gone, and good riddance!"

She swung around and grabbed Shane's hands, urging him to face her. "Shane, let me teach you everything," she said breathlessly. "I will teach you to read and write. I will show you everything that I know about running a cattle farm. We both have a lot to prove, not only to Josh, but also to my brother. Let's show them both just how wrong they are about everything."

Moved by Melanie's continued devotion to him, Shane smiled softly down at her. "You have done so much for me already," he said thickly. "How can I ask any more of you?"

"Shane, don't you see?" Melanie said, sighing. "It is not only for you, but also for myself. I love you. I want you to be happy. If you're happy, I'm happy!"

"Melanie, I already know much about reading and writing," Shane said. "In my youth, I picked up those skills when trappers and traders came through the village. And as for learning about cattle—I am of the outdoors. Early in life I learned everything about animals in the forest. Cattle should be no different."

Melanie laughed softly. "Longhorns are quite different," she said. "Tomorrow we shall ride among them. I will point out the differences. You will see just how far and wide your land stretches —land that your father bought and labored over, just like my father. At the beginning, it was not easy for either of them."

She eased her hands from Shane's and went to a window and drew back a heavy drapery. Looking out onto a moon-splashed land, she felt an emptiness assail her that she had become familiar with since her father's death.

"Our fathers labored so hard all of their lives and then they had to die," she said, stifling a sob. "It isn't fair, Shane. It seems that's the way it is in life. The parents work hard, then the children benefit."

She swung around and looked at Shane as he moved to her side. "Shane, let's enjoy life while we can," she said, her voice drawn. "One never knows about tomorrow. I hate to think what will happen when Josh comes back."

"He is my brother," Shane said hoarsely. "I am his. One day we will be of one heart and one mind. Until then, it is he who has to overcome the feelings that torment him. My heart is free of hatred for him."

Melanie jerked with a start from Shane's arms when the longhorns in the near pasture began to bellow loudly. She questioned Shane with her eyes, then drew the drapery aside again, to peer through the darkness. "Something is spooking them," she said. She watched some of the longhorns begin to move around restlessly, their long, curved horns picking up the shine of the moonlight.

"I'm sure it's nothing," Shane said, yet not convinced himself. He knew that he had many enemies and most were the sort that would resort to most anything to get even with him. There was his brother, Josh; Melanie's brother, Terrance; and Chief Gray Falcon.

But of all of the enemies that Shane could name, there was one who did not even know that he existed. Trapper Dan! It was Shane who hoped that their paths would cross. Shane had a debt to pay!

"I've got to leave, Shane," Melanie said, gathering up the dishes from the floor. "I'll look around outside and see what the disturbance is as I go."

Shane walked with her to the kitchen, where she placed the dirty dishes in a basin. Then she walked, arm-in-arm with Shane, from the house and to her buggy. The longhorns were no longer uneasy. The night was quiet, except for a slight breeze that whispered through the trees.

"I'll come bright and early tomorrow," Melanie said, standing on tiptoe to give Shane a soft kiss on the lips. She giggled softly. "You should be fit as a fiddle in the morning. You no longer have to sleep on the bed, though I would prefer it to the floor, myself."

"I'm going to accompany you home," he said, tilting her chin with his forefinger. "Things are much too quiet now."

"Darling, I'll be fine," she said, slipping away from him. She stepped up into the buggy and reached for the reins. "Now you just go back inside and get that good night's rest, for tomorrow I have lots planned for you."

She wheeled the horse and buggy around and

began to ride away, but then turned with a start when she heard a horse soon following behind her. When Shane rode up beside her and gave her a stern look, she smiled warmly at him, glad that he continued to prove to her just how much he did care about her.

· CHAPTER SEVENTEEN ·

White, fluffy clouds filtered the morning's first light along the rugged fence corraling the vast range. Pistols hanging low in holsters belted at his waist, Terrance stood on his porch, leaning against a tall column. Lifting a bottle of whiskey to his lips, he gulped down several mouthfuls, stinging his throat and then his gut. He peered across the land at two horses riding together and cursed low beneath his breath, recognizing Melanie and Shane as the riders.

Just as he had suspected would happen, the two were inseparable. Shane had succeeded not only at taking over most of the Brennan estate, but Melanie as well. Couldn't she see? He had blinded her with his wild charm! She'd been suckered in by him, hook, line and sinker!

Taking another drink, Terrance staggered down the steps. His footsteps were heavy in the dust of the road as he moved toward the stable. He ignored the watchful eyes of the cowhands as they busied themselves with the duties of the day.

"What'cha gawkin' at?" he shouted, finally realizing that he was being stared at. "Haven't you ever seen someone drunk before?" He motioned with the bottle toward the stable. "Someone get in there and ready my horse. I'm almost out of whiskey. I've got to ride into town and get me another bottle. If there's any of you ready to argue that point, speak up now or forever hold your peace!"

He laughed throatily, taking the last drink of whiskey from the bottle. Hiccuping, he pitched the bottle up into the air and quickly drew his pistol and fired at it. He cursed when he missed.

Spinning the pistol back into its holster, he reached for his horse as it was brought to him.

"Sir, I don't think you're up to ridin' today," the cowhand said, looking guardedly at Terrance as he tried to fit his foot into the stirrup, only succeeding at falling down on the ground.

"I didn't ask your opinion," Terrance said, rising to his feet, trying again. "I got people to see." He swung his hand toward the cowhand. "Give me a hand, dammit."

Shakily, he finally managed to get in the saddle. Slumped over, he rode away, taking another lingering look at Melanie and Shane. "Yes, siree," he mumbled. "I've got people to see. . . ."

* * *

Melanie's horse was moving in a slow, easy canter alongside Shane's as they rode across the wide pasture that separated Shane's land from Melanie's. Attired in a dark riding skirt and a white, long-sleeved cotton blouse, her hair drawn back and tied with a ribbon, Melanie clung to her reins. Giving Shane occasional troubled glances, she knew that he was aware of how the cowhands now under his employ had treated him earlier that morning when they left their bunkhouses. Their eyes cold, their footsteps heavy, they had gone on about their business as though he wasn't there. None had treated him with respect, gossip obviously having spread amongst them that Josh had left and that Shane was now in charge. To them, Shane was an Indian-lover. They acted as though they might get dirty by getting near him.

Trying to lighten his mood, Melanie swung her horse closer to Shane's. Where there were no cattle grazing, pink and white lady's-slippers graced the land, delicate in their loveliness. The sun was rising high in the sky, puffs of clouds scudding along the horizon.

"It's a beautiful day to be on horseback, isn't it, Shane?" Melanie asked. Her gaze moved over him. In his new dark, coarse breeches that fit against his muscled legs like a glove; a blue plaid shirt that was half unbuttoned in the front, revealing a froth of golden chest hair; and boots all shining and new thrust into the stirrups, wasn't he handsome?

His long blond hair was shining like summer wheat in the sunlight and was drawn back from his tanned face, hanging loose to his shoulders. His eyes were so blue, they seemed to be an extension of the sky.

With his gentlemanly demeanor, his politeness, he seemed the sort that anyone would trust at first sight. He was so clean and upright, how could anyone mistreat him? Why did there have to be so much injustice in the world? So many prejudices?

Shane did not respond. His jaw was tight, his eyes cold.

Sighing heavily, Melanie reached a hand to his arm. "Shane, I know how you must be feeling," she blurted out. "I'd feel the same. But those cowhands are fools. Don't let them get under your skin. If I know Josh, he's spread hatred among them purposely. He'd do anything to get you to leave. Please don't let him succeed."

"Tell me about the longhorns, Melanie," Shane said, ignoring her comments about the cowhands. He had known there would be obstacles in this new way of life. But that did not make the hurt sting his heart and insides any less when he came face to face with it.

But he would overcome it all.

To survive, he must.

His father had shown confidence in him by leaving him in charge of so much. He could not let him down! Shane believed that when a loved one died, they were not truly gone. Their spirits lingered somewhere overhead, observing. Just as the old chief watched Shane from somewhere, his true father was watching him now, also. Perhaps his father was holding his precious wife's hand in the hereafter, both observing the son they had loved with all of their hearts.

Melanie would not be put off all that easily. She wheeled her horse around and blocked Shane's further progress. "Damn it, Shane," she said, squaring her shoulders angrily. "Those men are under your employ. Don't let them get away with this. Let them know that you are the boss or give them their walking papers!"

Shane grabbed Melanie's reins from her and glared at her. "Woman, I know that you mean well," he said flatly. "But let it be. I will fight my own battles in my own way. Do you understand?"

Melanie flinched as though she had been slapped. Color rushed to her cheeks and tears burned at the corners of her eyes. She grabbed her reins back from Shane, gave him a hurt stare, then rode away from him, her horse's hooves a sullen thunder against the ground.

"Melanie!" Shane shouted, riding after her. When he caught up with her, his eyes were apologetic. "I'm sorry. I shouldn't have scolded you. I do know that you mean only what is best for me, but darling, there are some things you cannot teach a man. Self-respect is one of them!"

A strange sort of pain centered around Melanie's heart when she heard Shane's pleas. She had been wrong to become angry with him. That was the last thing he needed at this time. Her fingers tightened on the reins and her horse slowed to an easy canter again.

"Shane, I'm the one who needs to apologize," she said, brushing a tear from her eye. "I was insensitive to your feelings. Darling, I'm so sorry."

"Let us not talk any more of feelings today," Shane said, reaching over and cupping her chin within the palm of his hand. "You say you want to teach me about the longhorns. I am eager to learn."

"And I am perhaps too eager to teach you?" Melanie said, smiling weakly up at him.

"Only because your love for me is strong," Shane said, leaning to brush a kiss against her brow. He drew away from her and looked across the vastness of the land dotted with grazing longhorns.

"The longhorns came from a place called Texas?" he asked, admiring anew the animals with the glistening, curved horns.

Feeling as though everything was back in proper perspective again, Melanie relaxed her shoulders. She circled a hand on the pommel of her saddle and rested it there. "Yes, they are from Texas," she said, smiling. "They are trailed to New Orleans, and on up to Minnesota Territory by boat." She paused as she turned her attention to the cattle. "Longhorns are a profitable business. The meat sells at three cents a pound."

They watched together as cows and calves were cut from the main herd for branding.

"It takes a special pony to separate the cows and calves," Melanie explained. "The best cutting ponies are so alert and intelligent, their riders have little need of reins. As soon as the cowhand shows the pony which calf or steer he wants to cut, the horse's ears begin to twitch and its eyes stay glued on the animal being chased toward the branding iron. It knows what it's doing."

Shane watched as the branding irons were heated to a red-hot glow. Two men on horseback roped a calf by the hind legs and dragged it toward the fire. Working in teams, others wrestled the calves to the ground. Each calf was branded on the ribs and dehorned; the males were castrated.

This continued, the cowhands taking turns roping, branding, cutting, and earmarking.

Melanie and Shane rode among the longhorns, looking them over carefully. "On our farm, we castrate the calves only every other year," Melanie further explained. "In alternate years, all the males are left to breed."

She nodded and gestured with a hand. "As you can see, a quantity of Hereford bull yearlings have been placed among the longhorns," she said.

"Do you ever worry about stampedes?" Shane asked, seeing the fierceness in the eyes of some of the larger animals.

"That is the only true disadvantage of raising longhorns," Melanie said, frowning. "They have an extraordinary wildness about them that makes them nervous, easy to stampede."

She drew her reins taut, stopping her horse. "Do you see that longhorn over there?" she said, pointing one out. "His thick horns, set forward as they are, can be as sharp as any knife."

Shane studied the animal, his jaw set. Of all the longhorns he had seen, this one seemed the most untrustworthy. Mighty-antlered and wild-eyed, the bull even now seemed to be challenging Shane and Melanie for the right to the land that it grazed on. Its coarse-haired coat was a glossy dunnish-brown merging into black with white speckles and splotches on its rump, and a washed-out copper line down its back. It was tall, bony, flat-sided and thin-flanked, and grotesquely narrow-hipped. Its length was so extended its back swayed, its big ears were carved into an outlandish design. Its horns were most threatening in their size.

"Several bulls have taken up with our cattle and have become quite domesticated," Melanie said, watching this particular bull with care. "But this is not one of them. This is the one that Terrance has named Wild Thunder. I would suggest we ride on. I don't like the gleam in his eye."

Shane rode alongside Melanie as she rode away from the threatening beast. "Terrance gave the bull a name because he is fond of it?" he asked, forking an eyebrow at Melanie.

"On the contrary," Melanie said, laughing. "He hates that bull. Many a time Terrance has been cornered by it and the cowhands have had to go to his rescue. There seems to be some bad blood between my brother and that bull. I'm not sure why."

"Well, as I see it, it's because the bull is a good judge of character," Shane said, his eyes gleaming.

Melanie giggled, realizing that Terrance deserved Shane's comment. "As for the other longhorns," she said, looking at the innocent ones that stood peacefully around her and Shane. "I would say that unless frightened, they are safe enough to be around. When not eating, they are bellowing, moaning, or making some other ungodly noise."

She gestured with a hand toward a new calf staying close to its mama's side, grazing dew-covered grass. "No wild animal, or domestic either, that I know of, has as many vocal tones as the longhorn," she said. "A cow has one moo for her newborn calf, another for when it is older, one to tell it to come to her side, and another to tell it to stay hidden in the tall grass."

Melanie gestured with a gloved hand toward the fence. "This is where our acreage meets, Shane," she said. "Our farms are divided by this fence. Shane, did I say something wrong?" she asked, having seen a sudden coldness enter his eyes.

Shane's eyes followed the split-rail fence that staggered across the land, dividing it. Although he had been born white, his Indian instincts made him hate anything associated with fences. Fences not only divided the land, they also caused confusion in the hearts and minds of wild animals. Since fences were now sprouting up all across the land, many animals had been denied the Chippewa. This made Shane sad, yet he knew that this, as so much more, was something the Chippewa had grown to endure.

But he had to remind himself that he was no longer a part of the Chippewa. He had returned to where he rightfully belonged. He was a white man. He had to live by the white man's rules!

"It is nothing," Shane said, wheeling his horse around and riding away.

Melanie watched him for a moment, then rode after him. She was learning not to question his reasons for his sudden, withdrawn behavior. She knew that he was wrestling with the side of himself that was being forced into change. In time, she hoped, he would never again have cause to feel bitter or torn.

She followed him up the gentle slope of land to the butte, then drew rein beside the river, where he quickly swung himself out of his saddle.

Dismounting, Melanie went to stand beside Shane at the water's edge. Her eyes followed his gaze. She crept a hand into Shane's, joining him in watching a phantom-voiced loon as it swam gracefully through the water, then dove to a great depth to find food.

Lifting its heavy body from the water, it flew only a short distance and settled on the grassy embankment. The loon had short legs, located far back on its body, making it clumsy. It waddled awkwardly to a nest of dried grass and weeds and squirmed down onto two, bluish-gray, mottled eggs.

"Isn't that beautiful?" Melanie whispered, sighing. "If only life could be that simple for us, Shane. The loon truly has no worries in the world except for looking after her eggs."

Shane placed his hands on Melanie's waist and drew her around to face him. "Melanie, soon that will change for her," he reminded her. "Soon she will be responsible for two offspring. There are always predators waiting to steal away those who are most dear to a mother's heart."

"You are speaking of yourself and what happened to you, aren't you?" Melanie asked softly.

"Yes, and I am also speaking of Trapper Dan," Shane said solemnly. "He's out there somewhere. Melanie, surely I will get the chance to make him pay for all that he has taken from me. If only I knew where to begin looking!"

Melanie swallowed hard as she looked up into his troubled eyes. She had forgotten about having seen the trapper in St. Paul. But, even if she had remembered, she had vowed not to tell Shane! It was in Shane's best interest that he never discover that the trapper was anywhere close!

"Just forget about him, Shane," she said, slipping into his arms, hugging him tightly. "Please forget about him."

"Never," he said, then lifted her chin with a forefinger and lowered his mouth to her lips. "But if it were ever possible for me to forget, it would be because of you."

He kissed her with a soft, sweet passion, then walked her back to her horse and helped her into the saddle. She watched as he mounted his own horse, hoping that one day all of his pain would be gone. Should she tell him about Trapper Dan? If he were able to rid himself of the torment of that man, wouldn't that lessen the burden he carried around inside his heart?

No, Melanie still could not find it within herself to tell him. The dangers were too many.

* * *

Terrance walked through the hotel lobby, ignoring the stares of the fancily dressed women who brushed past him. Grabbing hold of the bannister, he moved clumsily up the staircase. He squinted and cursed beneath his breath. He had drunk too much alcohol to be able to focus on anything. He watched his feet as he lifted them from step to step, finding even that effort almost too hard to manage.

But he had to go to Josh. He had to get Josh to listen to reason! Josh had to help rid their lives of Shane. He was letting Shane get off too easy!

Finally reaching the second floor landing, Terrance stumbled along the corridor that was faintly lit by candles in sconces along the wall. He moved slowly, checking the room numbers on the doors, then smiled when he found the one he was searching for. Without knocking, he began fumbling with the doorknob and finally managed to get the door open. Laughing drunkenly, he fell into the room, then steadied himself and looked Josh square in the eye as Josh lay on the bed stark naked, a beautiful redhead beneath him.

"Whoops!" Terrance said, teetering. "Seems I've interrupted something." He bent closer, seeing the woman's eyes growing wide with embarrassment. "Do I know you, ma'am?" he asked, idly scratching his brow. "It don't seem like I've had the pleasure."

Josh looked good-humoredly up at Terrance. He looked no more sober, himself, with his thick stubble of golden beard and his hair all tangled and twisted. He reeked of alcohol. His eyes were bloodshot. "Damn it all to hell, Terrance," he said, drawing away from the woman and pulling a blanket up to hide her nakedness. "You never did learn the art of knocking before entering a room."

"Well, now, Josh, if that had been my sister in bed with you, I'd have most certainly knocked before interrupting," Terrance said, plopping down on a chair and sprawling his legs out before him. He spied an opened bottle of whiskey on the table next to him, grabbed it, and tipped it to his lips. But then slammed it back down on the table.

"But that isn't my sister and that's exactly what I've come to talk about. It should be Melanie makin' love with you, Josh. Not a whore from the streets." He waved a hand wildly in the air. "Ain't you got no brains, Josh? What are you doin' here instead of out at the farm tryin' to outsmart Shane? Your Pa called you lazy. Well, I'm beginning to think he was damn right."

The woman grabbed her dress and pulled it over her head, her face crimson with anger. She hurried into her shoes, then rushed from the room, slamming the door behind her.

"Well, thanks to you, that's one that won't be back," Josh said, pulling on his breeches. He stood over Terrance, glaring. "And as for outsmartin' my brother, that's exactly what I'm doin' by stayin' away from the farm. He'll soon realize he don't belong. Just give it time, Terrance. Give it time."

Josh shrugged himself into his shirt and buttoned it, then pulled on his boots. He eyed the deck of cards on the table beside Terrance. "I'm ready for a poker game," he said, winking at Terrance. "Think you're sober enough to outsmart me in poker?"

Terrance laughed as he rose shakily back to his feet. "Josh, I can outsmart you at anything, anytime," he said, grabbing up the deck of cards.

Josh combed his fingers through his hair, then leaned into Terrance's face. "Show me, you sonofabitch," he said, his eyes filled with sudden rage. He nodded toward the door. "After you, Terrance. I'm sure I'm not the only one who'd like to sit at the same poker table with you this afternoon. You're always smartin' off at the mouth. It'll be a pleasure to see your socks beat off today—preferably by me."

Terrance chuckled as he sauntered toward the door. "You never know who you'll run into at the poker table these days," he said, walking on past Josh into the corridor. "Like the other day. I played against this giant of a man with the godawfullest eyes. I ain't never seen the likes of them eyes. I enjoyed gettin' to know him, though. Seems we discovered we had some of the same interests in life."

"Who are you talkin' about, Terrance?" Josh asked, closing and locking his door.

"Oh, you wouldn't know him," Terrance said, giving Josh a half glance. "But maybe you should . . . ?"

Josh forked an eyebrow as he gazed questioningly at Terrance.

· CHAPTER EIGHTEEN ·

The moon was partially hidden beneath a haze of clouds as a figure stole stealthily through the night. Only a few longhorns stirred, welcoming the enticing smell of hay placed beneath their noses. Their tails swished contentedly as they began to eat, but one by one the tails slowed and the legs became wobbly. One by one, the longhorns eased to the ground. They plopped over onto their sides, their tongues hanging from the corners of their mouths, their legs stretched out stiffly, and their eyes fixed in a death trance.

Scooping up the remainder of the hay that was not eaten, the figure turned and moved cautiously away, making sure not to alarm the remaining longhorns.

* * *

Yawning and stretching, Shane rose from his pallet of furs. Nightmare free, his sleep had been pleasant. The smell of coffee brewing in the kitchen urged him into his clothes; he was growing fond of this drink that seemed to be habitual to the white community.

He looked into a full-length mirror and studied himself. Not only was he successfully conforming to the white man's taste in food and drink, but in clothing too. The coarse denim breeches and the blue-plaid cotton shirt fit him well. Even the expensive leather boots on his feet did not seem all that alien to him any longer.

But his hair was not yet changed, he thought, combing his fingers through his shoulder-length hair. In time, it must also be cut. But not quite yet. Parting with it would be hard. It had meant so much to him when he lived the life of an Indian.

Hearing the bawling of cattle outside his window made Shane go and look out at what he could now call mostly his. He weaved and grabbed at the windowsill. It had suddenly occurred to him that this was the first time in his life that he had actually owned anything except for his horse and weapons. He suddenly realized that the world was his!

His heart throbbed. "It is mine," he whispered, raking his hand over his face as though testing to see if he were actually there, experiencing this, instead of dreaming. "How can it be that suddenly so much belongs to me?"

Turning slowly back to gaze from the window

again, he firmed his jaw. "It is mine, and by damn, I am going to make the best of it," he said determinedly. "From now on I will face my new life with vigor instead of restraint!"

A commotion below drew Shane's gaze to several cowhands running toward the pasture. He squinted his eyes, trying to see through the early morning light, and watched the men stop and assemble around something on the ground. Shane could not tell what was drawing their keen interest. The light was poor this time of day. All that he could see was shadows. But the reaction of the men sent waves of alarm through him.

Grabbing his gunbelt and fastening it around his waist, the pistols heavy at his hips, he ran from his room and down the stairs. He could hear the shouts of the men as others ran from the bunkhouse to see what had been discovered in the pasture. Shane joined them, his breath raspy from running so hard.

When he reached the circle of gawking, cursing men, he elbowed his way through them, then stopped. His gut twisted and a bitterness rose up into his throat at the sight of the three dead animals, horseflies buzzing hungrily around them.

"I ain't never seen anything like it," one cowhand said, scratching his brow idly.

Shane only barely heard the comments being tossed around on all sides of him. He stared down at the dead animals.

The sound of an approaching horse drew Shane around. His eyes wavered when he caught sight of

Melanie riding toward him, her hair flying in the breeze, a question in her eyes as she looked at the circle of men, then at Shane.

Shane broke from the men and met her. As she drew rein beside him, Melanie's eyes locked with Shane's. Then she looked past him and saw the longhorn carcasses. Fear grabbed at her heart. If the cattle had been infected with a rare disease, it could run rampant through all of the animals on the adjoining farms. They could be wiped out.

"What's happened here?" Melanie asked, her voice sharp with worry.

Shane helped her from the horse and took her elbow as he guided her through the men. "Seems we lost a few head of cattle during the night," he said, his spine stiff. "But damned if I know why they died. There are no visible signs of illness."

"And they seemed to be all right yesterday," Melanie said, bending to a knee beside one of the longhorns. She had watched her father examine longhorns since she was old enough to be interested in them. She knew most signs of sickness, and close examination showed her nothing even remotely similar to any disease that her father had treated.

Then she grew cold inside when she opened one longhorn's mouth with her gloved hand. She had found something that her father had shown her only once during their years of owning cattle. A trapper who had happened by and who had been ordered from their property because of his crooked dealings had returned in the middle of the night and killed a select few of her father's prized bulls.

Melanie saw the same evidence of poisoning in this longhorn.

The tongue, the roof of the mouth, the coating on the teeth all were the same.

"In a way it's good news, Shane," she said, rising to her feet. She wiped her gloves on her skirt, gazing up at him.

"What is it?" Shane asked, placing his hands on her shoulders. "What have you seen that no one else has seen? Why did the cattle die?"

"It isn't a disease," Melanie said, sighing. "That is the good news."

"Why do you hesitate to tell me?" Shane asked. The men stood around them, also awaiting answers.

"The bad news is that you have been sabotaged," Melanie said. "Someone poisoned your longhorns, Shane."

Shane's jaw tightened. He dropped his hands to his sides and doubled them into fists. Turning, he looked toward Melanie's house, then up at the butte that stretched out into the forest. One of his enemies had made his mark.

But which one?

He walked away from Melanie, then turned and faced his cowhands. "Take these carcasses away!" he shouted. "Burn them!"

The cowhands stepped back away from him, their eyes filled with defiance.

"Those of you who do not wish to do as you are

told can leave!" Shane said, emotionless, looking them in the eye, challenging them, one by one. "You may as well accept who gives the orders around here now. You know that it isn't Josh."

When the men did not make an effort to heed Shane's warning, he went to the cowhand closest to him. With a low, throaty growl, he grabbed the cowhand by the throat and lifted him bodily from the ground. "Are you ready to voice your objection?" he asked, leaning into the cowhand's face. Fear distorted the man's features.

"No, sir . . ." the cowhand managed in a raspy voice, gasping for breath. "I ain't complainin'. Let me go. I'll do what you ask."

Shane jerked his hand away from the cowhand's throat and went to the next man and repeated the same performance. "Are you working? Or leaving?" he asked, challenging the man with a set stare, his grip firm on the man's neck.

"Let me go, you—you damn Injun lover," the cowhand managed, his voice a strangled gurgle as Shane's fingers tightened around his throat.

Shane's anger swelled to almost uncontrollable proportions, enraged by the cowhand's obvious loathing of Indians. When anyone insulted Indians, they were also insulting Shane, for in his mind and heart, they were one in the same.

Feeling Melanie's eyes on him, Shane refrained from attacking the cowhand. Instead he gave the man a shove, causing him to awkwardly fall to the ground. Placing a foot on the man's abdomen, pinioning him to the ground, he glared down at him. "Get your things and get out of here," he ordered. "Don't let me ever see you near my farm again."

Wild-eyed, the cowhand waited for Shane to take his foot away, then scrambled to his feet and ran to his horse and left in a frenzied gallop.

A sob froze in Melanie's throat. She backed away as the men fell in around the carcasses and began dragging them off. After they were gone, she went to Shane and took his hand. "I'm sorry this had to happen to your cattle," she murmured. "Of course, you are wondering who did it."

"In time, the truth will out," Shane said, watching his cowhands prepare the carcasses for burning.

"I've come to show you how farm ledgers are kept," Melanie said, knowing that Shane did not want to discuss this morning's tragedy. He surely felt helpless. It was hard enough that everything was new to him, without someone doing something like this to him!

Anger scorched her insides at the thought that it might have been Terrance! Would he? Or Josh? Was either of them capable of such an act as this? Or, could they be working together? Was their hatred toward Shane this intense?

"Ledgers?" Shane said, forking an eyebrow.

Melanie linked an arm through Shane's and began walking with him toward the house. "Entries must be made daily to keep up," she said, curling her nose distastefully when smoke wafted toward her from the burning carcasses. "My father said that I was a most skilled bookkeeper."

"I know of no ledgers, or where they are kept,"

Shane said in a grumble. "I will probably fail at that, also."

Melanie shot him a quick look. She frowned at him.

"Don't let doubts plague you," she scolded. "No one could have prevented this. How can you blame yourself?"

"It is because I am here that they are dead," Shane said, breaking away from her and striding into the house.

Melanie hurried after him, breathless as she reached him just outside the parlor. She grabbed him by an arm and forced him to stop. "Shane, you mustn't let anything stand in the way of your living here, where you belong," she said softly. "You mustn't let whoever poisoned the cattle see you defeated."

She tugged at his arm. "Come on, Shane," she urged him, giving him a wistful look through her long, dark lashes. "Let me help you. Please? I can find the ledgers. They are probably in a desk drawer. That's where father always kept his."

Shane looked down at her, his expression brooding. She gazed up at his bronzed, handsome face, feeling something mystical and magical suddenly weaving itself between them.

"Shane, what are you thinking?" she asked, a warmth blossoming within her as she saw his mood changing. His jaw was not as tight; his chin not as firm.

She gasped as his hands reached out to cup the roundness of her bottom through her soft, buckskin dress, and he drew her into the manly contours of his body. He crushed his mouth down upon her lips, his tongue plunging inside her mouth.

Her pulse racing, she twined her arms around his neck and was lost in passion. When he began gyrating his body into hers, she raised a leg and wrapped it around him, drawing him closer. She was flooded with a sweet desire that spread within her like a warm summer breeze, touching her all over with a lilting softness.

"I need you," Shane said huskily, drawing his mouth from her lips. He gathered her up into his arms and carried her toward the stairs. "I need you now, not tonight, Melanie. You move me in many ways with your sincere and generous ways. I am moved at this moment to make love with you."

Oblivious to servants standing in doorways watching, aghast, Melanie lay her head against Shane's powerful chest, the cotton of the shirt cool against her flaming cheek. She would not humiliate Shane in front of the servants by denying him this moment of need just because they were being observed. One humiliation a day was enough.

And wouldn't the servants have to get used to her presence in time? She and Shane were surely going to be married. In truth, wouldn't marriage be the answer to everything?

The bedroom reached and the door closed, Melanie stood before Shane, her blouse already unbuttoned. She became breathless as she observed him undressing, a garment at a time, matching those she removed from herself, until they were both standing nude before one other.

"We truly ought to be studying the ledgers," Melanie said, laughing lightly as she moved into Shane's embrace. She began running her hands across his chest, scarcely touching his flesh, then lower, across his abdomen.

Shane sucked in his breath and closed his eyes as Melanie's lips and tongue began making a hot, wet trail downward from where his thudding heart lay beneath his chest, lower still, to where his muscled thighs stiffened with building need.

"Shane, I love you so," Melanie said, brushing light kisses along his thighs, then daring to kiss that throbbing part of him that would soon send her to paradise.

"Melanie," Shane said thickly, twining his fingers through her auburn hair, guiding her mouth closer . . . closer . . . .

Melanie placed her hands to Shane's waist and urged him down onto the pallet of furs. Settling on her knees between his legs, she continued to pleasure him, thrilling her as she heard him groan and moan with pent-up ecstasy.

"Enough," Shane said in a growl. He took her by the shoulders and gently drew her up beneath him. Entering her with one fierce thrust, he began his skillful strokes within her. His lips suckled on her breasts, his hands excited her body.

She raked her fingernails along his back, to his thrusting hips, then splayed them against his buttocks. She kneaded his flesh in rhythm with his strokes. She could feel his excitement peaking, matching her own.

Gently coiling his fingers through her hair, he

guided her lips to his mouth. "You are all sweetness," he whispered. "How can I have found you? How is it that you are mine when everyone else hates me? How can you love me, Melanie? Do I not repel you at times when you think of my past? Most see me as an Indian lover and detest me for it. Tell me you don't, and never will, Melanie! Tell me!"

Melanie's eyes clouded with warm tears. She placed a hand to Shane's cheek. His lips were so temptingly close to hers, but for a moment she was denied the pleasure of being kissed by them.

"My darling, never doubt my love for you," she whispered, tracing the perfect outline of his lower lip with her forefinger. "How could I ever detest you, or be repelled by you? You are all that is good on this earth, and I am so lucky that you are mine!"

Shane gazed down at her for a moment longer, his eyes filled with dark emotion.

Then he buried himself more deeply within her and rocked with her, his muscles stirring and flexing down the length of his lean, tanned body.

Together they moaned, as a great surge of ecstasy claimed them both . . . .

Later, Melanie kissed his cheek softly. "Shane, whatever are we going to do about us?" she asked, giggling. "We shouldn't be here, you know. We have much to do. I have much to show you."

The magical spell between them was broken just as quickly as Melanie's words were spoken. Shane rose to his feet and drew on his breeches. "I will find out who killed the cattle," he said decisively.

He looked out the window, watching the thick, black smoke rising from the burning carcasses. "Surely it wasn't Josh. The longhorns belong to him, also. He wouldn't destroy something so valuable just to humiliate or scare me." He slipped into his shirt. "Yet, I don't really know my brother or what he is capable of, do I?"

Melanie began dressing. "And perhaps you never will," she said. "I've lived with Terrance all of my life and I still don't know him or how his mind works." She glanced at the window, shivering when she caught sight of the smoke. "Perhaps I wouldn't even want to. The knowing might frighten me."

"Tonight I will spend the night outside, keeping watch," Shane said flatly, brushing his hair back from his eyes with his long, lean fingers. "If anyone tries anything, they will have me to answer to, personally!"

Fear grabbed Melanie at the pit of her stomach. She splayed her hands against his chest. "Shane, please don't take this on all by yourself," she pleaded. "It could be dangerous. Let me call in the authorities—"

He interrupted her by placing a hand over her mouth. "I am my own authority," he growled. "It is partly my land. They are partly my cattle. I will protect it all in my own way. If anyone wants to kill any more of my longhorns, they will have to fight me to get to them!"

· CHAPTER NINETEEN ·

The moon was high, the hour late. Shane fought against falling asleep, pacing back and forth far enough from the longhorns so that his presence would not alarm them.

Peering through the shadowy night, he moved his eyes slowly so that he might catch any unusual, sudden movement in the pasture. Thus far, the night had been peaceful, disturbed only by the haunting, almost mournful cry of a loon in the distance.

Shane turned his eyes in the direction of the sound, and smiled, recalling the moment he and Melanie had watched the loon settle into its nest of eggs. The bird was patiently awaiting the birth of its offspring. Shane had to wonder if he would be as patient when he awaited the birth of his first child. Would this child be born to him and Melanie? Would they ever have that chance?

Or would one humiliation and failure after another make Shane flee this life? If not for Melanie, would he have left before now? Was she, in truth, the only thing holding him there?

He doubled his fists at his sides and firmed his jaw. No. His pride was at stake here! His pride and his love for Melanie were keeping him at the farm. It was damn well not the inheritance, for he had never had these sorts of riches while living in the wilderness, and he had been happy. He knew for a fact that riches did not make the man, or happiness!

The proof was in his brother and Terrance. Both men were tormented, driven, and power-hungry. Shane was none of those things, and until he returned home to life as it had been handed to him, he had been content.

Uncurling his hands from their tight fists, Shane stretched his arms over his head and yawned. A shudder coursed through him as he suddenly realized how cold it was at this hour of night, when a faint streak of light along the horizon revealed that morning would soon be upon this land of wild beauty.

Licking his parched lips, then wiping a hand across his face and inhaling a deep, weary breath, Shane began walking toward his house. It was obvious that no one was going to do anything to his cattle and that he had forced himself to stay awake a full night for nothing.

He looked through the darkness and saw faint

lamplight in some of the windows of Melanie's house. She was supposed to arrive early again, to continue with her teachings. If Shane were lucky, he might get two quick winks of sleep before she arrived.

He smiled wickedly. If he were really lucky, she would come to his bedroom and awaken him. She would not get off all that easily. He would show her how he expected to be woken up every morning once they were married. Making love was the best way to begin a new day.

In a few days he would ask her to marry him, Shane thought, taking the front steps two at a time. It made no sense at all that she was in one house and he in another. They should be together. They would be. Totally! *Ah-pah-nay.* Forever.

He jerked the massive oak door open, frowning. He just could not put the Chippewa language behind! It kept cropping up, as easily as breathing, it seemed!

Shane shrugged. The change could only be expected to be gradual. He stepped into the foyer, hesitated, and looked into the parlor. A kerosene lamp was dimly lighted, casting dancing shadows on the gilt-edged paintings on the walls, and onto the tall-stemmed crystal goblets that sat on a table against a wall that was filled with expensively bound books.

His gaze moved on around the room. The plushly upholstered sofa and matching chairs and the brocade drapes looked the sort of furnishings that Melanie would enjoy. This home would be hers, his wife's. Soon. Even if he didn't belong, she did. She would brighten up the place, her laughter filling the house with sunshine.

Yawning again, Shane climbed the stairs, blinking his eyes to keep from falling asleep on his feet. He heard only a faint sound of footsteps down below—the servants awakening for their full day of chores. Soon the smell of coffee would be drifting up into his room. Soon the sparrows would be singing in the trees just outside his window.

In an isolated part of Shane's pasture, a figure moved stealthily toward a lone longhorn bull standing with its head hung, its eyes closed as it dropped off into sleep. As the intruder drew closer, a knife poised in the air for the death plunge, a wooden pail carried in his other hand, he jumped with a start as the longhorn's tail began slowly swishing back and forth, as though the bull were fully awake again.

Taking quiet steps, moving in a wide circle around the longhorn, the man peered through the early morning light, testing the longhorn to see if it was alert enough to pick up on his scent.

Now directly in front of the longhorn, the man smiled devilishly, for again the bull's tail stopped swishing and his eyes were closed.

In a mad rush, knowing that hesitation could alert the bull and cause it to attack with its deadly horns, the intruder ran to the longhorn and plunged the knife into its side several times, so quickly that the longhorn did not even have a chance to let out a bellow of pain. Its body twitched and convulsed, then dropped heavily to the ground, dead.

Without hesitation, the man decapitated the longhorn, then set the wooden pail close to the bleeding carcass. He kept glancing over his shoulder toward Shane's house, then the bunkhouse, knowing that if he were caught, he would be shot on the spot.

After enough blood had dripped into the pail, the man moved stealthily across the wide breadth of the pasture, making sure to keep a healthy distance between himself and the remaining longhorns. One sniff of the blood and there would be a stampede, and this was not the time for it. If it became necessary, the stampede would come later.

The man climbed over the fence and tiptoed toward the stable. Smiling wickedly, he began pouring the blood across the ground in front of the stable, making a gruesome sight, and causing a hideous smell.

The pail empty, the man chuckled, then slipped away just as the morning sun began casting its golden rays across the land.

Carrying a wicker basket filled with fruit and cinnamon rolls, with a bottle of wine tucked beneath a red-checked napkin in the basket, Melanie left her house with a light step. Today, after she and Shane spent some time with the journals and looking over the herd, she would suggest they take time off for a leisurely picnic by the river. They needed as many light moments together as possible, to outweigh the heavy ones. She wanted Shane to experience more good than bad in his new life. She wanted to fill his life with happiness!

A shawl draped around her shoulders to ward off the early morning chill, and attired in a cotton dress trimmed with fine white lace, Melanie went to the horse and buggy that she had asked to be readied for her while she was eating breakfast.

Placing the picnic basket in the buggy, Melanie started to climb in, then hesitated. Someone was whistling a tune somewhere close by. Whoever it was seemed mighty happy so early in the morning. She would have to find out who it was; she liked to have cowhands under her employ who enjoyed their jobs.

Holding her shawl in place around her shoulders, Melanie almost skipped across the narrow drive, following the sound of the whistling. When she reached the stable, she went inside, then stopped, eyes wide, when she found that it was not a cowhand at all.

It was Terrance!

Unnoticed, Melanie stepped back into the shadows and watched her brother for a moment. It was obvious that he was not drunk. He was as steady as a broomstick as he stood among the thick bed of hay, tossing it with a pitchfork into the horses' stalls. His eyes were bright. His skin was of a good pink color. He was full of all sorts of energy.

It was wonderful to see Terrance sober and taking part in the actual running of Stanton Farm.

But why the change? Why was he so happy?

Melanie firmed her lips when she realized why her brother was so chipper. Always when he won at poker she could expect him to be this carefree, this full of energy. More than likely he had won big the previous day. It had even given him cause to take a reprieve from drinking for a while, to enjoy the simple pleasures of life.

"Well, well, what have we here?" Melanie asked, stepping out into full view. "My brother is actually working?"

Terrance dropped the pitchfork and turned with a start. He took a handkerchief from his hip pocket and began dabbing his brow with it. "Damn it, Melanie, you scared the hell outta me," he said, his voice drawn. "What're you doin' up so early? The stable boy came for your horse a while ago. I expected you to be leavin' soon." He looked her up and down. "You're not dressed for riding today, so I expect you've got something more delicate on your mind." He screwed his face up into a frown. "Like maybe some lovin'?"

Melanie refused to let him goad her into saying something she would regret. Inching her way around him, she patted his rear pockets. "Where's your cards?" she teased. "How much money did you win, Terrance? You're acting like you won a million dollars. I haven't seen you this happy in a long time." She stood on tiptoe and talked into his face. "What if you had lost as much as you've obviously won? Did you ever consider that?"

Terrance looked down at her, puzzled at her meaning for a moment, then laughed smoothly. He placed a finger to her chin and lifted it higher.

"You won't tell me your little secrets," he said in a low drawl. "I won't tell you mine."

"Secrets?" Melanie said, jerking away from him. "What do you mean?"

Terrance's eyes narrowed and his jaw tightened. "You damn well know what I mean," he said. He began pitching hay into the stalls again, this time with even more vigor. "What'cha teachin' Shane Brennan now? How to swindle his brother out of everything else he owns?"

Melanie's breath was stolen for a moment. Then she squared her shoulders and stared with contempt at her brother. "You are insulting," she hissed. "Terrance, I almost think I like you better when you're drunk! Your insults carry less meaning, for I attribute most of the things you say to alcohol. When you are sober, everything you say is from the heart, and sometimes your remarks are unbearable!"

Spinning around, suddenly sobbing, Melanie ran from the stable. Blinded by tears, she rushed to her wagon and climbed onto the seat. Flicking the reins, she ignored Terrance as he yelled at her, waving his arms frantically.

"You can't undo what you said," she whispered. "Oh, Terrance, what am I going to do about you?"

She made a wide turn in the lane and headed toward Shane's house. The sun was hotter than she had expected at this time of morning, and she slipped her shawl from around her shoulders and placed it on the seat next to her. She inhaled the wondrous fragrance of morning, suddenly exhilarated by it. She would place her thoughts of

Terrance aside. She would not let him spoil this day for her. It was another day meant only for her and Shane.

"I shall let nothing spoil it," she said, flipping her windblown hair back from her eyes.

As she grew closer to Shane's, her eyes widened in wonder when she saw the men congregating just outside the stables, staring at something on the ground. She was recalling the poisoned cattle. Surely that vicious act had not been repeated a second night. Shane had even said that he was going to stand guard through the night. No one could have gotten close to the farm, much less have wreaked such havoc again!

But as Melanie brought her horse and buggy to a stop close to the men, she soon discovered how wrong she was. The air was putrid with the stench of blood. The ground was covered with it!

"What on earth—?" she gasped, climbing quickly from the buggy. She made her way through the men and stared down at the ground turned crimson with blood.

Ken, one of the cowhands stepped to her side. "Miss Stanton, we found a decapitated longhorn in the pasture," he said. "Some sonofabitch slaughtered a prize bull and used its blood to scare the hell outta us, and he's damn well succeeded." He gestured with a wave of the hand. "Look at the men. It won't take much more to spook them into leavin'."

He glanced over his shoulder, at the house. "Josh needs to be here, damn it. Shane Brennan's done nothin' but bring us all a peck of bad luck."

249

He shuddered as he looked back down at the blood. "This looks like some Indian hocus-pocus to me." He looked slowly over at Melanie. "Wouldn't you say so, ma'am?"

Melanie's thoughts rushed to Chief Gray Falcon. Had he succeeded at eluding Shane in the night? Was he the one responsible for this latest vicious act? She truly didn't know how an Indian's mind worked, what acts of revenge they might use against someone they loathed.

"I don't know, Ken," Melanie said. She looked around her, at the men, then up at the house. "Where's Shane? Has he been told?"

"I don't rightly think that he knows, or he'd be here angrier than a hornet's nest," Ken said. "I reckon he's tuckered out from his long vigil through the night." He cleared his throat nervously. "He warned us all last night that he'd be hangin' around, watchin' for intruders in the night," he remarked, slipping his hands inside his front pockets. "He told us to stay put all night so that we wouldn't be mistook for a prowler and probably be shot because of it. Damn if any of us took one step outside that bunkhouse, Miss Stanton, not to even take a piss in the weeds. I don't rightly trust a man who's been raised by Injuns." His eyes darkened. "Ma'am, I don't see how any of us should be expected to."

Outraged by the man's obvious ignorance and his inability to tell the true, good man from the bad, Melanie stared with silent disgust at Ken, then spun around and headed toward the house. She went in without knocking.

Sighing heavily, hating to have to tell Shane this latest bit of gruesome news, she looked up the steep staircase, then rushed on up to the second floor. Sad for Shane, not able to even guess what his reaction would be to this latest revolting act, Melanie slipped into his room and tiptoed across to the pile of furs.

Standing over him, seeing him lying there so innocently asleep, stretched out on his stomach on his thick pallet of furs, she wasn't sure she could even tell him what had happened. At this moment he was at peace with himself, with the world. Soon she would change everything for him—again!

Settling down on her knees beside him, Melanie's eyes filled with tears. She reached a hand to his sun-bronzed face and touched him gently on the cheek. Asleep, he looked no more than a child, his sculpted handsome face catching the rays of the sun as they crept into the room from the gaping sides of the closed draperies.

Awash with pure adoration for him, Melanie studied Shane. His lips were parted, revealing his white, clean teeth. His eyes were closed, shuttered by thick blond lashes. His golden hair lay about his shoulders, wide and muscled. Her eyes traveled down his broad back, his tapered thighs, and his thin hips.

She could not help herself. She was drawn into lying down beside him, hugging him closely to her. "Oh, Shane," she whispered. "How can I tell you? Who is doing this to you? Who?"

Shane stirred. He raised his lashes and looked slowly to his side, then smiled when he discovered

Melanie looking him squarely in the eye. "I awaken from a dream of you, and you are here," he said, turning on his side to face her. He placed his hands to her waist and drew her against him. "Did you also dream of me? Is that why you have come? To make it real?"

Melanie wove her fingers through his hair and brushed a kiss across his lips. "Darling, we had plans for this morning, or did you forget?" she whispered. "I hadn't expected you would still be in bed."

Shane eased his hands from her waist. Moving to a sitting position, he rubbed his eyes and yawned. "I haven't been in bed that long," he said. "I was outside all night, guarding my cattle."

"You were?" Melanie asked, sitting up beside him. She began running a hand down the smoothness of his bare back. "Shane, exactly when did you come in and go to bed?"

"When dawn began to break along the horizon," he said, looking at her, suddenly aware of something different about her. Why the questions? Turning to her, he grabbed her hands. "Melanie, has something happened?"

Melanie swallowed hard and nodded.

Shane dropped her hands and jumped to his feet. In wide strides he went to the window and jerked the draperies open. He raised an eyebrow inquisitively when he saw the group of men assembled outside the stable.

Then his gaze shifted, and he saw the morning sun shining brightly on the pools of blood spread across the ground. He drew a shocked breath.

Melanie went to his side. "Somehow, after you came in and went to bed, someone did something horribly macabre," she said in a rush of words. "Someone decapitated one of your longhorns and brought its blood and poured it all over the ground close to the stable."

She placed her hands to his cheeks. "Shane, someone did this to frighten your cowhands," she murmured. "It was meant to scare them away so that you will be left alone to run your farm."

She looked from the window and her eyes narrowed in on Ken, recalling his assumptions. She looked slowly back up at Shane. "Ken suspected it was done by an Indian," she said, her voice drawn. "Could Chief Gray Falcon have done this terrible thing?"

Melanie could feel Shane grow tense at her suggestion. She did not know whether it was because he agreed that it could be the chief, or because he did not like anyone to suspect the Indians because he had been raised by Indians. To him it was a delicate subject.

"That is not the work of Gray Falcon," Shane said, looking solemnly down at her. "I was wrong ever to suspect that he could have been responsible for poisoning my longhorns. I know him well enough to know that he values the life of animals too much to kill them senselessly." He turned away from her and stepped into his breeches. "No, Melanie, it was not Gray Falcon. It was someone else whose values are as dim as his morals!"

"If not Chief Gray Falcon, then who—?" Melanie grew ashen with a thought. Her own brother! It could be! Hadn't he been behaving out of character only moments ago? He hadn't risen with the dawn in months to work on the farm. He hadn't been as cheerful in months!

She rushed to the door, and Shane looked at her, puzzled. "Where are you going?" he asked, slipping into his cotton shirt.

"I have someone to see," Melanie said from across her shoulder. "I have questions to ask!"

Shane watched her leave, full of wonder.

Melanie jumped from her buggy and ran into the stable. Terrance was just putting his pitchfork away. He turned with a start when Melanie cleared her throat behind him.

"What have you been up to?" Melanie asked, placing her hands on her hips. "I hope it's not what I'm thinking. If so, I can honestly say that I don't know you at all."

Terrance toyed nervously with the end of his mustache, eyeing Melanie closely. "If you're accusing me of something, you may as well just come out and say it," he grumbled. "What's got you in this mood, anyhow? You were on your way to see Shane. Why'd you come back home?"

"Are you saying that you don't know what I found when I arrived there?" Melanie said, lifting her chin angrily.

"Why the hell should I?" Terrance asked, waving a hand wildly in the air. "Am I supposed to be a mind reader, or what? You know I don't own a crystal ball, Melanie, and my game is poker, not looking into the future!"

"You're not at all amusing, Terrance."

Terrance grabbed her shoulders and glared down at her. "Are you going to tell me what's got you all riled up or do I have to go to Shane's and question him about it?" he asked, his teeth clenched.

"If you have to ask, then perhaps I was wrong," Melanie said, reaching to remove his hands from her shoulders.

She stared at Terrance, searching his face and his eyes to see if he was lying. She wanted to believe that he wasn't guilty of such a vile act, yet she could not help but suspect him.

But she would not come right out and ask him. If he was responsible, he would not tell her the truth, anyhow. If he was responsible, at this moment he was proving that he knew the art of lying well!

"Melanie, are you going to tell me what's bothering you?" Terrance asked, frowning down at her. "Why didn't you stay at Shane's?"

In Melanie's mind's eye she was seeing the spilled blood; she was envisioning the torment that Shane must be going through at this very moment. He needed her and she wasn't there! She must go to him!

She whirled around and began running from the stable. "If you want to know, come with me!" she said, then stopped and turned to face Terrance.

"Perhaps you can offer some advice to Shane as to what to do about the evil person who is destroying his cattle," she said, studying Terrance's expression again, trying to see his reaction to what she was saying. "Who knows? They might slaughter some of our cattle next."

Terrance seemed not at all moved by the declaration. Instead he put an arm around Melanie's waist and led her to the buggy. "Let's just see what happened at Shane's that's so terrible," he said.

· CHAPTER TWENTY ·

Shane stood watching his men pitch hay on the ground, soaking up the blood with it. His mind was tormented. Who was responsible for this latest macabre act?

He turned and stared at his house. Not a word had been heard from Josh. Could his absence point to him as the culprit? Would he be staying away purposely to draw guilt away from himself?

Then Shane's attention was diverted by the sight of Melanie and Terrance approaching in the buggy. His eyes narrowed, knowing that Terrance could be responsible. Terrance made no bones about not being pleased over Shane's arrival in his sister's life.

But could he be this determined to get rid of Shane? Was he this low? This vile?

Melanie reined the horse in beside the fence. She left the buggy and went to Shane, Terrance at her side. "Terrance has come to help in whatever way that he can," she said. "My brother is as appalled by this as we are, Shane."

She looked at Terrance again, her jaw firm. "Isn't that so, Terrance?" she asked.

Terrance shifted his feet and toyed with his mustache. "Yes, quite," he said, his voice drawn.

Shane studied Terrance, wondering. Yet he had already decided that Josh was the one he was going to narrow in on with questions this morning. As far as Shane was concerned, Josh had a lot to answer for.

"What can Terrance do to help?" Melanie asked, folding her hands together behind her. "Shane, what can I do?"

"Nothing," Shane said, brushing past Melanie into the stable. "I'm going into St. Paul. I've someone to see."

Melanie's lips parted with surprise. She started to follow him, then shuddered when she stepped into a pool of blood that was not yet covered with hay. Gasping, she lifted her skirt past her ankles and stepped over the blood, then raced into the stable. Shane was determinedly placing his saddle onto his horse.

"Shane," she said, "who are you going into St. Paul to see? Of course, it must be Josh, for there is no one else in St. Paul that you know." She placed a hand on his arm, causing him to turn and look down at her. "Do you think he's the one responsible for this, Shane? Do you?"

"Do you?" Shane said in a deep grumble. He looked past her at Terrance, who was standing among a group of the cowhands, speaking low, occasionally glancing Shane's way.

Melanie's eyes followed Shane's steady gaze. She recoiled inside, knowing that Shane must also suspect Terrance. Yet he had not openly accused him. Was it because Terrance was her brother and Shane wanted to save her embarrassment and torment should Terrance prove to be the guilty party? If it was Terrance, dare Shane wait for any reason?

She turned her eyes slowly back to Shane. "You asked if I thought Josh is responsible," she murmured. She lowered her eyes. "I cannot say."

Shane grabbed the horse's reins and led it on past Melanie. "Nor can I," he growled. "But I damn well intend to find out!"

Melanie ran after him. "Let me go with you, Shane," she said, reaching up for him. "I can unsaddle my horse from the buggy quickly. I won't delay you. I want to go with you."

Shane placed a foot into a stirrup and swung himself up into his saddle. "No," he said flatly. "I think I know where I might find my brother and it is not a place for a lady. This time I go into St. Paul alone."

Melanie circled her hands into tight fists at her sides. "Oh, Shane . . ." she whispered, watching him wheel his horse around and ride away.

Terrance sidled up close to Melanie and whispered into her ear, "Sis, you're making one damn fool of yourself over that man," he said. "Look around you. Don't you see yourself being gawked at?"

Melanie felt a heated blush rise to her cheeks. She glanced around and saw that the cowhands really were staring at her. She stamped a foot and went to her buggy. "Terrance, since you agreed so heartily to help here at Shane's, get to it!" she hissed, snapping the reins against her mare.

After taking a wide turn on the drive, she traveled briskly away, leaving Terrance standing with his fists on his hips, glaring angrily after her.

Sitting tall in the saddle, Shane rode into town. He looked from saloon to saloon. He knew the terms of his father's will and understood them all, even why Josh had been left less of their father's inheritance than Shane. It was a well-known fact that Josh loved his whiskey and poker too much. Even at this mid-morning hour, Shane expected that he could find his brother in a saloon, losing himself in his two favorite pastimes.

Securing the horse's reins to a hitching rail, Shane walked determinedly toward the saloon. He stepped up onto the wooden sidewalk, then flung the saloon's swinging doors aside and stepped into the room.

The stench of whiskey lay heavy in the air, intermingling with gray swirls of smoke, almost choking in its intensity. The room was noisy with laughter, cursing, the tinkling of a piano, and the clink-clink of coins.

Women in gawdy short skirts and plunging

necklines mingled with the men, giggling, kissing, fondling.

At the bar, Shane purchased a cigar. Then, leaning his back against the bar, he bit off the end of the cigar, spat the tip onto the floor, and thrust the cigar between his lips. The light of a burning match suddenly appeared and was placed to his cigar by a hand with long, lean fingers, their nails brightly polished. Shane looked up into seductive, dark eyes, feathered by thick, even darker lashes.

He accepted the light and puffed on his cigar, slowly looking the woman over as she dropped the burned-out match to the floor. She was nothing less than beautiful, yet not the sort that Shane was attracted to. Her dress was brightly-colored and scant, revealing all but the nipples of her breasts. There was a wickedness in the way she smiled up at him as she leaned into him, brushing her breasts against his chest.

"Somethin' else I can do for you, hon, besides light your cigar?" she asked in a seductive purr. She nodded toward the staircase. "I've got a room upstairs. Go with me and I could make you feel real good." She nodded toward a bottle of whiskey on the bar. "If you're the shy sort, we could sit down and begin with sharin' a drink or two." She bumped up against him again. "What do you say? A handsome fella like you'd be good to be around for awhile."

Shane placed his hands to her waist and moved her aside. He smiled slowly down at her when he saw rage fill her eyes. "Thank you for the compliment," he said, taking his cigar from his mouth, flicking ashes from it. "But I don't think I've got the time today for the sort of fun you're offering me."

Sauntering away from her, Shane thrust the cigar between his lips again. He peered intently through the smoke as he walked slowly from table to table, looking for Josh.

Seeing no sign of him in this saloon, Shane went to another and another. Then he finally found his brother in a saloon that sat squeezed in between two brothels.

Shane stood across the room from where Josh sat at a table, gambling and drinking, and looked at him disbelievingly. His brother's face was stubbled with golden whiskers. He wore a white, ruffled shirt and dark breeches, both of which were wrinkled and soiled with whiskey and food spills down the front. Standing behind him, a skimpily attired whore clung around his neck possessively.

Something akin to regret for his brother, for what Josh had let himself become, washed over Shane. It seemed that he had no pride. Yet, Shane felt as though he was to blame for his brother's misfortune. Josh had left his farm because of Shane! Why couldn't brothers live together? Work together? Did it have to come down to this?

Then Shane recalled what had brought him there. He had come to question Josh, to see if his brother was responsible for the recent mishaps at the Brennan farm. Did Josh gamble by day and wreak havoc by night?

Shane's eyes moved back to the woman who still clung around Josh's neck. He grew cold inside as he watched her motioning to a man across the table from Josh, giving him finger signals to tell him what was in Josh's spread hand of cards. The woman was helping the man cheat!

Taking slow, calculated steps closer, Shane positioned himself behind the man who was the recipient of the hand signals. He removed his knife from the sheath at his waist and waited for Josh and the man to discard, and for the man to drag in his winnings.

"Seems you've got a run of bad luck today, Josh," the man said, laughing boisterously as he reached out his hand and covered the coins with them. As he started to drag the coins toward him, Shane flipped the knife down beside his hand, causing the man to yowl with fright and jerk his hand back.

Cursing, the man turned and eyed Shane angrily. Slowly he pushed his chair back and rose to his feet. "You'd better have a good reason for doin' that, sonny," the man said, scowling at Shane as he slowly eased his hand toward his holstered revolver.

"I wouldn't do that if I were you," Shane said, eyeing the pistol. "My brother has a gun on you beneath the table."

The man's eyes wavered, looking from Shane, to Josh, then back to Shane. "Your—brother?" he stammered.

"That's what I said," Shane said, not taking his eyes off the man's hand, now frozen in mid-air.

"Josh ain't wearin' no gun," the man said, laughing nervously.

"Are you positive of that?" Shane said, grinning slowly.

The man kneaded his chin. "I didn't notice one before," he said.

"One way to find out is to test him," Shane said, inching his way around the table. He grabbed the whore by the wrist and held her immobile beside him. "But I think the best way to settle this is to have this little woman here admit to what she was doing to help you win against my brother."

The man swallowed hard. "I reckon you saw?" he said, dropping his hand to his side, away from his gun.

"You damn well know that I did," Shane said, shoving the whore away from him. "And so did everyone else. I guess you all wanted to see Josh Brennan lose today, huh?"

"Take the money, Josh," the man said, leaning down to shove the coins back over to Josh. "No hard feelings, I hope."

Josh had sat through all of this scarcely aware of what was happening. He had drowned his brain, and his ability to think straight, with alcohol. He looked up at Shane, blinking his eyes to clear his vision.

"Shane?" he said in a drunken slur. "What'cha doin' here? Huh?"

Shane looked down at his brother, pitying him. It did not seem possible that Josh could be capable of poisoning cattle one night and beheading a longhorn the next, for at this moment he was not even aware of what was happening around him. He had no idea, even, that his brother had saved him a lot of money—and perhaps even his hide!

Josh shoved his chair back and rose shakily to his feet. He touched Shane's face, then patted it. "Hi, Shane," he said, laughing oddly. "Wanna drink?"

Shane gave Josh a silent stare, then leaned over the table and scooped up the coins. He shoved them into his brother's front breeches pocket, then guided him from the establishment.

"Where's your room?" Shane asked, steadying his brother against him. "I've come to talk, but I don't think it's necessary any longer. I think I've got all the answers I need."

"My room?" Josh said, idly scratching his brow.

"I'd take you home with me, but I don't think you're up to the ride," Shane said. "You've got to sleep off the whiskey, Josh. Then we'll do some serious talking about your coming home where you belong."

"I belong here," Josh said, tossing an arm around Shane's shoulder. He nodded toward a steep staircase that led up to a room over the saloon. "My room is up there, Shane. Want to join me there for a drink?"

"Josh, knowing how you feel about me, I know you must be drunk to be offering me all these kindnesses," Shane said, his voice drawn. He let Josh place his full weight on him and began walking him toward the stairs. "I'll take you up to your room and get you settled into a bed and, by damn, Josh, you stay there until you're sober.

You're in no shape to do anything, much less gamble with men who are ready to take everything you own. Take my word for it, those men were ready to skin you alive."

"I'll beat 'em all to hell next time," Josh said, laughing boisterously. A keen dizziness overtook him. "But for now, I think I do need to get a few winks of sleep."

"And then some more," Shane growled, finally at the head of the stairs. He opened the door and half dragged his brother into a dimly lit room that reeked of whiskey and dirty bed clothing. He cringed when he looked slowly around him at the empty whiskey bottles and half-smoked cigars that cluttered the floor. The bed was covered with yellowed sheets, and roaches crawled along the walls and floors. A dark green window shade was pulled closed, emitting cracks of light through slits cut into its rotten fabric.

"So this is what you call home now, Josh?" Shane said, helping Josh to the bed and easing him down onto it. "How can you prefer this over living at the farm with me? Is being around me all that intolerable?"

Josh was no longer even aware of who was there with him, nor did he hear anyone speaking to him. He closed his eyes and fell into a deep sleep.

Shane shook his head, then left the room. He had found no answers; only a man whose mortality was being tested, it seemed.

· CHAPTER TWENTY-ONE ·

The loon sang its haunting tune in the distance as night fell, the sky a dark crimson backdrop for the flashing stars. Downcast, torn with mixed feelings about Josh, Shane unsaddled his horse and walked it to its stall. Lifting a handful of straw to his stallion's mouth, he watched him munch at it from his palm; his horse's brown, friendly eyes revealed his trust in Shane.

"If life could be like the bond between a man and his horse, no one would ever have cause to hate or mistrust again," Shane whispered, lifting his other hand to draw his fingers through his stallion's sleek, white mane. "You've been good for me. You've been dependable from that very first day I placed a saddle on your broad, strong back."

"Boss?"

A voice from behind Shane startled him. He dropped the remainder of the straw to the ground and eyed Ken warily, then took a wide stride toward him. "Have you done as instructed?" he asked. "Have you positioned men around the pasture to keep watch through the night?"

Ken avoided Shane's stare, looking down at his feet as he shuffled them nervously. "Boss . . ."

Shane placed a firm grip on Ken's shoulder. "When you speak to me, look at me," he said. "Do you understand?"

Ken raised his eyes quickly. He clamped his hands tightly behind him and met Shane's steady stare. "Not too many men were willin' to do that," he said. "They don't like what's goin' on here. They even expect some sort of Indian trouble. They know about you havin' stolen horses from an Indian chief and that you brought them here. They don't want to have any part of the Indian's revenge. They think it's already started by what's happened here."

"Chief Gray Falcon is not responsible for what's happened here," Shane growled.

"Now can you be sure?" Ken dared to argue.

Shane's eyes wavered. He dropped his hand away from Ken and went to the door to gaze down at the ground, where blood still stained the tramped earth. He did not give Ken any answers. He was beginning to doubt everyone and everything.

"Those who choose not to cooperate can come to the house and draw their wages," he said.

"Those who do cooperate—well, tell them I appreciate it."

Ken went to stand beside Shane. "Boss, those who don't like what's goin' on here have already left," he said. "They said to tell you they'd be back to collect their wages when Josh is here to pay them." He cleared his throat nervously. "Seems they don't trust your ability to give them what they've earned."

An instant rage tore through Shane. He walked away from Ken in slow, easy strides, not wanting to show the humiliation that he was feeling. When he reached the protective walls of his house, he closed the door and leaned against it, burying his face in his hands.

He kept telling himself over and over again that he had known all along that none of this would be easy.

Dispirited, yet determined that Shane would not be alone should another disaster befall him this night, Melanie stood among her cowhands, looking authoritatively at them.

"I've gathered you together tonight to ask your assistance on a delicate matter," she said, eying each of the men separately. She smoothed her hands down the front of her fringed buckskin skirt and shifted her knee-high moccasins nervously in the tramped dirt in front of her stable. "Gossip spreads fast, so I know that you are aware of what has been happening at the Brennan farm."

She began walking from man to man. "You know that Josh has left for a while and his brother

269

is in charge," she continued. "Well, it seems that someone doesn't approve of Shane, so attempts have been made to encourage him to leave."

She straightened her back determinedly. "Tonight will probably be no different," she said. "I would like for you all to volunteer to help Shane, should the need arise. I would like to ask each of you to sleep with your clothes and boots on, in case I come and ask for your help at a moment's notice."

She stepped closer and let her gaze move slowly from man to man again. "Is there any among you who has a problem with my request?" she asked.

"I do, Melanie," Terrance said suddenly from behind her.

Melanie turned with a start as Terrance approached her, his eyes lit with fire. "And why should you?" she asked shallowly, anger rising inside her.

"Haven't you heard?" Terrance said, stopping to tower over her. He leaned down into her face. She recoiled, smelling the stench of whiskey on his breath. "Most of Shane's men skipped out on him early this evening. I'm not going to ask our men to go and take their places. Do you want them to go over there and be killed by some crazy lunatic who seems to stop at nothing to frighten Shane? So far it's just been cattle that's been slaughtered. Who knows? Maybe tonight it will be a man!"

He squared his shoulders. "No, Melanie, I won't allow it," Terrance said flatly. "We pay our cowhands to fight our battles, not Shane's."

Melanie's head was spinning. She hadn't heard

about the men walking out on Shane. She had only chosen to ask her cowhands for their help in case Shane's were not enough to handle whatever problem arose.

And now? She had no choice but to ignore Terrance and order the Stanton cowhands to give Shane a hand.

She sighed heavily and shook her head with disgust. "Terrance, you couldn't go another full day without drinking, could you?" she hissed. "And I bet you're quite smug about what's happened at Shane's, aren't you? Well, just take your whiskey and smugness and leave me be!"

She turned and faced the cowhands. "I have as much right to plead for your help as my brother has to order you not to help," she shouted. "I know that puts you all in a bad position, torn with what to do! But it boils down to this. If you have any compassion, you will do as I ask."

She gave Terrance a half smile over her shoulder, then looked back at the men. "And don't forget who keeps the ledgers here at Stanton farm and who dishes out the wages," she warned. "It's not my brother! He doesn't know the first thing about ledgers or who gets paid what. My father taught me, not Terrance! If you walk away from me and what I ask of you, you will be walking away from your job!"

The cowhands glanced at each other, then stepped forward and offered a handshake to Melanie, affirming their trust in her.

She smiled as she shook their hands, thanking them each as they passed by her. Then she again explained what she wanted of them. They would sleep in their clothes and boots. They would keep a loaded pistol at their side. Their horses would be saddled and ready to ride.

As the lamps dimmed in Shane's house, the cowhands who remained moved from their assigned posts and met at the stable. They knelt down in a circle, facing one another.

"You know what this will mean to Shane," Ken argued. "You know what it will mean for you. You'll be out on your asses. It's mighty hard to find a job like this in these parts. There's not that many farms around who employ a good number of cowhands and who pay as good."

"You know damn well that if we wait around long enough in town, Josh'll be back in charge," another cowhand argued. "I'd say, let's leave this guy Shane to fight his own battles. He's the cause of the trouble here. Before he came, nothin' was goin' wrong. Now every night somethin' spooky happens." He looked toward the house. "I say it's because he was raised by Injuns. He's practically one of them!"

"Yeah, he even went and stole those damn horses like a savage would, from another savage," another cowhand grumbled. "There ain't no need in us waitin' around to have our scalps removed just because of somethin' that half-breed did. I say let's head out. We all have enough earnings to get us through a few weeks. I'm lookin' forward to havin' some fun with the wenches in town. Damn, just think of it. We can stay in bed humpin' all day if we choose to. What more could you ask for than that?"

Ken frowned. He could not tell the men that he liked Shane Brennan and wanted to do right by him. He had to go along with the crowd. Shane Brennan was not worth the sort of ridicule that Ken could expect if he stayed behind while everyone else rode away.

"All right, let's get our gear and leave," Ken said, rising to his full height. "But we've got to be quiet about it. Shane Brennan has ears like a polecat. He'll hear us if we ride out. One by one we've got to walk our horses away from the farm. Do you understand? Once we get far enough away, only then will it be safe enough to ride."

"Yeah, that's best," the men agreed, nodding.

Before long, everything in the pasture was eerily quiet. Only the longhorns stood there, their tails swishing, their horns glistening against the dark sky.

Melanie could not sleep. Fully clothed, she rose from the bed. She peered from the window toward Shane's house, and then at the pasture. Everything seemed peaceful enough. Perhaps she had been too hasty in asking her men to be on guard in case they were needed tonight. Perhaps the person responsible for the havoc at Shane's farm would not be so brazen as to show up again so soon. Surely they would have to know that Shane was sitting shotgun again tonight, waiting. She had not gone to see him tonight because of this. She did not want to disturb his plans.

273

"I can't believe that some of his men actually left him," she said, stepping back from the window. She began nervously pacing. "How can they hate him so much?"

A figure stole stealthily through the dark. When he got close enough to the longhorns to smell them in the darkness, he watched for any sudden movement on their part. Familiar with them, the man knew that when a steer bedded down, he held his breath for a few seconds, then blew off. That noise showed that he was settling himself for comfort. But when he curled his nose and took long breaths, it was a sign that he was sniffing for something, and if anything crossed his wind that he didn't like, there was likely to be trouble.

There was to be trouble tonight.

The air was suddenly charged with tension. A dun steer awakened and lifted his head slowly, rose to his knees, and looked around. He got to his feet and raised his nose to smell.

Another steer rose and stood rigidly still, expectant, then others, until the whole herd of longhorns were on their feet, motionless.

Hurrying, knowing that his life was at stake, the man placed a grotesque scarecrow close to the longhorns—a scarecrow with wings that moved up and down as the wind blew against them. The man scurried away, mounted a horse, and rode away from the scene of coming disaster.

A breeze caught in the wings of the scarecrow. They began to move up and down. A longhorn bull saw the wings moving. Frightened, it leapt into the air, then back down to the ground with a thud. He gave a grunt that sounded more like that of a hog than of a cow. Others followed. The pounding hoofs popped and clicked while horns clacked upon horns in the longhorns' desperation to flee from the grotesque scarecrow.

A stampede had started with the swiftness of a lightning bolt!

The steers smashed into the fence. The leaders piled up, while the cattle behind, forming a gigantic battering ram, rushed over them and surged over the fence, then through it, tearing it down from the top.

As they raced across the land, the cattle stretched out so that their bellies seemed to scrape the roots of the grass.

Shane heard the first bellow. Still fully clothed, he bolted from his pallet of furs and ran from his room. Taking the steps two at a time, he raced outside, then looked wildly around him. His heart sank. There were no riders in sight trying to stop the stampede. There were no cowhands there to prevent it. They had all deserted him! Each and every one of them. Even Ken.

But there was no time for regrets. Knowing that he alone had to stop the stampede, Shane broke into a run and swung himself up into his saddle. Taking the reins, he led his stallion from the stable, then sank his booted heels into the flanks of the horse and rode in the direction of what sounded like thunder echoing across the land.

Then he drew his horse to a sudden stop. He

looked disbelievingly at Melanie as she rode up and reined in beside him, then saw the swarm of her cowhands on horseback, jumping the fence, chasing the crazed longhorns.

"How did you know about the stampede?" Shane asked. "How did you get the cowhands to agree to come and help so quickly?"

"I'll explain later," Melanie shouted, her bay gelding pawing nervously at the ground. "Right now, let's do what we can to stop the stampede!"

"You stay behind!" Shane shouted.

"Shane, please don't tell me not to help!" she pleaded. "I want to! I know about stampedes! My father told me about some that he had experienced and how he stopped them!"

"Melanie, this isn't the time to get stubborn on me," Shane growled. He glared at her. "You stay behind. I don't want to have to worry about you. I've enough to worry about already!"

"Shane, while we're arguing, your longhorns are getting away!" Melanie shouted, exasperated.

Shane looked into the distance and saw that the cowhands were not having much luck at stopping the stampede. Having experienced crazed buffalo, even at age thirteen, he knew the art of what to do about them.

"Do as you wish!" he shouted, gesturing with a hand. "But be careful, Melanie! I love you!"

Melanie was overcome with warmth, knowing that Shane did not speak those words all that freely. But when he did speak them, they were from the heart. They were true!

"Shane, I love you," she said, then slapped her

reins and rode alongside him toward the stamped-ing herd.

"We've got to get around the cattle and circle the leaders," Shane shouted. "Swing the leaders around into the tail end of the herd."

Melanie nodded, trying not to show the fear that was gripping her insides. She knew the danger in the cattle's sharp horns! She knew the danger of her horse becoming spooked, possibly throwing her! Riding at breakneck speed through the night to check the stampede was the most dangerous part of a perilous job. Melanie depended on the sure-footedness of her horse. A spill meant certain death, with both horse and rider thrown in the path of the herd.

But she had to help Shane. No matter what.

The longhorns picked up speed. It was so dark, it was hard for Shane to see them in the distance, but he could tell by the noise that they were now running straight. There was no clicking of horns. What he was hearing was a kind of buzzing noise, loud and deafening. There was no use trying to turn them in the darkness. He rode wide, herding by ear, following the noise. Soon his ears told him that they were crowding and milling together, their heads jammed together and their horns locked.

Shane and Melanie finally reached the front of the stampede and began zigzagging across the front, directing its course. Melanie looked over at Shane as he began to chant.

"Wo-up, wo-up, wo, wo-o-o, wo bop, wo-o-oo boys. Be good, be good, wo-o-o-o, you wall-eyed rascals!" Shane chanted, as he had so long ago when riding after buffalo.

The lead cattle suddenly tried to halt, but there was no time. The rushing mob was at their heels, propelled by its own mass, and it plunged over the hesitating leaders. Some fell. The herd piled up, animals on the bottom being trampled to death.

Now the stampede was without direction, some cattle trying to run in a circle, bunches cutting off this way and that. While Shane and Melanie rode side by side, zigzagging across the front of the stampede, still attempting to direct its course with the cattle running too fast to be circled, an old cow suddenly let out a bawl—probably for her calf. In a minute, the whole herd was stopped and every animal in it was bawling.

Breathless, Melanie stopped alongside Shane. They stared at each other, then at the longhorns. "I've never seen anything like it," Melanie said, wiping her brow with the sleeve of her blouse. "But thank God for the favor!"

The cowhands came riding up and drew rein around Melanie and Shane, awaiting further instructions.

"Let's get them rounded up and back to the farm!" Shane said, looking from man to man. "And thank you all for your help. It won't be forgotten."

The longhorns were circled around and led back inside the fence. Even without being told to, several men jumped from their horses and began repairing the damaged fence. Some took a count of the dead animals. Others checked over the ones that had lived through the ordeal, to make sure they had no serious tears or wounds.

Melanie and Shane dismounted at the stable. As a cowhand came riding toward them, carrying something grotesque, they met his approach.

The cowhand reined in his horse and jumped to the ground, holding the scarecrow out before him. "Seems this was used to start the stampede," he said. "I found it close by the broken fence."

Shane took the scarecrow and examined it, then threw it to the ground and stomped away. He placed a foot on the lower rung of the fence and folded his arms across the top rung as he stared unseeing into the night.

Melanie went to him and touched his arm gently. "We knew it had to be something like that," she murmured. "Stampedes like this don't get started for no reason."

"I doubt if it will ever end, Melanie," Shane said, his voice breaking. "It just wasn't meant for me to come here. The cowhands were right to leave. I guess I should, also."

"Shane," Melanie said, gasping. "Don't talk like that! You can't leave. Do you want to let whoever is doing this to you win? You can't want that, Shane. You can't!"

Shane dropped his foot to the ground. He turned to Melanie and grasped her shoulders. "Go home, Melanie," he said flatly. He nodded toward her cowhands. "Take your cowhands with you. They've done their job. It is appreciated. But now I need time alone. To think."

"Shane—" Melanie protested.

"Melanie, go home and get your rest," Shane said, his jaw firm. "Tomorrow is another day. You have your own responsibilities on your farm. You need the proper rest to perform them."

"Shane, I'm afraid to leave you alone," Melanie said weakly. "You're acting as though you're ready to give up. Please don't leave tonight, Shane. Please?"

"Just go home, Melanie," Shane said.

Melanie stepped back away from him, numb. She knew that she had no choice but to leave. It was obvious that no arguing with him would change his mind. She had to take the chance that once he thought all of this over very carefully, he would know that he could not give up. The battle had just begun!

She instructed her cowhands to go home and get some sleep. She took another lingering look at Shane, then rode away, carrying with her an aching heart.

Shane watched Melanie until she was out of sight. Then he walked past the fenced-in land, out to the pasture where longhorns lay dead beneath the moonlight. Some of the carcasses of the steers were as flat on the ground as if their hides had been peeled off and staked out. They had fallen or got knocked down, and hundreds of hooves had trampled over them.

He looked at the fence. He would see that a new one was erected all across his land! It would be made out of logs, not rails! It would be laid ten feet high between heavy posts sunk deep into the ground. Heavy log buttresses would brace the fence all around from the outside. It would be a pen nothing could break down!

The bawling and lowing of the longhorns that had survived the ordeal was tremendous and drew Shane's thoughts back to the present. The sad refrain of the cattle was almost an extension of the sadness he was feeling in his heart. He had so badly wanted to make his new life work! Not only for himself, but also for Melanie.

But thus far, the odds were against him.

Someone hated him too much to let any of this work!

But who?

· CHAPTER TWENTY-TWO ·

The early morning sun cast its golden light upon the land and the lone horseman riding in a slow canter through the forest.

Shane had spent a restless night, nightmares causing him to awaken in beads of cold sweat. He had awakened feeling no better about life than when he had gone to bed after the stampede. He saw all of his attempts to adapt to the white man's life as useless, and thus far anything but pleasant. He had decided that for at least this one day he would leave his white man's life behind him and pretend that he was a part of the Chippewa again. He had slipped into his fringed buckskin breeches and moccasins and was now in search of a most perfect, private place in which to pray to the Great Spirit, to ask for strength and faith in himself!

He rode endlessly onward. The farther he got from his farm, the better. Today he must not have any connections with the white man. He must clear his mind and heart to pray. He would not even allow thoughts of Melanie to disturb what he must achieve today!

Serrated silhouettes of evergreens were reflected in a lake just ahead. Shane rode to the lake and dismounted close to it, looking around, admiring the serenity. Across the way, the early light of dawn glinted off wind-bent trees in a quiet cove. He heard nothing but the quiet splash of water as it coursed its way over sprinklings of rock that jutted up out of the lake.

"Yes, this is where I will spend my day," he whispered.

Dew sprinkled Shane's moccasins as he went to the embankment and bent to rest himself on his haunches. He looked around once more, then smiled. He had found the perfect place to pray and meditate. He had not found such a place of peace since he had left Canada.

Raising his arms above his head, Shane turned his hands palm-side-up and spread his fingers. He raised his eyes to the heavens and closed them. Taking several deep breaths, he began to pray.

But his eyes were drawn quickly open again when he heard something that was disturbing his first moment of prayer. It was the rattle of traps. A trapper was approaching.

Springing to his feet, Shane ran to his horse and led it behind a thick cluster of cedar trees. After securing it so that it would not wander along after him, Shane moved stealthily from tree to tree in the direction of the sound of the traps. He had to see where the trapper was placing the traps so that he would not lead his stallion into one when he left the lake. If Shane had to part with his horse, it would be like parting with his own soul!

Seeing movement ahead, Shane sprang behind another tree and stiffened himself against it. Stealing a glance, he was now able to fully see the man. He was large and sported a thick, gray-streaked rusty beard, and was dressed in sweat-stained buckskins. Carrying several steel traps, he passed close to Shane, unaware of being watched. A break in the trees overhead allowed the morning light to spiral downward onto the man's face, fully revealing his features to Shane.

Shane's insides tightened and a strange sort of pressure, like a band being squeezed about his head, momentarily dizzied him. He knew this man! It was the eyes that made Shane recognize him. They were the same eyes that had haunted Shane since the day of his mother's death!

His heart pounding hard, Shane turned his eyes away and pressed his back up against the trunk of the tree, splaying the palms of his hands against the rough bark until it began cutting into his flesh. It took all of the restraint that he had learned from the Indians in his youth not to cry out! He gritted his teeth and closed his eyes, trying to block out the day the man with the peculiar eyes had crouched over his mother and stripped her delicate finger of her wedding band!

But it was impossible! He would never forget!

Then another thought struck him, like a bolt of lightning reaching from the sky to impale him at the pit of his stomach. Not only his mother had suffered at the hands of this evil man, but also Cedar Maid! Because of Trapper Dan, Cedar Maid too was dead!

Shane's hand crept slowly to his sheathed knife. Slipping it free, he turned to wait for Trapper Dan to get close enough to attack. The trapper would die slowly from his wounds. He would lie in the forest, bleeding to death, prey to any animal that would come sniffing, searching for food. Instead of the trapper ensnaring an innocent animal in his trap's steel teeth, the trapper would experience teeth just as sharp—the animal's!

Shane's eyes wavered and his heart skipped a beat when, after turning to watch the trapper again, he discovered someone else walking close to the tree he lurked behind. He hadn't seen her before. Leading a horse that had more traps secured on it, she must have been lagging behind, only now catching up with her companion, the trapper.

Blinking his eyes, unable to believe what he was seeing, Shane lowered his knife to his side and looked more intently at the Indian woman. He did not recognize her, yet he knew that he wouldn't. This trapper who was responsible for one Indian woman's death would not return to the same village for another. He had surely gone to a village far from Gray Falcon's!

As Trapper Dan and his woman came closer, Shane moved stealthily from the tree for a greater cover behind some flowering bushes. Spreading the leaves and flowers aside, he looked up at the woman as she passed only a few feet away from him. She was beautiful. She was young. And she did not seem all that unhappy to be with the trapper! She did not walk with her eyes downcast, as one who was sad. She looked straight ahead, a softness in her dark eyes. If Shane killed the trapper, what would she do? She would be a witness to his crime.

Shaking his head, Shane settled down onto the ground and buried his face in his hands. What should he do? The man he hated with every fiber of his being was only footsteps away, setting traps in the forest not a day's ride away from his farm. He should be able to take his revenge. But he could not. Because of the Indian woman, he could not.

Trapper Dan and the Indian woman had gone past him, and Shane began quietly following along behind them. He had to see where the trapper lived. He could plan his revenge later!

One by one the traps were set, until there were no more on the horse. Shane held his breath as the trapper swung himself up into his saddle, then reached and pulled the Indian woman up behind him. They rode away slowly, giving Shane the opportunity to continue following them on foot. When he spied a cabin up ahead in the forest, he jumped back behind a tree and waited for the trapper and his woman to go inside.

Breathless moments passed while Trapper Dan watered down his horse and gave it a bunch of hay to munch on. But finally both he and the woman were inside the cabin.

Shane crept to a window and looked in furtively. Everything seemed so normal. Trapper Dan lit a fire on the hearth. The woman set a pot of water into the flames. Then she turned to Trapper Dan. Shane watched guardedly as the woman slipped the trapper's buckskin shirt over his head, then kneeled to remove his boots. Shane's eyes narrowed as he saw the woman pull the trapper's breeches down, to reveal a large erection.

Hating the trapper even more fiercely, Shane witnessed the lust in his eyes as the woman stepped out of her buckskin dress, revealing a shapely bronze body with lovely breasts, a tapering waist, and a triangular bush of raven hair at the juncture of her thighs.

A bitterness rose into Shane's throat when he saw the Indian woman climb onto a bed, obedient to the white man. He momentarily turned his eyes away when Trapper Dan plunged himself inside her and began thrusting wildly, his grunts and groans reaching Shane's ears through the crude walls of the cabin.

He listened for any sign of the woman being uncomfortable, hoping that would give him a reason to believe that she would welcome rescue.

But he heard none. Perhaps she was even enjoying being with the trapper.

Perhaps she loved him . . . .

"How could she?" Shane asked himself. He jerked away from the window. It took all the willpower that he could muster not to go inside the cabin anyway, to get his revenge now! He had waited twenty-five years! How could he pass up the opportunity?

But he did not want to take the chance of hurting the woman.

It would come later, he told himself. He moved stealthily away from the cabin, entering the shadows of the forest again. For now, he must get away from there.

Seeing the Indian woman had brought back too many memories. Shane wasn't ready to return to the stiff, white house in which he now resided. He longed for his wigwam, the life that he had once known when, at the rising sun, he knew what the day would have in store for him. Indians did everything with a pattern, a plan. The white man's life had nothing in order. And he still did not know who was trying to make life even more difficult for him at the farm. Should he allow them to succeed at running him off?

For now, he wanted to be at peace with himself and nature. He needed time to contemplate this latest discovery. He had much in his life to sort out.

Avoiding all the traps that had been set in the forest, Shane went back to the lake where he had originally planned to pray and meditate. He jerked his horse's reins free and swung himself up into his saddle. He couldn't stay there. He had to move on.

He had to put many miles between himself and the trapper.

Shane rode with abandon for some time, until the pines began to cast long shadows all around him. He rode away from the forest and across a meadow where dew was already capturing reflections of the evening sky. The air was cooling. It was time to stop and build a fire.

Choosing an isolated spot beside a river that snaked its way down from a mist-mantled foothill, Shane dismounted. After building a campfire and a makeshift lean-to, he took his saddlebag from his horse and settled down on a blanket beside the fire.

Smiling, he reached inside the saddlebag and withdrew a cigar, his deck of playing cards, and a silver flask of whiskey.

He lit the cigar and dealt out two hands of poker, then opened the flask of whiskey. He removed his cigar from his mouth long enough to take a quick drink of whiskey, then held the silver flask up before him.

"Here's to you, old chief," he murmured, pretending his old friend was there beside him.

Melanie sat before the fire in her parlor, trying to concentrate on her embroidery work. But it was hard. She had only a short while ago gone to Shane's farm to see how he was faring after the stampede and had discovered him gone. The same fear that he was going to escape back to his other way of life had stabbed at her heart, but she had to have more faith in him than that. She would give him time before she panicked. He would come to terms with himself. He was not the sort to run away from a fight.

But she had looked around the farm and understood why a man would throw his hands up in the air and walk away. All of Shane's cowhands were gone. The longhorns that had been killed during the stampede still lay across the land. Josh still wasn't there, to make things right.

She had promptly gone to work with a small crew of men, doing what she could. When Terrance had showed up, looking for her, she had put him to work, even though he grumbled all the while he burned the stiff longhorn carcasses. When Shane returned home, he would find everything in place, as though he had a whole crew of men seeing after his farm.

"I certainly hope you're pleased with yourself," Terrance grumbled, lumbering into the room. He went to the sideboard and poured himself a glass of whiskey. "I'm plumb tuckered out from that work you forced me into at Shane's. Damn it, Sis, why should we be doing his chores? We've enough of our own to keep us busy from sunup to sunset."

"You haven't got one ounce of pity in you for that man, do you?" Melanie asked, giving Terrance a flash of fiery eyes. "What if you were in his shoes, Terrance? It's just a twist of fate that he's where he is in life. He's a wonderful, very likeable man. If you'd give him half a chance, you'd see that too."

"What if he isn't back tomorrow, Melanie?" Terrance asked, moving to stand over her. He leaned down, close to her face. "I'm not going to Shane's again and do what he should be doing himself. If you ask me, he's run off like a scared puppy with his tail tucked beneath his hind legs."

Melanie challenged his steady stare, laying her embroidery work on the table beside her. "You'd like that, wouldn't you?" she said. "Behind my back, where I can't see you snickering, I bet you're laughing over all of Shane's misfortunes."

She placed a hand to Terrance's chest and shoved him away from her, then rose to her feet. "Well, go ahead and laugh," she said. "Shane will be back. He'll make things work."

Terrance followed her out into the foyer. He grabbed his hat from a chair, where he had absently tossed it. "You can waste all the time you want to worrying about that man," he said. "But I've better things to do."

Melanie spun around to face him. "Now let me see," she mocked. "Just where are you off to? It wouldn't be a saloon, would it?"

Terrance plopped his hat on his head and, laughing, left the house. Melanie sighed heavily and began climbing the stairs to her room. Suddenly she felt drained, empty, and so very much alone.

Where was Shane?

Didn't he know that she would be worried? Did he care so little about her state of mind?

Then she felt guilty, knowing that he was the

only one who mattered. He had the battles to fight. Her only battle was for him!

As Melanie reached the upstairs landing, a sudden shudder swept through her. She stopped and looked from side to side. Somehow, she did not feel alone. There was a sense of foreboding in the air all around her.

But why? She and Terrance had been home long enough to bathe, eat and relax before the fire.

But when they were gone earlier, had someone gotten into the house? Was he hiding there now?

Her eyes brightened. "Shane?" she whispered, taking hasty steps toward her bedroom. Had he been here all along, waiting for Terrance to leave?

Melanie hurried into her bedroom and searched with her hand for her kerosene lamp beside her bed so that she could light it.

But as she searched through the darkness, a hand suddenly gripped her wrist painfully, then jerked her hard onto the bed.

"Shane?" Melanie asked, her voice quavering.

She peered upward through the darkness and made out a man's shadow. The man's hand tightened around her wrist. His body pinioned her against the bed.

"Shane, you're hurting me!" she cried. "You've never been rough before. Why are you now?"

"Bee-sahn-ee-I-yah-mah-gud! Silence!" a voice said threateningly in Chippewa.

Melanie gasped. This was not Shane! It was an Indian! He had obviously waited for her to be alone.

But why? Did he plan to rape, kill, or abduct her?

Could it possibly be Shane's enemy, Chief Gray Falcon?

Scarcely breathing, Melanie awaited her fate, for she could not move with the Indian pressing so hard down upon her.

· CHAPTER TWENTY-THREE ·

It pained her where the Indian held Melanie's wrist clamped to the bed. His body, stretched atop hers, was beginning to feel like lead. His breath was hot on her face, as though tongues of flames darted out at her from a fireplace. His hand, now held tightly against her mouth, kept her from crying out. Why was he keeping her immobile for so long? The passing moments felt like hours!

She wanted to cry out, to alert the servants!

Her eyes widened. The servants! That's why the Indian was not taking her away just yet. He was waiting for the house to become quiet, for all of the servants to go to bed, so that he could steal her away without anyone's seeing or hearing him. No one had heard the earlier struggle, for the Indian had been swift and silent.

Breathing hard, Melanie's gaze went to the window. If the Indian waited long enough, Terrance would arrive back home!

But her hopes quickly waned, for she could be almost sure of Terrance's condition when he did return. He would be stinking drunk and would not notice anything awry—not until morning, and that would be too late!

Suddenly the Indian was all movement. He had acquired a buckskin gag from somewhere and secured it around Melanie's mouth. Then he was grabbing her up into his arms!

Melanie fought the Indian as he held her tightly within his steel grip. She pummeled her fists against his bare chest. She kicked. She tried to cry out through the foul-tasting fabric tied around her mouth. When she tried to reach for it, he knocked her hand away.

Then, just as the Indian began walking hastily toward the door, Melanie made a lunge and grabbed at a bead necklace that hung around his neck and tore it away from his body. Beads sprayed in all directions—too many to stop and try to gather them up!

Melanie smiled smugly up at the Indian as he uttered several Chippewa phrases barely beneath his breath. When Terrance discovered her gone, he would at least know an Indian had done the ghastly deed. And when Terrance went to Shane and told him of the abduction, Shane would guess which Indian was responsible. Shane would rescue her! She knew that he would!

She winced with pain as the Indian's lean,

strong fingers dug into her body and carried her from her room. The light from the wall sconces in the corridor was dim, but the candles reflected enough golden light to enable Melanie to finally get a look at her captor as he stole quietly toward the staircase.

She looked first at his face.

Painted with frightening black zigzag lines across his nose and cheeks, the face beneath the paint was of a dark copper tone. His cheekbones were high and sculpted, his eyes were midnight black. His black, coarse hair was drawn back from his brow with a beaded headband.

Pressed hard against his bare chest, Melanie could manage only a slight movement to her head downward to see what he wore. Her eyes widened over her gag. He wore only a scant loincloth! Beneath the soft fabric she could see the identifiable outline of his manhood.

Knowing now how quickly he could rape her once he had her out in the wilderness, Melanie again began desperately fighting him. But it was all in vain. He did not seem even aware of her fists pounding against his bare flesh, or of her wildly kicking legs. He had come to abduct her, and it seemed that nothing was going to stop him!

The house was left behind and Melanie watched with wild eyes as the Indian ran with her through the dark until just ahead, a pearl-white horse shone in the darkness like a great white ghost. Melanie groaned as the Indian sat her roughly onto a saddle of blankets, then mounted behind her and held onto her as he rode away, toward the butte in the distance.

Melanie cast a pleading stare over her shoulder at Shane's house that sat dark in the distance. Was he home yet? Was he sleeping soundly on his pallet of furs in his bedroom? Oh, if only he were! If only she were there with him! If what was happening to her were only a nightmare and she would awaken soon in her lover's arms!

The campfire was burning low. Cards lay upturned on the ground beside the empty silver flask. Shane was snuggled between blankets, sleep having finally claimed him. Suddenly his body twitched and he moaned aloud. In a dream, he was hearing Melanie crying out to him. He could see her outstretched arms, beckoning to him. She wore a sheer, white garment that billowed around her as she moved farther away from Shane, looking as though she were being carried by the wind.

Shane broke out in a cold sweat as, in his dream, he tried to run after Melanie to save her, but found it impossible to run. His legs seemed frozen to the ground. He screamed her name. Over and over again he screamed her name.

"Melanie!" Shane cried, this time out loud, awakening himself from the fretful nightmare. His heart was thundering inside him. He jerked himself up into a sitting position, his eyes wild as he looked frantically around him. The dream had seemed so real! It was as though Melanie had been there, crying out for him!

Shane inhaled a nervous breath, then sighed. He raked his fingers through his golden hair, straightening it back from his eyes. He looked up into the heavens that were just lightening with the promise of a new day.

"I must return home," he said, rising quickly to his feet. "But I must go to Melanie first. Perhaps my dream was an omen! What if something has happened to her?"

He grabbed his cards and silver flask up from the ground and thrust them inside his saddle bag along with his blankets. As he secured these to his horse, his thoughts went to Trapper Dan. In time, he would finally avenge his mother's and Cedar Maid's deaths.

But for now, Melanie was his main concern.

Mounting his horse, Shane bent low over its mane and rode away at a brisk gallop.

Terrance awakened with a throbbing headache. Groaning, he lifted one leg from his bed, and then the other. He hadn't thought to close his drapes after arriving home after midnight, and the sun now poured in through the windows, making Terrance teeter with the shock of the brightness entering his bloodshot eyes.

Cursing beneath his breath, he struggled into his clothes, then his boots, almost toppling over when he found it hard to balance himself.

Fully clothed, he lumbered to a peg on the wall and yanked his gunbelt down and fastened it around his waist, the pistols heavy at each hip. Last night, when he had arrived home, he had been met by several of his cowhands. They had been out searching for Wild Thunder. The bull had kicked a portion of the fence in and had escaped. Terrance was determined to hunt the bull down himself, and this time he would put a bullet through its heart. The bull had been nothing but trouble, almost human in its obvious hatred for Terrance!

"I'll show him this time," Terrance grumbled, fidgeting with the doorknob, then jerking the door open when he finally got a firm grip. "The whip hasn't been enough to show that damn bull who's the boss around here. A bullet is the sort of medicine he needs."

Sauntering from his bedroom, he saw that Melanie's door was ajar. An eyebrow raised inquisitively when he saw something on the floor just inside the door. Going into her room, he bent to one knee and started picking up colored beads. Then he looked toward her bed and saw the distinct signs of a struggle in the rumpled sheets.

His heart grew cold, again studying the beads. Then he found a piece of thin leather, the sort that Indians used in stringing their necklaces.

Growing ashen, Terrance thrust the beads and thin leather into his pocket. He ran from Melanie's room and went through the house questioning the servants. None had seen Melanie since the last evening. Her personal maid had wondered why she hadn't slept in her bed, or why it was so unkept. She even commented on having seen Indian beads scattered across the floor.

The sound of a horse approaching drew

Terrance's attention. He rushed to a window and looked out and saw that it was Shane. Anger flared in his eyes. Cold hate caused the features of his face to become distorted. If anything happened to Melanie, it was all Shane's fault. The presence of Indian beads in Melanie's bedroom pointed to only one thing—that Chief Gray Falcon had decided to take out his hatred for Shane on Melanie!

Blinded with rage, Terrance broke into a run and jerked the front door open. Grabbing a pistol from his holster, he ran down the steps and fired it wildly at Shane as he was dismounting close to the porch.

"It's your fault!" Terrance screamed, tears streaming down his face. Out of bullets, he threw the pistol at Shane, who dodged it easily. Terrance fell to his knees on the ground, sobbing and hitting his doubled fists into the earth. "Damn you, Shane. Damn you all to hell."

Stunned by this strange sort of greeting, Shane looked down at Terrance for a moment, then saw more in Terrance's attitude than mere hate for himself. A coldness soared through him. Melanie. The dream. Something had surely happened to her!

Shane went to Terrance and drew him roughly to his feet. "What has happened?" he asked, his pulse racing.

Terrance struggled to get free. He raised a fist and attempted to hit Shane, but Shane was too fast and grabbed the fist in mid-air.

"Where's Melanie?" Shane growled, looking toward the house, then back at Terrance.

"She's gone," Terrance sobbed, wiping his nose with the back of a hand. He jerked away from Shane and slipped his hand inside his pocket and withdrew a handful of Indian beads. "I found these in her room. There must have been a struggle. It was surely Chief Gray Falcon."

Shane turned quickly and mounted his horse in one leap and began to ride away.

"I want to go with you!" Terrance shouted, running after Shane.

Shane looked over his shoulder at Terrance. "You are not capable of watching over your sister when she is in your house!" he shouted. "You are surely not capable of fighting for her in an Indian village! Worthless man, drown your worries in whiskey again! That's all you're good for!"

Terrance teetered to a stop and wiped his mouth with the back of a hand, Shane's words stabbing him like a knife into his gut. Downhearted, he turned and walked slowly back to the house and up to his room. He threw himself across his bed and cried until he fell into a fitful sleep.

Melanie blinked her eyes nervously. She had not allowed herself to go to sleep while traveling on the horse with the Indian, and now she was limp with exhaustion. Every bone in her body ached from being held so tightly against the Indian for so many hours.

Dawn's glow was seeping through the night fog. If Chief Gray Falcon was her abductor, his village should be reached soon. Shane had said that the Chippewa village was not even a sleep away from their farms, which in the white man's terms meant that traveling by horseback it would not be a full day and night away. Her abductor had traveled without stopping—not for a drink, not to stretch, not for anything.

She looked over her shoulder and gave the Indian an angry scowl. The only decent thing he had done for her was to remove the damnable gag after they had traveled far into the forest. The buckskin cloth had tasted so vile that even now she could taste it on her lips!

"*O-nee-shee-shin gee-gee-shayb,*" Gray Falcon said, looking down at Melanie as he caught her glaring at him. "Soon we reach my village. You will be fed and then you can rest." He smiled. "You are stubborn, woman. You should have slept instead of forcing yourself to stay awake."

Melanie's eyes widened in disbelief. This was the first time the Indian had spoken to her since the one brief moment when she had discovered him in her bedroom. To her amazement, he spoke English. And he did not seem at all threatening. His tone was gentle.

"Who are you and why did you do this to me?" she asked in a rush of words.

Gray Falcon ignored her, not liking any woman making demands on him. Especially not Shane's woman. After watching Shane's house for many days and nights and seeing Shane with this woman so often, he felt no doubt that she was his woman!

To satisfy his lust to avenge Shane's having stolen from him, Gray Falcon had stolen something of more value to Shane than horses and pelts!

When Shane discovered Melanie missing, he would see that Gray Falcon was the more clever of the two. He would come for his woman and this did not matter to Gray Falcon. The pleasure would be in watching Shane humbling himself to come and speak for her! He would not enter the village with fighting on his mind. Shane loved the Chippewa people too much.

No. When Shane came, it would be in peace. It would be in full humility. Gray Falcon would be the victor!

Melanie sighed. "I see that you are not going to answer me," she said sullenly. "So I will let you know that I have already come to my own conclusions. You're Chief Gray Falcon, aren't you? You've done this because Shane stole horses and pelts from you. But I can't fathom what your plans are for me. Shane would surely kill you should you harm me."

When Gray Falcon's eyes narrowed and grew dark with some hidden, secret emotion, Melanie winced. Chills coursed through her. His gaze was so cutting! "That's why you abducted me, isn't it?" she gasped. "To draw Shane to your village so that you can kill him?"

Again Melanie tried to escape his iron grip. She squirmed and wrestled, but lack of sleep, made her too weak to continue the struggle. She breathed hard and slumped over the arm that held onto her around her waist.

"I'm too tired," she moaned. "I'm so . . . sleepy. . . ."

The struggling had drained the last bit of strength from her. No matter how hard she tried, she could not keep her eyes open any longer. The drone of the horse's hooves making a steady sound on the ground lulled her to escape her discomfort and fears by finally drifting into the welcoming black void of sleep. . . .

• CHAPTER TWENTY-FOUR •

A great clap of thunder awakened Melanie with a start. She jerked her head up and recoiled when she was abruptly reminded of her circumstances. Her heart pounding, she looked around her. She was in an Indian wigwam, and she was alone.

Her gaze lowered as she reached her hands out before her. She was not bound or gagged. Could she possibly escape? The dwelling in which she was imprisoned was dark except for the soft, dancing glow of a fire in a firespace.

"It must be night," she murmured. "I slept all day!"

Her knees weak with fear, Melanie rose to her feet and moved quietly to the closed entrance flap. She reached her trembling fingers to the flap and slowly lifted it, then froze with fear when she discovered a hefty brave standing with his back to the wigwam, guarding it.

She looked past the brave. Tiny fires were scattered everywhere in the Indian village, throwing weird shadows among the domed bark houses. The odor of meat cooking from somewhere close by came to Melanie with a change in the wind, causing her stomach to growl painfully.

She looked around, assessing her chances of eventual escape. Men and women milled about outside their houses, dogs barked, and children played. A pang of loneliness for Shane stung Melanie's heart. He probably knew all of these people. He had once been a child who played among them. He had grown up knowing them all and sharing their customs.

Knowing these things, Melanie could not find it in her heart to hate these people in whose village she was being held captive. There was only one Indian to blame—Chief Gray Falcon!

"But where is he?" she whispered. "Why has he left me alone?"

Drunken laughter drew Melanie's attention to a group of men sitting around a larger outdoor fire. She peered intensely at them, stiffening when she recognized that a white man sat among them. It was surely a trapper. Great piles of furs were spread out on the ground, being admired by several Indians.

A bitter hate grabbed at her insides as she sorted out Chief Gray Falcon from among the men. Then she was again seized with fear, for the chief was tipping a large jug to his lips. He was drinking whiskey!

"Oh, Lord, what if he gets drunk?" Melanie whispered, placing a hand to her throat. "What will he do with me then?"

She looked up. The sky was pitch black, brightening erratically with great bursts of lightning. Another vicious streak of lightning in the heavens and an ensuing burst of thunder, shaking the matted floor beneath Melanie's feet, made her drop the entrance flap as though she had been shot.

Dispirited, she went to the fire and settled down on a bear pelt before it, her gaze moved slowly around the wigwam. The roof was sloped both ways from the peak where a smoke hole gaped open, and there were posts set into the ground to hold the roof solid. Cords of skins were strung between these posts and were weighed down by all manner of skins and weapons and baskets of woven grass. Along the walls were piles of skins.

An empty kettle was suspended over the fire from a tripod; a high rack stood near the door with uncooked meat draped over it.

Cedar boughs were spread on the ground and covered with rush mats, and great bear pelts hung on a far wall, under which lay more pelts rolled up, perhaps used as bedding. Many highly-colored parfleche bags, in which she thought the chief's personal possessions must be stored, lay about the outer walls of the dwelling, and impressive bows and pouches of arrows lay close to the fire, not far from where Melanie sat.

Her gaze stopped at the weapons.

Should she . . . ?

But that thought was quickly cast aside, for suddenly she was no longer alone. She turned her head with a jerk and watched Chief Gray Falcon enter the dwelling, teetering. Melanie's jaws tightened, recognizing the signs of drunkenness. She had witnessed it often enough in her brother!

Afraid, she began scooting backward as Gray Falcon went and stood over the fire. His dark eyes branded Melanie as he stared down at her, then his gaze was drawn elsewhere when a beautiful young squaw came into the wigwam, carrying water in a wooden basin.

Melanie surmised that this was Blue Blossom, of whom Shane had made mention while relaying his story to her about stealing the pelts from Gray Falcon's wigwam.

Melanie slipped farther back into the darker shadows of the wigwam, then stopped when she could go no farther. She leaned her back stiffly against a pile of bear pelts, watching the squaw begin to attentively bathe her chief. First she bathed the paint from his face, then moved the cloth to his massive copper chest.

Melanie scarcely breathed as she watched the squaw place her cloth into the water and then remove the chief's loincloth and moccasins, leaving him totally naked. Chief Gray Falcon's dark, penetrating eyes burned into hers as he watched her with a sort of amused interest, a mocking smile lifting the corner of his lips.

Embarrassed, stunned, and frightened, Melanie turned her eyes away, knowing now that the chief was being readied for a seduction.

Her own!

Her gaze went to the bows and arrows again. But she knew that she did not have a chance in hell of getting to use them. She could still feel the chief's eyes on her, watching.

A great flash of lightning showed through the smoke hole overhead and the ensuing burst of thunder made Melanie grab herself with her arms. She hugged herself, trembling, then looked slowly around when she heard the rustle of feet close beside her. It was Blue Blossom. She was changing the position of the smoke hole opening, for it had just begun to rain in torrents outside.

Her chore finished, Blue Blossom knelt down beside Melanie. She touched her face softly. "Do not be afraid," she whispered. "Nothing is going to happen to you. My chief is now going to get needed rest. He drank too much of the white man's firewater. I soon will bring you food to eat. Then you can rest again also."

Grasping this sudden chance at friendship, Melanie moved closer to Blue Blossom. "You speak English so well," she whispered, ignoring Gray Falcon's continued stare. "You do know Shane, don't you?"

"Yes," Blue Blossom said softly, lowering her hand to her lap. "We in this village all know and love Shane. And you do, also. I know why you are here. Is Shane well?"

"Very, but I am sure that by now he knows that I have been abducted and is very angry," Melanie whispered harshly.

"I know," Blue Blossom murmured, moving back to her feet. "I must ready my chief for his sleep."

The instant friendship gave Melanie a measure of hope, yet she knew that she must not expect anything from this woman who was being so attentive to her chief. She would most definitely not help Melanie escape!

She scooted back against the pelts again and observed the rest of the ritual being acted out before her eyes. She watched Blue Blossom spread some sort of oil over Gray Falcon's body, then wrap thick pelts around him. Next she spread a great heap of furs on the floor beside the fire and gently helped him down atop them.

After Blue Blossom spread another fur over him, she stepped out into the rain, but returned shortly, soaked, carrying a tray of food that she had protected from the rain by a covering of buckskin.

"Eat," Blue Blossom said to Melanie. She uncovered the food, displaying a mixture of boiled rabbit, baked fish, and fruit. "I must sleep beside my chief to keep him content."

Melanie nodded, stunned by Blue Blossom's sweet, generous nature. She plucked a piece of fish from the wooden tray and began eating it ravenously. Her gaze watched Blue Blossom's every movement, not at all surprised when she unashamedly undressed and dried her slim body off in front of her. Melanie was in awe of Blue Blossom, in how she so dutifully crept beneath the furs, to then mold her body against Gray Falcon's.

Melanie continued to watch and eat, then soon realized that both Chief Gray Falcon and Blue Blossom were sound asleep. Would this be the time to escape? Was the brave still guarding the wigwam, even though it was raining?

Shoving the food tray aside, Melanie crawled past the two sleeping figures. Rain splashed onto her face and into her eyes as she lifted the entrance flap. Wiping the rain from her eyes, she found that the brave was still standing there.

But she smiled smugly when she saw him look up into the sky, then jolt with alarm when another zigzag of lightning forked its way overhead, then straight down into the earth not far from the village. Surely he would give up his post soon and seek a drier, safer shelter! She would keep an eye on him.

But for now, the food was too tempting. Her stomach still gnawed with hunger. She crawled back to the food platter and began to eat an apple.

Unaware of being soaked to the bone or of the lightning popping and cracking all around him, Shane crept through the rain toward the Chippewa village. When he was only a few feet away he stopped and lunged behind a tree, having seen a brave standing guard outside Gray Falcon's wigwam.

Shane's jaw tightened and his eyes became two points of fire. The presence of a brave standing guard outside the chief's wigwam was proof that something unusual had happened.

"She's there," Shane whispered, doubling a hand into a tight fist.

He hugged himself and hunched over in the rain. It was now falling so hard it was as though pellets were hitting his body. He looked at the brave again, knowing that he could be no less uncomfortable. If luck was with him, the brave would seek shelter—at least for a while!

A smile lifted Shane's lips. He was right. The brave glanced nervously over his shoulder at the Chief's dwelling, and then in the direction of his own wigwam. In a matter of minutes he was fleeing toward it.

Shane stepped cautiously from behind the tree and made sure the brave went into his wigwam. When he did, Shane broke into a run until he was behind Gray Falcon's dwelling. Drawing his knife from its sheath, he inched his way around to the front, then leaned his ear to the entrance flap, listening. There was no sound except for Gray Falcon's snores.

Again Shane smiled. He recalled when Gray Falcon was a youth and had spent evenings in the forest with his friends, Shane among them. Gray Falcon had always kept everyone awake by his snoring. It seemed that he had not grown out of that habit—as he had not grown out of his jealousy of Shane!

"If he so much as touched Melanie, I shall slit his throat!" Shane told himself, his fingers clamped so hard around the handle of the knife his knuckles were white.

Anxious to see if Melanie was there, Shane slowly shoved the entrance flap aside and stepped into the wigwam. His eyes widened and his heart melted when he saw Melanie stretched out asleep on one side of the fire on a layer of mats, while Gray Falcon and Blue Blossom slept on the other. Gray Falcon had not harmed Melanie and it was obvious that he had no intention of doing so. He still slept with Blue Blossom.

Feeling much calmer, Shane went to Melanie and knelt down over her. He looked at her for a moment before awakening her, at this moment understanding just how much he loved her. It was a love that knew no limit to its endurance, no end to its trust. This sort of love would still stand, when all else had fallen. Shane would be half a man without her. He understood at this moment that he was ready and happy to place all of his past behind him for her sake.

Reaching a hand to Melanie's hair, he stroked his long, lean fingers through it. When she awakened and looked up at him, no words were spoken, nor were they needed. Her happiness was in her eyes, and in her smile. She moved into his arms and hugged him tightly.

Shane looked at Gray Falcon and did not hate him as much at this moment as he had thought he would when gazing upon the man who had stolen his woman!

Yet Shane had to let Gray Falcon know that he

had been here! That Shane was the one who had taken Melanie away from him!

When Shane saw Gray Falcon's hand lying at his side, palm side up, an idea struck him. There was one sure way that Gray Falcon would know that it was Shane! And it was the best proof of all, because it would say more than that! Gray Falcon would see proof of Shane's having given up all claim to a part of the Chippewa world! Shane would leave that which was most sacred to all Indians—the long locks of his hair! When he parted with his hair, he would be saying a final farewell not only to Gray Falcon, but to the old chief and his old life.

Shane slipped slowly away from Melanie. He stared down at his knife and his heart pounded, for since he had been a part of the Indian culture, he had learned to take pride in the length of his hair. It meant strength to the Indians. It was a cause for great pride.

Melanie paled as she looked from the knife to Shane. She started to reach for the hand that held the knife, to stop whatever he was considering, but she was too late. While he gritted his teeth and his eyes showed a strange sort of torment, he began cutting his hair.

Placing a hand over her mouth to muffle a gasp, Melanie watched until Shane had his hair cut clear around, from one side to the other, until its length was that which would lie just above the collar line of a shirt when he wore one.

Tears streamed down her face as Shane took the locks of hair and placed them gently in Gray

Falcon's outstretched hand. She did not know the meaning of the gesture, but she could tell that this ceremony Shane had chosen to do was very important to him. He hesitated before backing away from Gray Falcon, reaching a hand back to the hair, as though he was almost reconsidering leaving the hair.

Then Shane turned his eyes to Melanie. He went to her and placed a bear pelt around her shoulders and over her head and led her out into the rain. Lifting her up into his arms, he ran with her from the village. The rain was blinding in its force and cold in its sting, but he carried her through it to the forest and his horse. Placing her in the saddle, he mounted behind her and they rode off into the darkness.

Lightning continued to tear the heavens apart with its white heat. Thunder echoed through the forest. When lightning hit a tree and split it in half just ahead, and it fell with a loud thud in the stallion's path, the horse reared and whinnied, throwing Melanie and Shane to the ground.

Melanie cried out with pain, grasping hard onto consciousness. She reached for Shane, who lay too still in the mud.

Slowly her hand dropped to the ground and she too drifted into the black void of unconsciousness.

· CHAPTER TWENTY-FIVE ·

There was now only distant, muffled thunder. The air was sweet with after-rain; the leaves of the trees were heavy with crystal droplets. Melanie awakened slowly to a sense of something warm stroking her cheek.

As she became more aware, she felt strong arms encompassing her. In flashes, the last moments before unconsciousness claimed her came to her. The flight from the Indian village. The pounding rain. The terrible thunder. The lightning! The horse rearing, tossing her and Shane from the saddle!

"Shane!" she gasped, tensing her body. She sighed heavily and relaxed when she looked up into the crystal blue eyes gazing lovingly down at her. She snuggled more closely into his embrace. "You're all right. God, you're all right."

"And you?" Shane asked, weaving his fingers through the wet tendrils of her hair.

"Just a bit achy," Melanie said, shivering as the damp night air reminded her that her clothes were wet and clinging. "I'm mainly cold."

She looked around her. Thank goodness the rain had stopped. Shane's handsome stallion was calm now, resting beneath a tree, nibbling the wet grass. Then she became aware of a strange sort of roof over her and questioned Shane with her eyes.

"This is a lean-to," Shane said, smiling his understanding down at her. "I built it quickly, to get you out of the rain."

"How long was I unconscious?" Melanie asked, easing away from Shane. She stretched her arms over her head, then smoothed a hand across both of her ankles. Despite the aching, she seemed to be in one piece. "How long were you?"

"Not long," Shane said. "The fall just stunned us."

He cupped her face between his hands and leaned closer. "Now that you are awake and I know that you are going to be all right, I would like to leave you long enough to build us a fire to ward off the night chill," he said. "We will stay long enough for you to get warmed, and then we must get you back to your home."

"Yes, Terrance will be sending out a posse for me, I'm sure," Melanie said, frowning. "If he even realizes I am missing. He stays drunk for the most part nowadays." She drew her knees up before her and hugged them to her chest with her arms. "I so fear for him, Shane. No good can come from his habitual drinking."

"No, none," Shane agreed, rising to his feet. He was recalling Terrance carelessly firing at him, but he would not worry Melanie about it. She had been through enough tonight. "I will build that fire now."

"Shane, thank you," Melanie said. "Thank you for everything. Had you not come . . ."

Shane looked down at her. "But you knew that I would," he said, reassuringly. "And I did."

Melanie gestured with a hand toward his hair. "Your hair," she said, swallowing hard. "Shane, you cut it. Why? I know how proud you were of your hair or you would have cut it earlier."

"It had to be done for many reasons," Shane said flatly. "To Gray Falcon, many things will be made clear when he awakens and finds my locks of hair." He smiled suddenly. "I only wish I could be there to see his reaction!"

Laughing softly, Shane turned and began a search for dry wood, finding enough for a small fire beneath thick layers of leaves that hugged the trunks of the trees, and beneath outcroppings of rock at the foot of the butte under which the lean-to had been built.

Soon a fire was burning warmly. Melanie moved closer to it, letting the heat envelope her body.

"Remove your clothes," Shane said, slipping first his moccasins off, and then his fringed breeches. He stood naked over Melanie, reaching for her hand. "You must get your clothes dry before we continue our journey homeward."

Melanie nodded. She rose to her feet and trembled inside as she slipped off first one garment, and then another. She hugged herself as she watched Shane carefully hang her clothes on the ends of the lean-to, so that they hung low over the fire. Then Shane went to his horse and removed two blankets from his saddlebag. When he returned, he placed one of the blankets around her shoulders, and one around his own.

Enjoying the warmth of the blanket, Melanie followed Shane's lead and sat down beside the fire again. The fire cast shadows onto his handsome profile and into his blue eyes, turning them golden. Just looking at him could steal her breath away. Just his touch would melt her insides!

But there was something amiss about him tonight that made her keep her distance. Though he had achieved a major goal, he still did not seem content. She had to believe that it was because of the ritual he had performed with his hair.

Or was it because he was tormented anew by having been in the Chippewa village and not being able to stay, to greet his friends? Would he forever be tormented because of having been sent from the village so unjustly?

"He did not harm you in any way, did he?"

Shane's sudden question, his eyes now on her, fixed and angry, made Melanie flinch. Then her insides mellowed when he placed a hand at her nape and began caressing her there with his fingers.

"No, he didn't harm me," she said, leaning into his hand. "But when he began drinking heavily, I became afraid. I expected him to rape me at any moment."

"I doubt that he would have," Shane said, looking away from her, into the fire. He was recalling his youth, when young girls from other tribes had openly pursued Gray Falcon because he was next in line to be chief and they wanted to share in such a noble life. Gray Falcon could have had them all, but did not. Though plagued by ugly jealousy, he was a man of morals. He had made his choice of woman now, and she apparently had joined with him willingly.

An involuntary shiver raced across Melanie's flesh when she recalled the moments alone in her bedroom with Gray Falcon. It would have been so easy for him then to assault her. He had held her pinioned to the bed for what seemed hours!

But he hadn't.

"No, I don't think he would have, either," she said in a rush. "His main concern was you, Shane. He abducted me only to prove to you that he could."

Letting her blanket flutter down from her shoulders, to drape loosely about her arms, Melanie moved to her knees before Shane. She looked at him, her eyes filled with questioning. "Shane, where were you all day yesterday?" she asked.

Shane's gaze moved over Melanie. In the soft light of the fire, in the wide innocence of her eyes as she gazed intensely up at him, she looked so vulnerable—yet so ravishingly beautiful. Her hair picked up the flame of the fire in its folds, highlighting it in soft reds as it spilled over her creamy shoulders and down her back. The upper curves of her breasts were bare, tempting his lips to touch them.

Melanie's insides were growing hot with passion as Shane gazed down at her. His eyes branded her. His dark, finely chiseled face was taut with emotion.

Something compelled her to reach her hands to his blanket, to slowly lower it from his shoulders. When it dropped away and settled in a heap on the ground, his muscles stirred down the length of his tanned body as he, in turn, reached and took her blanket away from her.

At this moment she desired no answers from him.

She desired only him.

Drifting toward Shane, Melanie's heart pounded. She knew that what she had gone through today, and all yesterdays, had been worth it, if the end result was this moment alone with Shane. If there were no tomorrow, even that did not matter.

There was now. Only now.

Shane drew her into his embrace and held her tightly against him, her breasts pressed into his flesh, rendering him almost mindless. "Are you still cold?" he asked, his voice husky.

"How could I be cold?" she whispered, brushing her lips across his mouth. "Shane, your mere touch sets me afire."

Their bodies strained together hungrily as

321

Shane took her mouth by storm. His fingers ran down her body, caressing her, then clasped the softness of her buttocks. Lifting her, he guided her onto his lap.

Drugged by his kiss, Melanie slipped her legs around him and straddled him. She arched and cried out against his lips as he drove swiftly into her.

Melanie's blood quickened as Shane's thrusts propelled her into another world, a world of ecstasy. When his lips left her mouth and dipped low to flick over her hardening nipples, she held her head back and moaned with pleasure. His fingers raked lightly down her spine, over her silken hips, back around again to her buttocks.

Cupping her with his hands, he pulled her down harder against him as his strokes quickened. As his hardness filled her even more deeply, it touched that innermost part of herself that she had only recently discovered, that which knew the wonders of fulfilled longings . . .

Again Shane kissed her.

He tingled in anticipation, yet fought to go more slowly, to savor the swimming sensations that loving her always caused within him. He reverently breathed her name against her parted mouth; his lips brushed her throat.

Melanie was aware of how Shane's body suddenly hardened and tightened. She knew that his release was near. As his mouth came down over hers demandingly, his fierce, fevered kiss triggered a fire in her. She abandoned herself to the wondrous ecstasy flooding her senses. She trembled, her hands moving over the slope of his hard jaw, through the shock of his golden hair.

With quick, eager fingers, Shane cupped Melanie's breasts. As the peak he had sought was reached, he held his head back and emitted a loud cry that filled the dark void of the night.

Melanie clung to him as he shuddered violently into her. She closed her eyes, lost to everything but rapture.

Breathing hard, Shane lifted Melanie from his lap. Gently, he draped the blanket around her shoulders again. He gazed down upon her, trying to hide his torn emotions from her astute eyes. Although she had just shown again how much she loved him, and he had discovered anew how important she was to him, Shane was troubled about their future. It had disturbed him terribly to have to steal into the Indian village like an enemy. The more he thought about it, the more he resented Gray Falcon for denying him his rights.

He had cut his hair to prove something to Gray Falcon, but had the act proven anything to Shane? Could he ever truly conform to this new life he had chosen?

He wanted to—but only for Melanie.

Should he allow a woman to be that important to him? And what of her welfare? Hadn't she been drawn into Gray Falcon's vendetta against Shane? Would it be best to take her safely home, then go on his way, alone? He had brought nothing into Melanie's life but confusion.

And wasn't it time to settle this thing with Trapper Dan?

Sensing that Shane was troubled, Melanie touched his cheek in a soft caress. "Darling, please tell me what's wrong," she murmured. "Perhaps I can help. I owe you so much, Shane. Because of you—"

Shane gently covered her mouth with his hand. "You owe me nothing," he said, devouring her face with his eyes, memorizing her for all lonely nights of his future. "It is I who owe you. You have given me so much. I, in truth, have given you so little in return. Only confusion and danger!"

Melanie crept into his arms, her blanket dropping away from her. "Oh, Shane, how can you say that?" she asked softly, placing her cheek to his bare, solid chest. "You have given me a direction in my life—a true reason for my existence. Until you came, I was only half a person. Now I'm whole. I awaken each day with a song on my lips. Darling, you are that song. You are my life."

Guilt sprang forth within Shane for even thinking of abandoning her. She would never understand. She would never forgive him!

"I love you so, Melanie," he whispered, his breath hot on her ear. "Always remember that."

Melanie stiffened. She drew slowly away from him and gazed up at him questioningly. "Shane, you say that as though there is a double meaning to it," she murmured. "Why, Shane? Why?"

To change the subject, Shane once more pulled the blanket up around her shoulders. "I'm sorry if I seem distant," he apologized. He thought fast, trying to hide his true thoughts from her. "But I have something that lies heavy on my mind and heart." He glanced over at her. "You remember the trapper? The one who killed Cedar Maid? The one who stole from my mother after she was killed in the massacre?"

Melanie's insides went cold. Again she was reminded of having seen a man in St. Paul who fit the trapper's description. She had chosen not to tell Shane about the man. Had she been wrong?

"Yes, I recall the man," she said, her voice drawn.

"Melanie, I saw him yesterday," Shane said, raking his fingers through his hair.

Melanie tensed. "You did?" she said guardedly. "Where?"

Shane looked over at her, torment in his eyes. "He lives near our adjoining farms," he told her. "He sets traps for animals in the forest. He lives with an Indian woman!"

Melanie gasped. "What are you going to do?" she asked.

"I will take you home, then make plans for the trapper that will finally give my heart peace," he said, staring gloomily into space. "But I must spare the woman. She is not at fault for the evil the man has done."

Melanie could not help but think back to how she had found Cedar Maid, her brown eyes fixed in death. She shuddered at the thought, then looked slowly at Shane. "This Indian woman," she murmured. "Was she paid for also with a bride price?"

Shane nodded. "I am sure of it."

Melanie shuddered again, finding it hard to

envision any woman willingly marrying the man that she had seen. His vile stench and wild appearance had turned her stomach.

Shane crept an arm around her waist. He urged her to her feet and offered her her clothes. "It is time to travel onward," he said, again looking toward the sky. "The storm has passed. Soon the sky will be lightening with dawn."

Melanie hurried into her clothes that were still damp, but thankfully not clinging wet. A great uneasiness swept through her. She did not like Shane's mood. What did he have planned for Trapper Dan?

Why must he place himself in danger again—and again, and again?

· CHAPTER TWENTY-SIX ·

Having worried about Shane the whole night, Melanie hurried into a long-sleeved blouse, a heavy riding skirt, and a buckskin jacket. She left her house without eating breakfast and walked determinedly toward the men who were milling around outside the bunkhouse, drinking coffee.

"Boys, I think I've got to ask for volunteers again," she said. The chill morning air stung her nose and the wind lifted her hair from her shoulders, whipping it around her face. "Shane Brennan is still without cowhands. Until more are found, he needs help at his farm. Chores are going undone now. That can't continue for much longer or the whole farm is going to suffer."

A coldness seized her when she saw most of the men turn their eyes to the ground, ignoring her.

Then she understood the reason why. Terrance was suddenly there at her side, looking down at her with utter contempt.

"What the hell are you doing, sis?" Terrance said in a controlled voice.

"You don't really have to ask, do you?" Melanie said, turning to talk up into his face. "And you're darn well going to try to stop me, aren't you?"

Terrance waved a hand into the air toward the men. "All of you get to work!" he shouted. "There's been enough horsing around here the past few days to last a lifetime! What are you getting paid for? Damn it, get to work!"

Melanie stared at the men as they splashed the remainder of their coffee from their tin cups onto the ground and walked away, grumbling beneath their breaths.

She then turned and stared angrily up at Terrance. "Why do you have to be so—so mean?" she asked incredulously. "Terrance, you know as well as I that we can spare a few of the men. If not for Shane, at least think of Josh. Josh still owns a portion of the farm. He'll suffer losses, as well as Shane."

Terrance's lips lifted into a smug smile as he challenged her with a set stare, then turned and sauntered away from her.

Melanie's temper flared even hotter, and she rushed to him and grabbed him by an arm, stopping him.

"You hope they do lose the farm, don't you?" Melanie accused him. "You want to be there to take it off their hands, don't you? You won't even have to force Josh on me anymore. That won't be necessary. You will have the farm and an unwed sister, to boot!"

She dropped her hand away from him. "Well, brother dear, you will find that you are wrong on both counts," she said. "Your sister is going to be married, but to the man you would least want her to marry! And I won't allow you to force the Brennan farm into bankruptcy. I'll do anything I can to stop you!"

She turned and began running toward the stable. She had to get to Shane and encourage him to go into town today and hire himself a new crew. Not one more day should be allowed to pass without filling his pasture with men branding the longhorns, herding the cows, and repairing the fences!

Even if she had to go into town herself and do the hiring, it would be done!

Quickly saddling her horse, Melanie swung herself up onto it and rode away. She looked at the sky, thankful for the rising sun giving warmth to the air. She looked ahead, seeing no smoke rising from the Brennan chimneys. Had the house servants also fled?

She damned Josh beneath her breath.

His head throbbing, his tongue thick, Gray Falcon awakened from his drunken stupor. Blue Blossom was still at his side, asleep. The morning light was pouring in through the smokehole in the ceiling.

Turning to rise, Gray Falcon stopped short and

stared at something that had fallen from his hands. He stared unblinkingly at the floss of hair that lay golden against the dark bear pelts. He reached his fingers to it and touched it.

"Golden hair . . . ?" he said, running his fingers over the hair. "How did it . . . ?"

Then his gaze moved quickly upward. Now that he was coming out of his drunken state, he remembered his captive. His eyes darted around the dark recesses of the wigwam and his gut twisted when he saw that Melanie was nowhere in sight. She was gone! She had escaped!

Again he looked down at the hair. A slow, lazy smile lifted his lips. "Shane," he whispered. "He came. He stole his woman away from me. He cut his hair and left it for me to find. He is clever! He is even more cunning than I!"

He rose into a sitting position and lifted the hair up into his hands. His smile faded, knowing that Shane had cut his hair for more than one reason. It was a way of showing Gray Falcon that Shane had severed his ties with the Chippewa forever!

A pang of regret stung Gray Falcon's heart. Were the games, the challenges with Shane truly over? Now that they seemed to be, Gray Falcon was not at all happy. There would now be a void in his life, and he was sorry now that he had forced Shane's hand.

Perhaps he should offer a truce to Shane, he thought, still studying the hair, sad that Shane had actually parted with it. Perhaps he should offer himself as a brother to him. Did it take this, to make him realize just how important Shane really was to him?

Blue Blossom stirred at Gray Falcon's side. She leaned up on an elbow, the blanket falling away, revealing her thick breasts. "*Ah-neen-ay-kee-do-yen*?" she said, smiling up at him.

Then she suddenly remembered the captive and shot her eyes around and gasped when she discovered that Melanie was gone. She looked guardedly back at Gray Falcon. "White woman," she said softly. "She is gone."

"*Ay-uh*, she is gone," Gray Falcon grumbled. He gazed at the golden hair that lay within the folds of his hand. "And Shane is also gone. Forever."

Blue Blossom stared down at the hair, recognizing it. She placed a hand to her mouth, stifling a sob.

A great bellowing across Shane's pasture met Melanie's approach. Worried, she looked at the restless longhorns, then at Shane's house and the yard that surrounded it. Everything was too quiet.

But of course, it would be, if all of the cowhands had deserted the farm.

Yet, where was Shane? Now that he had returned her safely home, she had expected to find him slaving away at his farm, trying to keep up with everything!

A sick feeling grabbed Melanie at the pit of her stomach. Had he left again? If so, where had he gone? Had he decided to leave all of his misery behind after all, or had he gone to find Trapper Dan's?

She brought the buggy to a halt and leapt from it and ran into Shane's house. More silence met her there. She ran up the stairs to Shane's bedroom and gazed with longing down at his pallet of furs, recalling the passionate moments spent there with him. Then she drew her mind back to the true reason she was there.

"He's gone," she whispered, placing a hand to her throat.

She rushed from room to room, just to make sure, then stopped when she came to Josh's bedroom. She inhaled the familiar fragrance of his cologne, which still clung to the drapes and bedspread. Her eyes narrowed angrily as hate rose within her.

"It's all his fault," she hissed. "If not for Josh and his attitude toward Shane, none of these things would have happened."

Racing toward the staircase, Melanie now knew what must be done. She had to go to St. Paul and find Josh. Come hell or high water, she had to find him and bring him home. By damn, he would make things right! He would even go and search for Shane and give him whatever assistance he needed, if she had to force him to do so at gunpoint!

She rode away from Shane's farm and went to her own and attached another horse to the back of her buggy. When Terrance came outside and demanded to know what she was up to, she paid no attention to him.

* * *

Shane took several gold coins from his pocket and tossed them on the table in the blacksmith shop in St. Paul. "I will double this amount if you can find some dependable men who are willing to work as cowhands at my farm, under my employ," he said, giving the blacksmith a firm stare. "Tell them to come tomorrow morning. They will be well paid and fed for their services. My bunkhouse is better than some in these parts. During the winter months, the men will have a place to keep warm by a blazing fire. I will pay you well, Smith, if you will do me this service."

The blacksmith, tall and lanky, smoothed a hand across his bald head, eying Shane critically. "I heard that Josh had a twin brother and by damn, this time gossip was right," he said, spitting over his shoulder. "If I didn't know that Josh was over there in that saloon drunk and all whiskered up in the face, I'd think I was speakin' to him, instead of you."

"I am not here to be compared to my brother," Shane said, resting a hand on a holstered pistol. "I am here to make sure my farm does not go one more day without cowhands. Do I take those coins back, or do I leave them?"

"You keep callin' the farm your farm," the blacksmith said, spitting over his shoulder again. "Until you showed up, it was Josh's. Whose is it now? Yours or his?"

Shane's shoulder muscles tightened. "That isn't any concern of yours or anyone's," he said. "It is between me and my brother." He leaned closer to the blacksmith's face. "Smith, do you or don't you want my coins? I can go somewhere else. It does not matter to me who I make richer."

The blacksmith cupped his hands over the coins possessively. "By sunup tomorrow you'll have yourself enough cowhands," he said, smiling crookedly up at Shane. "By sunup tomorrow."

Shane nodded. "I appreciate it," he said, turning and leaving.

When he was out on the street again, he looked toward the saloons, then at the building where his brother made residence. He had thought that Josh was going to come home after their last confrontation. Apparently he had been wrong.

He went to his horse and swung himself up into his saddle. He was too lost in thought to notice a horse and buggy speeding into town, stirring up dust behind it. He mingled with the other men on horseback along the busy thoroughfare and made his way in the opposite direction, to the edge of town. He had one chore behind him and one more to go. He had a score to settle. With Trapper Dan. But he must first go and try to speak to the Indian woman, to see if he could persuade her to leave the trapper, so that she would not come to any harm when Shane finally got his revenge.

Melanie elbowed her way along the crowded sidewalk, unsure of which saloon she would enter first. Even the thought of mingling with the sorts of people who frequented those sinful places made her cringe, but to help Shane, she was ready to face any sort of uncomfortable situation. For Shane, she would do anything!

Before she shoved the first swinging door aside, Melanie stopped and took a deep breath. Then, mustering up the courage required for the task at hand, she stepped into the establishment. Choking on the thick smoke that was spiraling like heavy fog through the air, she covered her mouth with one hand. With her free hand, she waved the smoke aside and walked toward the sound of coins clinking and men laughing. She remembered the other time she had been in this saloon and she heard the sound of cards shuffling. She became unnerved when she stepped up to a table and found herself staring down, face to face with Josh as he turned and looked up at her as she approached the table.

"Melanie?" Josh said in a drunken drawl, blinking his eyes to be sure that he was not seeing things. "Melanie, is that you?"

Melanie stared at Josh, scarcely believing what she was seeing. His face was covered with thick, golden stubble. There were dark hollows beneath his bloodshot eyes; his face was gaunt. She looked slowly up at his hair. It was greasy and uncombed. His expensive white silk shirt was stained from food and drink. The collar was grimy, and a strong stench of perspiration rose from his armpits, proving that he had been without a bath for some time.

"Josh, I could safely ask if that is you," Melanie said, shaking her head with disgust. "Never did I think that you could let yourself look like this. You—you have always been so immaculate."

Josh laughed drunkenly as he rose to his feet, clumsily knocking the chair to the floor behind him. He reached for Melanie, then fell awkwardly forward when she stepped out of the way. "My little Melanie," he said, grabbing for her again and missing again. "Do I sense that you care just a little bit about me?"

Melanie cringed as he took another step toward her. "Josh, I didn't come into this hellhole for anyone but Shane," she snapped angrily. "He needs you, Josh, and by damn you're going to forget this life of gambling and drinking and behave as a brother should behave."

She grabbed his arm and gave a hard yank. "You're going home, Josh," she said, forcefully moving him along through the gawking crowd. "You're going to have a bath and drink a gallon of coffee to sober you up, and then you are going to go and find Shane and give him a helping hand."

Josh frowned. "Give him a helping hand?" he said in a drunken drawl. "Who says?"

"I do," Melanie said, giving him another hard yank. "Now come along. You don't have any choice this time. You're going to do something for someone besides yourself. Your selfish days are over as far as I'm concerned."

The men at the table that Josh was leaving began to laugh and poke fun at him. Josh hesitated and looked over his shoulder. His gaze settled on the half-emptied whiskey bottle and the stack of coins that were his. He started pulling back from Melanie.

"I'm not finished with my whiskey," he whined. "I'm not through playing poker." He reached a hand back over his shoulder. "Give me my money! Give me my whiskey!"

The men ignored him now and resumed playing cards.

Melanie tugged and pulled with all her might until she had Josh out on the sidewalk. "There's my horse and buggy," she said flatly. "Come on, Josh. Walk on your own. Don't force us both to make fools of ourselves. I felt fool enough just having to enter that terrible place. I don't want to set the whole city of St. Paul's tongues to wagging about both our families any more than they are already."

Josh staggered. He grabbed for Melanie. He squinted down at her. "I've got one helluva headache," he confessed. "Damn it, Melanie, I need to go someplace and lie down." He looked up at the stairs that led to his room. "Come on, Melanie. Let me go to my room and get a few winks of sleep before riding on that rickety buggy. I just might puke."

Melanie shook her head. "If you think I'm going to let you sidetrack me into going to your hotel room, you're crazy," she said, shoving him toward her buggy. "Get in the buggy. And Josh, if you dare get sick in my buggy, I'll kick you out onto the road and make you walk home. Do you understand?"

Josh pulled himself up into the buggy and held his face in his hands. "You're a hard-hearted woman," he said, groaning as she climbed in beside him and slapped the reins against the horse's rump. "Please go slow, Melanie. Please . . ."

Melanie smiled wickedly at him and sent her horse into a hard gallop over the dusty road. When the buggy hit a pothole, she laughed to herself when Josh's eyes widened and he covered his mouth with a hand. She could see his throat constricting and knew that he was terribly ill. It would do him good to have to suffer like everyone else!

But she stopped to let him be sick in a clump of bushes alongside the road. After that, Josh climbed to the back of the buggy and stretched out and fell into a restless sleep. Melanie drove on, more slowly.

Stealing stealthily across the stretch of land that led from the depths of the forest to Trapper Dan's cabin, Shane tensed when he heard the trapper laughing. He went to the window and peered inside. The trapper was straddling the naked Indian woman, rutting her vigorously. Shane looked at the woman's face to see if she was enjoying it. His insides grew cold when he saw that she was passive, her eyes fixed on the roof rather than the man who held her.

Shane turned away, his teeth clenched. He had come to speak with the woman and that was impossible now. So, he would at least achieve another part of his plan. He would steal some of the trapper's traps. He had plans for them, later.

"I will speak with the woman another time," he whispered. "But I will. I must. It is obvious to me now that she is not with him willingly!"

· CHAPTER TWENTY-SEVEN ·

While Josh lay prone on the bed in his room, snoring, Melanie began filling a copper tub that she had dragged to his room. She glared at him. She would sober him up if it was the last thing she did! She had to get him to listen to reason, but while his brain was soaked with alcohol, there was no getting through to him.

Melanie went downstairs to the kitchen and pumped more water into a bucket. She sank a finger deep into the water and smiled to herself, realizing just how cold the water was as it came up from the deep well in the ground. If this cold water didn't sober Josh up, nothing would!

The bucket filled to the brim, Melanie groaned and held onto the small of her back with her free hand as she began climbing the stairs again. She looked up, mentally counting the steps, tired from the many trips she had already made with buckets of water.

But this was the last. There was enough water in the tub to give the drunken sot a good soaking.

Now would come the true test. Could she even get Josh to the tub, to get into the water? Drunk, he was a dead weight.

The last step finally taken, Melanie leaned into the weight of the water and carried it on into Josh's bedroom. She started to pour it into the tub with the rest, then looked at Josh with a lingering stare, and reconsidered. She needed this last bucket of water for another purpose.

Setting the bucket aside, beside the tub, Melanie took a deep breath and stretched out her aching bones. Then she went to the bed and shook Josh.

"Wake up!" she shouted. When he stirred only enough to lick his lips and emit a crude hiccough, she shook him again. "Damn it, Josh, wake up. I didn't go to all of the trouble of dragging you up those godawful stairs to your room just to let you go to sleep in your bed. I have other plans for you. Get up. If you don't, I'm going to drag you to the tub and put you in the water headfirst!"

Suddenly Josh slung a heavy arm around Melanie's waist and yanked her down atop him. With dark intent in his eyes, he coiled his fingers through her hair and drew her lips to his mouth in a wet kiss.

Melanie was momentarily stunned, having thought that he was too drunk to be a threat to her. But she was wrong. He knew damn well what he was doing. His free hand was roaming over her with obvious purpose.

Doubling a fist, Melanie slammed it into his chest, and then his jaw. His reaction was swift. He yowled painfully and released her hair. She grabbed the opportunity and jerked herself free, then jumped from the bed.

Her eyes were lit with fire. "How dare you!" she hissed, panting. "I didn't come here to be man-handled!"

Josh rubbed his jaw and leaned up on an elbow. "Why'd you go and do that for?" he drawled. "I didn't mean anything by an innocent little kiss."

"That wasn't an innocent kiss and you know it," Melanie said, eying him venomously. Her gaze raked over him, shuddering at his soiled, disheveled appearance. "I'd like nothing more than to leave this room and never see you again, but I can't. I've come here for a purpose and I'm not going to leave." She nodded toward him. "Josh, get on your feet and take off your clothes."

Josh's eyes widened. He rose slowly to a sitting position, a sneer on his face. "Why it'd be my pleasure," he said, wobbling to his feet. "Then maybe you'll let me try and kiss you again." His gaze roamed over her suggestively as he began unbuttoning his shirt. "You goin' to join me in the bath?" His eyes gleamed, suddenly not all that drunk after all. "We'd have fun, Melanie. Perhaps you'd even forget Shane once you see what I have to offer."

Melanie began to feel uneasy as Josh placed his thumbs to his breeches and began lowering them.

"On second thought, maybe you'd best take a bath with your clothes on," she said shallowly.

Josh continued undressing. "Now who ever heard of anyone taking a bath with his clothes on?" he said, chuckling. He stepped out of his breeches, revealing his nakedness to Melanie's nervous eyes. He looked up at her as he sat down on the edge of the bed and yanked one boot off, and then the other. "I'm doin' exactly what you said, Melanie. I've taken my clothes off. Now I'm going to take that bath." His eyes gleamed. "Are you going to scrub the filth and stench of whiskey off me?"

"The whole point to having you take a bath was not only to clean you up, but also to sober you," Melanie said, turning her back to him. Her heart pounded, afraid. "Seems you are sober enough to clean yourself, Josh." She started toward the door, intent on escape. "After you take the bath, come downstairs. I have much to talk over with you."

Suddenly she felt a hand grip hard onto her wrist. As she was forced around, she looked up into blue, leering eyes. "Josh, don't," she said, her voice weak. "You don't want to do this."

"The hell I don't," Josh said, grabbing her around the waist and yanking her to him. "Melanie, there isn't anything you can do to keep me from having you. I've wanted you forever. You're in my room. There's a bed handy. I'll never get the same opportunity again."

Melanie eyed the tub, and then Josh. She moved into action. Splaying her hands against his bare chest, she gave him a powerful shove, then watched gleefully as he lost his balance and fell backward into the water. She laughed as he yelled and reached desperately for the sides of the tub, his eyes wild from the shock of the cold water.

She reached for the bucket and coiled her fingers around the handle. "If you think that's cold, just wait until you feel this," she said, dumping the bucket of water over his head.

His reaction was not at all what Melanie expected. After the initial shock of the dousing, he came out of the tub like a clap of thunder, his eyes spitting fire.

Melanie's insides froze. She turned and started to run but Josh was there, his fingers biting into the flesh of her wrists.

His horse loaded down with several of Trapper Dan's steel traps, Shane rode up the lane to his house, then leaned over the pommel of his saddle when he recognized Melanie's horse and buggy. Smiling, expecting to find her in the house awaiting his arrival, he nudged his horse in the flanks with his heels and rode up to the porch. Swinging himself out of his saddle, he rushed into the house.

"Melanie?" he shouted, looking from room to room. "Melanie, where are you? Have you been here long?"

When he didn't find her anywhere, and she did not respond in any way, he scratched his brow idly. A noise like the rustling of feet overhead drew his eyes upward. Then a loud shriek split the silence.

"My God! Melanie!" Shane gasped, taking the stairs two at a time.

He followed the sound of Melanie's sobs. He flung Josh's door open and paled when he saw Josh struggling with Melanie on the floor. For a moment time seemed to stand still as Shane looked at Josh's naked form now pinioning Melanie to the floor, a knee nudging her legs apart while a hand raised her skirt.

Shane's gaze swept to Melanie. Her face was red and scratched by Josh's stiff whiskers as he attempted to kiss her. Her eyes were wild.

Then all that Shane could see was red. With a low growl and flying feet he went to Josh and twisted his fingers through his brother's thick golden hair. With one hard yank he had Josh away from Melanie. With a firm foot on Josh's abdomen, Shane pinned his brother to the floor.

With marked fear in his eyes, the pulse at the base of his throat pounding, Josh pleaded with Shane. "I didn't mean nothing by it, Shane," he cried. "She's the cause! She's the one who came to my room. She told me to undress. What's a man to think when a woman out and out asks him to undress in his own bedroom? Wouldn't you think the same thing if it happened to you? Wouldn't you take advantage of it? Shane, I've wanted her for so long! It's unfair that I can't have her!"

Shane ground his heel harder into Josh's abdomen, causing him to groan with pain. "If Melanie was in your room, it sure as hell was not for the reason you assumed," he growled. "You know

345

that, Josh. Father failed somehow in teaching you manners." He smiled slowly, his eyes twinkling. "But maybe I can teach you a few." He kneaded his chin thoughtfully. "Now just where do you think I should begin?"

"Just let me go," Josh begged, sweat pearling his brow. "I didn't want to come back home, anyhow. Melanie dragged me here. I'll leave again. Just let me up. I'll show you just how damn fast I can get out of here."

Melanie moved shakily to her feet. She straightened her skirt and glowered at Josh, then looked at Shane. "Let him go," she said, her voice quavering. "The only reason I brought him home was to make him go and search for you and help you. Shane, you're home and obviously all right. We don't need Josh!"

Her eyes faltered as she once again looked down at Josh. "Unless he can get the hired hands to return and work for you," she said. "If Josh were here, your cowhands would return."

"That isn't necessary," Shane said, lifting his foot away from Josh. "I have my own ways of getting cowhands. By sunup tomorrow, there will be enough to tend to all of the chores around here."

"How—?" Melanie gasped. "Is that where you were? In town? You weren't out searching for Trapper Dan? I even thought that perhaps you had left again, for good. Shane, I'm so glad that you didn't."

Distracted, Shane looked away from Josh. Melanie watched, horror-struck, as Josh lunged for the knife that was sheathed at Shane's waist. She ran to Josh and kicked him in the groin, causing him to drop back to the floor weaponless, howling with pain.

Shane went to Melanie and drew her within his arms. "I'm sorry you have to become involved in my battles," he apologized. He tilted her chin with a finger. "Thank you, though, for everything you have done."

"Where were you this morning?" Melanie asked, looking up at him with adoring eyes. "I was so worried."

"In St. Paul," Shane responded, gazing raptly down at her. "I paid the blacksmith to round me up some men. Then I went to—"

"You sonofabitch," Josh said from between clenched teeth, interrupting Shane. "Don't you know? Melanie wanted me to return to the farm because you don't have the brains to run it, ever. You're responsible for all of the men leaving. What are you good for, Shane? As I see it, you should be back in the wilderness living with the savages, because you are one of them!"

Melanie grabbed Shane's arm quickly, stopping him from attacking Josh again. "Shane, leave him be," she urged. "Let's let him go. We don't need him."

"No, he won't get off that easily," Shane said, bending to one knee beside Josh. He grabbed him by the throat and drew him up close to his face. "I'm tired of listening to him saying that I'm a savage and that I am ignorant."

Shane leaned down into Josh's face. "It's time

for me to prove a few things to my brother," he said thickly. "Josh, I challenge you to a duel. We'll see who is the most cunning. If I lose, the farm is all yours. If you lose, the farm is mine. And you will treat me with respect. Do you hear?"

Melanie paled. She looked from Shane to Josh, then back at Shane. "Shane, no!" she cried. "Please don't! You can't have a duel with Josh! One of you will be killed. Please don't. I can't bear the thought of losing you!"

Josh reached a hand and removed Shane's fingers from around his throat. Coughing, rubbing his raw flesh, he backed away from Shane. "A duel?" he said thinly. "Shane, I—"

"Don't break out into a nervous sweat over my challenge," Shane said, laughing lightly. "No one is going to get killed, because we won't be using guns. I am challenging you to a game of poker, Josh. It will be a duel of cards and wits!"

Josh smiled slyly up at Shane. "You want to challenge me in a game of poker?" he said, reaching for a blanket from the bed to cover his nakedness.

"Exactly," Shane said, squaring his shoulders.

"I accept the challenge," Josh said, moving slowly to his feet. "Gladly."

Melanie and Shane exchanged quick looks. She smiled at Shane, he at her. She knew Shane's skill with cards.

Josh apparently didn't.

"But for now, if you don't mind, I'm going to return to St. Paul," Josh said, going to his armoire to choose fresh clothes. "Perhaps I had better get some practice in before you get the chance—maybe—to beat me." He looked smugly at Shane.

"Tomorrow, Josh," Shane said, walking Melanie toward the door. "I'll meet you in St. Paul. Have a table ready." He looked over his shoulder at Josh. "Now I would make a suggestion. Stay sober. You are going to need all your senses when you play your brother in a game of poker."

"You scare the hell outta me," Josh said, chuckling. "You've lived in a damn Indian village all your life. Where could you pick up any skill at poker?" He gestured with a hand around the room. "Brother dear, you'd best enjoy your night in this house, for it will be your last!"

Melanie wanted so badly to brag to him about Shane's prowess at the poker table, for she had no doubt that Shane would win. She had seen Shane play poker. She had seen a man get so riled because of his skills he had drawn a pistol on him!

Yes, Shane would be the winner. She smiled as she left the room with him.

When they got outside and Melanie saw the traps on Shane's horse, she looked up at him with questioning eyes. "Darling, where did you—?"

"I stole them from Trapper Dan," he said. "When the time is right, after I get the new cowhands settled in here at the farm and I have some free time again, I plan to use the trapper's traps on him. He will see the sort of pain he has caused many an innocent animal that has lain for

349

hours before being taken from a trap. It will be a slow and painful lesson. I will watch him suffer and enjoy it!"

Melanie turned her eyes away, not wanting to envision the sort of vengeance that Shane was talking about. The cows bellowing in the distance gave her cause to change the subject.

"Shane, I'm going to spend the rest of the day with you," she said, turning her eyes back to him. "I'm going to help you do whatever has been neglected the last couple of days. It will be fun working side by side with you."

Melanie walked alongside Shane as he led his horse to the stable and unloaded the traps. He hid them beneath a stack of straw, then spun around and glowered at Josh as he came to the door.

"Now ain't you two a pair?" Josh chuckled, saddling himself a horse. "Melanie, are you going into the wilderness with Shane to live as a savage with him after he loses at poker with me? I can just see you now—walking around with a papoose hanging on your back!"

Shane's eyes darkened with a quick anger. He took two wide steps forward, a fist doubled, but Melanie intercepted him by stepping in his way. "Ignore him," she urged. "He only continues to show his ignorance—his uncouth ways. Let him go. Tomorrow he'll never have cause to mock you again."

"See you tomorrow!" Josh shouted, swinging himself up into his saddle. "And don't fret none. I'll be as sober as you!"

Melanie grabbed for Shane's hand and wrapped her fingers around it. "Tomorrow, darling," she said softly. "Tomorrow."

· Chapter Twenty-Eight ·

The moon spiraled its light through Shane's bedroom window, silvering Shane's bare back as he lay above Melanie, gazing down at her, smiling softly. "You smell of many wonderful things," he whispered. "Like spring rain, like the sweetness of milk. The bath we shared after our long day of work is something that I would like to repeat, often. Once we are married, this is the way I would like to end every day. Sharing a bath with you, then licking your skin dry with my eager tongue."

"Shane, that's shameful," Melanie whispered, smoothing his damp hair back from his brow.

"What's shameful?"

"That you wish to lick my skin dry after our baths," she said, giggling.

"Are you saying that you did not enjoy it?"

"You know that I did," she murmured.

"That is all that matters," he said, watching her expression as he gently stroked her leg, behind her knees, and her calves, the sureness of his caress firing her desire.

Melanie bit her lower lip to stifle a cry of ecstasy when Shane's fingers teased a circle around her belly, up to her breasts, just missing the nipples, then made his way down her body again, until he reached her throbbing center.

As he began to stroke her hardening flesh, Melanie caught her breath, not daring to breathe. With quick, eager fingers he brought her almost over the edge into total ecstasy.

Then he braced himself with his arms, his hands catching Melanie's, holding them slightly above her. He kissed her eyes and nose, every place that he could reach. A white heat traveled through the sinews of his thighs and across his back, and he was unable to hold back any longer. He pressed his mouth to her parted lips and kissed her hotly as he plunged his hardness inside her and began his eager thrusts.

His loins were aflame. His heart was beating wildly.

Great surges of warmth flooded through Melanie. Her hands moved to Shane's buttocks. She splayed her fingers across his tight flesh and enjoyed the muscled feel of him as he stroked within her. Her hips responded, thrusting toward him. Each of his strokes promised more, assuring fulfillment. Tremors cascaded down her back. She shivered.

And then it felt as though she were filled with some great, warm light as a rush of ecstasy claimed her. Shane drew his lips away and burrowed his face between her breasts, groaning as his body spasmed and his own joy peaked.

Afterwards, they lay next to each other, pressing tightly together. Melanie caressed the long line of Shane's back and trailed her fingers over his buttocks, then encircled them around his velvet-textured shaft. It still pulsed, as though alive. She slowly caressed it, eliciting a moan of pleasure from Shane as he breathed hotly against her cheek.

"If only things were better between you and Josh," Melanie said, sighing. She looked at the deck of cards that lay on the floor beside the bed. "But I'm glad about one thing. I'm glad you are having a duel with cards instead of guns!"

Shane leaned away from Melanie and reached for his cards. He sat up and began shuffling them. "It's going to be interesting, Melanie," he said, chuckling. "My brother soon will learn that his smugness is misplaced."

"I doubt if he will ever change," Melanie said, shaking her head. "Since boyhood he's been impossible. I truly believe it will take more than a game of poker to make him change."

"Whether it does or not, at least one main decision will be reached," Shane said, stacking the cards. "Only one of us will own the farm. That seems to be the sole problem here. Josh does not want to share in the ownership, though I cannot understand why. It is a large farm. There is so much land, so many cattle! Sharing is in my blood.

354

I learned to share from the Chippewa. Did they not share with me after rescuing me from the forest? They shared their lives—everything!"

"Until Gray Falcon became chief?" Melanie asked, touching Shane gently on the arm as he lay down beside her again.

"Until Gray Falcon," Shane grumbled.

"If only we never had to leave this bedroom," Melanie whispered, melting inside as Shane moved his lips to her breast and nibbled at the nipple with his teeth. "There would be no problems and sorrow. Only wonderful joy, Shane. Wouldn't it be heavenly?"

"You're worrying about what your brother is thinking about you staying the night with me, aren't you?" Shane asked, leaning up on an elbow and looking down at her.

Melanie rose to a sitting position and drew a blanket up around her. With a forefinger, she began tracing the lines of the moonlight across the bear pelt beside her. "I don't worry too much about what Terrance says or thinks anymore," she said sadly. "Shane, since father's death, Terrance has changed. I hardly know him."

She swallowed hard. "I sometimes blame myself," she said, her voice strained. "Perhaps if I weren't so strong-minded, so bullheaded. Perhaps I should just step back and let him run things as he sees fit."

She looked at Shane. "But that could prove hazardous. The way he drinks . . ."

A strange sort of reddish-orange glow wavering along the ceiling drew Melanie's attention, causing her words to die on her lips. She moved slowly to her knees, the blanket falling away from her. "Shane, do you see—?"

Shane was already on his feet and drawing on his breeches. "Damn it," he growled. "Something outside is on fire."

Horses whinnying and longhorns bellowing drew Melanie's eyes quickly to the window. She jumped up from the pallet of furs and rushed to it. She gasped and placed her hands to her throat. "Shane, it's the stable!" she cried. "It's on fire! Flames are shooting from the sides!"

When there was no response from Shane, Melanie turned around in a jerk and discovered that he was gone. Her heart pounding, she rushed into her skirt and blouse, but didn't take the time to yank on her boots. She hurried from the room, down the stairs, and outside.

The sight of the fire in its full capacity momentarily rendered her numb. When she caught sight of Shane racing from the burning building, shooing horses from inside it, she broke into a mad run and joined him. Her feet stung as she stepped onto falling, burning debris. Her lungs ached from the smoke. Her eyes burned.

But still she worked earnestly alongside Shane, fighting the smoke and fire until all of the horses were rescued.

Afterwards, they stood disconsolately as they watched the fire rage out of control. Flames burst through the roof, then spiraled like orange streamers of satin against the dark velvet sky of night.

"If only the cowhands hadn't left," Melanie

said, her voice hoarse from the smoke. "The stable could have been saved."

"My new cowhands will build another," Shane said flatly.

"But it's so horrible!" Melanie cried.

"In my lifetime I have learned to accept many losses," Shane said, his voice drawn. "So shall I learn to accept many more. That is what life is all about, Melanie. Gains and losses."

He slipped an arm about her waist. He looked down at her through singed eyelashes. "My loss tonight is nothing in comparison with my recent gain," he said. "You are the most favored gain of all!"

Melanie leaned into his embrace and sighed languorously. "Darling, that is so sweet," she said, sighing. "I just wish that I could do something to help find the one responsible for all of your misfortune. But how?"

"You have already done enough in my behalf," Shane said, drawing away from her. "And I can never thank you enough for it."

"Never do you have to thank me for anything," Melanie said, looking devotedly up at him. "I do everything with love."

"I couldn't ask for anything more than that, now could I?" he said, gently cupping her chin in the palm of his hand. Then he looked past her, into the gloom of night.

"The horses have scattered," he said in a low growl. "I had best see to them."

He went to his horse and mounted, Melanie following along after him. "Melanie, it would be best if you went on home," he said. "It's going to take a good portion of the night for me to round up the horses and get the longhorns settled down."

"I could help," Melanie said, firming her chin as she looked up at him.

"You've done enough," Shane said, circling his reins around his fingers. "Go home and clean up." He looked down at her bare feet. "Doctor your feet. I'm sure they got burned."

Melanie nodded; her feet were stinging. "I was foolish not to have taken time to put my boots on," she said, lifting one foot and slowly rubbing the sole. "But you needed me. Some horses may have died had I not helped you as quickly as I did."

"I'll see you bright and early in the morning," Shane said, wheeling his horse around. "Nothing is going to stand in the way of that poker game."

"No, nothing," Melanie said. She smiled and waved at Shane as he rode away from her. Then she climbed into her buggy that she had not yet taken time to separate from her horse before she and Shane had gotten carried away in their bath and lovemaking.

Shoeless, too bone-tired to go back inside Shane's house to get her boots, she directed her buggy around and drove away. She looked across the pasture, only barely able to make out Shane on his horse in the darkness. Her heart went out to him. Would his troubles ever end?

Her face smudged with black ash, her lashes singed, Melanie entered her house, limping. Her feet stinging, she climbed the stairs slowly. When she got to the second floor landing, she stopped and looked at Terrance's door. It was closed. Was he already in bed? Somehow that didn't fit Terrance's personality these days. He had become a night owl, boozing it up, gambling and more than likely lifting many a woman's skirts way into the night.

Curiosity getting the best of her, Melanie opened Terrance's door. The splash of light pouring into his room from the wall sconces in the corridor revealed that her brother was in bed. She shrugged and started to leave, but stopped short when a faint aroma of smoke wafted across the room from where her brother lay.

Melanie sniffed, then felt blood rush to her face as rage filled her. She caught sight of a boot sticking out from beneath Terrance's blanket where the blanket had slipped away from the slick leather. She could even see a portion of his breeches leg! The scalawag was still dressed and very obviously feigning sleep! There could be only one explanation. Didn't the aroma of smoke in the room condemn him? He had not been caught at the scene of the crime, but he was no less guilty of it! Terrance was responsible for the fire at Shane's farm! He had more than likely returned home only shortly before Melanie. When he had heard her arrive, he had felt trapped and had fled to bed fully clothed just in case she stopped at his room to question him!

Melanie's gaze was drawn to another object that lay in the path of the candles' golden light—the barrel of one of Terrance's pistols as it lay on the table beside his bed!

Perfect! Melanie thought to herself, smiling devilishly as she began tiptoeing across the wooden floor. Absolutely perfect!

Her fingers did not tremble at all when she picked up the pistol. It was as steady as her heartbeat, for she was determined to get answers out of her brother, no matter what she had to do to achieve it. He would realize her absolute devotion to Shane when he discovered the pistol thrust into his back.

Never would he forget it, either!

Bending over Terrance, Melanie was aware of his forced, shallow breathing, absolute proof that he knew she was there, only pretending to be asleep for her benefit! He surely thought that she would take one look at him and leave. Never would he expect her to do otherwise!

As she bent down closer to him, an overpowering aroma of smoke rose up into her nostrils. The evidence was there, so strong, he could not deny it.

"Terrance, you aren't fooling anyone any longer, about anything," Melanie said, placing the barrel of the pistol square between his shoulder blades. When he jumped with alarm, she held her hand firm, not letting the pistol waver one inch away from him. "Now you're going to tell me everything. Do you hear? You can't wiggle your way out of this one, you snake! Lord, Terrance, you set the fire tonight. Admit it!"

"Melanie, damn it, what do you think you're doing?" Terrance asked, sweat pearling his brow.

"Move that gun away from me. You don't know enough about firearms. That fool thing'll go off before you know it."

"Perhaps that would be best," Melanie said, her voice finally quavering. "Terrance, all along you've been the one doing those terrible things to Shane. How could you? Don't you know that you could go to jail if he chose to bring charges against you?"

"Melanie, I don't know what you're talking about," Terrance said, giving her a glance over his shoulder. "You didn't see me tonight. You're mistaken. I've been here all night. You should be proud of me. I'm stone sober!"

"Terrance, tonight I would rather have caught you drunk than here in bed fully clothed, lying through your teeth," Melanie said, easing the pistol away from him. She lay it aside and sank down into a chair. "Terrance, the more you lie to me, the more disillusioned I get about you."

She raised her eyes and glared at him as he lit a kerosene lamp at his bedside.

"Terrance, can't you smell yourself?" Melanie snapped. "You reek of smoke. You know why. I know why. It's no use lying about it."

Terrance's eyes wavered. "All right, so I was there tonight," he finally admitted. "I did start the fire. I had to! I'm damn sick of waiting for Shane to get his fill and leave! God! You'd think he'd have given up long ago. But don't put the full blame on me. If Shane decides to press charges, I won't take the full rap alone. Someone else was in on it."

"Terrance, what are you saying?" Melanie gasped. "Who are you talking about? Don't tell me that you and Josh—"

Terrance interrupted. "No," he said, fidgeting with his mustache. "It wasn't Josh. He didn't have the guts to help me." He cleared his throat nervously and gave Melanie a half glance. "It was Trapper Dan. The man Shane hates with a vengeance."

Melanie blanched, finding this all almost too hard to comprehend. Then she rose quickly to her feet and stood over Terrance, her hands on her hips. "How could you?" she stormed. "How could you be in cohoots with such a vile man? And why was he willing to help you? How on earth did you ever get acquainted with him?"

"I met him in a saloon."

"And?"

"We got to talking."

"And?"

"The trapper was eager to make some extra money. So I agreed to pay him if he'd help me rid the area of Shane Brennan."

"Did you tell him of Shane's acquaintance with him?"

"Yeah."

"So?"

"This made him more than eager to see Shane leave the area. Shane is also a threat to him!"

"Oh, Terrance," Melanie cried, clenching her hands into tight fists. "Shane is no threat to anyone! Why can't you see that?"

"He is a threat to everything I had planned for

my future," Terrance said. "To our future, Melanie. Everything has changed since his arrival. Everything."

"Things can't always go the way you want," Melanie said, looking down at Terrance, hearing in his voice the small boy she could remember from so long ago.

A part of her was softening toward him. Another part still almost wanted to kill him! "You can't control other people's lives, other people's destinies, as if you were God," she said. "You have to learn to bend, to share. If you weren't so blind, you'd see that you are the only reason for the confusion these past weeks—not Shane!"

"So what do you plan to do about all of this?" Terrance asked, raking his fingers through his hair again. "Are you going to tell Shane? Are you going to turn me in to the authorities?

"No—not just yet, anyhow," Melanie said, sighing deeply.

"Then what?" Terrance asked.

"You're going to take me tonight and show me where the trapper lives," Melanie said, frowning down at Terrance. "Then I shall go and see what I can do about him myself—but after tomorrow. I've something else planned for tomorrow."

"Oh? And what's so important about tomorrow?" Terrance asked. "But, of course, it has to do with Shane, doesn't it? Doesn't everything you do anymore?"

"Yes, it has to do with Shane," Melanie said.

"Anything you'd like to tell me about?"

"Shane and Josh are meeting for a duel."

"What?" Terrance gasped.

Melanie laughed. "Not with guns," she explained. "With cards. They are playing a game of poker. The winner will get everything. The farm. The house. The land. The cattle. Everything. That will settle their differences once and for all!"

"Well, I'll be damned," Terrance drawled.

"As for you, Terrance?" Melanie said, "you're going to show me where Trapper Dan lives. And then you're going to clear out. I'll talk to our lawyer soon and see how the inheritance can be divided up. You will get your share. But you won't live under the same roof with me any longer. I don't trust you. I'll hire someone to look after my interests."

Terrance bolted to his feet. "You can't do that!" he gasped.

"You just watch me," Melanie said, firming her chin.

"I won't let you."

"If you try to stop me I guess I'll have to go to the sheriff and tell him that my brother is guilty not only of burning his neighbor's stable, but also of stampeding his cattle." She paused and smiled smugly down at him. "Need I go on?"

"Melanie, I never thought you had it in you," Terrance said, shaking his head. "You'd do this to your own brother? What'd Pop think if he were alive?"

"If only he were," Melanie said, sighing. "None of this would ever have happened. He would have had his eye on you all along. He'd have known you were up to no good that very first night! I sus-

ected it. I should have acted on it as Pop would
ave done. But I wanted to think the best of you,
errance. I was wrong to."

"What can I do to make you change your
mind?" Terrance asked in almost a whine. "The
arm is my life! I can't leave!"

"Your twisted love for power got you where you
re today," Melanie said, walking toward the
loor. "As I see it, there's nothing you can do to
nake me change my mind."

She looked over her shoulder at him. "I'm going
o go and wash up and change into something
nore comfortable. I won't take long. Don't you
ither. I want to see where Trapper Dan lives, then
ome home and try to get some rest. I want to be
resh for tomorrow. Shane is depending on me."

• CHAPTER TWENTY-NINE •

Melanie paced the parlor floor. Shane had en couraged her not to go into St. Paul to watch th poker game. A saloon was not the proper place fo a lady, even though Melanie would be there for purpose other than that which drew the sorts o women who could be found there regularly.

She had argued with Shane, yet in the end finall acquiesced because she knew that he had enoug on his mind without her causing him undue stres:

Stopping to stare at the clock on the mante Melanie sighed. The hands on the clock seeme not to have moved at all since the last time sh looked. The minutes were dragging into hours.

She went outside to stand on the porch. Sh lifted her hair from her shoulders and let th summer breeze caress the nape of her neck. Th sound of hammering drew her gaze to Shane's farm. The new cowhands had arrived. The stable was being rebuilt.

Her gaze traveled back to her own farm, seeing the activity of her cowhands doing their chores. A feeling of apprehension swept through her with the realization that she was now in total charge of the cowhands. With Terrance gone, all the responsibilities of the farm rested on her shoulders. If she did not succeed, the end result would be the same as if Terrance had gambled the farm away on a reckless game of poker.

She could lose it all.

Her thoughts went back to the previous night, when she had told Terrance he had to leave, and later, when he had shown her where Trapper Dan lived.

"Trapper Dan," she whispered, peering up at the butte that reached into the dark depths of the forest. "Perhaps I should go there now after all, instead of later to plead with the man. If I could talk him into leaving the area, not to be seen or heard from again, even pay him a good amount of money to leave, Shane wouldn't have to chance being hurt by challenging him."

She placed a finger to her lip. "Should I?"

She exhaled a nervous breath. "I'll wait a while longer," she said, moving back into the house. "If Shane doesn't come soon, I'll go and talk with Trapper Dan."

Plopping disconsolately into a chair, Melanie picked up her embroidery piece and began to work on it. She grumbled to herself when she pricked a finger. She hated to sew! She would rather be outdoors in the sunshine! When she got married and had children, would she be content caring for them? Would she not long to be with Shane, to do everything with him, side by side? It seemed that when that time came, she would have to make adjustments as Shane was now doing in his new life. If he could do it, so could she.

Perhaps it would not be so bad to be ladylike all of the time, instead of being called a tomboy forever.

Terrance slouched down low over a glass of whiskey at the bar, his eyes squinting as he peered through the haze of smoke toward the group of men standing around a table, waiting for Josh and Shane to begin their poker game. Terrance had decided to come and watch. A lot depended on the winner today—perhaps even Terrance's future. If Shane lost, Shane would leave and everything would get back to normal between the Stanton and Brennan families. Melanie would have no choice but to forget him. She would more than likely turn to Josh. For sure, she would come begging for her brother to return and run the farm!

Taking another quick gulp of whiskey, Terrance shuddered as it rolled down the back of his throat, burning it. He got a glimpse of Shane at the table as a man stepped aside. Hate grabbed Terrance at the pit of his stomach as he looked intensely at Shane who sat so smugly smoking a cigar and shuffling cards, his back straight, his blue eyes gleaming.

Terrance's thoughts went to the previous night, when Melanie had forced him to take her to point out Trapper Dan's house to her. There was no telling what she planned to do with the information, except perhaps tell Shane about him and take him there.

But Terrance had decided not to go and warn the trapper that he could expect trouble just yet. If Shane lost today, there would be no need to warn anyone. Shane would be gone. He would be out of everyone's lives. Even Trapper Dan's.

Setting his glass aside, Terrance inched toward the crowd of gawking men as Shane began dealing the cards. Smoothing his mustache with a finger, Terrance watched eagerly, not doubting who would be the winner. Shane had been raised with Indians, and Indians were not known for their skills with cards.

He smiled to himself as he looked at Josh, whose smile was broadening with each card he picked up.

Shane puffed on his cigar, eyeing Josh warily, then began picking up his own cards, one by one. First a two of spades, then a jack of hearts . . .

Before Shane picked up another card, he drummed his fingers on the tabletop and stared down at the cards that still lay face down. Five-card stud. Only three cards to go. So far he had nothing that even resembled a winning hand.

He reached for a bottle of whiskey and poured himself a glass. Taking a sip, he continued looking at the cards. In his mind's eye he was remembering the many hours that he had sat beside the fire in Chief Standing Tall's wigwam playing with these exact cards. They were the old chief's cards. If Shane looked hard enough he could see where the paint had been rubbed off at the corners by him and the chief through the many hours of their playing poker.

Setting the glass back down on the table, Shane glanced over his shoulder. He was not looking at the men who stood there, watching. Something else had caused his attention to be drawn from the task at hand. It was a presence of sorts, as though the old chief were there, his dark eyes twinkling.

Shane lifted the glass again. He nodded and smiled over his shoulder as he made a sort of mock salute with the glass, then swallowed the whiskey in one gulp.

"Shane, you've three more cards to pick up," Josh said, frowning. "What's the matter? Don't you know how to play?" He chuckled low and tipped his whiskey glass to his lips, emptying it in large gulps.

Shane looked across the table at his brother. He smiled slowly at him, then continued picking up the cards. One by one he placed them in his hand. He was careful not to show any sign of having drawn the three cards that gave him a winning hand.

His gaze moved from card to card. Three jacks, two twos. Josh could get better, but with five-card stud, it usually took several tries.

"Well, I'd say it's about time," Josh said.

"How many cards are you going to discard, Josh?" Shane asked, slapping his cards face down on the table before him.

Josh plucked two cards from his hand and shoved them into the middle of the table. "Two," he said, watching as Shane dealt him two more cards.

Shane lay the deck of cards aside again and watched Josh's expression as he fit his cards together in his hand again. Nothing. He could tell nothing about his brother's reaction. Josh was being careful.

Then Josh glanced at Shane. "How many do you discard?" he asked, folding his cards back together.

"None," Shane said nonchalantly.

"None?" Josh gasped, then he smiled sarcastically. "You took none because you don't even know what is worth keeping or throwing away."

"I wouldn't be so sure, Josh," a man across the way said. "Looks to me like he knows damn well what he's doin'."

"Yeah," several voices agreed.

"Anyhow, Shane, I've got openers," Josh said, scooting several coins out into the middle of the table.

Shane puffed hard on his cigar, squinting his eyes when the smoke spiraled up into them. He looked at Josh's cards held tightly in his hands, then up into his brother's eyes. It looked as though Josh thought he had a winner because he was looking damn smug.

Or was Josh looking so smug because he truly believed that Shane was stupid enough to challenge him to a game of cards without knowing how

371

to play himself? It was Josh who was the daft brother, it seemed.

"I'll call you," Shane said, scooting coins out onto the middle of the table. "And I'll raise you." He dropped several more coins in the middle of the table.

"Damn," Josh said, cocking an eyebrow quizzically as he looked over at Shane. He followed Shane's lead, matching the amount of money he had placed in the middle of the table. Then he watched, breathless, as Shane revealed his hand to everyone as he lay them down on the table, face up.

"Show 'em, Josh," Shane said, tipping his chair back, rocking slowly back and forth on the hind legs.

Josh paled as he studied Shane's cards, then slapped three kings on the table. "Seems you got lucky," he said thickly. He cringed as Shane dragged in the winnings.

"Your turn to deal, Josh," Shane said, slipping his cards over to his brother. "Better luck next time."

Shane slowly stacked the coins before him, purposely rattling them to draw Josh's full attention, to torment him.

Then the card game continued. Shane won hand after hand. He could see a cold, silent rage and humiliation in his brother's eyes, the smug smile replaced by a dark frown.

Suddenly Josh threw the cards on the table and burst up from his chair. Shoving the spectators aside, he stormed toward the door. Shane grabbed the cards and slipped them into his pocket and followed Josh from the saloon. He grabbed Josh by an arm and swung him around to face him.

"Let go of me," Josh said, jerking his arm free. "Haven't you humiliated me enough? Just go on to your farm, Shane. You've won it fair and square."

"Josh, come home with me," Shane said. "For me the poker game wasn't so much to win the farm and take it away from you, but to prove to you that I could. Come home, Josh. Though I won at cards today, I do not want to deprive you of anything. I know how it feels to be deprived, to lose everything. It happened to me at age four."

Shane placed a hand to Josh's shoulder. "Let us live as brothers," he said softly. "We will share everything equally." He smiled slowly. "Except for Melanie, of course. She is mine, Josh. She is going to be the mother of my children."

Josh's mouth was agape, finding Shane's generous offer hard to comprehend. Josh knew that if he had been the victor he would have laughed in Shane's face and ordered him to leave!

But now?

Now what should he do?

With every fiber of his being, Josh wanted to return to the farm, to be a part of the everyday excitement of watching it grow. It had been his life for as long as he could remember. These past weeks it had been hard to live away from it.

Yet, he still could not envision himself sharing everything equally with Shane. He could not accept the fact that Melanie would more than likely marry Shane. If she did, she would move into the

Brennan mansion. That would mean that if Josh returned, he could only observe her from afar. He would have to watch her going into Shane's room each night. Realizing what would be going on behind the locked doors would be more than he could bear! He did love Melanie. With all of his heart.

Josh broke away from Shane. "Go to hell, Shane," he growled. "And take Melanie with you! I don't need either of you. Do you hear?"

Disbelieving, Shane watched Josh shove his way angrily through the crowded sidewalk. He wanted to go after him and try one last time to convince his brother that they could be friends. Their father would want it that way. So would their mother. It was not right for brothers to be enemies!

Especially not twin brothers.

Then Shane looked at his horse, loaded down with traps hidden beneath a blanket. The true reason he had not wanted Melanie to accompany him into town was because he had planned to go to Trapper Dan's immediately after the card game. Had he won or lost, he had planned to go to the trapper's cabin and finally get his revenge.

He had waited long enough!

The man would be forced to remember that day long ago when so many innocent people were slain for the meager belongings the men had taken from their boat and bodies. Shane was going to tear the trapper's cabin apart to search for the ring that had been stolen from his mother's finger.

He did not expect to find it.

But nevertheless, he would never rest if he didn't at least search for it.

Turning to look at Josh one last time, Shane was torn. But words and time seemed wasted on his brother. It would be up to Josh to make the next move. He knew that he would be welcome at the ranch, that he would still have possession of what was rightfully his.

In two wide strides Shane went to his horse. He untied the reins from the hitching rail and mounted. Wheeling his stallion around, he urged it into a lope along the crowded thoroughfare. When the edge of town was reached, he sank his heels into the horse's flanks and broke into a gallop along a narrow, dusty road toward the dark shadows of the forest.

His only concern was the Indian woman. How could he prevent her from being harmed?

Discouraged, feeling as though he himself had participated in the poker game and lost, Terrance stepped from the saloon and watched Shane ride away. His eyes squinted narrowly as he studied the blanket at the rear of Shane's stallion. It was hiding something bulky beneath it.

He twirled the end of his narrow mustache as he tried to figure out what Shane was transporting. If he didn't know better he would think it was traps! He had seen Trapper Dan carry the same sort of bundle on his horse.

"Trapper Dan!" he said, gasping. He took a shaky step forward and leaned against the support post at the front of the saloon. "I've got to get to Trapper Dan and warn him about Shane. Even about Melanie! Now that Shane won the poker game, he sure as hell won't be leaving these parts. He'll be here now until hell freezes over!"

His mind fuzzy from alcohol, Terrance stumbled from the sidewalk. He laughed nervously when he came near to being trampled by a horse and buggy as its owner swung it away from him, just in time. His hands trembling, his knees weak, Terrance grabbed his horse's reins from the hitching rail and tried to place a foot in the stirrup. Each time he tried, his boot slipped out again.

"God damn it all to hell," he muttered, trying to force himself to focus his full attention on the stirrup. He laughed throatily when he was finally able to get his foot in.

He pulled himself up into the saddle and straightened his back. He teetered dizzily, then managed to get his horse out among the other horsemen. Not wanting to take the same route that Shane was taking, he took off in another direction, hoping he could get to Trapper Dan first.

If not, who was to say what would happen? Who would die?

He smiled crookedly. By damn! Maybe Trapper Dan would get the best of Shane! This could be the best way yet to rid himself of that half-savage!

"Yes," he whispered. "It could really happen! Trapper Dan's killed many a man in his time. One more won't matter none!"

* * *

Melanie drew her hair back and secured it with a ribbon, then slipped into her buckskin riding attire. The waiting had become too intolerable! She wanted so badly to go into St. Paul and learn the results of the poker game, but she couldn't because Shane had adamantly told her he did not want her to.

So, while she had this time to kill, she would make good use of it! It wouldn't take her long to get to Trapper Dan's. She would plead her case, pay him well, leave, and surely be home before Shane returned.

She did not want to let herself think about the possibility of Josh being the victor. If he was, Shane would lose everything again. That would be unjust, for Shane had just been given his rightful place in life—the way it should have been since he was four years old.

To lose it all again would be worse than unjust!

· CHAPTER THIRTY ·

Trapper Dan's cabin was within view through the trees. Shane dismounted behind a thick cover of brush and secured his reins, then moved stealthily on toward the house, breathing shallowly. One hand was on his knife sheathed at his waist; the other grasped his slim rifle firmly.

Moving to the back of the cabin, hugging the wall with his back, Shane listened for voices in the cabin. All that he could hear was some hammering.

Taking a quick step he went to the window and quickly scanned the inside. His eyes lit up. Trapper Dan was alone. He was absorbed in repairing traps. It would be easy to slip into the house and shoot the bastard.

But that would be too simple. Shane had other

plans for him. He wanted him to suffer slowly while he died.

The sound of someone singing from somewhere close by drew Shane's quick attention from the trapper. He followed the sound with his eyes and got a glimpse of the Indian woman in the nearby river. She was immersed in the water, all but her head. She was taking her morning bath.

This made things much simpler for Shane. He had worried about her welfare. Now he had the chance to warn her, to make sure she did not get in the way of whatever might transpire here if Shane's plans went awry.

Moving back into the forest, taking a wide circle around where the cabin's clearing reached into the forest, Shane crept to the river's edge. He hid behind a tree as the woman left the water and slipped her buckskin dress over her head. Then he made a dash for her and had his hands clasped over her mouth before she had time to cry out with fright.

Drawing her backside against the front of himself, pinioning her there as he held his hand firmly over her mouth, Shane leaned his mouth to her ear. "I'm not going to harm you," he whispered. "I have come to help you. After today you won't ever have to look at that damn trapper's face again, much less be obedient to his wishes. Nod your head if you understand that I am your friend and have no intentions of hurting you."

Her wet, glossy black hair smooth and sleek against Shane's face was reminiscent of Cedar Maid's beautiful hair. The thought of Cedar Maid made him more determined to carry through with his plan.

The trapper would die slowly. And painfully.

The woman nodded her head. Shane removed his hand from her mouth. She turned wide, dark eyes to him as she swung around to face him.

"Who are you?" she asked, seeing something familiar about him, yet unable to put her finger on what, or why.

"Why do you do this thing?" she added in barely a whisper.

Shane cupped her cheek gently within the palm of his hand. So much about her reminded him of Cedar Maid. But wouldn't any lovely Indian maiden? The reminder of Cedar Maid would always be there in any Indian woman he saw. He sorely missed her.

"I don't have time to explain everything to you," Shane said, looking over his shoulder at the cabin. He could still hear the hammering. The trapper was still too occupied to know what was happening out here by the river!

Shane looked down at the petite maiden again. "The trapper paid a bride price for you?" he asked, frowning.

"*Ay-uh*," the woman said, nodding. "Enough so that my father parted with me willingly. My father is poor. Horses and trinkets given to him by Trapper Dan made him feel rich!"

"Yes, I would imagine," Shane said thickly. He looked her up and down, then looked into her dark eyes again. "You speak in the Chippewa tongue. Where is your village?"

The woman pointed. "Two sleeps away," she said, tears forming in her eyes. "But I can never return. I have been soiled by the white man's hands."

"Yes, I understand," Shane said. "Your name?"

She cast her eyes downward. "My name was left behind at my village," she murmured. "Trapper Dan give me a new name. He calls me *Ee-qway-zance*, Girl." Slowly her eyes lifted to Shane's. "That name is ugly!"

Shane nodded. "Very ugly," he said. "After today you can live in my house and you can choose any pretty name that you wish. That name will be yours *ah-pay-nay*—forever."

Girl's lips parted in a slight gasp. "You spoke in Chippewa!" she said. Then she smiled suddenly up at him. "I know you! You are the man with the blue eyes and golden hair that my father told me about! You live with the Chippewa!"

"I did, but no longer," Shane said, again glancing toward the cabin. He turned back to Girl and took her hand and led her to his horse. "You stay hidden here. No matter what, don't you leave this spot. Do you understand?"

Girl nodded. "I understand," she whispered, her voice anxious. She grabbed for Shane's arm. "Your name is Shane! I remember now!"

Shane smiled down at her, then turned to his horse and began removing the traps. His arms full, he moved stealthily back in the direction of the cabin. Hearing the continued hammering inside the cabin, Shane felt safe enough to begin placing the traps in the undergrowth in front of the cabin.

After covering the traps with fallen pine boughs and leaves, Shane ran back to cover.

"You set traps for Trapper Dan?" Girl asked, inching over closer to Shane.

"Yes, for Trapper Dan," Shane said dryly. "Traps are for animals, aren't they? I think I'm going to catch a large one quite soon."

Just as he was about to shout Trapper Dan's name to draw his attention, he could not believe his eyes when he saw Melanie suddenly there on horseback. He had been too absorbed in setting the traps to notice a horse approaching!

"God!" Shane gasped, rushing from behind the bushes and waving frantically at Melanie as she dismounted and began walking toward the cabin. "Melanie! Stop!"

Melanie stopped with a start and looked disbelievingly at Shane as he came running from behind the thick brush. He had not been in St. Paul all of this time playing poker—he had come to Trapper Dan's!

"Shane—" she said, then spun around and stared at Trapper Dan as he came to the door and opened it with a bang.

"What the hell's goin' on out here?" Trapper Dan asked in a growl, a rifle aimed at Melanie.

Then Trapper Dan saw Shane approaching. "Josh?" he asked, then realized his mistake. "It's you, the brother," he snarled. "Get outta here or I'll shoot 'er. You ain't got no business here."

"Put the gun down, you weasel," Shane said, still approaching. "You haven't got any argument with Melanie. It's you and I who have a score to settle."

"I should've made sure there were no survivors hidin' in the bushes the day your Ma died," Trapper Dan said, not lowering his rifle. "Guess I've got to do it today." Then he motioned with his rifle. "Step aside, young lady. I've got better use for my firearm."

"If you plan to kill Shane, you'll have to kill me first," Melanie said, trying to hide the trembling in her voice.

"It'd be a waste to kill someone as purty as you," Trapper Dan said, leering at Melanie. Then it came to him that Girl should be finished bathing. Where was she? Without averting his eyes, he leaned his head sideways and called over his shoulder. "Girl! Where are you, Girl?"

Girl stepped out into view. She walked boldly to Shane's side. "Shane come to rescue me!" she shouted. "I never stay with you no more!"

"Why, you bitch," Trapper Dan snarled. He took two steps from his house, then his face contorted as he stepped into one of the hidden traps. The steel teeth of the trap snapped shut onto one of his legs, throwing him to the ground. Blood spurted in all directions. Trapper Dan screamed with pain and dropped his rifle. As it fell to the ground, it discharged. Melanie screamed and fell to the ground in a heap.

"Help me!" Trapper Dan screamed in a painful gurgle. He clutched at the trap. "Girl, come and help me! You're my wife! You can't leave me here sufferin' so!"

Shane bodily set Girl aside. "Don't go any closer to the cabin," he ordered. "Only I know where the traps are set."

He rushed to Melanie, his heart pounding. He searched over her frantically for a gun wound, then sighed with relief. She had not fallen from a wound. She had fainted!

Grabbing her up into his arms, Shane carried Melanie to where he had his horse reined. Girl followed him and knelt down beside him. "Let Girl help," she said.

Shane kissed Melanie's cheek, gave Girl a trusting look, then went back and stood over Trapper Dan. "You will die slowly," he said. "You will have time to remember all the settlers you killed the day my mother died. You will remember how Cedar Maid died, and why. You stole too much from me, trapper. Now you will pay!"

Sweat was pouring profusely from Trapper Dan's brow. His face was twisted grotesquely with pain as blood continued to flow from the jagged wounds of the trap. "Free me," he begged. "I will pay you well!"

"I do not need anything that belongs to you," Shane said. He glanced at the cabin. "But I have come to claim that which was my mother's. Trapper, you had better hope that I find it among your things or I will bring another trap and place your other leg in it. You think you are suffering now? Think of the suffering two traps will cause!"

"I don't know what you're talking about," Trapper Dan said, breathing shallowly, already feeling lightheaded from loss of blood.

"You stole my mother's wedding ring the day she died," Shane accused him. "But of course you don't recall just one tiny ring. You stole many things that day!"

"A . . . ring . . . ?" Trapper Dan said, coughing. "A ring . . . ?"

"Yes, a ring."

"I have many rings."

Shane leaned over Trapper Dan and grabbed hold of his thick red hair. He gave it a hard yank. "Tell me where you keep them," he growled.

"Only if you promise to release me," Trapper Dan said, looking Shane squarely in the eye. "Release me. I'll tell you."

Shane raised a hand and slapped Trapper Dan across the face. "You are in no position to bargain," he shouted. "You are going to die, Trapper Dan!"

Trapper Dan closed his eyes. His head bobbed clumsily forward when Shane released his hair.

"I don't need you to tell me where the ring is," Shane said, moving around the other traps, then on into the cabin.

A vile stench, a mixture of dried urine and perspiration, made Shane's nostrils flare. The cabin was cluttered with all sorts of debris. The furniture consisted of a crude table and two chairs, a bed with yellowed, wrinkled blankets, and a storage cabinet.

Shane went to the cabinet and searched it first. He started throwing pans, books, papers, and jars from it. He looked inside boxes, finding odds and ends of all sorts. He went to the bed and dumped it over, then stopped and stared down at a wooden box that had been hidden there.

Moving to rest on his haunches, Shane lifted the box and rested it on his knee. His fingers were trembling as he removed a pin that was holding the lid in place, then slowly raised the lid and peered down at an abundant assortment of ladies' and men's rings, brooches, diamond-encrusted combs, men's diamond stickpins, and necklaces of various gems.

Hatred swelled within Shane. No doubt every jewel had been taken from someone he had killed. Now Shane wondered if letting him die slowly within the jaws of the trap was a horrible enough death for him. Perhaps he should be scalped alive. Shane would gladly do the honors if it were not that he could not let Melanie witness the act.

"Melanie," he said, reminded that he had left her in a deep swoon. He must hurry and go to her. He had to reassure her that everything would be all right. Soon his vengeance would be complete.

One by one he sorted through the rings. He would know his mother's. When he was small, he had admired the ring. She had explained that it sealed the bond between her and his father. It was a symbol of their love. Often he had looked at the inscription on the inside of the ring. He hadn't been able to read it, but as he ran his finger over the inscription, his mother had told him that his father had engraved a message of love to her before he gave it to her on their wedding day. He could not recall the exact inscription, except that his mother's and father's name were written there, also.

His heart raced when he picked up a gold wedding band. He closed his eyes and ran his fingers along the inside. A great warmth spread through him when he felt inscribed words etched into the gold. "Mama," he whispered. "Tell me about it, Mama. I want to hear it again."

His mind went back to the last day he had seen his mother. While traveling in the boat, she had removed her ring and entertained him by telling him about it again, and reading the inscription to him. If he thought hard enough, he could hear her soft, sweet voice even now. Tears sprang from his eyes and a deep sob tore from his throat. At this moment, he missed his mother more than ever. This ring brought her closer, as though she were there, embracing and comforting him.

Wiping a tear from his cheek, Shane placed the ring before his eyes and read the inscription. It read: "To Amy, my true love, forever and ever. Jared."

Shane brought the ring to his lips and kissed it, then clutched it hard within his hand as he rose to his feet. Leaving the cabin, he stopped and bent over Trapper Dan. "You sonofabitch," he hissed. "I found my mother's ring. Not only my mother's, but many more."

Shane coiled his fingers through Trapper Dan's greasy red hair and gave a hard yank. "I lived with the Chippewa for most of my life because of you," he growled. "Did you know that I learned the art of scalping quite well? Perhaps I'll take your scalp to place on my scalp pole."

Trapper Dan grimaced and looked up at Shane, wild-eyed. "You've got what you came for," he cried. "Your mother's ring! Let me go. I'll never cause you trouble again."

Shane straightened his back and stared down at the blood still oozing from the wound, the severed bone protruding from the skin at a strange angle. "No, I don't think you will be causing anyone else heartache," he said smoothly. "Soon that leg will become gangrenous. You shouldn't last long after that. That is, if you last through the night without something wild coming to feast on your leg." Shane smiled slowly at Trapper Dan. "Or perhaps on your face?"

"Oh, God, have mercy," Trapper Dan cried, reaching a hand to Shane.

"At this moment I don't even know the meaning of the word mercy," Shane said. He turned and made his way carefully around the ring of traps he had set.

"You're no better than the savages you lived with!" Trapper Dan shouted.

"No, I guess not," Shane said from over his shoulder. "And I have you to thank for that, don't I?"

He broke into a run, then stopped when he saw Melanie walking toward him. Safe from the threat of the traps, he hurried to her and drew her into his arms. "It is done," he said, his cheek resting in her hair. "Vengeance is mine."

"You're all right?" Melanie murmured, pulling

away, looking him up and down. She smiled. "Yes, I can see that you are."

"And you?"

"I feel foolish."

"Why?"

"For having fainted."

"It was the blood?"

Melanie smiled sheepishly at him. She placed a hand to her stomach. "Perhaps not," she said softly. "Perhaps it was because of something wonderful."

Shane gazed at her hands resting over her stomach, then he looked quickly up at her. "Are you saying . . . ?"

She interrupted him. "Yes, darling," she said, snuggling close to him again. "I think I am with child."

Shane held her tightly. "Nothing would make me happier," he whispered, then he held her away from him. He held out his clasped hand and opened it. He revealed the gold wedding band. "This was my mother's. Now it will be yours."

Melanie placed a hand to her throat, choked with emotion. Tears streamed from her eyes as she let him place the ring on her finger. "You found it?" she murmured. "This is truly your mother's?"

"It was among Trapper Dan's belongings. But now it is in its rightful place."

"It is so beautiful," she murmured. "I will wear it proudly."

"We must have the wedding ceremony soon," Shane said. "You must carry a child beneath your heart with a husband at your side!"

Girl stepped meekly into view behind Melanie. Shane saw her and eased Melanie from his arms, turning her to also see the Indian woman. "Melanie, I hope you don't mind that I have invited Girl to live with us," he said, beckoning for Girl to come to him. "Trapper Dan paid a bride price for her and she cannot return to her village. I now realize that I should have taken Cedar Maid with me when I left. Perhaps if I take Girl in, that will make up for my ignorance."

"Girl?" Melanie said, looking questioningly up at Shane. "That is her name?"

"She left her Indian name behind when she left her people," Shane explained, looking down at Girl as she now stood before him and Melanie. "Trapper Dan has called her Girl while she lived with him. She thinks that is the name he assigned her."

Melanie looked at the beautiful Indian woman and smiled. "Would you like a different name?" she asked softly. "One more suited to you?"

"*Ay-uh*, that would please me," Girl said, smiling from Shane to Melanie.

"Daphne is a name that I have always loved," Melanie said, moving to Girl. She took her hands affectionately. "Would you like to be called Daphne?"

Girl nodded anxiously, her eyes beaming. "That is pretty," she said. "I will like being called Daphne."

Shane looked at Melanie questioningly, suddenly struck with wonder over Melanie's coming to

Trapper Dan's cabin. How did she even know the man?

"Melanie, why were you coming to see Trapper Dan?" he asked suddenly.

Melanie's eyes wavered. What would he think when she told him that she had known for a long time that Trapper Dan was in the area—that she had been shown only yesterday where he resided! What would he do when he discovered that it was Trapper Dan, and Melanie's brother, who had been the cause of all of Shane's torment? She had so wanted not to be in the position of telling him, especially about Terrance.

Someone yelling for help in the distance reprieved her momentarily from revealing truths to Shane that would make her uncomfortable. Shivers rode her spine when another shriek filled the air. It was a cry of stark fear.

Melanie's insides grew cold as she looked quickly up at Shane. Had he recognized the voice?

She had!

It was Terrance! He was in trouble!

"Shane, it's Terrance," she said, looking anxiously in the direction of the cries. She ran to her horse, grabbed its reins and mounted. "I must go to him. He's in danger."

Though she had sent Terrance away, there was no doubt that she still loved him, for at this moment her heart was pounding with fear for him. No matter what he had done to Shane, she wouldn't want anything to happen to him. He was her brother.

Melanie's hair blew in the breeze as she rode away. When she heard Shane on horseback behind her, grateful tears burned at the corners of her eyes. He had every reason in the world not to help Terrance, yet he was prepared to.

But would he, if he knew the truth?

• CHAPTER THIRTY-ONE •

Melanie rode hard, then drew her reins tight, stopping her horse when she finally saw Terrance only a short distance away from her now. A sick feeling swept through her. Terrance was on his horse, a bluff at his back, cornered by Wild Thunder, the Stantons' prize longhorn which had escaped only a few days ago.

Melanie stifled a cry of fear when she looked away from Terrance at the longhorn. Angry and frightened, its bloodshot and bulging eyes were burning like bull's-eye lanterns. A great Brindle bull, Wild Thunder was seven years old and at the apex of his prowess. His powerful neck showed a great bulge just behind the head. A big dewlap accenting his primeval origin. He seemed mad through and through, having taken a position on a rise of open ground perhaps a hundred yards from Terrance.

Melanie could tell that the longhorn had been pawing dirt for a long time. As she watched him, scarcely breathing, he lifted the dirt with his forefeet so that it went high up in the air and fell in part upon his own back. He often stopped to hook one of his horns—the "master horn"—into the ground, goring down to a kind of clayish damp that stuck to the tip. He even hooked both horns in, one at a time, and kneeling, rubbed his shoulder against the ground.

His powerful lungs bellowed out streams of breath that sprayed particles of earth away from his nostrils. Now, with earth plastering his horns, matting his shaggy frontlet, and covering his back from head to toe, he was a spectacle.

"Melanie, for God's sake, do something!" Terrance shouted, afraid to move. The longhorn was hellbent on attacking him!

Terrance watched Shane ride up next to Melanie, an Indian woman clinging to him. "Shane! Kill the damn longhorn!" he shouted, his voice ragged. "Shoot him!"

Melanie pleaded with Shane with her eyes. "Shane, what can we do?" she asked, all cold from fear inside. "One false move and the longhorn will attack Terrance. My brother won't have a chance!"

"Inch your horse back slowly," Shane said, guiding his backward. "Then slip slowly from the saddle. Right now the longhorn isn't even aware that we're here. His eyes are on Terrance only."

Melanie followed Shane's lead. They moved

their horses back a safe distance, then slipped slowly from the saddles. Daphne stayed put, too afraid to move.

Shane lifted his rifle from the gun boot on the side of his horse. "Melanie, I'm going to have to kill the longhorn," he said, his voice barely above a whisper.

"I know," she said, moving to Shane's side. "It's a shame, though. He's one of our handsomest bulls."

"Turn your eyes away," Shane said, raising his rifle. "It won't be a pretty sight."

"I'm afraid for Terrance," Melanie said, biting her lower lip in frustration.

"Turn your eyes away, Melanie," Shane said flatly, his finger on the trigger.

Melanie took one last look at the longhorn. He was talking to himself, his truculent head swaying. Hoarse and deep, like thunder on the horizon, he mumbled *uh-huh-uh-uh-uhing*, then raised his head in a loud, high defiant challenge, combining a bellow from the uttermost profundities with a shriek high and foreign.

He was pawing up more dirt, lunging his horn in as if to rip out the guts of the earth.

Melanie turned away from the sight, trembling.

"Terrance, I'm going to shoot the longhorn," Shane said, holding his rifle steady. "But it would be best if you could move your horse away from the steer. He's going to make a mighty lunge when the bullet sinks into his flesh. Once he's shot, be ready to burn leather and get the hell out of there."

"I don't need instructions, Shane," Terrance

said, sweat streaming from his brow. "Just do it, damn it!"

"I can't shoot him until you move your horse away," Shane said, his teeth clenching angrily. "You'll be signing your own death warrant if you don't do as I say."

"Who taught you so much about longhorn habits?" Terrance said, his contempt for Shane showing even in the eye of danger.

Melanie swung around and glared at Terrance. "Terrance, for once can't you put your feelings for Shane aside?" she said, her voice quavering. She circled her hands into tight fists at her sides. "Do as he says. Your life is at stake here!"

Terrance eyed the longhorn warily. His spine stiffened when he saw the animal's horns all shining and sharp. He knew that bulls kept their horns sharpened for bloody work by rubbing them against trees and brush, and whetting them in the ground. Wild Thunder was muttering and pawing, all pluck and vinegar, ready for a fight.

"I'm afraid to move," Terrance said in a whine. "Damn it, I don't think I have a chance in hell of escaping that damn bull's wrath."

"No, you don't if you don't move farther away from him," Shane said, impatience thick in his voice.

"All right, damn it," Terrance said, his hands trembling as he flicked the reins and nudged his heels into the flanks of his horse.

But he was too slow. The brute wheeled to attack. Before Shane had the chance to fire his rifle, Terrance's horse was met full in the side by the bull's horns.

Her throat too frozen in fear to scream, Melanie felt faint as she watched in mortal terror as both horse and rider were lifted for one instant into the air, and then came down in a heap together. The horse was dead, one horn completely through its body, the other caught in the bones of the chest. One of Terrance's legs was between the horns of the bull, pinned fast between his head and the body of the horse.

The horse's body was impaled on the bull's head, fastening it to the ground. Terrance lay on the bull's back.

Pain shooting through his pinned leg, Terrance began to flail his arms wildly in the air, crying and yelling as he struggled to get free. He gazed at the bull. It was breathing hard and frothing at the mouth. Terrance could feel its mighty heartbeat against his body, just waiting for it to begin a hard struggle to be set free. At the moment, it seemed to be stunned by the predicament it had gotten itself in.

Shane stepped slowly toward the twisted mass of horse, longhorn, and man. He was afraid to shoot the bull, lest the longhorn's struggles further injure Terrance.

Instead, he lay his gun on the ground and took his knife from the sheath at his waist. He crept up to the steer and with lightning speed he opened the bull's jugular vein and waited for him to slowly bleed to death.

He then cut off the bull's horns. His muscles cording and straining, he finally managed to pull the bull off Terrance. He lifted Terrance in his arms and carried him toward Melanie, then lay him on the ground beneath the shade of an oak tree.

Melanie fell to her knees beside Terrance. She cradled his head on her lap, feeling a bitterness rising into her throat when she saw the condition of his leg. It was crushed. Splinters of bone protruded through his pants, revealing bloody, mangled flesh. "Terrance, Terrance," she cried, tears flooding her eyes.

"At least he's alive," Shane said, kneeling down beside her.

"Thank you for saving him," Melanie said, sniffling back more tears. "It would have been so easy for you to have ignored him. He's been nothing but a thorn in your side since you returned home."

"Well, perhaps some, but he's done nothing all that terrible that would make me want to see harm come to him," Shane said, wiping the longhorn's blood from his knife onto the grass at his side.

Melanie's eyes wavered, knowing more than Shane did about her brother's ugly activities. She looked down at her brother, who had drifted into unconsciousness, the pain surely having rendered him almost mindless.

She stroked his brow. How could she hate him at a time like this? She had almost lost him! She felt partially responsible, for she had driven him away! She should have been more understanding!

If she had been, perhaps this would have not happened to him! Now he was surely going to be a cripple for the rest of his life. And all because of her!

Terrance's eyes blinked slowly open. He grimaced with pain, his face flushed. He looked from Melanie to Shane. "Thanks," he said, then laughed awkwardly. "But I sure as hell wish you could've thought of a better way to rid my life of that damn longhorn. My leg hurts like hell."

"We're going to get you to a doctor," Shane said. "I'm going to make a travois for transporting you." He started to rise, but was stopped when Terrance placed a hand to his arm.

"Shane, I owe you my life," Terrance said, blinking back tears. "Thanks. Thanks for everything."

"You're not out of the woods yet," Shane said. "If we don't get you to the doctor quick, you could lose more than your damn leg." He started to rise, but was stopped again by Terrance clasping onto his arm. His fingers dug desperately into Shane's flesh.

"Shane, there's something that needs to be said, in case I don't pull through this thing alive," Terrance said, swallowing hard. "It needs telling, Shane. Please take the time to listen."

Melanie placed her hands to her mouth, sobbing, as she looked down at her brother who was ready to confess everything to Shane.

Oh, what if he died? She felt as though she had failed her brother! She should have found a way to help him with his drinking and gambling. He had seemed tormented, but never had she been able to understand exactly why.

Was it too late? Was the longhorn going to succeed at ridding the world of the man he had most hated after all? If so, a part of her would die along with him!

"We don't have time for talking, Terrance," Shane grumbled.

"We've got to take the time," Terrance said, grabbing at his leg as a crushing sort of pain shot through it. The hand that still held onto Shane clasped harder, desperate to purge his soul of that which could make him burn in hell if he didn't.

"Then, damn it, Terrance, get said whatever it is that needs saying," Shane grumbled.

"Shane, I'm sorry for all the trouble I've caused you," Terrance said, swallowing hard. "I was wrong about you. Damn it, you could've stood by and watched that damn longhorn gore me to death. Instead, you jumped right in there, ready to help. I didn't deserve your help."

Melanie caressed Terrance's brow. "Terrance, this isn't the time," she pleaded. "You can tell Shane everything later."

Terrance looked up at her. "There may not be another chance," he said sullenly. "I've got to say it now." He looked slowly back at Shane. "Shane, all that's happened to you lately? It's been me doin' it."

Shane gulped in a quick breath of air. He glared down at Terrance as he continued to speak, recalling his first impression of Melanie's brother. He had thought then that Terrance was a coward! All these devious acts behind everyone's backs now proved his cowardice!

"I had help from someone else, but I am responsible for your barn burning and the stampede," he said, licking his parched lips. "Everything, Shane. Everything!"

He looked up at Melanie, then turned his eyes back to Shane. "But, as I said, I didn't work alone," he said weakly. "I paid Trapper Dan to help me. He was with me all along. If he wasn't actually helping me do the dirty deed, he was standing watch." He swallowed hard again. "He's as much at fault as I was." He looked over Shane's shoulder, at the Indian woman. He recognized her. She was Trapper Dan's wife! "What's she doin' here? She's—"

"Yes, she lived with Trapper Dan," Melanie said, interrupting. "But she won't any longer. She's going to live with me and Shane."

Terrance's eyes widened. "You . . . and . . . Shane?" he said in an almost whisper.

"Yes, we're going to be married," Melanie said, smiling over at Shane. "Soon."

Then she frowned down at Terrance. "We've got to get you to a doctor," she said. She gave Shane a quick glance. "You mentioned building a travois. Perhaps you'd best get to it. I don't know how much longer Terrance can hold out."

Shane started to rise, but was stopped again by Terrance grabbing his arm. "I was on my way to warn Trapper Dan about you," he said shallowly.

"Seems you're too late," Shane said, easing his arm from Terrance's grip. "Just like you, he's met with an accident. But he hasn't got someone willing to see that he gets proper doctoring. He's going to die a slow, painful death, Terrance. The sort that he deserves."

"You probably think I deserve the same sort of death now that you know everything," Terrance said, wincing when he was flooded with renewed pain.

Shane glared down at Terrance. "Yes, perhaps I do," he said flatly. "But because you are Melanie's brother, I am forced to do what my heart does not tell me to do." He stood over Terrance, his doubled fists on his hips. "You are lucky. You are being given another chance."

Melanie covered her mouth with a hand and cried softly as she watched Shane begin cutting the limbs off willow trees and putting together a travois. Never had she loved him more than now.

Melanie sat at Terrance's bedside in his bedroom, bathing his feverish brow with a dampened cloth. Doc Raley had come and gone. The amputation had been quick, yet gruesome. The leg had been removed from the thigh, and now hard times were ahead, whether or not Terrance's body could adjust to the shock it had just been put through. A fever now threatened him more than the longhorn bull during its most fevered pitch of anger!

Shane stepped to Melanie's side and placed a comforting hand on her shoulder. "Have faith," he said reassuringly. "Your brother has a strong constitution."

Melanie placed a hand over Shane's and squeezed it affectionately as she looked up at him through misty eyes. "You are so kind," she murmured. "You don't have to be here, you know."

"I am here because you need me," Shane said, then turned with a start when someone else entered the room. He questioned the stranger with a forked eyebrow, seeing two mighty holstered pistols weighting him down at his hips.

Melanie moved quickly to her feet. "Sheriff Morgan?" she said, stunned by his presence. "What's wrong? Why are you here?"

Sheriff Morgan removed his hat and came into the room, overpowering in his two hundred and fifty pounds of brawn and muscle. "Sorry to intrude on your private moments with your brother," he said softly. He looked Shane over slowly. "But I'm here to see Shane. It's about his brother."

He looked directly into Shane's eyes. "By God, I cain't get over the resemblance. You and Josh are identical, ain't you?"

"What about my brother?" Shane said, brushing aside the small talk.

The sheriff twirled his hat around, between his fingers. He looked at the floor. "The news ain't good," he said hoarsely. He rose his eyes slowly back up again and met Shane's steady stare. "Son, I need you to come into town and identify the body."

Melanie teetered for a moment. She grabbed for

Shane's arm and steadied herself. Shane paled. Something grabbed him at the pit of his stomach, as though a sledge hammer had hit him there.

"What are you saying?" he said, his voice drawn.

"Seems your brother has played his last game of poker," Sheriff Morgan said sullenly. "He got careless. Someone pulled a gun on him and blasted him clear to kingdom come. He didn't know what hit him." He cleared his throat. "It's required that the next of kin come and identify the body. It's at the undertaker's. Then you can talk with the undertaker about the arrangements that need to be made."

Shane was in a state of shock, filled with regrets and memories of long ago, when brothers behaved as brothers and loved one another! He had hoped that it could be the same again once Josh thought more about things and was able to accept Shane into his life!

"No, it just can't be!" Shane said, between clenched teeth. "It isn't fair!"

He turned away from the sheriff and buried his face in his hands. Melanie crept an arm around his waist and hugged him tightly.

"Shane, Shane . . ."

• CHAPTER THIRTY-TWO •

Sunshine streamed through lace-draped windows. Light flooded through double doors that had welcomed the guests to the Brennan mansion.

When they entered they had walked past big covered Delft jars on black and gold Italianate brackets. The room in which they all now stood was complex with hot accents—rose-strewn chintzes and a Bessarabian rug, and gilded Italian side chairs in a brilliant red weave, with Edwardian needlework pillows. The floor boards were mostly bare.

The house was lavishly decorated with great masses of flowers. The staircase was garlanded with roses and other blossoms, filling the house with a sweet, heady fragrance, mingling with the aroma of freshly baked rolls wafting through the hall from the big kitchen.

The marriage ceremony was performed in the back parlor, where the windows opened onto a large garden whose gnarled old pear trees were heavy with ripe fruit. A low breeze disturbed the silence and gentle petals of autumn flowers in the garden, a lush bouquet of colors.

Melanie stood clasped by the golden light, like the sweetheart of the sun, as she looked adoringly up at Shane, the minister with an opened bible standing before them. She wore a white Venice lace and silk satin gown with a Queen Anne neckline, long sleeves, and Alencon lace framing her face, falling back into a long train that hugged the floor around her. She carried a bridal bouquet of miniature pink roses, the pink of her cheeks seeming to be their reflection.

With one sweep of her eyes she saw Shane as someone wonderfully handsome in his double-breasted coat that had a fitted bodice and flared skirt with a split in the back, its lapels curved almost like a shawl. His dark trousers were worn down on his shoes, even touching the floor in the back with straps under his feet. His coat fit him perfectly, emphasizing the broadness of his shoulders, his shirt front was dazzling white, with an abundance of ruffles spilling over his gray waistcoat. His hair caught the rays of the sun in its folds, making it appear more golden than usual.

The moment was magical, something that Melanie had wanted from the moment she set eyes on Shane. She had often doubted that she and

Shane would reach this day, for one thing after another had stood in the way of their happiness. Even the latest death had postponed this precious moment. They had been forced to wait until a respectable amount of time passed after Josh's funeral, so much that Melanie was beginning to show that she was with child.

"I now pronounce you man and wife," the preacher said, closing his bible. He clasped his bible in one hand and placed it behind him, smiling from Shane to Melanie. "You may now kiss the bride."

Behind Shane and Melanie, Terrance leaned heavily into his canes, one in each hand, his artificial leg balancing him as well as if it were a true leg. He smiled from Melanie to Shane. He had been wrong about so many things. All along Shane had been the true answer to the dilemma that Terrance had found himself in since his father's death.

Now that Melanie had married Shane, she would live with him and the farm was back in Terrance's control. To hell with wanting to get his hands on a portion of the Brennan estate. He felt lucky to have anything.

He eyed his wooden leg. Damn it, he had almost mastered it. One day he would even ride a horse again!

The only thing that he deeply regretted was Josh's death. Yet something good had come from it. Terrance no longer gambled or drank. Those vices had been the cause of Josh's early demise.

The same fate would not come to Terrance Stanton!

Shane turned to Melanie. He looked down at her with a gentle passion, his blue eyes sparkling with happiness. He smoothed the lace back from her face and placed his fingers on her cheeks. He leaned down and touched her lips wonderingly, aware of many eyes on them as the guests looked on, moved.

Melanie's insides melted as her lips met Shane's. She twined an arm about his neck and kissed him softly, aware of the guests from St. Paul and surrounding farms watching, seemingly happy with her choice of husband. No one seemed to mind that Shane had been raised with Indians.

It seemed to Melanie that finally that part of his past was behind him. He rarely spoke of the Chippewa. Daphne was the only reminder, and she was adapting well to her new life. She even stood watching the ceremony in a silk gown, flounced with yards of lace, her dark hair spiraling in long coils of curls down her perfectly straight back.

Melanie drew away from Shane, looked up into his eyes again, and smiled. Then she turned to gaze warmly at Daphne. Deliberately, she tossed her bridal bouquet in Daphne's direction.

Daphne's eyes lit up and she smiled widely as she caught the bouquet and hugged it to her chest.

But there was a trace of sadness in her eyes as one hand slipped down to her stomach. Melanie was not the only one who was with child. The trapper had impregnated Daphne before she had been rescued.

Laughing giddily, Melanie went to Daphne and hugged her. "Everything is going to be all right," she whispered. "One day you'll find a man who will give your child a father. Until then, you will share your child with me, Shane, and our child."

Daphne draped an arm around Melanie's neck. "*Mee-gway-chee-wahn-dum*, thank you," she whispered. "You are so kind. I love you, Melanie."

"I love you, too," Melanie whispered, then drew away from her and went to stand at Shane's side as people began to mill around them, offering a congratulatory handshake.

Soon Melanie's jaws began to ache from her incessant smiling. She gave Shane occasional glances, seeing the radiance in his eyes, proof of his happiness.

Then there was a thundering of hoofbeats outside. Melanie and Shane exchanged wondering glances, then moved, arm in arm, down the long corridor and outside onto the wide veranda that ran along the entire front of the mansion.

Melanie's insides froze when she saw the mass of Indians on horseback who now stood motionlessly before the house, especially when she recognized Chief Gray Falcon among them.

She welcomed Shane's possessive arm around her waist, recalling so vividly that night when she was abducted.

"Gray Falcon, you are disturbing my wedding day," Shane said, looking his old friend over carefully. Gray Falcon wore his fanciest headdress of at least a hundred feathers tumbling down his back in a profusion of colors. His clothing was of white doeskin, bedecked with colorful beads and porcupine quills shaped in many colorful designs. He carried no weapon. His usual stoic expression showed something akin to friendship, his jaw and lips relaxed.

"Why have you come?" Shane asked. "It has been many sleeps since I left my hair in your hand to prove that I no longer wanted any part of your life. I feel no different now."

"I have come in peace, bearing many gifts," Gray Falcon said, nodding toward many horses that were being led toward Shane and Melanie. "My scouts brought me news of your wedding. The gifts are for your wedding. Please take them in friendship."

Gray Falcon gestured toward a great strawberry roan that a brave was singling out from the rest. "Come, my brother," he offered Shane. "I give you my best horse! Get on his back with your woman and come with me to my village!"

Shane's eyes narrowed as some Chippewa braves began securing the horses' reins to a hitching rail. "Remove the horses!" he shouted. He gestured with his free hand toward them as he stared coldly into Gray Falcon's eyes. "I need nothing from you anymore. Go. Your friendship comes too late."

Chief Gray Falcon frowned and leaned over his pommel. "Gray Falcon was wrong about many things," he said in an almost whisper, his voice drawn. "Gray Falcon misses your companionship. Come home, Shane. We can have a new beginning!"

"Can't you see that I am now married?" Shane said, squaring his shoulders. He drew Melanie close to his side. "This is my home." He looked down at Melanie, a softness in his eyes. "This is our home."

Again he looked up at Gray Falcon. "Please go, Gray Falcon," he said thickly. "We have nothing else to say to one another. You are responsible for too much ugliness in my life. It is not easy to forget Cedar Maid. It is not easy to forget that you abducted my woman, or that you sent me away when I did not want to go!"

"So you send me away?"

"Yes. Now. Please leave."

Chief Gray Falcon stared into Shane's eyes a moment. *"Gah-ween-nee-nee-sis-eh-tos-say-non,"* he said, his voice a monotone. *"Mee-suh-ay-oo!"*

Gray Falcon then wheeled his horse around and began riding away. He shouted to his braves for them to follow him, the horses trailing behind them.

Shane watched, feeling as though a part of his heart was being torn in shreds, for he so wanted to join the braves. He so wanted to tell Gray Falcon that all was forgiven! He hungered for the hunt on horseback with his Chippewa companions! He hungered for the wigwam, and the feeling of freedom that living in such a simple way gave him.

Shaking his head to clear his mind of such

troubled thoughts, Shane turned his back to the departing Indians. He swallowed hard, then looked down at Melanie.

His gut twisted strangely when he saw a look of knowing in her eyes. Had she truly read his thoughts only a moment ago? Did she know how badly he wanted to join the Chippewa, become a part of their lives again?

But did she also know that if that ever could have been possible, she would still be a part of that life? She could live in that wigwam with him. She could bear their child there and sit by the fire, nursing him.

"Darling, I think we should join our guests again," Melanie said, seeing something akin to torment in her husband's eyes. She knew what had caused it. Why had Chief Gray Falcon arrived today, of all days, to bring back memories that haunted Shane? To make him hunger for that which he could no longer have? Why—oh, why?

"Yes, it would be best," Shane said, guiding her back into the house. The aroma wafting from the massive dining room was mouth-watering. "It is time to feed our guests, wouldn't you say?"

"And then afterwards?" Melanie giggled, clinging to Shane as they moved into the back parlor. "What then, my darling husband?"

"I have a surprise awaiting you, my darling wife," Shane said, smiling down at her.

"What?" Melanie asked, her voice lilting.

"It would not be a surprise if I told you, would it?"

"Well, I guess not," Melanie said, laughing softly.

The guests welcomed them, and then proceeded into the dining room. A Waterford crystal chandelier set off the large, airy room. A long, dark mahogany table was set with Sevres porcelain. Platter after platter with mounds and mounds of food were set along the table. There was marinated beef tenderloin, broccoli swimming in melted cheese, ham loaf baked with a tangy tomato sauce glaze, sweet potatoes, fresh rolls with butter, and jam and apple butter. Dessert was sitting on a sidetable—peach shortcake, Melanie's favorite.

As everyone sat down at the table, they found a tall glass of lemonade besprigged with mint awaiting their pleasure. A string quartet played just outside on the lawn, the music wafting through the open windows with the gentle breeze as light and airy as the Liszt étude that was being played.

It was the end of a wonderful day. Melanie ate slowly as she gave Shane occasional glances. He seemed still in a sort of fog. She attributed that to Chief Gray Falcon. Was he now regretting that he had not accepted the chief's apology? Would he forever regret it? Would that overshadow their night filled with surprises and the promise of gentle lovemaking?

She hoped not. One's wedding night came only once in a lifetime.

Yet she knew that she would perhaps have to live under the shadow, always, of Shane's past. She had been foolish to think that he had totally left it behind.

Everyone was gone. The night was like wide water, without sound. Shane swept Melanie up into his arms and began ascending the graceful, curved stairway with bronze rails and delicately turned balusters, also of bronze. As he looked at her, words were not necessary. He could see in her eyes and in the way her pulse beat at the hollow of her throat the excitement building within her over what was to come on their wedding night. Though they had shared many intimate moments before their wedding vows had been spoken, they still looked forward to this new sort of sharing—this sharing of a total commitment!

"Oh, Shane, I feel so sinful," Melanie said, clinging around his neck. Her hair drifted down behind her, almost touching the floor as she held her head back.

"Sinful?" Shane said, forking an eyebrow. "Why would you? We can now boast of being married!"

Melanie's eyes gleamed into his as she straightened her back. "Darling, I know that we are married," she said, their eyes meeting and holding. "I feel sinful because I am so deliriously happy!"

"Oh, I see," Shane said, chuckling. He stepped up on the second floor landing and began walking down the corridor that was lighted by soft flickering candles in wall sconces.

Melanie's eyes flickered over the door that was usually Shane's as he passed it by. She looked back up at him. "Where are you taking me?" she asked. "Why aren't you taking me to your room?"

"Be patient," Shane said, going to another room and nudging the door open with his shoulder. He stepped inside. The room was flooded with candlelight.

Melanie's breath was stolen as he carried her on to a large bedroom that boasted a fourteen-foot ceiling. A carved double bed, canopied with white lace, stood in the middle of the room, while all around the room were deep, comfortable, thick-cushioned chairs and sofas.

Off the room, Melanie could see something that made her want to cry. Shane had seen to it that the adjoining room had already been made into a nursery. She could see a baby's crib, gaily colored wallpaper, and an assortment of all the toys that a child could want!

She looked up at him and placed a hand to his cheek. "Darling, darling . . ." she whispered, then sighed with pleasure as he laid her down on the bed, upon a layering of crisply-tailored sheets. She watched him begin to undress, then sat up on the bed and began matching him, removing her clothes piece by piece.

When he joined her on the bed, she accepted him atop her. There were no preliminaries. He plunged himself inside her and began his slow strokes.

"Shane, are you going to sleep with me at

night?" she whispered, running her fingernails up and down his spine.

Shane drew partially away from her, looking down at her with puzzlement. "You think that I wouldn't?" he said, his eyes darkening with emotion.

"Well, I know how you feel about beds," Melanie said. "And this most certainly is a bed."

"This is our bed," Shane corrected, brushing his tongue along her lower lip. "Never shall I let you sleep alone in it. Never."

"But the pallet of furs—?"

"Gone. Just as Gray Falcon is gone."

"Will you be happy without either?"

"Very."

"Then that is all that matters," Melanie said, sighing deeply.

"Let us make love," Shane said, kissing the column of her neck lightly. "Let us share our feelings for one another with our child even as our child sleeps in your womb."

"Yes, darling," Melanie whispered, shimmering with ecstasy as he resumed his sweet strokes within her. "Let us always share everything with our child. Then let's give our child a brother or sister as quickly as possible. No child should be raised alone."

"Yes, brothers should love one another from their very beginnings," Shane said, then swallowed hard when his thoughts went to Josh, sad over his loss. "Perhaps we shall even have twins, Melanie."

"That would be wonderful," she said, weaving her fingers through his hair, hearing the soft melancholy in his voice. "That would be wonderful."

They held each other with exquisite tenderness. They made love slowly, wonderfully.

· CHAPTER THIRTY-THREE ·

Seven Months Later

Heavy with child, Melanie stood at the parlor window looking across quiet fields under skies the color of shadows, past fences hushed in snow, and at gullies mantled by the snow-laden branches of oaks and maples. The lane that led to the Brennan mansion was dusted with white and marked with the tracks of wooden wheels and horses; here and there fresh horse manure lay steaming in the chill morning air.

Melanie hugged herself when snow began falling again, first in slow, soft swirls, and then in blizzard strength. She looked toward the herd of longhorns in the corral, barely visible through the haze of snow. As many as could stayed huddled together, close to the barn.

But out on the range, those that weren't as

fortunate were looking possible death in the eye each night. Some had not survived, the ones that weren't as strong having frozen solid in the cold blasts of winds that came like the wrath of God from the north. If the snow deepened and the temperatures lowered tonight, more deaths could be expected.

Thus far there had been a record snowfall. At times, the yearling heifers had hopped over the fences like grasshoppers. The snowfall had caved in buildings. Sometimes the snow melted off the hay shed and slipped into the feeders.

Melanie turned when she heard footsteps behind her. She smiled and welcomed Shane's embrace as he moved to her side to join her at the window. "Shane, the weather is worsening," she murmured, snuggling closer to him. "I'm worried about the cattle at both farms. The loss could be great if the snow gets worse and the temperature drops again."

Shane looked past the cattle, up at the butte that stretched out into the dark depths of the forest. Though he was as concerned about the cattle as Melanie, he could not help but shift some of his concern to the Chippewa. In weather like this, when animals could freeze in their tracks, the Chippewa could suffer from starvation. He had seen it before, when a baby born in mid-winter could not survive because its mother's milk was not nourishing enough, because the mother had not eaten properly herself.

It was surely the same now for the people that he loved. There had been too many snows, too many freezes! He was finding it hard to block out thoughts of how it must be in the Indian village even at this moment. He could see them huddled around a fire made of wood scraped from beneath layers of snow. He could see the leanness of the braves' bodies. He could see the longing, the hunger in their eyes.

"I must go to them," Shane blurted out, suddenly swinging away from Melanie. He began walking away from her, his steps determined.

Melanie turned and stared at him, not understanding. Them? Whom was he referring to? The cattle? He had never been this concerned before about them. He had done what was humanly possible to save them, and then had reconciled himself to the fact that losses could be expected. Everyone knew that the weather this winter had been the worst in years. No one expected to come out of it without losses.

Melanie followed Shane from the room and stared in wonder as he slapped his gunbelt around his waist and fastened it, then grabbed his heavy, quilted buckskin jacket and jerked his arms into the sleeves.

"Shane, where are you going?" Melanie asked, grabbing his hand. "What are you going to do?"

Shane looked down at Melanie, suddenly realizing what he was doing without any thought for his wife, who was heavy with his child. He swallowed hard and placed his hands on her swollen abdomen. He smiled when he felt their child kick against his firm grip and then move slowly.

Melanie placed her hands over Shane's and

smiled up at him. "It won't be long now, darling," she said proudly. She laughed softly. "As much movement as there is, it could be twins. Yet my father said that I was an active child while within my mother's womb. Would you believe that he said I even kicked one of her ribs out of place?"

"Yes, I believe that you would be as feisty and unpredictable even then," Shane said, running his hands over her round belly.

His eyes shadowed in thought as he looked over his shoulder at the window, and his insides tightened when he saw the thick veil of snow that continued to fall.

He looked down at Melanie again. "Darling, there is something that I need to do and it cannot include you," he said. "You must stay behind and protect our unborn child. Stay in the house and keep warm. Eat plenty of nourishing food. I will return in time to witness our child's birth."

Melanie paled. She took a shaky step back from Shane. "What do you mean, you will return?" she said, her voice drawn. "Where are you going?" She looked toward the window and a shiver stung her when she saw the fierceness of the storm outside. She pleaded with her eyes at Shane. "You can't." She slowly shook her head and placed a hand to her mouth. "You can't be planning to . . ."

She lunged into Shane's arms. "No!" she cried. "I won't let you! You can't travel to the Indian village in this weather." She drew away from him and studied the haunted look in his eyes. "Oh, God, that is where you plan to go, isn't it? I know how concerned you have been over the people at the Chippewa village. I know you fear for them. But, Shane, you just can't leave in this blizzard to go to them. What good would it do?"

Again she crept into his arms and hugged him to her. "Shane, I thought you had forgotten your past," she cried. "You have seemed so content."

Shane placed his hands to her shoulders and eased her away from him. "Never will they be entirely from my blood," he said. "Especially now, in their time of need." He looked at the window, hearing the bellow of the longhorns. "We have meat that could keep many of the Chippewa alive. We have milk for the babies! I must take it to them!"

Melanie wiped tears from her eyes and choked back a sob. "But, Shane, what of me? What of our child?" she said, her voice breaking. "If you go out in that blizzard, I may never see you again! If you lost your way . . ."

"Never would I lose my way," Shane said in a low growl. "Not even in the worst storm! Now let me pass and sort through our cattle and choose which of them I will take to the Chippewa." He placed a hand to Melanie's cheek, caressing her trembling chin with his thumb. "Our loss will also be our gain, darling. Our hearts will be at peace, always, remembering the lives that will be saved because of our gesture of friendship."

Melanie sniffled and wiped more tears from her cheeks as she looked up into Shane's eyes. "You are such a compassionate man," she murmured. "You are so good." She crept back into his arms.

"How can I deny you this that you ask of me when I know you are doing it from the goodness of your heart?"

"Then I can go with your blessing?"

"Yes, but please hurry back to me. I could not bear it if anything happened to you."

"Our child will see my face the moment it is born," Shane whispered, burrowing his nose into the jasmine scent of her hair. "I promise you that, Melanie."

"Shane, if I weren't pregnant, I would go with you," Melanie said, hugging him tightly.

"I'm sure you would give it a try," Shane said, chuckling.

"No, Shane, not just a try," Melanie said sternly. "I would go with you."

Shane nodded. He knew that she would. He tilted her chin upward and directed his mouth to her lips. He kissed her long and sweet, then spun away from her. "Now that ought to hold you until I get back," he said, plopping a heavy, wide-brimmed hat on his head.

Melanie walked him to the door. They embraced one long last time, then Shane opened the door and the snow that had drifted against it tumbled inside.

Shane turned and eyed Melanie as snow blew in on her lovely, innocent face. "Go and sit by the fire and rid yourself of the chill," he said, then closed the door, separating them from each other, for days, perhaps weeks.

Melanie ran to the window and watched Shane

423

trudging through the snow toward the bunkhouse. She sighed with relief. He was not going to attempt to travel alone. He was going to recruit help.

Snow still clinging to her eyelashes and hair like minute crystal pellets, she rushed to the fireplace and knelt down before it. Her eyes blurred with more tears, knowing just how cold Shane was going to be while battling the raging storm.

Could he, in fact, freeze in the saddle, as some of the cattle had frozen in their tracks in the pasture? Oh, would he truly return to her and their unborn child? Was fate going to take him away from her after all?

She had fought so hard to win him!

The snow was deep and blowing, and Shane's breath froze as it escaped his mouth, crystalizing on his chin and lips. But he pushed relentlessly onward. Crouched low over his horse's mane, he looked over his shoulder at the men trailing the cattle behind him, and at the wagon, upon which had been placed many bales of hay so that the cows would have something to feast upon while giving their sweet milk to the Chippewa babies— at least until the snows stopped falling, and grass began to grow in the early spring. The rest of the longhorns would be slaughtered as soon as they reached the village.

Everyone, even the cattle, seemed to be faring well enough. It seemed as though something or someone were there protecting them. Perhaps the old chief's spirit was watching over them. His people depended on the safe arrival of the steers.

Turning his eyes back ahead, peering at the snow-shrouded, low-hanging branches of the trees, Shane's gut twisted at the sudden mournful wails wafting through the air. His hair bristled at the nape of his neck, knowing that the village was near. The people were in mourning! That meant that someone important had died, or was near death!

Nudging his knees into the sides of his stallion, Shane forced his steed to move faster. He could hear his horse's labored breathing as it pushed its legs through the snow, so white it blended in with it. He could see his horse's breath crystalizing on its mouth and the hairs of its chin. He could feel its muscles cording beneath his clamped legs, knowing the effort it was making to please and obey its master!

"That'a boy," Shane whispered, running his gloved hand over the horse's mane. "Just a little farther and I'll have you beside a fire. Your bones will get warmed." He nudged his knees again into his steed's side. "Come on, boy. You can do it. Just a little bit farther."

Through the trees ahead Shane saw the communal fire, then the wigwams that sat in the snow in a circle around it. No one was outside their dwellings. Nor did Shane see any horses in the corral.

Was he too late? Should he have come sooner?

But the weather had only recently grown this severe. The Chippewa usually stored foods of all kinds to last the duration of the winter.

The continuing mournful wails pierced not only

425

Shane's ears, but his heart. As soon as he was within running distance of the village, he swung himself out of his saddle. He could make better time without his horse. He had to see who was being mourned for! Normally, if the whole village was in trouble, it suffered in silence. The sort of wails that Shane was hearing were only performed when someone of great importance was dying.

Suddenly Shane saw his friend, Red Raven, step from Chief Gray Falcon's wigwam. Their eyes met and held, and then they began running toward one another. They lunged into each other's arms and embraced tightly.

"What has happened?" Shane asked, drawing away from Red Raven. He glanced over at Gray Falcon's wigwam, then into his friend's dark, fathomless eyes. He clasped his hands onto Red Raven's buckskin-clad shoulders. "Why are you here, my friend? You departed from this village long ago!"

"I am here because I was summoned," Red Raven said solemnly. "I am Gray Falcon's cousin. I am next in line to be chief."

"You were summoned here to—to become chief?" Shane said, his voice shallow.

"*Ay-uh*, that is so," Red Raven said, looking over his shoulder at Gray Falcon's dwelling, then back at Shane. "My cousin lies near death."

Shane paled, his heart sank. "How?" he said, his blue eyes imploring Red Raven. "He is so strong! How could he, of all of the people of the village, be the one who is dying?"

426

"He is not the first," Red Raven said, lowering his eyes sadly. "Many of our people were tainted by poisoned animals found dead in traps in the forest."

Shane was taken aback by this discovery. He exhaled a heavy breath, afraid to ask the next question. Was this not the act of someone as careless and vicious as Trapper Dan? Trapper Dan would be the sort to leave poisoned meat near the traps to lure the forest animals out of their winter shelters. The trapped animals would then poison anyone who ate them! Trapper Dan always only wanted their pelts.

Shane held his face in his hands. When he had investigated to see if Trapper Dan had finally died from the loss of blood, his body was gone and Shane had surmised that either an animal had dragged it away and had feasted upon it, or someone had found him and had buried him. Never in his wildest dreams had he thought the man would survive his wounds!

He looked slowly up at Red Raven. "Who is responsible for the poison?" he asked, his voice drawn.

"The braves are on his trail now," Red Raven said, doubling a fist at his side. "It is the same trapper who paid a high bride price for Cedar Maid! It is Trapper Dan!"

A sick feeling invaded Shane's insides. He turned abruptly away, afraid that he was going to retch. He cursed himself for being the careless one this time. He should have shot Trapper Dan! The proof would have been there for all to see and Trapper Dan wouldn't have had the chance to harm any more innocent people!

Then Shane brushed aside Red Raven and hurried into Gray Falcon's dwelling. He saw Gray Falcon lying on a raised platform, already decked out in his finest doeskin outfit, colorful beads resplendent across the fringed shirt and leggings. His hair was drawn back and his face was already painted with vermilion, his eyes closed, sunken with death's approach.

Shane went and stood over Gray Falcon. Tears streamed from his eyes, recalling how his childhood friend had tried to recapture their friendship on Shane's wedding day. Being too stubborn and proud, Shane had forbidden it! Childhood friends had become distant adult friends when jealousy clouded Gray Falcon's reasoning. Then Shane had sent Gray Falcon away. And now Gray Falcon was dying!

"Gray Falcon?" he said, falling to a knee beside the platform.

Gray Falcon's eyes did not open, but he reached a shaky hand to Shane. "You . . . have . . . come," he whispered. "That is good."

"If I had known of your trouble, I would have come sooner," Shane said, unable to stop the trembling in his voice.

"You are here now," Gray Falcon said, his voice so slight that Shane had to lean forward to hear. "That is all that matters." His eyes opened slowly. He looked at Shane. "Red Raven will now be chief. It is only right. I have not had sons."

"Nor have I," Shane said, clasping hard onto his friend's hand. "But I shall. My wife is with child."

Gray Falcon's lips quivered into a smile. "Even with child is she beautiful?" he asked, coughing.

"*Ay-uh*, even with child," Shane said, looking over his shoulder as Red Raven came into the wigwam and knelt down beside Shane.

"Gray Falcon, Shane has brought good meat to our people," Red Raven said softly. "He has even brought cows to give our children milk. Because of Shane many lives will be spared."

Gray Falcon nodded slowly. Tears sparkled in the corners of his eyes. "That is good," he said. "Thank you, Shane." He licked his parched lips and blinked his eyes. "Oh, Shane, it is with a sad heart that I leave you! We have missed so much valuable time together because of my jealousy and spiteful ways! Will you ever truly forgive me?"

"I have forgiven you," Shane said, swallowing back the urge to cry. "*Ah-pah-nay* I forgive you. Do not enter the hereafter with sadness in your heart." He placed a doubled fist to his chest, over his heart. "You should enter triumphant! Your father and mother will be there to greet you! Tell them I think of them often!"

"*Ay-uh*, Gray Falcon will tell them," he said, his eyes closing heavily. "Sleep. I . . . must . . . sleep."

Shane placed Gray Falcon's hand on his friend's chest and rose slowly to his feet. Tears near, he turned and embraced Red Raven. "My friend," he said thickly. "My friend."

The muffled sound of horses approaching in the

snow drew Shane and Red Raven apart. They exchanged questioning glances, then left the wigwam. Shane's insides stiffened when he found himself suddenly eye to eye with Trapper Dan, who was hanging like a sack of potatoes over the back of a horse, his hands tied behind him, icicles hanging from his nostrils and his bare fingers.

Shane's gaze then moved to the trapper's legs. He should be missing one.

Shane smiled lazily when he saw a wooden peg in place of the leg that had been mangled in the trap.

Then he met Trapper Dan's steady stare again, the blue and brown eyes reminding him again of that fateful day long ago past, the day of the massacre.

"Have mercy!" Trapper Dan yelled. "I didn't mean nothin' by leavin' poison meat for the animals. The Injuns shouldn't have stole the animals from my traps! It's not my fault they did!"

"But they did, and now even Chief Gray Falcon lies near death," Shane said, taking a step closer to the trapper. "How is it that you are alive? I left you for dead!"

"A trapper friend of mine came to visit and found me," Trapper Dan said, his voice thinning. "He took me to the doctor and all that I lost was my leg, not my life!" He glowered at Shane. "No thanks to you! I should've come and cut your throat, but I thought I'd best hightail it out of your area. I came to these parts and took my chances with these heathens again! I should've known better! I ain't got a chance in hell of survivin'."

"That's correct," Shane said, looking up at the braves who flanked the horse on which Trapper Dan had been tied. "Let him down. I've a score to settle. This time I'll make sure the bastard is dead."

Trapper Dan emitted a loud shriek as he was cut loose and fell with a thud into the deep snow. He tried to get to his feet, but his wooden peg kept slipping in the snow. He stopped and looked up at Shane, trembling. "What'cha got planned for me?" he asked, his eyes wild.

"Help him up," Shane said, his eyes narrowing as two braves helped Trapper Dan from the ground. "Take him over there by the fire." He chuckled low. "We shall test his endurance."

"What?" Trapper Dan gasped, moving clumsily along as he was half dragged to the communal fire. "What 'cha goin' to do? I cain't stand pain!"

"No one likes pain," Shane said, bending to a knee to withdraw a burning twig from the fire. "Chief Gray Falcon lies near death, his insides eaten up with poison. Do you not think he is in pain?"

While the men held Trapper Dan in place and forced the fingers of one of his hands open, Shane placed the burning twig in the palm and watched the fire moving closer to the trapper's flesh. "Cry out. Give us cause to call you a woman," Shane said solemnly. "Then comes another test."

Though Trapper Dan was trembling from the fierceness of the cold, sweat began to bead up on his brow. He watched the twig burning closer, closer. He tried to shake his hand, to remove the twig, but his hand was being held immobile by the braves.

He bit his lower lip as the fire began to burn along the flesh of his hand, sizzling as it blended with the snow and ice on it.

Then the snow and ice melted away and all that the trapper felt was the burning, searing heat of the fire!

In one powerful yank he jerked away from the braves. Now balancing himself well on his wooden peg, he grabbed a knife from the sheath of one of the braves. He twirled around and lunged for Shane, the knife poised for its death plunge.

But Shane was too quick. He had withdrawn his own knife and watched as Trapper Dan fell right onto it.

The knife completely imbedded in his clothes and stomach, Trapper Dan looked wildly up at Shane, grunting, then fell slowly to the ground, his eyes staring straight ahead in a death trance.

Shane stared down at the trapper, finding it hard to believe that this was the last time that he would ever have to look into those eyes. He took a deep breath, shook his head, and went back inside Gray Falcon's wigwam with Red Raven at his side. Together they sat down beside Gray Falcon, looking solemnly down at him.

"Is Trapper Dan truly dead this time?" Shane suddenly blurted, looking over at Red Raven. "I did kill him, didn't I, Red Raven?"

Red Raven placed a hand to Shane's shoulder. "He is dead," he said, smiling.

A slight moan drew their eyes back to Gray

Falcon. Shane's insides turned cold as he watched Gray Falcon's body twitch and convulse strangely, then become much too quiet. His fingers trembling, Shane placed a hand over Gray Falcon's mouth. When he felt no breath, he gave Red Raven a look of knowing.

"I am now chief?" Red Raven said, as though he doubted the truth of this moment.

"I know that you left the village, never to return," Shane said, rising to his feet along with Red Raven. "And that you never thought Gray Falcon would be the one to summon you back, to declare to your people that you would soon be chief. But it has happened. You are chief! You will carry the title well!"

"If only you were here to share the future of my people with me," Red Raven said, placing a hand on Shane's shoulder.

"That is not my destiny," Shane said, sighing. "Melanie and our children are my destiny." He smiled slowly at Red Raven. "Once you have seen your people through these hardships of winter and death, will you come to my house and pay a visit?"

Red Raven nodded. "*Ay-uh*, many times I will make a visit," he said.

"There is someone I would like you to meet," Shane said, in his mind's eye seeing Daphne and how she looked all swollen with child. Like Melanie, she was even more beautiful. Red Raven would make a wonderful husband—a wonderful father!

"Oh?" Red Raven said, forking an eyebrow.

"We will talk of it later," Shane said, swinging

an arm around his friend's shoulder. "Let us now join in mourning with your people."

"The burial rites must be swift," Red Raven said, walking from the wigwam beside Shane. "We have much meat to prepare. We have milk to feed my people's children!"

"Milk from a black cow is more healthful than that from a cow of any other color," Shane said. "I have brought only black cows to your people."

Red Raven hugged Shane fiercely. "Thank you, my brother," he said thickly. "*Mee-gway-chee-wahn-dum* for everything. Because of you, much is now possible for my people." He swallowed hard. "For our people, Shane. For our people."

· CHAPTER THIRTY-FOUR ·

Four Years Later, Mid-June

The day was delightful, soft and bright, with a brisk wind from the southwest. The air was heavy with rich, earthy scents.

Shane loaded a huge picnic basket at the rear of his buggy and offered Terrance a smile as Terrance helped his wife, Daphne, up into their buggy. After giving birth to two children already, Daphne was heavy with child again.

As far as Shane was concerned, things had not worked out as planned for Daphne. She and Terrance had fallen in love. Their courtship had been brief. Before Red Raven even had a chance to meet her, she was already married to Terrance.

Surprising to Shane, however, the marriage was working out. Terrance treated Daphne's first child as though it were his own, and he could not be more attentive and caring to a woman as he was his wife. She had seemed to change him into a gentle man overnight, into a man of heart—most definitely into a man who now had compassion for all Indians, since his wife was a full-blooded Chippewa.

Puffing, pregnant again, Melanie waddled down the front steps of her home, balancing her round ball of a stomach between her hands. She was perfectly content to be a wife and mother, having long ago left her tomboyish ways behind her. Her four-year-old daughter, Sara, came skipping down the steps beside her, carrying her baby doll wrapped in a blanket. Sara would be no tomboy.

Sara giggled flirtatiously when she saw Daphne's four-year-old-son, Jonathan, peeking at her from behind his parents' buggy. Oh, how she adored his copper complexion, his devilishly brown eyes and high cheekbones. He looked so Indian, and Sara was intrigued by all Indians. She loved to travel to the Chippewa village to visit her "uncle" Red Raven and "aunt" Blue Blossom. Married now, they had the tiniest baby girl named Sunshine!

"Come along, Sara," Shane said, sweeping his daughter up into his arms. "You and Jonathan can play hide-and-seek later. Right now we must take ourselves for a ride into the forest for that picnic your mother and I promised you."

"Is Jonathan's sister, baby Elizabeth, going?" Sara chirped, placing a hand to her father's freshly-shaven cheek.

Melanie, eight months pregnant, went to Sara

and smoothed some of her golden locks of hair back from her brow. "No, she's not going, honey," she said softly. "Daphne and Terrance thought it best to leave their baby home. Jonathan tests their patience enough on these outings."

Shane sat Sara down in the back of the buggy alongside the picnic basket, then swung his arm around Melanie's thick middle. He leaned her back up against the side of the buggy and gazed into her eyes. "Happy?" he asked, amused at how much weight she had gained while pregnant this time. She was like a little butterball, all bouncy and sweet.

Melanie stood on tiptoe and brushed a kiss across Shane's lips. "Very," she murmured. "Darling, how can I not be? When passion calls, you are always there."

Shane's mouth closed over her lips. They kissed as though it were the first time.